COLLECTED EDITION I
SHORT BITS

THE FIRST FOUR VOLUMES IN A SPECIAL ILLUSTRATED EDITION

BELINDA CRAWFORD

Published by Hendrix & Faust, Publishers in 2024
Text copyright © Belinda Crawford 2024

www.belindacrawford.com

ISBN: 978-0-6459318-1-5 (ebook)
ISBN: 978-0-6459318-5-3 (paperback)
ISBN: 978-0-6459318-2-2 (collector's edition hardback)

This one is dedicated to
a couple of legends,
Emma Morris &
Mike Dobey.

Books by Belinda Crawford

The Hero Rebellion
(Hunter)
Hero
(Race)
Riven
Regan

The Echo
Cold Between Stars
Dark Between Oceans
Echo Between Worlds
(Brother)

Demons & Battleskirts
Volume 1

Collections
Short Bits, Volumes 1–5
I Am Maggie, Volume 1

CONTENTS

INTRODUCTION

It's been two and a bit years since I published the first *Short Bits*; two years of learning and (dare I say it) growing as a short story author. What I was learning wasn't so much how to write a short story (although there was some of that in there) but in giving myself *permission* to be a short story writer.

The whole idea behind *Short Bits* was to force me out of my comfort zone, and sending that first bundle of stories off to my editor sure did the job*. I was a nervous wreck, and I swear, despite knowing she liked my other work, it was a good hour before I gathered the courage to open her return email.

There's nothing quite as nausea-inducing as having a professional critique your work.

She loved the collection, and not only that, she put to rest some of my fears that my short stories weren't actually short stories. Phew.

Needless to say—two years and four volumes in—I got over the whole "you're not a short story writer" thing. Actually, I didn't just get over it, I *smashed* that little voice whining, "these aren't short stories! *And* they suck!" Take *that* inner bitch-critic!

This collected edition represents that journey from nervous wreck to… Titan? No, too big. Steamroller, perhaps? Runaway horses? I don't know, something suitably unstoppable and a little reckless.

Whatever it is, I hope you enjoy it, and the stories contained herein.

At the beginning of each story, you'll find a brief introduction with a special multimedia experience. Exclusive to the *Collected Edition*, the multimedia experience is an extra behind-the-scenes glimpse into my writing process, including a short video introduction, soundtracks and visual inspiration.

When I was putting the collection together, one thing I tossed up was in what order to put the stories in. Should I group them by genre, by theme or some random assortment of... well, randomness? In the end, I went with genre, from epic fantasy through to space opera, and within those genres... well, you'll see.

Happy reading!
Belinda

*By this time, Amanda had already earned my creative trust by coping with the weirdness of The Echo series. And loving it. Just saying.

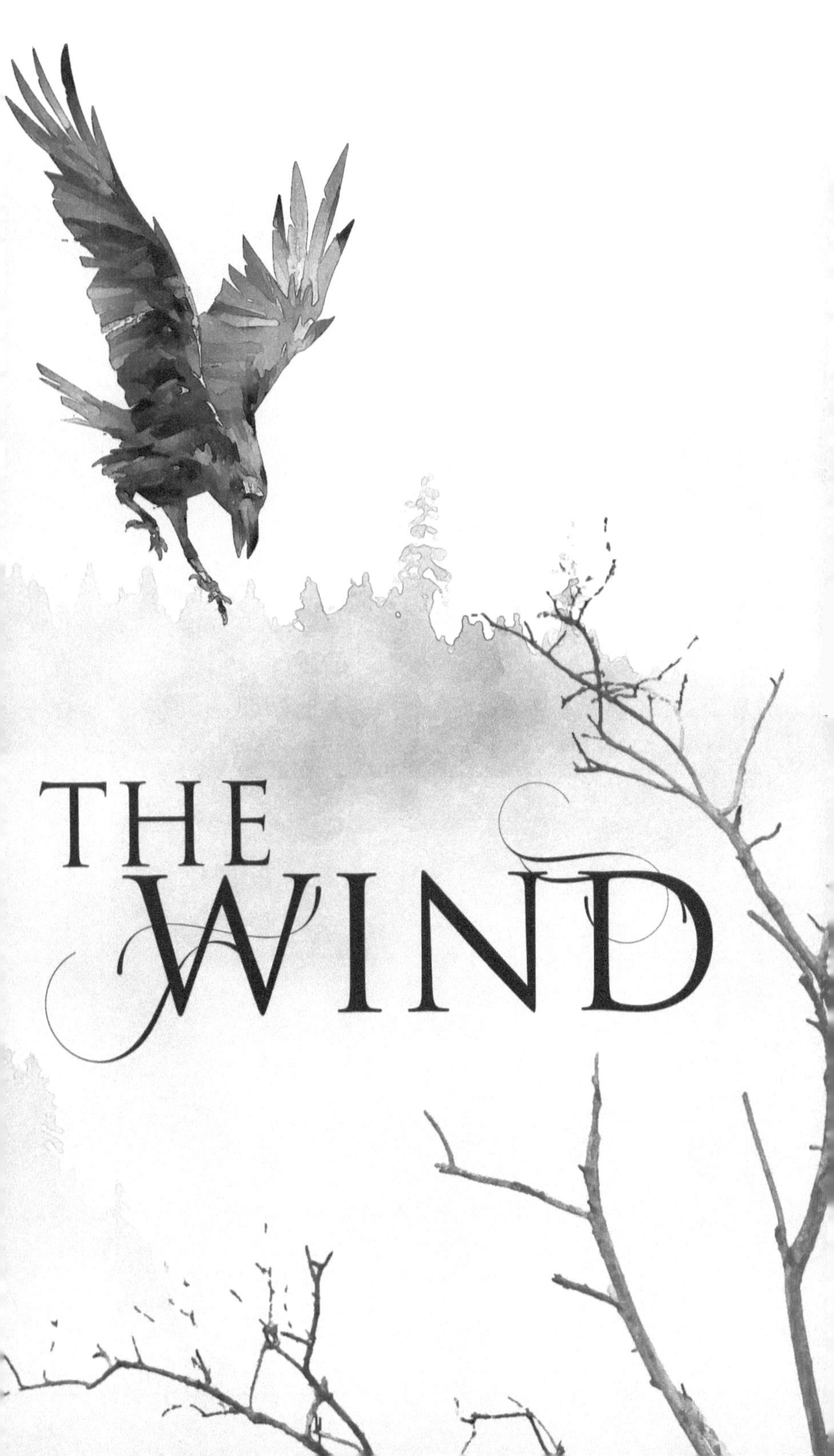

THE
WIND

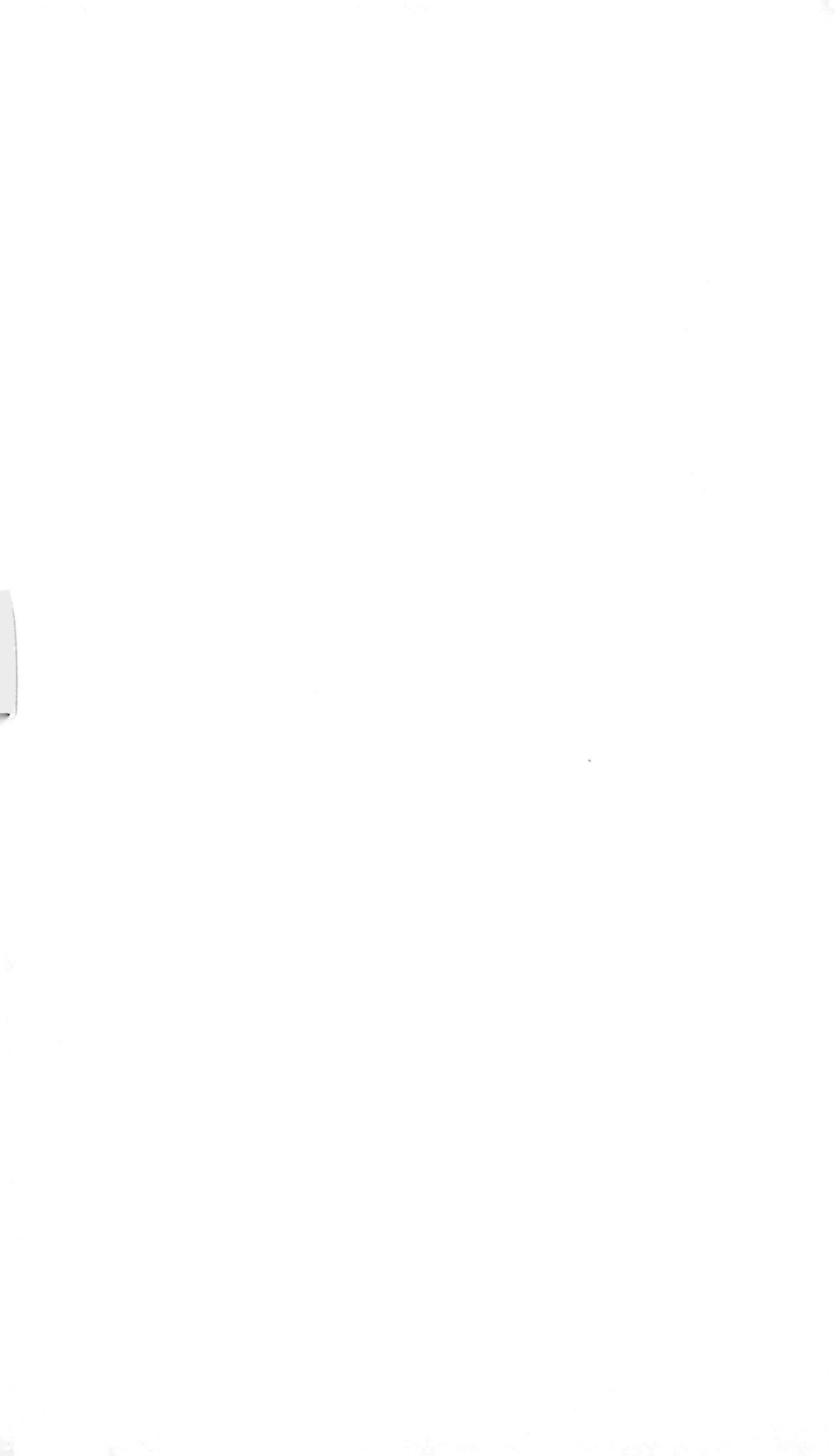

INTRODUCTION

Should you have some familiarity with Norse mythology, or one of the many variations of it in popular culture, you might recognise the main character, S'Ahn as a Valkyrie. If you're not familiar… well, you know now.

Now and then, a particular idea gets stuck in my brain, and I work on it, a bit like a piece of cud, or chewing gum. It gets turned into all sorts of knots, sprinkled with all kinds of sparkly toppings, reused, recycled and eventually spat out the other end, sometimes in multiple retellings.

The Valkyrie is one such, and it's been stuck in my brain long enough for me to take the idea of Odin's shield maidens and give it my own, darker spin. In *The Wind*, and the three stories following, I'll introduce to my latest and (if I say so myself) most exciting version.

 Learn more about the writing of *The Wind*. Scan the QR code for the audio commentary, soundtrack and more.

THE WIND

The wind whispered her name. It wrapped around the pale, snow-laden branches of the gnarled tree above, age clinging to its flaky bark, its wide-flung arms and twisted trunk. It sighed through the bare twigs, the tiny buds waiting to burst as soon as the frost gave them leave, and played with the ends of her hair.

S'Ahn.

She lifted her face to the breeze, the frozen chill long-since embedded in her cheekbones, and drew deep of the earth, the sweat, the blood that rode in on it. That twisted through her nose, hit the back of her throat—the ice freezing the heavy copper tang to the back of her tastebuds—and burst in her lungs. Thorns shot through her rib cage, a bloody rose nestled against her heart, feeding on pain, adrenaline and the moans of the dying.

The wind tugged, pulling at the long, ragged ends of her war braids, casting loose stands of dirty chestnut hair across her lips.

S'Ahn, it said again.

She dug her talons into the dirt, felt the tree's roots under the sharp, black tips, the blood-churned mud squishing between her black, scaly toes.

The wind slipped under her breastplate, the heavy leather scratched and scarred, through the rough woollen tunic underneath—the once rich red fabric a dull, muddy mauve—and slid cool fingers along her ribs, working its way upward to her shoulders and the heavy, feathered appendages erupting from the pale skin.

It rustled the short, downy black feathers close to her skin, slipped in among the longer, glossier ones that dragged in the mud.

S'Ahn. On the battlefield, the moans rose, following the wind under the woven leather band trapping her hair over her ears. *Choose*, it said, and pulled; a hard tug from the middle of her gut.

She stumbled, jerked forward by the call, only a hand on the old pale tree saving her from falling to her knees. Thick black nails dug deep into the flashy bark, sap oozing around her fingers, mixing with the blood embedded in the skin.

Choose, it said again. Harder, meaner, wrapping around feathered wings and twisting—a miniature tornado ripping glossy black feathers from her back. The moans rose higher, a cacophony of pain and death drowning her heart, pulling her to walk among the bodies, highlighting the bright, shiny souls waiting to be plucked from decaying mortal flesh.

Another yank and lurch forward, nails still dug in the tree, sap clinging to her fingers. *Obey.*

Above, a pale streak, more dark wings catching the air as Olia descended from the sky, the battle sister hitting the field with the force of a comet, taloned feet shredding dead and dying alike.

Olia knelt, gauntleted hand passing over a warrior's dead face, sweeping up the glow above it, wrapping it around her fingers before shoving them in her mouth.

Other battle sisters strode through the muddy field, long flight-feathers dragging in the mud. Their faces—dark and light and golden—were streaked with dirt and blood; their hair—twelve different shades of black and brown and blonde, long and short and frizzy—were uniformly snarled by wind and caught up with sticks and twigs, their gazes unfocused, their eyes mad. Like Olia, they stalked the dead, gathering souls, scooping them up and feasting.

But not all the souls, only those worthy, the golden ones

shimmering like the ice riming the tree's tightly closed buds. Not the others, the greys and blues and pinks, pale and faded, still clinging to dead flesh.

The wind barrelled into the back of her legs, ripping her hand from the tree as her knees buckled. Mud spat, sticking to her thighs when she hit the slush.

Obey, the wind demanded. *Choose.*

The rose in her chest bloomed, thorns sinking deeper into the crack in her soul, the giant chasm only partially healed, the two halves of herself held together with little more than gossamer threads.

Choose. Thunder rode on the wind, even as lightning flashed across the storm-clouded sky. *Now.*

Another gust of wind, pushing her down—hands in the mud, war braids tumbling over her shoulders—scooting under her wings and trying to snap them open, to spread the giant raven feathers wide and catch the air. To lift her out of the mud and onto the battlefield. With her sisters, with their mad, blind eyes and roses buried in their breasts, spreading their poison, and their pain.

Like it did in hers, daggers driving into her ribs, her spine, her spleen, molten iron running under her skin, trying to burn away the memories, the hard-won threads binding her selves together. It was coming, the madness, the rage, the lust for blood and battle. Throwing herself back into bondage the only way to make the pain stop.

Mama. Another voice. Smaller. Gentler. A memory rising from the carefully healed halves, the combined pieces of herself. *Mama.* A small, soft hand on her face, sweet daisy-scented breath, a smile like the sun rising.

Choose! The voice boomed in her ear, the command digging deep, ripping at that little voice, that soft hand, even as her talons ripped at the mud, at the tree buried there. At the stones and earth. *Choose!*

The rose grew, the pain growing with it, stealing her breath, her sight, the wet, cold earth squishing between her fingers. The little voice...

Mama...

Tattered and fading, trailing on the breeze.

She reached for it, lifting a hand from the mud, stretching her fingers, snagging the silvery threads in her claws, wrapping them around and around.

S'Ahn. The wind played with her feathers, twisted through her braids, wound past her jaw to the outstretched hand, tugged at the threads.

She moaned. All the words she could manage.

It tugged again, twisting and pulling at the threads.

She held them harder, claws digging into her palm, anchoring the little voice to her blood, welling through the skin.

S'Ahn. It wrapped the threads up in its chilly clutches, lightning flitting through the loose chestnut hair around her face, chilling her cheeks, freezing her teeth. Gathering, gathering, a storm roiling around her knucklebones, cracking over her fist, arcs of power stabbing at her wrist. More blood, more pain.

But she did not loosen her hold, instead, strained her ears for that little voice, clawed at her memory for the soft hand and the daisy breath.

The breeze became a gale, ripping at her wings, feathers snatched from their mooring, more pain to join the rest, war braids lashing her face, the rose... The rose pushing it roots deep into her heart, squeezing, thorns shredding. Blood in the back of her throat. And still she held to the silver threads, her claws buried deep in her palm.

The storm pulled harder, spits of mist becoming icy daggers to open new wounds in her cheeks, to slice lips and chest and arm. To shred the little voice—

Choose!

A command, the wind a hard, merciless hand wrapping around

her wrist, crushing the bones.

Choose!

A blow to her back, to the tender spot between wings, the sharp down-gust driving the breath from her lungs.

She gasped.

Let go.

No.

But even as the thought crossed her mind, as the word tried to pass her lips, the rose took hold. Its thorns sliced the stitches holding the halves of her soul together, its sweet, cloying scent winding through her nose, creeping over her tongue, warming her insides with pain and lust and power. A heady battle-filled power, a desperate need for the iron-rich tang of violence and death. To join her battle sisters in scooping the rich, golden shimmer from fallen warriors, the tangy, tingling slide of them down her throat, and then the warmth, the glow as they went beyond her, into the place after death, the place where—

Mama.

Silver caught in the armour joint around her knuckles, a thin, tattered wisp...

The wind gusted, twisting back around her hand, loosening the thread. It drifted free...

She grabbed for it.

Another icy, airy foot between her wing joints

She fell, chest and chin in the mud.

It was gone, twisting away, caught in the storm...

...but the rose was there, filling the holes, pushing her to her knees, her hands, propelling her towards her sisters—

A flash of midnight, wings—miniature, arm-length copies of her own—a bird diving out of the sky, piercing the storm. It's long sharp beak wide, snatching the silver out of the twisting air, catching an updraft, corkscrewing back round to hover, for just a heartbeat, far above her, a shadow against the storm, before it dove straight for her.

Kill it, the air commanded.

She snarled, legs bunching, talons digging into the mud in preparation to leap, to catch the bird in her pointed claws and feast on its small, feathered body—

Silver caught the light, trailing from the raven's beak.

Mama, it said.

She hesitated.

The bird—a raven, glossy and dark—evaded her grasp, landed on her shoulder its talons, as razor-sharp as her own, sinking through leather armour into the pale flesh beyond. It thrust that wisp in her face, the tattered silvery end brushing her cheek, gliding over her lips.

Daisies in her nose, the sweet earthy scent blooming on the back of her throat, sliding down down down.

The rose, thorny shoots rising up up up.

The two meeting, tangling.

The rose drawing blood, the daisies whispering: *Mama. Mama. Mama.*

The raven's dead black eyes opening wide, its wing a gentle caress on her neck.

Mama.

Hand trembling, fighting the dual urges to hold and to rend, she reached for the thread fluttering under her nose—

The raven ate it. A lunge and a gulp, throwing back its little black head, the silver thread disappearing down its gullet like a fat, grey worm.

She screamed, one of the few sounds left to her. Long and painful, the rose spilling out her mouth, thorny lashing tendrils, desperate for something to hurt and to kill.

The bird screamed back, a long and lonely *caaawww,* too big for its little chest, too loud, too piercing. It beat back the torrent boiling from her own mouth, twisting and tangling with the rose, slicing the thorns, the thick green stems, and rushing down her throat.

It tasted like earth, like the mud at her knees.

She choked, her claws at her throat, leaving long, dirt-encrusted scores in her flesh as she tried to dig it out, to let the air back in.

The *caw* reached her centre, the rose behind her breast, and like the cry was the bird's beak, it reached in and ate it.

Silence.

Her face was back in the mud, nose and mouth pressed to the cold, wet slop, the stuff on her tongue, smeared over her chin and cheeks and breast. Hands fisted in it.

A flutter. The bird in the mud beside her, head twisted, a beady black eye fixed on hers, that sharp, black beak hovering a hairsbreadth from her face.

It sang—*caw*—the music softer, gentler. *Caw. Caw.* And somehow, the more she heard of it, the more it sounded different, sounded like that soft whisper of *mama*.

Caw.

Mama.

Caw.

Mama.

The bird butted her brow with its head. *Caw*, it sang again.

Beneath her breast, behind her ribcage, she breathed. Heart beating against her chest. No stabbing pain, no thorns embedded in her ribs, in her spine and spleen. She breathed again, deeper, harder. Tasted not the cloying sweetness but the earthy scent of daises, felt the flutter of soft yellow petals, the woolly caress of soft green leaves. And in her soul... silver threads bound the halves of herself, ragged and thin, fragile, but there, straining against the yawning chasm that was... Was her. The woman without a name.

The cold wind whispered, *S'Ahn.*

She got up.

That was not her name.

The raven fluttered to her shoulder, talons sinking back through leather to flesh.

S'Ahn, the wind whispered again, tugging at her wings, the wet, muddy length of her braids.

Out on the field, her battle sisters had straightened, no longer walking through the dead, kneeling and scooping and eating. Staring instead at her, alone under the winter-rimed tree with its tiny, frosted buds.

The raven ruffled its wings.

Lightning rippled across the doom-laden sky.

S'Ahn, ob—

Caw. Right in her ear, drowning the words, the pain that came with them. *Caw.*

Obe—!

Caw!

She looked to the sky, the storm raging across it, the fury swirling the clouds, a tight corkscrew forming above her, ripping at the tree. The air a hammer getting ready to smash her once more to her knees.

She felt more than saw her battle sisters move, powerful legs striding across the field, stalking over corpses as easily as the mud, their wings no longer dragging behind them but mantled, their expressions no longer blank but fierce. The madness in their eyes not just banked but a bloody inferno spilling down their cheeks, twelve shades of pale and dark and gold.

Obey—

Caw! Caw, caw, caw.

Retribution gathered above, no longer a hammer but a spear, lightning forming at its tip, ready to strike her down, to rend the daises blooming in her soul.

Her sisters, heartbeats away, their arms outstretched, their hands clawed.

She launched upwards, into the storm, and screamed defiance.

Maelstrom

INTRODUCTION

Inspiration comes from many places, although the inspiration for this story came while I was on the treadmill, listening to a rather punky rock number.

'Devil' by Fight the Fade immediately brought to mind someone hiding from a relentless, violent pursuit. And while the song would otherwise bring to mind dark, urban areas—factories, nightclubs and deserted parking lots—a short story I'd written previously (*Woman in White*, which follows *Maelstrom*) meant I had snowstorms on my mind.

Learn more about the writing of *Maelstrom*. Scan the QR code for the audio commentary, soundtrack and more.

MAELSTROM

She came with the storm.

Appearing out of the absolute white, all alabaster skin shadowed by dark gale-snarled hair, ivory robes seemingly made from the snow itself, long ragged ends whipped in the wind. Only her eyes and the blood smeared across her face held colour—a furious green jade against brilliant red.

The blood stained her face from forehead to chin, drawn on her pale skin in four long, thin lines, as if with fingers—over eyelids and nose and lips—and perhaps they had been, but the eight men huddled around the little fire could not tell.

They saw only fury in the storm-born woman, only death in the snarl pulling at her lips. They shivered even as they jerked to their feet, as they pulled comrades upright and yelled, 'Ware, ware! The devil comes!'

And though the words left their mouths, though the eight stood shoulder to shoulder in the little cave, they heard only the soul-shredding wail of the wind whistling though the gaps in the boulders they'd piled in the entrance, and the fury in the storm outside. Or maybe it was the woman's roar, maybe it was *her* fury, her bloodlust reaching across the blinding, biting cold to pierce their hearts.

Maybe that piecing wail wasn't the wind but the souls of the broken bodies they'd left in the small, crude hut in the valley. The little girl in her torn dress who'd bled out on the dirt floor, the boy pinned to the rough timber wall, the sword that held him there nearly severing arm from shoulder.

It didn't matter. Nothing mattered now, although they did not say that aloud, even as hands tightened on sword hilts and magic played across knuckles. All that mattered was surviving the coming onslaught, was getting down this cursed mountain with their lives and their prize intact.

Storm and woman flew over the boulders, the stoney barricade little more than an inconvenience. Among them in a moment, steel and fury swirling with the snow, with the ragged ends of her robes, impossible to tell where woman began and the elements left off.

The clash of steel, the crunch of bone, screams cut short by gurgles of blood. The eight fought, six steel blades dancing through the snow-laden air, magic lighting up the cavern with brilliant flashes of white and blue, a complex choreography through which the woman spun and slashed.

Their swords passed through air and fabric, drew thin lines of blood across her white robes, her cheek, her back, but she did not stop. For every wound in her own flesh, the twin axes in her hands inflicted three on theirs, the wide crescent blades soon thick with blood, their intricately carved, leather-wrapped hafts slick with it.

The woman made no sound as she ripped through the men— slicing tendons as readily as throats and bellies. The storm was her voice, the wind the gut-wrenching howl trapped in her throat, the stabbing hail her pain, the biting cold her fury.

The little fire guttered under the onslaught, flames pushed left and right even as the first of the eight hit the hard ground, and then the second and the third and the fifth. Only when the woman was done, when the eight lay on the cavern's cold, stoney floor, their blood feeding the ground, their lungs drawing their last ragged gasps, did the fire straighten.

She straightened with it, blood dripping from the crescent tip of her axes, staining hands and her long white sleeves, even as the rain and mud clung to her hems. Madness lit her eyes, and she spun, desperately seeking another victim for the rage filling her chest, but there were none.

Impotent rage exploded from her chest in a loud, piercing scream. The storm howled with her, the hate and bloodlust in her veins, the acidic bile of old wounds spilled from her mouth. The gale whipped it about to smash against the boulders and cavern walls. And in the broken, pitiful sounds that bounced back, the woman saw not herself but the little girl with her dress all bloodied, and the boy, fingers bent and broken were someone older and stronger had wrested a rare prize from his grip.

A prize the eight had taken, a prize they had died for, a prize—

Boots crunching stone.

The rage in her chest sang, no longer impotent, no longer thwarted with a new target to unleash itself upon. She twisted about, joy stretching her lips, lighting her heart even as she raised her axes and—

And stopped, frozen in a heartbeat by the old, rusty dagger laying across the new man's palm. The short, straight blade was chipped and scratched, and the leather wrapping the plain wooden handle was stained and loose in parts, shabby to the point of falling apart. It would barely slice parchment let alone skin, and yet the sight of it, the ancient russet stains deep in the join between hilt and blade, froze her to the core.

'S'Ahn,' the man said and his voice, a deep echoing baritone, cut through the storm's fury, the wail of the wind. His hand wrapped around the hilt, little finger first, then second then third, his thumb—the joint old and gnarled, stiff with age—closed last. He lifted the blade, and the fire found places to gleam even on that dull, pocked surface, shaking in his unsure grip.

Her eyes followed every movement, every twitch of the light reflected in the knife as if they were slices in her flesh. As if they were the Underlord come to steal her soul.

'S'Ahn,' he said again, only this time he whispered the name, *her* name. By rights, the gale should have picked up his voice and scattered it to the heavens, drowned it under the storm's fury, but his thin, pinched lips were pressed to the blade, and the blade...

The twin axes fell from nerveless fingers, clattering against the bloody stone. She pressed a hand to her breastbone, to the ragged scar hidden under torn and muddied robes, and felt the man's voice as if it were inside her, vibrating in the channel once carved by that rusty blade.

'S'Ahn, Keeper of the Thirteen, I command you to hear me.'

'No.' The denial was a moan, a plea ignored by the wind.

'Hear me.' With his other hand he gripped the blade. She felt his hand, the blood flowing from his palm, as if it were inside her, squeezing her heart. 'Hear me,' he said again, 'and obey.'

She fell to her knees.

WOMAN IN WHITE

INTRODUCTION

Woman in White is the first story I wrote with Valkyries, not that it's immediately obvious. It was also my first attempt at channeling my (slight) obsession with east Asian television shows into my writing. I love the martial arts fantasy genre (called xianxia) in particular. There's something about all that flowing fabric, fantastical kung-fu and *drama* (soooo much drama!) that sucks me in every time.

I don't know why, but probably because it was unexpected, this story seemed the perfect opportunity to introduce my Valkyrie.

 Learn more about the writing of *Woman in White*. Scan the QR code for the audio commentary, soundtrack and more.

WOMAN IN WHITE

The rustle of wings and the harsh, alien craw of an unseen bird had drawn him into the ancient Snow Forest. Its shadow led him through the green of the outer forest—the maples a riot of colour against the green stalwart pines, their leaves turning red then yellow as winter marched toward the mountains. The bird's call had continued as the mountain trees thinned before the giant black pillars marking the edge of the inner forest. Its *caw caw caw* had rung off the slabs of granite, tall as two men and twice as thick, untouched by either the bleak mountain winters or time, marked only by the spells carved into their glossy surfaces.

He had hesitated before he crossed that threshold. Stood with his hands clasped tight within the billowing sleeves of his dark blue outer robe while the sharp sting of fate tip-toed up his spine. Then the bird had cawed once more and some shadow had moved in the snow-covered forest, a flutter of wings within bare, twisted branches. That tug, the sharp sting of fate, had moved him forward.

There had been no gradual change from the delicate touch of natural winter to the glacial white of the land beyond the pillars. There was the green meadow and then there was snow, divided as if a sword had fallen from the heavens and driven the two forests apart. And where, in the outer forest, the rich scent of earth and loam rose with every footfall, and the sweet trill of larks graced the ear, here only the soft *shush* of his robes and the beckoning *caw* accompanied his feet.

He walked until the bright green and autumn colours of the outer forest were far behind, until the cold had crept through the seams of his boots and frost clung to the dark hem of his robe. He walked until the bare, ancient branches of the forest where a cage above and the breeze was thick with the sighs of long-dead souls. He walked, led by the shadow of the unseen bird, its harsh cry ringing like the clash of swords and the screams of men. He walked until he came upon a clearing, the branches above giving way to a small circle of open sky, the sun harsh, the air cold enough to frost his breath.

In that clearing, a woman lay in a puddle of white, her robes and skin a few shades darker than the snow. Foreign not just to the forest, but the realm, her face a study in stark, square lines and the heavy folds of her clothes unlike any he had seen—the fabric plain and unadorned, bound at the waist by a delicate cord of silver. Nevertheless, the snow cradled her like something precious, the soft drift a pillow on which she slept, her dark lashes resting on bloodless cheeks, her hair a shadow against the brightness.

If not for that dark walnut spill, he would not have seen her, so well did she blend into the snow-shrouded forest. The relentless sun and harsh moon had long since bleached the ancient trees, leaving the trunks a million shades of grey and white. No blooms softened the stark grey-white with a soft blush of pink, no leaves graced the delicate branches or sighed in the icy wind. No birds sang, no rabbits foraged, no wolves stalked. No life trod here, not since the war a millennia ago.

Not even the unseen bird, with its eerie cry.

Nothing save the woman, her chest rising and falling in slow, gentle movements, sleeping where she did not belong.

The forest was a place... not of death, because if one unsheathed their eyes and looked below the surface, they could see life pulse deep in its heart. Slow, languid, as close to death as sleep could take it but still there, still... waiting.

He looked at the way the woman nestled into the land.

Waiting and perhaps finding.

The thought chilled his blood.

He stopped, the hem of his silk robes flirting with the white, woollen spill of hers, and he looked. Looked through the veil of sleep and cold, let his eyes sink through fabric and skin and bone, all the way down to the soul.

Power pulsed around the woman, as slow and languid as the Snow Forest itself but different. Hot where the trees where cold, rich with death and blood, the gory scent of a battlefield where the forest air was crisp and cutting, smelling of nothing more than the ice itself. And still... and still the forest curled around her and pulsed in response to the slow, steady beat of her heart, the frigid silver threads of its magic caressing her cheek and winding around her arms.

One of her hands was outflung, her palm open, fingers gently curled, and even though her eyes were shut, her face was turned towards that open, empty palm as if she was looking at something. Something precious.

He knelt, robes spilling about his feet, his hand a warm, pale gold against the cool ivory of hers.

He touched that upturned palm, cupped the strong yet delicate fingers in his. What had she been looking at? What had those long, elegant fingers held onto as she slipped into the slow fog of almost death?

He leaned closer, drawn by the rise and fall of her breath, the utter colourlessness of her cheeks, the bones of her face sharper, her jaw squarer, eyes deeper set than other women.

She did not belong here, neither on this mountain nor in this forest nor this land. In so many ways, she did not belong.

And yet here she was, an exotic, dangerous mystery crumbled at his feet.

He traced a thumb over the dark swoop of her brow, and felt, as his flesh brushed the meridian, the heavy thump of boots on hard-packed dirt, heard the echo of drums and the fierce rush of wings. War trampled his spine and chilled his soul, even as it doubled the beat of his heart and brought the flush of anticipation to his skin.

The sounds of battle in this place, in this moment, curling around this strange woman with her outflung hand. Nothing good could come of them. He should leave her here. Even if he had not seen the pain and death in her aura, nothing peaceful grew in this forest, and that she was here now, as the stars above changed and the Lord of Fate grew anxious...

And still... and still.

Destiny skittled over his back.

He slipped his arms under her and rose.

She was both lighter and heavier than he expected, her frame willowy, delicate and yet that cold dark warning in his heart, the icy prick of fate, weighed her limbs, made her head rest heavy on his shoulder, her breath shiver across his neck.

He stood in that secluded clearing, with the bony fingers of the Snow Forest arching above, and knew, as he stared at the pale peaceful face, that this was the end.

MIRROR

INTRODUCTION

Mirror is the last Valkyrie tale in this collection, or at least, the last of this version (they appear later, starting with *Don't Die*). It is not, however, the last story in the tale. Rather, the three shorties you've just read and the one you're about to form the start of S'Ahn's story.

Having *Mirror* wrap up the four is a lucky accident. Originally, it wasn't included in the Collected Edition but, thanks to the Kickstarter Heroes who helped bring this special edition to life, it's here. I, for one, am glad *Mirror* not only rounds out the tale (with a lot of holes, of course) but also gives a glimpse into the larger story; a clash of pantheons and a reclaiming of power.

shivers It's going to be exciting.

Learn more about the writing of *Mirror*. Scan the QR code for the audio commentary, soundtrack and more.

MIRROR

The bitter wind twisted around her ankles. It played with the ends of her outer robes, the fine white wool billowing around her knees, the delicate inner robes—a pale cloud of blue—flying between them. It caught in the wide, open cuffs of her sleeves and lifted the chestnut curtain of hair from her back, blowing strands across her face. It brought with it the cold, fresh scent of mountain pines and the chill nothingness of snow.

The same chill shivered through her soles, pouring upwards from the glacial black ice beneath her soft leather boots—more suited to dark oak floors and smooth, pebble-lined paths than the mud and leaf litter that stained her hems—even as the wind bore snow across the lake, eddies of delicate white scudding across frozen water.

War came with the snow, pounding drums and marching feet, the low mournful cry of the horn. So familiar to her and yet so alien to this place, more used to the lilting call of the flute.

It was a shadow in her vision, a mirage waiting on the edge of her awareness, the clank of shields, the rattle of swords and axes, horses churning the ground, warriors shifting and stamping on the water's northern edge. While to the south...

She didn't not look. She *would* not look, and neither would she listen. Instead, she shut her ears to the moans carrying across the ice, the quiet sobs and prayers for the dead, and gave her attention to the lake. She let the icy black mirror clasp her tight, the dark and cold rise through her feet to take hold of her resolve and freeze it in her chest.

Stars played in the mirror, twelve brilliant lights out before their time, shining in the grey sky, uncaring of the sun struggling to rise over the mountains and cast its blood-red glow across the clouds.

The stars grew larger. Soon they would eclipse her vision. Soon they would become comets with blood-crusted armour, and the mirror would shatter under their talons.

But not yet. Until then, there was just her and the woman staring back from the thick, cold mirror.

The woman in the lake who looked like her, wearing the same flying robes, her hair the same wind-snarled chestnut, her jaw square, her skin pale, pale white. The same determination written across her face, drawing her deathly pink lips tight, but not the same eyes... The reflection's eyes weren't green but molten gold, bleeding long, ragged tears down her cheeks like fingerprints.

The bloody tracks matched the ones on her body, tracing over shoulders and chest and throat, a delicate pattern of torn flesh, the last traces of the magic that held her in, that had made her safe and tame and obedient. The iron and power embedded in the ink that had once decorated her body was gone, even if, deep in her being, the final threads of it remained, binding her to mortal flesh, robbing her of what was hers.

In the lake, the stars burned.

Not for long.

On the northern shore, swords bashed against shields, while behind...

And maybe too long. Maybe not soon enough.

It was not meant to happen like this. The army that should have been on the southern shore was too far away, waiting uselessly for the horde that stood before her now, and instead... Instead, only these few. Dead and bleeding at her back.

And her. Power trapped in a mortal shell, still bound, still broken.

Was it enough?

She weighed the power, let it pool in her hands and swirl between her fingers, a golden mirage playing around her knuckles even as she steeled herself against the vicious stab in her gut – the last, strongest part of the restraints pulling back against the use.

Warmth trickled down her back, trailed over her shoulder blades, tickled as it wound its way over her wrist, between her knuckles. It would seep through her robes soon, an intricate scarlet knot against the brilliant white, trailing across her shoulders and around her ribs. An echo of what lay beneath.

Would they see it, the army laid out along the lake's long, icy northern shore? Was the god there? Would he know? Could he stop it? Reforge the bindings, restart the millennia of servitude and lay waste to the fragile flutterings of hope?

She wanted to look, fear twisting through the pain, making her heart race. But no, she hadn't seen the flash, felt the *pop* as a god materialised.

The reflection glared at her. A challenge. A dare.

Don't look, don't waver.

The stars blazed one-by-one in the ice even as, on the northern shore where soldiers clanked their shields and raised their voices in song, a sudden, brilliant light blazed.

A god had come.

Don't look.

A god would see.

Don't let them guess.

A god would *know*.

The first comet struck.

The ice shook, a giant white crack splitting the darkness, shattering her reflection.

Another comet followed. And another, and another.

Whomp. Whomp. Whomp.

Four then seven, then ten and twelve.

Ice flew, shards stinging her face, her hands, even as wicked black talons dug into the lake's surface.

The wind died.

All was still.

No sound carried across the lake, no horses stamped, no shields clanked. No chants or drums, not even the mournful horn.

Just the ice, groaning.

The woman in the mirror was gone. Only those bleeding, molten eyes remained.

She looked up.

The first comet snarled, crimson lips pulled back over gritted teeth, the massive raven wings at her back vibrating with rage. Madness had long since obliterated reason from the comet's eyes while pain had drawn her face and robbed her tongue of words. Just like the ink-green lines tattooed from forehead to chin, all the way past the grey-furred neck of her tunic and under her chest plate, had taken her freedom.

Similar lines, now weeping gashes, had once caged her.

Around her, the other comets waited, long bloodied spears in their hands, the same pain-born insanity twisting their faces, the same rage shivering half-mantled wings, the same impatience making them kneed the ice with their talons. The same iron binding their souls.

She knew that madness, it lived in her, in her marrow, in the clash of swords in her blood, the thud of boots in her heart, the sweet copper on her lips.

The rents in her flesh burned, the broken shackles under her skin tightening, links pulling through her soul, fire flowing in their wake.

Obey, the pain said. *Submit. Serve.*

Don't leave, said the first comet's mad green gaze.

Come with me, she said back.

On the northern shore the god laughed, the sound thunder, the force of it sending ripples across the lake.

We can't, said the first, even as lightning flashed through her tattoos and those green eyes turned red.

She laughed, the god in her voice.

Spears struck ice; twelve sharp spiked ends sending up new shards, clumps of white clinging to wooden shafts turned black with gore.

On the northern shore, swords struck shields again, the rhythm changing, no longer a slow, steady march, but a frenetic *clang clang clang.*

Behind, she sensed more than saw the battered and broken few stumbling to their feet, swords clutched in tired hands, feet dragging across blood-churned snow.

Time was gone.

Now was the time.

She reached deep into herself, following the magic shimmering around her fingers, past the broken bits, the sting of iron, the shackles clinging to her soul… to the quiet, seething core and *pulled.*

Power answered, a sudden surge—

Pain. Broken shackles burning, fresh blood flowing from her wounds as they struggled to hold back the magic.

She pulled harder, knowing the god was watching through First's mad red eyes, *feeling* the sharp crack of it under her skin, hearing it in the clamour and *clang clang clang* from the north. Knowing she had to do this now, now, *now* before the god bounded across the ice and—

The wind changed, a soft familiar *shush* picking up not from the bitter north but the south. From behind. Beyond the ring of raven wings and mad eyes. From the shore where prayers and moans rose, where the few waited, sighing their song of hopelessness and determination.

A different music skidded across the ice, the sharp snap of robes, the orderly clink of swords, the quiet hum of expectation. Of hope. Of faith.

A gentle 'S'Ahn' whispered across the width of a dozen fields.

Underfoot, the ice moaned under the weight of a new body.

Fear. Real fear. The first she had known in centuries bloomed. The kind that robbed the lungs of breath, that turned knees to jelly and stoppered sense, tried to cease thought and cage action.

The power in her stuttered.

The god, watching through First's eyes, laughed.

Anticipation shivered through the comets, rustled their glossy black wings, tightened dirt-encrusted hands around spears and through them... Through them, the god on the northern shore watched. Waited. The hunter singing his dogs to the kill.

No.

She stepped back. The hot, battle-maddened breath of a comet washed over her, the sharp, hard plates of a gauntlet pressed into her spine. Underneath, the mirror lake sang with cold, the ice moaning under the comets' talons, the echoing *crrrrack crrrrack crack* as new fractures spiralled outwards from the sharp, bloodied points.

She *pulled*.

Power surged anew, washed between the gaps in her soul, twisted through fragile mortal veins, burning as it went. Fire enveloped her hands, hungry white-gold licking her fingers, cauterising the wounds across her shoulders and chest, lighting up her eyes.

Blood ran down her cheeks, tear tracks burning through flesh.

'S'Ahn.'

No.

Not this time.

Power rippled the air on a thrum like a hummingbird's wings, accompanied by the sharp tang of ozone. Above, a shield descended, a golden sheet spreading outward to encompass the middle of the lake. Where she stood. Surrounded by comets.

By kin.

By sisters.

First looked up, snarled at the barrier. Caging them, sure as the iron inked into their flesh.

The comet beside First leapt skyward, wings whipping snow and ice into a storm. A third followed, and a fourth.

Arrowing for the shield, hammering it with spear tips and claws, every strike a new pain tearing her insides, new blood weeping from old wounds.

First pushed her face into S'Ahn's and snarled. Those mad red eyes could skewer bone, sure as the spear in her sister's fist.

She grabbed the spear, holding First in place, both her hands wrapped around the smooth, fire-hardened haft, one above and one below her sister's fist. It was a ridiculous contrast in this form, her fists the size of a child against First's, her fingers pale and delicate without the same weathered roughness or scared and calloused knuckles.

But it was not brawn she needed now, was not the ferocious stare or the bowel-loosening war cry.

It was the pain and the magic that came with it.

She pulled it out of her soul, ripped the last pieces of the restraints free from her insides, the iron and magic tearing as they came out, blood flowing from the wounds across chest and back, white robes turned red with the pattern of wings. With the pain came the magic. Not the hot, furious rush of before, the battle-maddened fury of the warrior – the same anger and pain that glazed First's eyes. This was a different power. A different magic. A brilliant, cold rush sweeping up from the depths of her being, bursting through the fissure that kept her two selves apart, and bursting from her fingers, her eyes, her back.

Wings tore through the rents in her flesh, the rush of them sending the comets behind her tumbling, the force of them blowing back hair, rocketing across the lake ice on a silent explosion.

First and the others beside her stumbled, arms shielding faces, pointed spear ends slammed into the cracked and crazed mirror.

They snarled. Rage once more consuming bloodied features.

The ice was no longer cold under S'Ahn's feet; she rose into the air on the sweep of wings to rival the comets' glossy black. But where theirs drank the remaining night, shimmered blue and grey in the coming dawn, hers were the sun, golden red and fierce. Same as the power curling over her fingers and spilling out her eyes, eating mortal flesh from the inside out.

From the northern shore came a godly yell, anger laced with denial. It *boomed*, splitting the air and then lightning descended from the sky, a viscous *crack*.

It hit, pierced her breast, shot all the way through spine and guts to lance the ice below.

The lake shattered, shards spewing upwards, outwards.

She didn't feel it, or maybe it blended with the other pain, maybe the cold eating her veins ate the lightning like it consumed flesh. She didn't know, didn't care.

The cold was splitting her apart, burning blood and hair and skin.

There was not much time.

But then, there had been too much time already.

Eons.

Days.

Hours.

A whisper from the south, the deep lilting *S'Ahn* shivering through her feathers, curling around her wrist, turning her chin.

But she wasn't S'Ahn. She'd never been S'Ahn. She was someone else, the guardian, the thirteenth, the brilliant, blinding sun come to rip away the dark and turn lightning to ashes.

And she would do that, would burn until the lake was a desert, until the snow-capped mountain peaks ran with rivers, the north's army a bone yard and all that remained of her was less than ash.

She would burn and the iron caging her sisters would burn with her.

Reprisal

INTRODUCTION

I cannot tell you how many story ideas I've had because a movie or television show pissed me off. I swear, there is no better way to start the plot bunnies rolling than subjecting me to a questionable story, especially if it's chauvinist. Forget red flag in front of a bull, this is blank blinking cursor in front of writer.

The impetuous for *Reprisal* came as I was watching a terrible teen movie about a bunch of high school dudes with magic. It's only redeeming features where the eye-candy and a rather chauvinist plot device where only men could wield magic, which ticked me off. Big time.

I mean, why do only guys get magic? And such a sucky (like literally, using it drained their life force) kind of magic at that?

Anyway, me being me, I came up with a counter. *Reprisal* is it.

 Learn more about the writing of *Reprisal.* Scan the QR code for the audio commentary, soundtrack and more.

REPRISAL

The mare's leg is laid open to the bone. Her skin and sinew separated in one jagged stroke from shoulder to knee. She stands lopsided on the other three, sinking into the stall's carpet of straw, her head drooping and her ears wilted. I lay one hand on her nose, gently stroking the white blaze, her lead in my other hand.

Jack is crouched by the wound, his hands bloody. There is an edgy tension in my limbs as my husband's mouth thins and his brow furrows like the freshly tilled fields. He shakes his head. My heart sinks.

He puts his hands to his knees and pushes himself upward. 'She'll have to be put down.'

I stroke the mare's nose. She is a faithful creature, placid with age and years of hard labour. Without her, the fields would not be tilled nor grain taken to the village market. 'We can't afford another horse.

'We'll make do.' Jack looks past me, toward the open barn door. 'I can hitch Daisy to the plough.'

I follow his gaze. The cow awaits her morning milking, lazily swatting flies, untroubled by my son's clumsy pets of her broad shoulder. Her honey-coloured coat is again glossy and her udder full after the lean months of winter but unlike our neighbour's oxen, she is small and delicate.

I turn back, raising my eyes to Jack's. 'There's another way.'

Jack's shoulders tense and the centres of his eyes grow large till only a thin line of blue rings the black. He stares at me for several long seconds and I smile softly, willing him to agree. The Reverend's sermons, full of shaken fists and dire warnings, have frightened us all, inviting suspicion into the village. Our friends and neighbours peer from around their curtains and hold themselves ready to point and cry alarm at the slightest hint of devilry, but there is little choice. We need the mare.

Finally, Jack shakes his head. 'It's too dangerous. If the Reverend should find out...'

'There's no one here to carry tales.' I widen my smile, gesturing around the barn, empty except for us, the horse, and little Devon petting the cow.

His lips tighten. For a moment, I fear he will refuse and wonder what I will do if he does.

Jack nods but his expression remains grim as he holds out his hand for the lead. I place it in his palm and step around him to the mare's shoulder, touching it lightly just above the wound. The unmarred skin is warm and smooth, her chestnut coat silky beneath my fingers and for a moment I stand there, the dusty scent of horse strong in my nose.

I crouch and place my other hand on the mare's knee, a bare inch below the ragged tear. Here, her coat is tacky with blood as it seeps from the wound and an iron tang mixes with her dusty scent.

I close my eyes. A few moments of concentration as I summon the coil of warmth that lives in my belly. It shivers and then leaps to my will, flooding through my chest in a rush that lightens my head.

I take a breath, quieting the magick before drawing it through my hands and sending it into the animal's flesh. The warmth twists and turns, wrapping itself around veins and muscles, pulling them together. It is not enough though, the injury is too great and my power too small, so I steel myself and reach down through my feet and into the earth, seeking more. It comes quickly, flowing hot and rich, burning its way through my hands and into the horse. Behind my lids I can see skin knit together, unblemished and whole, and my head spins.

My eyes open and I smile, barely noticing the grass at my feet, brown and dry, its life taken for the mare.

There is a gasp from behind me. I turn. Euphoria vanishes.

Little Devon stands at the stall's gate, jumping and waving, and next to him—Oh Dear Lord—next to him in her heavy black skirts is Hetty Jones, the storekeeper's wife, a hand over her mouth and a covered basket hanging from the crook of her arm. Her wide brown eyes stare at me with such fear that I think my heart may stop.

Beside me Jack moves, taking a step forward, his face as pale as mine. Hetty's eyes snap from me to Jack, to his outstretched hand. She stares at it like she would a snake, or the Devil himself. She draws back, her eyes growing wider.

'Hetty,' Jacks says and takes another step forward.

The basket falls to the ground, a crock of honey spilling from under the white covering.

Hetty runs.

☾

I stumble in the dark and my heart leaps before I recover my footing.

I pause, clutching little Devon closer, terrified of dropping his precious weight and just as terrified of the stillness of his form. I squeeze my eyes shut and send a prayer to God that my magick wasn't too much.

The mob had come so fast, so much faster than we had thought. Hetty's feet must have flown her to the Reverend. There had been no time to pack the cart, less to hitch it to the mare and take ourselves to safety. Only my magick had allowed our escape, allowed us to slip past the storekeeper waiting at our back door with a torch.

There had been so much confusion, so much fear, and the mare had taken all of my magick to heal. I had reached past the empty tangle of power in my belly, reached once more for the earth when little Devon had clutched at my leg. Thick and rich the power poured through me, igniting the spell on my lips and wrapping confusion around the storekeeper's eyes. My son sank to the ground at my feet, his face pale, a small part of his life absorbed by the spell.

For several moments I stood horrified, looking down at my son's crumpled form. Then Jack yelled at me to run and I scooped little Devon into my arms, feeling his heart beat against my chest, and fled, dashing past the storekeeper's sightless eyes.

Now the breeze at my back brings the whiff of burning wood and my heart leaps. I glance over my shoulder and see the vague glow of the mob's torches over the rise. They are gaining on me.

A faint noise escapes my lips as I look frantically toward the tree line. I have to reach it before they top the rise or all is lost.

Jack is already gone, taken by the mob. I heard our front door splintering as I ran, and knew my husband was not running behind us as he had promised. I dashed through darkness toward the barn, Devon still clutched close, his arms and legs dangling limp by my sides. I reached its dense shadow and turned. The mob had surrounded our house, lighting the night with fire, the Reverend at their head.

People spilled from the front door and my heart clenched when I saw Jack struggling in their midst. They jerked to a halt before the Reverend. The old man leaned forward. Jack screamed. I wanted to scream with him and bit my lip till it bled. I saw Jack crumple, disappearing behind a curtain of bodies. The Reverend shouted and raised something that glinted in the torchlight. I didn't see him bring it down, instead I turned and ran. From behind me Jack screamed again.

The field is soft and my feet sink and slide in the furrowed earth. I cross the field as fast as my sodden skirts allow. My breath comes in rasps and the faint taste of blood coats the back of my throat. My limbs are tired and Devon is heavy in my arms, but the knowledge of the mob at my back and the memory of Jack's horrifying screams keep me moving.

Faster, faster until I fear tripping over my own feet. Twice I risk a look over my shoulder and each time the glow over the rise is brighter. The tree line is close but not close enough. My heart pounds in my ears, louder and louder as I run. It's not loud enough to drown the sudden braying of the hounds.

Oh my Lord, let me reach the trees before they see me.

Only a dozen yards before I'm safe and again I glance over my shoulder. My blood freezes and my feet with it. A silhouette, torch in hand, stands against the sky.

Instinctually, I clutch Devon tighter.

They've found me, oh dear Lord in Heaven, they've found me!

A movement from the figure on the rise sends liquid fire through my veins and I start to run.

I hear a shout and fear lends speed to my feet but the short distance to the trees still seems like a mile.

☾

I crouch lower in the hollow of the firs as the mob draws near.

The dogs run in circles, my magick has confused our trail, leaving them no scent to follow. I squeeze my eyes shut as the glow of the torches approaches.

If they see us, it is over. They will hang me just for being born, and my son... I clutch Devon closer feeling him breathe, warm against my neck.

Oh Merciful Lord, please protect my son from what I must do.

They can't see us, they can't see us.

Behind my eyes Devon blazes with life, so much closer and so much brighter than the earth and roots below. I grit my teeth, fighting an unholy instinct to draw on Devon for my spell, and touch the earth instead, feeling the pull in my belly as the magick comes. It wraps itself around our place of refuge, twisting and turning around the hollowed-out trunk, playing tricks with the moonlight until we're obscured from sight.

They can't see us, they can't see us.

I rock as I repeat my chant, my eyes closed tight against the sight of the mob milling in confusion like their dogs. Soon the chant is all I can hear, all I will allow myself to hear.

They can't see us, they can't see us.

Somewhere in the distance I am aware of the Reverend's voice. It reverberates against the trees and for a moment I am back in the small church, sitting on the hard pew as he stands at the pulpit. Standing as straight as his stooped shoulders will allow, his knuckles white, the wrath of the Lord on his face and promises of damnation on his tongue.

'She's bewitched your dogs, Johnson, you can't deny her perfidy now!'

I squeeze my eyes tighter and think harder to drown the sound of his hated voice.

'... confounded the dogs...'

'She can't go far...'

☾

Dawn breaks before I let the magick fade.

We are alone now. Above me a bird sings in the morning and I look up, spying the white spotted breast and cinnamon wings of a thrush. From somewhere comes the furtive rustling of leaves and something soft and round catches my eye. A hare hops an arm's length from our refuge, its brown sides quivering as it sniffs the air. Its ears twitch once, twice, before it drops its head and paws at the litter of leaves and grass.

For the moment we are safe.

I look down at my son. His soft blonde head rests against my chest. Warm relief twists through me and I press my lips to his curls before resting my cheek against the top of his head and hugging him close.

'Devon,' I say. The hare's long ears twitch at the sound of my voice. My son does not respond. 'Devon.' I look down, noting his pale cheeks and the darkness under his eyes. My heart clutches, something nameless and terrifying crawls into my throat.

My hand shakes as I lay it against his cheek. It is cold. Too, too cold.

'Devon?' My voice rises, becoming strident. The hare lifts its head, ears alert.

I tilt my son's head. It lolls against my arm. His face is lax, without expression, his lips blue. I press my fingers into the juncture between head and neck.

Oh Dear Lord, please, please, please.

☾

I leave my son in a cold grave under the branches of a sapling pine. It will grow. I have ensured that no blade will leave a mark on its smooth trunk. The hare and a nest of starlings paid the price for my spell.

I am cold inside, my innards are laid out next to my son and there is nothing left in me to feel. The coldness is its own comfort though, has its own voice, its own urgings.

☾

The village square is grey, silent, tomorrow giving way to today on the crow of the cock. I stand beneath the oak at its centre, no longer cold, no longer empty. A day and night have passed since I left Devon under the pine and I have used the time well.

Now, this morning under the oak, I wait for the villagers to wake and discover the things I have taken during the night.

A shutter clatters. A candle flickers in the general store.

My breath shortens and my shoulders tighten.

The wind rustles in the leaves above me and from somewhere distant a cow lows. Closer, I hear birds flutter and call. Of the villagers I hear nothing and my chest pounds and squeezes. I take a step forward, then another, willing, hoping, waiting.

It rings out, high and piercing and piteous, a wail from the little house behind the store, full of pain and grief. The storekeeper's daughter has found her parents, cold and still like my little Devon.

I smile and wait for the others.

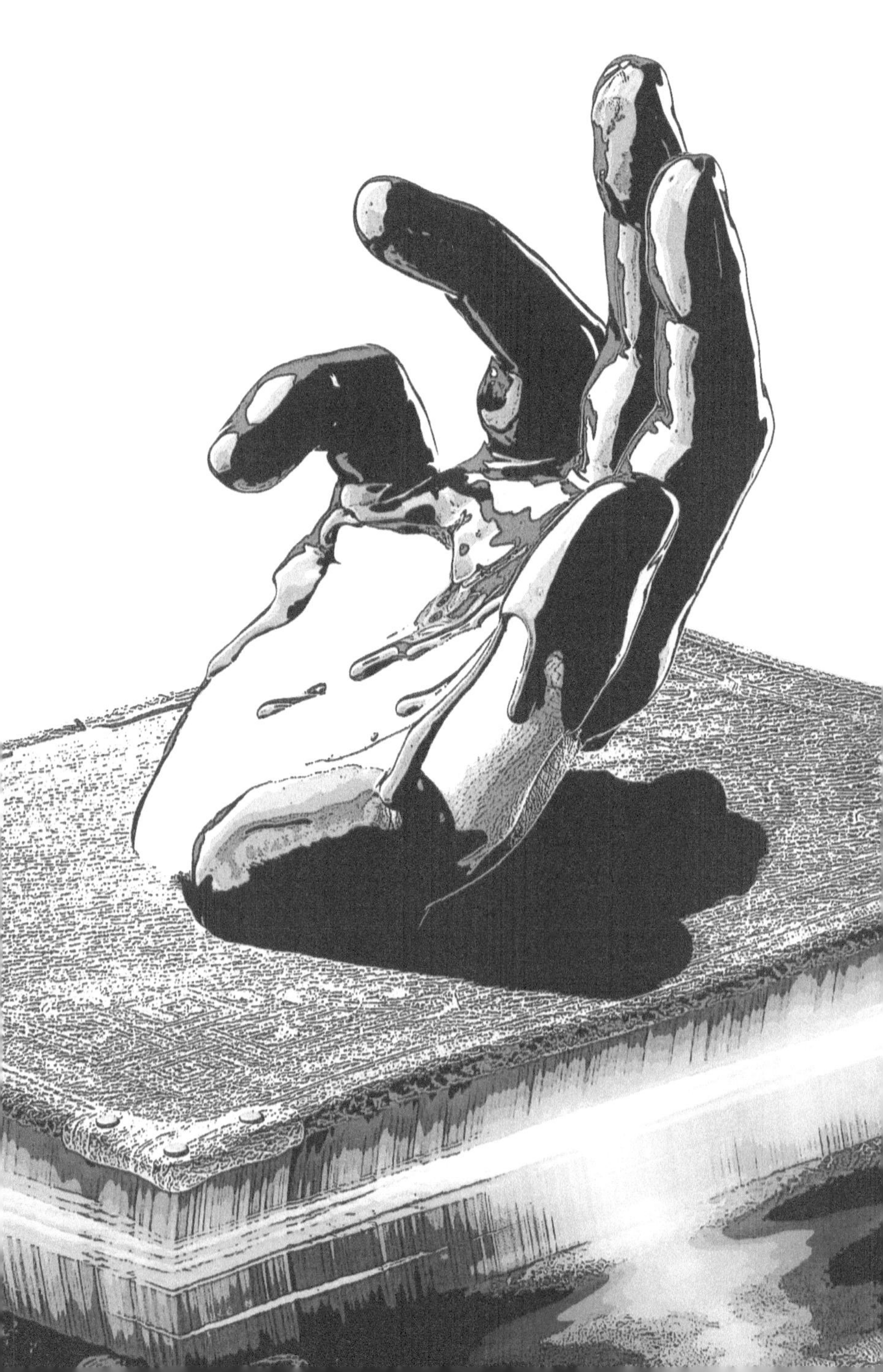

LITTLE BLACK BOOK

INTRODUCTION

This story is weird. When I first wrote it, it was one of those little bits of daydream fluff that didn't really *fit* anywhere. Usually, my stories kind of slot into one another, particularly the science fiction ones, but this… it was an orphan, a poor, lonely kid all on its own, just existing.

However, in the two years since it was written, *Little Black Book* has gained a few siblings (one of which follows this story) and settled into a universe of its own. It's a weird universe, a strange Australian-flavoured urban fantasy without were-creatures, vampires or even urbanity.

 Learn more about the writing of *Little Black Book*. Scan the QR code for the audio commentary, soundtrack and more.

LITTLE BLACK BOOK

The little black book was old and tattered, the pages yellowed, edges crumbled—eaten by the rats and other bibliophilic vermin that had infested her aunt's attic.

Not anymore though, not after the fire.

Niyha turned the book over in her hands and wondered if her aunt had done the same, had ever sat in the little hothouse out back and just stared at the faded leather, run her fingers over the words carved into the surface.

"Prina Kolaeda."

Prina Kolaeda. The name sent a shiver down her spine, or maybe that was just the way the letters seemed to writhe. The plain block print stamped into the leather—the faintest hint of gold still clinging to the corners—shouldn't be able to twist around itself and wind around her fingers, but it did. The "P" slipping up over her knuckle, the tail on that final "a" reaching out to entangle her thumb as if to suck her into the journal too.

She shook the letters off and forced herself to put the book down. It was harder than it should have been, her fingers cramped, muscles pulling, tendons standing on end as a little voice in the back of her head screamed at her to hold tight. It was deep and commanding, a hook reaching down into the pit of her, trying to rip her soul out through her mouth.

Niyha breathed—in through the nose, out through the mouth—and concentrated on the cry of the crows in the trees, the sigh of the soot-laden breeze, the distant rumble of cars. She breathed again—in, out—and built a wall between herself and the voice, tall and thick. It screamed one last time, a desperate lunge for the small gap at the top of the wall then died.

Her fingers relaxed, and the book plopped into the garden bed, sinking into the old soil—more dust than loam now and covered in a fine layer of ash.

'Are you happy?' The voice spoke from behind, twisting out of the dead arms of her aunt's wisteria, branches that had once been full of green, now little more than decaying twigs.

'Are you?' she whispered back.

Corrian moved out of the dark. Tall and slim, with a hard face almost as ancient as the stones beneath Niyha's sandals, even if age had forgotten to carve the matching lines into his skin. 'Yes,' he said. 'I am.'

Niyha nodded, gaze lifting from the book to the house. The fire had razed it to the ground but had left the fireplaces with their chimneys standing—three silent, blackened sentinels marking the boundaries of the old building.

She wouldn't miss it, wouldn't miss the way the veranda creaked, giving away her every attempt to escape, nor how the old weatherboard siding with its faded yellow paint had shoved splinters under her fingernails. But she would remember them more fondly than she would the shrill screech of her aunt's parrot and the sharp slap of the old woman's hand.

Niyha rubbed her cheek, still feeling the sting of that last imprint, the ragged burn of hooked nails dragging over flesh.

Corrian settled beside her, the long black ends of his coat flaring out either side, knees together, long bony fingers—nails hooked and as black as her aunt's had been—laid on his lap.

'Are you happy?' he asked again, voice soft, like feathers.

'Yes,' she said, but her voice was a whisper, hesitation and guilt thick in her throat.

Corrian cocked his head, a sharp sideways movement that

looked strange on a human neck. He stared at her, eyes black as his nails, the iris swallowing the white until only a thin rim of it remained. He stared at her and didn't move, the sharp slashes of his eyebrows half raised. There was no reproach on his brow, no disbelief or anger, nothing but patience.

Tension shivered up her back, made her shoulders tight and her feet restless. She looked away, away from Corrian, away from the ruins of the house, seeking out the hypnotic spin of Old Lady Anise's windmill in the distance.

'You are not happy,' Corrian said. She felt the garden bench's old slats shift with his weight, and the absence of his stare like a laser shifted from her shoulders. 'It is okay, humans are often conflicted.'

'I'm not conflicted. She was... she was a...' She wanted to say "monster" or "devil", even just "evil" but the words caught in her throat, bottled up behind that last memory of her aunt, the way the fire had run up her legs. So fast. The blue-green flames wound around her waist, her shoulders and head, and then *whomp* it consumed her, not so much burning as collapsing in on itself before eating its own tail, sucking her aunt into the book.

Niyha's fingers itched, the urge to trace over the letters hewn into the leather strong.

She was free now, free of her aunt, free of the house and yet… and yet—

A thick brown twig nudged the book out of reach.

'Best to leave that.' Corrian nudged the book a little farther away. 'Perhaps best to let the earth have it, hide your aunt away, safe in the soil.'

Niyha nodded. The thought of knowing it was here, her aunt's evil bound in the old, crumbled pages, made her skin crawl.

'And what of the—' She was going to say "house" but a shift in the breeze brought the scent of ashes and she stopped herself. 'What of the land? What will I do with that?'

It was hers now, by both human law and witch, written down in ink and blood, plain and bold. Every worthless inch, from the old wrought-iron gate out front to the thin ribbon of the creek out back, and the book sinking into the soil.

The thought of it, of what she'd done for it...

The text on the journal writhed, and for a second Niyha sensed her aunt reaching out to her, hand wreathed in blue-green flames.

Oh Goddess. She thought confining her aunt in the journal would free her, but now... The blood rushed from her face, leaving the ice of dawning horror behind. No one would buy the land, and without money Niyha couldn't afford to leave, stuck here as surely as her aunt was in the book.

Corrian looked up, sharp, sudden, like he hadn't thought that far ahead, but she knew better. Crows always had plans within plans, they were Morrigan's favourite for more than their mastery of chess.

'We will pay you.'

'What?'

Corrian nodded, a strange double bob more suited to a bobble-head than a humanoid. 'Yes, we will pay you for the land. One hundred stones and you will fly away like you would have if she had not been.' He nodded again. 'Yes, it is settled.'

'What? But—'

He hummed, low in his throat, the sound a trill away from being a song, a serenade to welcome in the morning. Other hums rose from the surrounding trees, shadows passing over the hothouse's old, frosted glass ceiling.

Magic played over her skin—the gentle silken flutter of wings buffeting her cheeks, the prick of talons through her shirt, the musty scent of feathers in her nose—and then it was gone. Where the book had been was a pile of brilliant glittering stones, opals of every size, shape and colour, some as small as her pinkie others large as a twenty-cent piece, and one... Her fingers trembled, made the rising sun dance under the opal's skin as she picked it up, lighting it like the ocean caught in the stone, shards of teal playing in the dark blue depths of its heart.

The tear-drop shaped gem fit into her palm, whispered of distant places.

'Corrian.' She breathed his name, wonder and gratitude trying to fight through the shock and fear in her voice. 'This is too much, these opals are worth a fortune.'

He shrugged, and in that moment as he shifted his shoulders and shuffled his feet, she glimpsed the crow's stark black plumage under his form. 'They are stones,' he said. 'We cannot eat them.'

He shifted again, the blue-black sheen of feathers flashing in the dawn light as he wriggled on the bench. He looked skyward, and she read impatience in the snap of his movement.

She closed her hand around the blue opal and held it to her heart. 'Thank you.'

Corrian smiled, his human form fading in a swirl of mist and wings, leaving just the trill of his voice and feather behind. 'Fly, little bird,' he said. 'Fly.'

CORPSES &DEMON HORSES

INTRODUCTION

I loved writing *Corpses & Demons Horses*. It's *Little Black Book's* next-oldest sibling and when I first started considering whether I'd created a new rural urban fantasy universe. A lot of *Corpses*, and indeed the other stories in the world (none of which are in this collection, you'll have to wait for *Short Bits Volume 5* #sorry-not-sorry), are taken from my own experiences, much more so than any other tale.

For instance, Dog's love of smelly substances and the missus's disgust at such are reflections of my mum and her dog, while Horse's uppityness comes direct from the antics of my own trusty steed, and Shetty... The small, fluffy pony breed known as the Shetland came by its reputation honestly.

 Learn more about the writing of *Corpses & Demon Horses*. Scan the QR code for the audio commentary, soundtrack and more.

CORPSES & DEMON HORSES

'What should we do with the body?'

'Niyha's paying good money.'

'For what?'

'The eyes.' Magpie paused, cocked her head in one of those weird, sharp movements that always made Dog's skin crawl. 'The toes.'

He considered the corpse's feet, bloated and purple with death, skin starting to slip from its time in the water. There was still pink polish on the nails, a fat-cheeked feline inked on the bridge of the right foot and a shiny bracelet around the ankle. The rest of the corpse was naked.

Dog sniffed and then wished he hadn't. Not even the milk-rich smell of cow shit or the earthy wet of the river—running brown with the sediment pulled of freshly tilled paddocks, an iridescent chemical stain snaking through it—could cover the stench of rotting flesh.

'I ain't carrying it,' he said. Normally he would, the scent of dead shit made the missus wild, but there were shades of dead, and this one was on the uncomfortable threshold of fresh dead and not-quite-dead enough. Plus, he was pretty sure the stomach was going to pop, either that, or the human'd swallowed a sheep whole just before it died. A squirmy, expanding sheep.

With maggots.

He shuddered just thinking of the scrubbing if he got that shit in his fur or on his shirt. Not just scrubbing but scolding too, and the cold hose. The missus'd probably tie him up on the back of the ute again and drive into town.

To the Dog Wash.

With the Demon Dryer.

The second shudder wracked his spine all the way from the tip of his head to arse, almost popping his tail out of his human flesh.

Magpie shifted, sharp and jerky, still new in her human flesh and awkward with it. The shirt and shorts he'd only just managed to shove on her—if only so the local humans didn't go looney again and the missus stayed off his tail—didn't sit as well as they had when they'd set off from the backyard. It took a little time to settle into human flesh, and Magpie'd done pretty well, but he reckon'd she'd be sprouting wings to go with the feathers in her hair before long.

She flexed her bare feet, black and scaly, just four toes and too-long to fit into any of the human shoes Dog'd had stashed under the porch. At the moment, she was contemplating her own feet then the corpse's and then her feet again, neck snapping to and fro, and Dog had to look away.

The way the feathers sticking out from under Magpie's white hair kinda *slapped* on her shoulders, like puppy *crack crack cracks*, was too much. Made him think of the sheep hocks the missus had stashed in the bottom of the chest freezer, like he wouldn't scent them out under all that ice-cream and pizza.

'I cannot carry it,' Magpie finally said. 'It is too big for me.'

'No shit,' he muttered. For a bird—and maybe even for a dog, he admitted to himself on occasion—Magpie was pretty bright, but sometimes he wondered if all that time above the ground starved her brain of oxygen.

Even in human flesh, Magpie was a pip-squeak.

Dog crouched beside the corpse; female and young, he thought, although it was hard to tell with its flesh all puffy, straightening out the lines humans tended to get. They weren't many marks on it, and the scent, though enough to ruffle his hackles, didn't carry the sweet tempting sliminess of dog bait.

It was in good condition, and Niyha'd probably pay good bones for more than just its eyes and toes, especially if it was in one piece.

He slapped his knees and rose. 'I'm going to get Horse,' he said, already squelching through the ankle-deep mud toward the house.

'Horse does not like dead things,' Magpie said. 'Remember the sheep?'

Dog stopped, one foot lifted. Yeah, he did. He'd tagged along on one of the missus' and Horse's strolls. The sheep carcass had been pretty ripe, a good few days dead in the sun, the stomach and guts hollowed out—he'd scented Fox on that—perfect for a nice roll. And he'd been doing that, planning a little wash in Horse's trough to rinse the smell off enough the missus wouldn't catch whiff, when Horse'd blundered in.

The uppity fucker had gone sideways, all big-eyed and snorty like he didn't enjoy a good roll in the mud himself, and the missus had landed on her arse.

That had *not* been a good day.

Stupid horse.

He growled, thought about it a second. 'I'll get Cow.'

Magpie clacked her tongue. 'Sun's going down.'

Fuck. Cow'd be lining up for milking, and real irritable too if he tried to pull her out. He rubbed his side. Might even land a kick.

'Goat then,' and he turned back to walk away—

'It was shearing day last week, and you nipped one of her kids in the muster.'

Crap.

'Sheep—' he began and then cut himself off when Magpie cocked her head and gave him a look that made *him* feel stupid. But yeah, he'd earned that one.

Missus'd cornered one of the flock's elders the other day and now most of him was in the freezer, under the ice-cream and pizza. The rest… Dog licked his chops, the elder'd tasted pretty good, a little strong on the back of the palate, but that's how it was with the old ones.

But if Horse and Cow wouldn't come, and Goat and Sheep were mad at him, that just left…

Dog's short russet-brown hair quivered as his human ears slid up his skull and got longer, only to flatten. 'Shetty,' he said. And no, his voice *did not* waver and that was *not* his tail growing out of his arse at just the thought of the shaggy little demon.

Magpie nodded. 'Shetty,' she said back. Firm. Confident without a lick of fear, in the way only a creature that could fly could be. Fly, safe and high out of the reach of the Spotty One's teeth and hooves.

Dog shuddered. 'I ain't getting Shetty.'

He turned from the house, squelched back through the mud, and stood over the bloated corpse. Puffy cheeks, stomach like one of the human balloon things, right before missus added too much air. Just one good jostle and *pop*, except it wouldn't be air bursting out of that stretched white skin, it'd be guts and other gooey things.

Getting in his hair, sliming his skin.

The missus'd go cow-shit.

But there was Niyha and all her bones…

Dog rolled his shoulders, forced his tail back inside his human skin, bent and dragged the corpse's arms over his back.

The Dryer was better than the small demon horse, at least he'd get to stick his muzzle in the wind on the way into town, bark at a few stupid birds, piss on a few tires. Good times.

Better than Shetty.

Anything was better than Shetty.

Letters I'll Never Send

INTRODUCTION

Like the Valkyrie, *Letters I'll Never Send* is another instance of a particular story idea being stuck in my head for a really long time. It all started with an old-ish TV series called *Veritas: the Quest* (which *didn't* piss me off, except for only getting one season) and a role-playing game (I forget what it was).

It's rattled around in my head for almost as long as the Valkyrie and various spin-off have popped up in any number of places, but most notably here. The main character in this version is older and more awesome than the original, with strange powers (that she was never meant to have) and a rather large chip on her shoulder.

 Learn more about the writing of *Letters I'll Never Send*. Scan the QR code for the audio commentary, soundtrack and more.

LETTERS I'LL NEVER SEND

He stands with his back to the office, the vaulted ceiling, the heavy dark wood panelling and couch, the desk and the giant lion head embossed in metal above it. He stands there, bathes in the setting dusk and looks out over the city, the skyscrapers piercing the horizon, the residential towers a carpet of brown and grey at his feet.

Many would call this day's end, but his short black hair is still damp and his white shirt and tailored vest still carry the scent of laundry. The coffee in the small green cup cradled in his scarred hand is dark and bitter, and the flat silver rings on his square-tipped fingers with their manicured nails flash in the dying light.

He does not like "mornings", as he thinks of this time of day, he would rather be with the woman in his bed, waking up in other ways. But here he is, and even if he does not like it he can take the moment—the quiet before the chaos begins anew—as the peace it is.

There is little enough to be had.

He raises the coffee to his lips and contemplates the darkening city.

Behind, a door glides open and hard shoes *clack* on the dark cherry floorboards before they're muffled by the Berber rug.

The presence at his back is silent and stoic, waits without fidget as he finishes the coffee and returns the cup to the matching saucer sitting atop an antique sideboard.

'What is it?' He speaks without turning.

Stars pop over the city as the sun falls and electricity takes hold.

A large document envelope is thrust at him. It gleams under the office lights—still dimmed to better witness the coming night—in the way of a sec-package, the tech threading the silk-like plastic affording it a security almost as invincible as the material itself.

He takes it in one hand, the other slipping into his pocket, gaze skimming over his name and ident code on the front, turns the envelope over and stares at the back. Where the sender should be. And isn't.

A glance up, meeting Gvida's poison-green eyes with a single raised brow, he hefts the envelope.

Gvida shakes his head. 'Sent anonymously through a registered courier. They have no records.'

He considers the envelope, thin and flat, no thicker than a half-centimetre. 'Is it safe?'

'It passed all the scans: no biologicals, no explosives.'

He nods, turns the envelope over again. There are ways to fool the scans, and while there are enough who want him dead to try, few are intelligent enough to succeed, and of those... There were easier ways to get the job done.

He retreats from the windows, walking between the long square lounges to the desk, pressing his thumb to the envelop's seal as he does. The seal pulses as it reads his print, then a sharp prick as it takes it his blood.

In the ten strides it takes him to reach the leather desk chair, the envelope is open and the lights embedded in the ceiling have brightened, turning the office to day even as the city outside sinks to night.

He flicks the envelope open, draws out the sheaf of papers inside, and sits.

He sits for a long time.

Above him, the metallic lion bust—maw large enough to swallow him whole—roars in silence.

The paper is real. Old-fashioned lined paper, the edges yellowed, the grain rough, creases where it has been folded and unfolded in neat, horizontal thirds. There are no intelli-fibres embedded in its surface, no holo-sheen or nano-chips in the corners but it is not the age of it that stalls his brain, not the hotel logo printed at the top or the address half a world away at the bottom. It's the words.

Written in blue ink, the handwriting slanted and almost illegible in places, he's skimmed the first line, and the second, not understanding, impatient to get on with his day and then…

He slumps against the chair back.

There's not enough air in the office; his chest is tight, mouth dry, papers crumpling in his fist.

Gvida hovers on the other side of the wide desk. 'Sir?'

'No one disturbs me,' he says.

There is a nod; Gvida always nods, but he doesn't care, he only cares about the letter in his hand.

ONE

[A name is written the top of the page, but it's been crossed out over and over again, until all that's left is a messy black rectangle.]

I'll never send this letter, you'll never see it; I'm not writing it for you, I'm writing it for me, a farewell letter to the girl I used to be.

You should know that before I begin, just like you should know I'm not sorry for leaving, not then, not now.

Did you understand why? Did you care? I mean, I know you cared, but did you care because I was gone or because you lost face when I did?

I could never tell if your feelings for me were real, were for *me* or if they were for Father, to meet his expectations. You made it seem they were for him; the way you'd brush my shoulder, how you'd take my hand. Gently, like you were afraid to get close, as if my half-blood would wash off on you. Or worse, like I was a duty, the mongrel our fathers shackled you to, to tie the clans together and keep you in place.

Then there were the other times, when it was just us and you thought no one would see. Those times made me believe.

Until they didn't.

Did Father make it difficult for you when I ran? Did he summon you to the office, stand you in front of the desk with the blinds all drawn so he was silhouetted by the dusk? Did the sun pour through the window in all those shades of red? Did he stare at you with those cold eyes and try to peel your brain? Did he demand you find me, bring me back and lock me in chains? Did he make you suffer?

Did he?

Sometimes, I wonder. Usually when the nightmares start or the music shakes the floor from the nightclub downstairs; when I can't sleep. I imagine you standing straight and tall, facing Father, pretending like the sun doesn't blind you, that you can actually *see* his face, the anger in his eyes instead of just feeling it. I remember what that felt like, can't forget it; a weight like the sun itself is burning through the window, carving a hole in my chest.

And the times when he wasn't furious... Those are the times that feature in my nightmares, not even the things I've seen or done in the passing years can completely erase those.

It was always better to see his eyes, to know if they matched the sun or if they were cold. Always better to be prepared.

So I imagine how it must have been for you, and I pray he was furious, I pray he yelled and pointed and punched. I pray you left that office with bruises and a split lip, or even a broken jaw, and not something else. I pray he wasn't cold. That you didn't feel time and space seizing in the face of the soul-devouring black hole that is his other emotion.

I know he didn't kill you. I saw you in that little village near the Hanoi border. I was sitting in the dirt, under the banyan tree, hugging a threadbare blanket against the night. You walked right past me, out of place in your custom shoes and suit, your hair swept back in a midnight wave. You looked the way you always looked in public—tall and confident, wearing that expression, the one that said you'd seen the world and found it wanting.

If you'd seen me, would it have changed?

I was afraid you would see. All you had to do was turn your head and lower your chin. It'd only been a year since I ran, and I'd had... difficulties, was hungry and sick and injured, but I hadn't changed that much. Still kept my hair short then, hadn't coloured it, hadn't gotten my first implant, hadn't started wearing the glasses or the ear cuffs, didn't have the bodysuit or the bracers that hide me now.

Maybe it was because I *was* sick—thin, grey even—that you didn't recognise me. You wouldn't have been expecting what I was then, what the months and the fights had made me. You would been looking for the princess, the little girl who followed you around the compound, the older one who tugged on your shirt, the teen who blushed and just about fainted the first time you kissed her.

I wasn't her by then. The fights made me tougher, meaner, showed me just how much of Father was in me. How much darkness he passed along with the black hair and brown eyes. I see it sometimes, after a job, that soul-sucking oblivion. It scares me.

Maybe now, if I went back, I could stand in front of Father's desk and match him, black hole for black hole. If we did, would Father and I both walk out or would you be left mourning a boss, or a former-lover?

I couldn't stay there, in that house, in the city or anywhere within reach of him. I am not my mother. Maybe if I had been, maybe if I'd had the force of her resolve, the strength of her personality, the resilience, things might have been different.

Maybe. So many maybes.

I didn't want maybes, and so I ran; ran hard and fast and as far as my wits and the little cash I had would take me.

It wasn't far, not at first, but then the fights found me and things... changed.

They changed a lot.

I'm still not coming home, and I'm still not sorry.

I'll never be sorry.

—T

TWO

CJ,

The fights changed me, or rather, they were the catalyst.

Did you trace me there? Did you see the cages, the "dorms" with the bars and padlocks on the outside? Did you see the bunks? Charitable to call them bunks, more like canvas sheets strung against the walls. There were no blankets, no sheets or pillows, not unless you earned them, and even when you did, you still had to keep them.

I was... lucky, I guess. Ma had made sure I could fight, and Father... If it weren't for him, the things he taught even when he hated me, I might not have made it the first week let alone the first month. Or the one after that.

I died in that place, I died a thousand times. Over and over.

After the first few times, dying gets easier, losing little bits of the person you were seems as natural as the sunrise. It's the first death that hurts the most, the one where you lose hope.

That first death almost killed me—dead for real, not just the metaphorical deaths that came later. It was a shank in the hand of my only friend that did it, the handle of an old plastic fork right in my stomach. I almost bled-out on the shit-covered concrete, the cold was in my bones, the dark stealing my vision. I was sad at first, scared. The girl who stabbed me had been my rock, my safety, even if I'd only been a warm body in the way of the new comforts she wanted. The ones I'd earned through pain and violence yet hadn't learned to keep.

I would have them given to her if she'd asked, but she didn't. She took. She stole.

She died, true-dead, on the concrete next to me.

I watched the life go out of her eyes and waited for my turn.

And then I saw you, not the real you. If you'd been there, I wouldn't be here, writing this nonsense on this shitty motel-room pad, knowing I'm never going to send it. I'd be back at the compound, or true-dead in the family crypt—is there really much difference between the two? One is a death of the soul, the other the body.

I'd rather be the latter, even if the former meant being with you.

It was that first death that gave me life. Watching Amelia gasp out her last, the blood bubbling over lips, her mouth gaped like a fish, that was the moment that gave me strength. As her eyes went still and her mouth slack, I shed hope, the last few vestiges of wishful thinking; I killed the silly girl waiting for you to show up, riding in with your suit and Father's men at your back. Every inch the heir to his empire.

If you had, I'd have gone back happily, gratefully, falling all over myself to be out of that place, with those people, and I might never have left.

I'm glad you didn't come. I give *thanks* that you didn't because I was born in that moment.

I dragged myself up off that concrete, I ripped the shirt off Amelia's corpse and stuffed it against the hole she'd made. I washed it myself, bound it myself. I endured the chills and sweats that came after. I died and I came back, different. The first change, the hardest.

The one where I decided, *truly* decided, I wanted to live and living meant doing things that hurt, things that were hard and dark and dirty. It was the first step; the first death of many.

That place was full of death. My second came when I took my first life. I hadn't wanted to. I'd resisted for weeks, climbing the fight ladder from the little exhibition matches, the ones that happened even before the punters came—the bloodthirsty crowd who liked the hollow thunk of fist hitting flesh—to the warmups, before they threw in the paid matches, the ones with the real money.

Ma always told me I had talent, that the fight was engraved on my DNA, bred into my bones and that training only refined it. She was right, but she never spoke to the will, the desire to win, to do violence. To end someone.

I never had that. I *ran* because I didn't have that, because I didn't want to be Father, because I felt his darkness slithering inside me. I didn't want to be him. I wanted to be Ma, noble and pure; it wasn't until later I knew different, that my vision of her was that of a little girl.

The man wasn't the first I'd killed, Amelia had taken that trophy, but she'd been a reflex, an accident almost. I hadn't meant to kill her, she'd stabbed me once, drawn her arm back for the second strike and I'd just... finished it. My chopstick to her jugular. But the second man... he was on the cage floor, shattered knee, fractured rib, crying at the pain, and I'd stared at him, then up at the controllers and the referee pointing his thumb at the ground.

Kill or be killed. That was the law of the fights. The violence and broken bones were the punters' foreplay, death the climax, and they liked nothing better than seeing a virgin pop her cherry.

I crushed his thyroid, stood on it. Felt it go. That little *crunch* under my bare foot.

That was my second death and the beginning of my true self. My journey to the dark.

To Father.

—T

THREE

J,

When I was a girl, I wanted to be like Ma; beautiful, strong and confident, that otherworldly glow around her. You only had to look at her to know there was something special about her, something *different*.

Was that what attracted Father in first place? Did he know what she was then?

You used to tease me about how much I wanted to be her, would laugh when I dressed up in her clothes and stole her makeup. I got you back though, painted your face like a clown and didn't say a word. You didn't know a thing until Ma came home, and she kept a straight face right up until Father...

No one hid things like Ma. She could keep her face straight as a ruler or smile at you even though her heart was breaking. I could always tell though, there'd be a look in her eye, the tears turning them a darker shade of emerald, and then she'd go to her suite, or take one of the cars out of the garage, and cry in silence, where no one else could hear, or see. Except me.

I always knew.

Ma wouldn't close the door on me, like she would on Father or Nan or the other handful of people she considered friends. There were never that many of them, not after Nan died. I guess I took after her in that respect.

I haven't turned out like Ma, not all the way. I'm not beautiful anymore, and while there is strength in my arms and the same power in my veins, I'm lacking in other ways. In compassion. In mercy.

I lost those, right after I abandoned hope.

The fights started that, Father accomplished the rest.

As much as I hate the man, I understand him now, better than I ever would if I'd stayed.

It's funny, isn't it? How I ran to get away from him, from the control he had over my life, and yet... yet I'm here, I'm... this. Me. Father's little mongrel princess all grown up, a chip off the old genetic tree, just not the one he expected.

He wanted a mini-Ma, a perfect package of grace, intelligence and *power*, someone to tie the families together. Guess he didn't know the real Ma either, or maybe he just thought the killer could be trained out of me; ballet instead of Krav Maga, poetry instead of firearms, literature instead of survival.

Would Ma be proud? Before, I never feared that she would be anything but proud, but now... I'm not like Ma. Ma had boundaries and I... I have conviction. Purpose.

Father has those in spades. Would *he* be proud? Would he approve of me now, or would be still want the little princess?

Useless to wonder, I'm never going back. Never going to see him, not even to spit in his face.

I never knew what Ma was, she didn't tell me. I guess she would have, when the time came, but I wasn't there. I was in Bhutan, in the mountains and snow.

It came on slow, a few strange things at a time—a mirage in the corner of my eye, burnt bark on my tongue, lemons in my nose, the scents and flavours always changing.

A fever had gone through the village I was staying in at the time, and it'd grabbed me hard; I spent days in a sweat, unable to tell hallucinations from dreams, dreams from memories. So when the change started, I thought it was the fever again, coming back for another bite. Except it lasted not days or weeks, but months, and no matter what drugs I took, how many folk remedies or how many rites the witch doctors tried, it only got worse.

I made my way through the mountains starting at ghosts and spitting out tea that'd suddenly turn sour on my tongue. I smelled dogs where I should have smelled dumplings, went to sleep on hammocks that felt like nails. After the second village tried to stone me as witch, I learned to hide it, and I made my way north, looking for answers.

I never thought to call Ma, maybe if I had... but I was scared.

Scared of the way she'd look at me.

I miss Ma, miss her so much. It's a hole in my heart. I could see her, an anonymous note sent to her hotel while she's on one of her trips. All I'd have to do was drop a code word, a day, a time or I'd stand on a corner or under a streetlight as she got out of a car and she'd *know* I was there, with that weird sixth sense she has.

She'd slip away from her guards, we'd meet, hug, cry. Talk, just like we used to.

I could do that, I could have done it any number of times. I've stood on a dozen sidewalks, outside a dozen hotels and *tried* but... There's a worm in my heart, a vicious, poisonous thing that whispers "she won't love you anymore, she'll look at you and her eyes will go straight through, see all the dark, shitty things you've done, and you won't be her daughter anymore. You'll be *his*."

You will tell me that's not true, it's just my imagination, my guilty conscience imagining things, that Ma will always love me. But she doesn't love Father anymore, does she?

— T

FOUR

[The letter is crumpled, like someone ripped it from the writing pad in a hurry. Bloodstains mar some of the words, including the name at the top, the ink running into the red-brown like it hadn't been dry when the blood hit making it unreadable. There are the whorls and twists of fingerprints in the marks, matching the line along which it was crumpled.]

Why haven't you married? The families must be pressuring you to secure their fortunes.

There are no shortage of candidates; it's hard to escape them, or you, plastered all over the newsfeeds. Nightclubs, restaurants, boardrooms, that rather memorable shot of you and a blonde in the women's bathroom. It's like a direct feed into my systems, like no matter how many burners I go through, how many idents or phones or network accesses, you're there. Front and centre, reminding me.

Was it me? Did you really take our engagement to heart? Did you *really* believe?

That... makes me sad.

If it is me... get over it. I'm not coming back, not even when you're dead.

I haven't married, just in case you wanted to know.

Why would you want to know?

It doesn't matter, these aren't for you anyway. I don't even know why I keep the letters. I should burn them; isn't the act of writing them meant to be the catharsis? Spilling my guts on a blank page instead of opening my veins a second time. That's what these are meant to be about, and yet… Here I am, carting them around with me from place to place.

I tell myself that's because there are so few, and the envelope is small, shoved right down the bottom of my bag, hidden under the flap, that I forget about them.

It's not true, or not entirely true.

They're always there, just like you're always there, on the feeds in your expensive suits, looking down that long blade of a nose at the world. And no matter how many times I have to run, I always remember the bag.

I always *come back* for the bag.

I shouldn't. It'd be smarter, safer to leave it, let the bastards tear apart the jeans and t-shirts, the holey shocks and the worn shoes. They won't find anything, all the important things are in my head.

Except the letters. But the letters don't matter, right?

I'm good at lying to myself.

Really good.

But you should know that. Or maybe you don't? Maybe that was something I came to later, during that time after the fights but before I became… me. This. Ma's fairytale warrior, twisted by Father's darkness. Maybe.

You remember Ma's stories? The ones about the women clothed in white and gold, who'd stalk the night, hearing the cries of the lonely and helpless, meting out justice for the betrayed and abused? It took me awhile, after the villagers with their stones and the waking dreams, after I realised I wasn't sick, that I was just… different. Like Ma.

It took me awhile, but I realised Ma wasn't telling me bedtime stories, she was telling me about us, about my grandmother, and her mother and so on and so forth all the way back to the first of us. Whatever we are; those of us with Ma's magic.

I haven't found a name for us yet, I've searched—libraries, folk tales, art, history—found traces, but no name. I've come to wonder whether or not there is a name. Did we ever have one, or are we just our mother's daughters and that is that?

It doesn't seem possible, but then, half the things I can do don't seem possible.

I wish I'd seen Ma's powers. I want to know what they look like, what *she* can do and if it's different from what *I* can do. I want to know just how much of Father is in me, how much of my magic he's *twisted*.

Maybe I will. Maybe one of those days when I'm outside her hotel, I'll follow her and I'll watch, far enough away that she won't sense me. I'll know then, and if the light that comes to her fingers is white and gold, well... I'll have my answer.

I told you about my second death, in the fights, when I killed for the first time. Not an accident, but with purpose.

The fights had many more little deaths for me—of kindness, of mercy, of pride—but it wasn't until after, that the third one came.

It wasn't even a new death, more like a return of the first.

At some point in the years after the fights, I'd begun to hope again, even with the villagers and their stones. It wasn't rescue or family I hoped for, it certainly wasn't you in your shining Mercedes with Father's posse at your back. It was for me, that in my soul, despite the things I done, the people I'd killed, that I was still good. That Ma would still look at me with pride. And love.

And then I used my power for the first time, *really* used it.

I'd made it to Russia by then. Gone through the Himalayas and the Mongol plains. Buses, trains, hitch-hiking, even a horse once; I took whatever got me closer to that forest in Ma's stories, and when I got there...

The woman who walked through that forest did not wear skirts of white and gold, her footsteps did not toll as the churchyard bell, and they were not cries of gratitude that followed in her wake. I wore hiking boots that left a blister on my big toe, jeans soaked to the knee in mud and the only cries in my wake were that of the crows, coming to feast on the carnage left behind.

That was my third death, when I knew it wasn't Ma in my soul. It was Father.

—T

FIVE

[The letter is written in grey pencil on foolscap, the page lined and a little yellow. There's a red margin line on the left side with neat punch holes, while the edge is ragged, as if the page was torn from a notebook. The bottom right corner carries a faint brown stain, like someone has wiped dirt off the surface, and a darker stain covers the name at the top, leaving just a 'J' and 't' legible.]

They came for me again. It was close this time. They're getting better at tracking me down, and so they should, after three long years.

They found me— No, correction, they're *after* me because of the thing in the forest, the crows and the blood and the screaming. If I'd known then what I know now... But it wouldn't have made a difference. They'd have come after me eventually, I'd have given myself away, missed a surveillance drone or been slow scrubbing my footprint. The only way I'd have been free of them was to be shackled to Father.

Like Ma.

As much as she hates him—and I know she hates him, I see it in the feeds, in every glamour shot, every paparazzi snap, every vid, it's in her eyes. As much as she hates him, she stays because she knows.

If I'd known... well, if I'd known I'd have known what I was, what I could do, things might have been different right from the start.

Can you imagine Father's reaction to the magic? Can you imagine what he would do with it?

I can. It used to scare me, it *should* scare me, except I've done those things, left entire compounds screaming their sanity away. And that's not even the worst, because once I did those things, the *moment* I twisted my abilities in that direction, I imagined worse things.

I do an impossible thing and... pop, there's the next impossible thing in the front of my brain, just waiting for me to reach for it. It's as if the knowledge is locked in my DNA, and maybe it is, who knows.

There were no textbooks in the forest, no grimoires or wizened women in hidden caves. I'm left to work this shit out on my own. Unless I let the hunters catch me.

I've considered it at a time or two. They came for me, after all, knew enough to keep their distance and stay out of the shadows. If I didn't sleep in fits and starts, they'd have got me the first time, or the second. Hell, even the third. Those first six months after the forest, they came thick and fast.

Men and women in street clothes, a little too clean and not ripe enough to fit in amongst the addicts and whores. The only ones who hadn't known it were the idiots themselves, and the tension had rippled through the neighbourhood like a fucking wave. It was amazing they didn't pick up on it.

There's a burn scar on my back from that night, just another in the collection, it's not even that big – a few inches long, a half-inch wide, flame-shaped of all things. But even though it's not the biggest, or hurt as much, or nearly killed me—although the scent of scorched flesh is one that hangs in my memory; barbecue is no longer a favourite—it's one of the handful I remember most; one of my marks of learning.

I was used to surviving—the fights, the years on my own... Father—but I wasn't used to being hunted. And don't even call what you and Father attempted after I ran "hunting", that was a poor cousin to what these people do. These people are pros; they're patient, smart, wily in ways a fox could only wish. And they learn fucking fast.

Almost as fast as me.

Although, after the last time...

They only have to get lucky once.

They know what I am, know what Ma is and where we came from, *how* we came from it, and they know what I *should* be able to do, and they were ready for it. "Should" being the key word. I'm not sure if I should thank Father for that or curse him anew.

The hunters were after the righteous warrior, a woman in white and gold helping the helpless, and what they found... I think I made it this far, this long because they didn't truly know what they were dealing with. In all our confrontations, I've never left any of them alive, my control over the dark... There was none, not in those first two years, and after that... Well, I thought I'd lost them; I'd moved continents, changed names, IDs, faked my own death and stayed in places not even fit for rats. Stayed so low, for so long... And then I'd settled down, relaxed a little, found a guy who reminded me of—

And that was the kicker. Three years, eight months and seven days. That's how long it took them, how persistent they were. And in that time... They learned some things, the kind of things that made me wonder just where they got their information.

Did some nicely dressed Europeans turn up at the mansion, CJ? Did they ask Father questions? Did they see Ma?

Did they come to you?

I will kill you if you told them. I know it's not fair, not after all this time, not with you not actually *knowing* and yet... Betrayal hits deep, CJ, and stings like a bitch.

But not as much as I do.

Pray I never come back.

– T

SIX

I'm not sure I can run anymore.

I'm tired, Jon. So tried. It feels like my feet are rooted to rock and my hands... There's so much darkness on my hands, so much blood. I can't get them clean, no matter how much I wash or what lies I comfort myself with.

Maybe if I could sleep... but sleep comes with its own problems. If not nightmares, or the anxiety of the hunters getting closer—always closer—then it's the power itself.

In Ma's fairy tales, the warrior heard the cries of the helpless on the wind, and the way she described them... I always imagined dust motes sailing through sunbeams, or fireflies on a moonless night, something external. Not the constant muttering, the screams and pleading in my head. Is that Father's doing, his contribution to my DNA? Or did Ma lie to me with those fairy tales?

I hope she didn't lie, I hope the things that come for me when I close my eyes are all mine. I hope that for Ma, the messages come to her on sunbeams and fireflies.

I miss Ma. Miss the way she smells, the rich scent of the perfume she likes – does she still like it? I tracked a target through a department store the other day, dodging security even as I cornered the bastard in the men's toilet, and the perfume aisle... Security just about had me there. A mistake I wouldn't have made before, but now...

The darkness drags at me. I just...

The hunters are getting better, closer each time they strike. They're looking for me now, I can feel them stalking the construction site – three men, four women, two in the truck parked just outside the chain-link fence. The ones in the truck have the drones, a merry little squadron of the things buzzing through the buildings.

They haven't found me yet, they're not even sure I'm here. I can tell, feel it inside of me. Not just how far away they are, or the weapons hanging off their belts, but their heartbeats, their *smells*.

All I have to do is breathe and let the dark out.

I've been tucked up in this hole since I took out the bastard in the department store. I prepared for it. The moment his body was discovered, so was I. It's got that way now, the way the dark works, it's hard to disguise it. And I'm tired of disguising it. Tired of hiding.

I'm thinking of letting the hunters win.

Maybe they have answers. They know about Ma and even if they don't know exactly what I am, then they should have a place to start, an idea of what I'm *not*. And maybe, just maybe, I'd finally get some sleep.

I miss sleep.

[There is a line and the ink changes, no longer blue but black. The writing changes with it, still slanted and spiky, but hurried and messy where the previous passages are slower, the spaces between words larger, the loops and whorls bigger.]

I've left the construction site. I let the hunters find me, stood out in the skeleton of that shopping mall and waved at the drone. I even put my hands out wide and knelt when they approached.

I was going to let them take me, going to get the answers and the sleep I needed and then... That fucking whisper. It crept up behind and showed me the things the lead hunter liked to do. Nasty things, and not just to others, it showed me what he wanted to do to *me*. To Ma. To all the women like us.

He died last.

I took my time.

He did not end well.

I'm still tired. My feet still drag and my hands still ache, but I won't stop, I won't give in.

I need to know more, and to do that, I need to go back to the forest.

That's where the hunters found me, where Ma's tales lead, where the dark first stained my hands. That's where the answers are, and I was a fool to run so far from them.

Who knows, maybe going back will throw the hunters off, maybe it'll give me a few weeks, a month, even a year of breathing space, time to do whatever it is I need to do. Whatever answers the forest holds, something in me says it won't be enough, won't quite *fit*. Whatever I learn there won't be the end, but a start is better than what I have now; guesses, fairytales and violence.

You won't hear from me for a while. I'm going to stop writing these, or at the very least burn them, stop carting this fucking bag around with me like a security blanket. Tomorrow, I'm going to clean myself up, wash the blood out of my hair, dig the mud from under my fingernails, change into the clothes I took off one of the hunters, and waltz into the first registered courier I see.

If something happens to me, you'll get these letters. I don't know what you'll do with them, I don't care, but I want you to know, even if it's only to make you wish *[the sentence is scratched out, the pen marks thick and deep, almost tearing the lined paper]*.

I hope you don't get these, I hope you're always left wondering what happened to me, whether or not I'm going to pop up when you're old and grey, and make your life interesting.

Pray for me.

—T

SEVEN

Jon,

I found it, and just like I knew it would all those months ago, it was just the beginning.

The answers the hunters have, lead to more questions, more sleepless nights.

I thought I was the darkness, that Father had somehow made me this way but there's more to it, stories Ma didn't tell, reasons why the hunters came after me time and again. I was right when I thought they wouldn't have gone after Ma like they did me, wrong to think that they knew about her, more wrong to assume that it was Father keeping them at bay.

If they'd known about Father…

They know now.

Prepare yourself, CJ. They're coming.

So am I.

—T

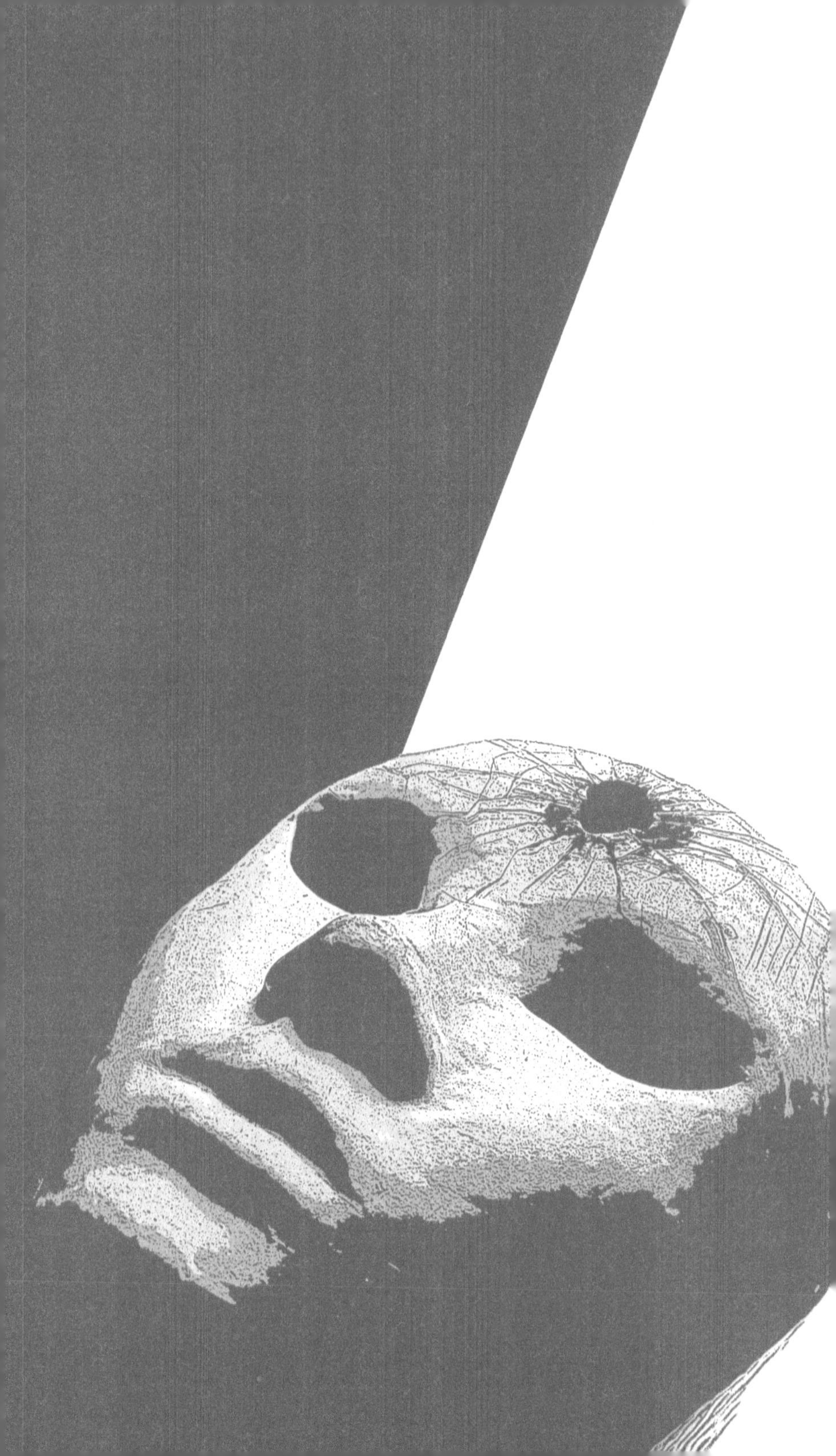

THE LAW

INTRODUCTION

This is an example of the same idea popping up in multiple places. The main character here is a spin-off of the heroine in *Letters I'll Never Send*; in fact, you could even suggest that it's same story set in an alternate universe. Honestly, I was aiming to have one follow the other chronologically, but then the end happened and… Yeah, you'll know when you get there.

About the end, as soon as I realised where it was going, I fought it, like… I just did not want to go that way but… *sighs* the muse works in mysterious ways.

By the way, if you enjoy this story, thank my Kickstarter Heroes. As with *Mirror*, *The Law* wasn't originally included in the *Collected Edition*, but the Heroes kicked some serious butt and got it here.

 Learn more about the writing of *The Law*. Scan the QR code for the audio commentary, soundtrack and more.

THE LAW

The music pulsed through the floor, the heavy beat riding through the soles of her boots and into her bones. Ahead, dancers and drunks and waiters parted around Dale like the big black man was Moses commanding the Red Sea. She moved in his wake, gliding through the nightclub, a dark, commanding shadow in a long, hooded coat.

Women in short, tight skirts, men in dark pants that hugged their arses, and shirts that showed off their chests—muscled or not—that might have argued with Dale, took one look at her and stepped back. They might not see her face, hidden under the deep, protecting hood, chin and mouth obscured by the plain black face-mask, but they knew Death when they saw it.

Tonight, Death's head ached. The sharp scent of too much perfume and the darker one of too much alcohol invaded her nose, made it itch, while the bright, strobing dance lights tried to pierce her eyeballs, even under the shadowing hood.

Tonight was a mistake, but even Death was as the mercy of fate, or in this case, the Council.

Dale stepped to the side.

The sea ended at a thick black rope.

Two men stood behind it, in the same sleek, dark suits as Dale, right down to the discreet bulge under their left arms – although not, she suspected, the less obvious bulges at his spine, or the ones at his ankles or his wrists, hidden under expert tailoring. And they certainly did not fill out the neat, sharp lines as well as her bodyguard, although they tried, straightening their spines, pulling at bottom of their jackets and lifting their chins.

The one on the right—a shade taller than the left, his hair shaved at the sides, the black mop atop a little sleeker, the single earring dangling from his lobe a little flashier, his suit a little shinier—threw his shoulders back, looked down his fat, stubby nose and jerked his chin in her direction. Arrogance wrested from the gun against his ribs.

'It's a private party,' he said, half-shouting over the bone throbbing music. 'Who are you?'

She didn't look up, not after the first glance, didn't turn or cock her head to the side. Her head hurt too much, and the night had just begun. Besides, Dale was there.

'She's invited,' he said. Her bodyguard didn't raise his voice, and yet his words travelled, splitting the music, the too-loud voices and the throb behind her eyes.

The idiot on the right jerked his chin again. 'I need a name.'

'You know her name,' Dale said. 'Your bosses are waiting for her.'

Right idiot sneered. 'They're not waiting for a skan—'

The suit on the left was already unlatching the rope, and she was stepping through before the other completed his insult.

Right idiot grabbed her—

And was on the floor a second later, his body a single, tight convulsive knot curled in on itself.

She slipped the little stunner back under the coat's wide cuff as she swept past, casting a single, brief glance back at Dale.

He nodded, green eyes sober.

The mess would be cleaned before the door in front of her closed. The door the other suit—the subtle one, with the exquisite stitching around cuffs and lapels, the fine detail in his shirt collar and the discreetly expensive cufflinks—was opening. He bent at the waist as she passed, a half-bow with arms straight at his sides.

'Judge,' he said, the title falling off his lips, the reverence thick in the air as she passed.

'Not today,' she whispered back, and stepped into the green-lit hell beyond.

○

For Hell, it was quiet. Thick soundproofing cut out the music from the nightclub beyond, still visible through the one-way floor-to-ceiling window, while the richly draped walls muffled the low, polite rumble of male voices within.

It did nothing for the tension.

Animosity filled the large, private room, just like the two men—the originals to the carbon copies outside—filled the long emerald couches, each in various states of sprawled. More suits, professional muscles like the ones guarding the door, hovered around the edges; faces stoney, eyes flicking left and right and everywhere in between, suspicion rolling off them in giant, palpable waves.

The door *snicked* shut behind her.

Every eye turned her way.

No one spoke.

The tension ramped up a notch, the heavies—three to a side—transferred their suspicion to her. She felt their eyes, trying to see under her hood, to penetrate her coat's long, enveloping skirt and tailored sides. Brief glances, for the most part, assessments carried out in moments, judging height and weight and gender, weighing her short, lithe frame and the delicacy of her gloved hands against their own brawn and looking away. Dismissive.

Only two sets of eyes stayed on her. One of them belonged to the man on the couch closest to the big plate window, the boss of the grunt probably still curled around his guts on the floor outside. Dinesh Yu, underboss of the Pan family. The other set of eyes...

The other set stood behind the man on the couch opposite.

Chen Jingtai's were the only eyes that hadn't weighed her, his attention hadn't shifted from his rival. Instead, he sat with ankle crossed over knee and his arms spread across the back of the green couch like he owned it – and perhaps he did. She hadn't checked to see who owned Delicatessen, it did not concern her, not tonight. She wasn't a Judge tonight.

Hosting a Judgement at his own extravagant nightclub would suit Chen Jingtai, the arrogance of it, the carefully-calculated disregard for Council rules.

It would *all* suit him.

A single chair sat between the two long green couches, facing them. The minimalist wood with its old, straight, slatted back and no arms, was at odds with the padded couches and glass and steel tables. An austere antique in the midst of luxury. It did not belong.

A message.

For her?

From whom?

She moved to the chair, paused a moment, hands resting on the wooden back.

A smile crossed Dinesh Yu's broad, square face.

From him?

She sat—coat spilling around her, the long skirts pooling either side of the unpadded seat, hood still shadowing her face—and folded her hands in her lap.

Seconds passed.

She did not speak.

Neither did anyone else.

The heavies twitched.

Dinesh Yu leaned forward and poured a measure of dark, golden liquid into a heavy crystal glass.

He rose, a smooth graceful movement.

'My lady Judge.' His voice was deep and warm as he offered her the glass. 'Welcome,' he said, still smiling.

She let the glass hang.

A heartbeat.

Two.

His eyes—a pale hickory—narrowed, his smile tightening.

'The Judge doesn't drink, Yu.' Chen Jingtai spoke, ankle still crossed over knee, arms still spread across the back of the couch, gaze still focused on his rival. His posture made his coat gape and lifted the hem of his sweater, exposing a thin slice of neat golden skin above his waistband, and she wondered how many new scars had joined the others marring his chest. 'She's a set of ears for the Council. I doubt she even breathes.'

If she were there as the Judge, that would be true.

Slowly, she took the offered glass—

Most wouldn't have noticed the tension in Jingtai's shoulders, the ripple as his abs contracted.

—lifted it under her hood, held it to the mask across her lips… and watched Jingtai's dark-gold skin turn a shade whiter.

And now she knew, the chair had been his idea.

Rule breaker.

The rich, heady scent of old brandy curled through her nose, promising warmth and smooth golden fire in her belly, even as the sensors in her mask told other tales.

Like the tracking compound mixed in with the aged oak and fermented barley.

But why? It was not for her. Everyone knew better than to try drugging a Judge.

Not that she was a Judge.

Behind her, the door opened.

The heavies that had dismissed her so readily, stiffened like a bear had just claimed the room.

The only eyes left on her were the ones behind Jingtai.

Shen Ru had always been smart.

Maybe the tracking compound had been their idea. They were cautious like that.

'It's why I'm so old,' they'd like to say. And why Jingtai, He-Who-Liked-to-Play-with-Fire, was still alive.

Dale's shadow at her back, tall and broad and menacing.

She handed him the drink.

Begin, she said, lips moving silently against her mask, words transmitted not by her voice but the digital web wrapped around her being. The nanites and sensors in her clothes, the chip behind her ear and the others in her fingers, spiderwebs across the back of her hands.

Receipts pinged against her interior matrix, even as the two men across from her flinched. Dinesh hiding it behind a quick smile, Jingtai looking away, discomfort a brief flash across his face.

A Judge's voice was never comfortable, even if it was silent.

But she was not a Judge, even if the transmitters and vocals were the same.

The ones who knew different, did not tell tales.

Dinesh Yu sprawled back along his couch. 'There's nothing to discuss,' he said, and there was ice in his drawl. 'The Chen clan intruded on our territory, the Council must make a ruling.'

They have, she said. *That is not what we are beginning.*

'Then if this is not a mediation...' The heavy cut crystal glass stopped its movement, Jingtai's attention no longer on the brandy swirling inside. His voice went low. 'What are you here for?'

Behind Jingtai, Shen Ru stiffened, tension rippling from them to the other heavies like an ill tide.

She did not speak.

The answer was clear enough.

The sensors in her coat and hood tracked the eyes, the hands, had already highlighted the guns and knives strapped to backs and wrists and ankles. It spread them before her, a vision of danger only she and the AI—a hundred kilometres away and deep underground—could witness.

'You're not a Judge,' Dinesh Yu said. The drawl was gone from his voice, the warmth from his smile, leaving just the steel behind. Dead hickory eyes, an implacable jaw.

Tension coursed through Dale.

The Council has ruled, she said. She reached for her hood, gloved hands—the nano-transmitters glittering within the thin leather—pushing it back, exposing the mask that covered her face, the braids held tight to her head, the wires shimmering through them.

Chen Jingtai—

Pain engulfed her.

There was a time when her life had not been ruled by pain. A brief time, a moment between the desperate, shitty heartbeats of adolescence and adulthood. A moment when she thought she'd found a home, and if she'd been allowed to keep it, she'd have been happy there, content in the role others had made for her.

Or, at least, that's what she used to tell herself when the pain became too much.

She'd been younger then. Softer.

In love.

But now...

...but now the nightclub's quiet, soundproofed, private room was full of bodies in various states of dead. Some moaning, some staring at the dark, glossy ceiling, the gilt cornicing and baroque lovers embracing within the clouds their last sight in life.

It seemed appropriate, fitting in a way that only partially satisfied the gremlin in her soul.

The gremlin would never be satisfied.

She'd given up on that when she'd given up on lying to herself.

The gremlin made her job easier, gobbled up the pain and gave her purpose, gave her drive. Made it possible to stand in the midst of the shattered tables—glass crunching under boots, a shard of it embedded in her left bicep, just below her shoulder—and bare metal table frames that had once supported it—the imprint of the thick square metal blooming across her ribs—and ignore everything but Chen Jingtai.

The Chen underboss had not moved.

Shen Ru had, her sensors tracked them, deconstructed the pistol aimed at the back of her unprotected head, told her the calibre and the composition of the bullets in the old-fashioned magazine.

Dale moved in the shadows behind Shen Ru.

Even Dinesh Yu had run, three of his bodyguards throwing themselves at her while their boss dashed for the door hidden behind the decorative mirror. It was them on the ground, moaning and dying.

Dinesh had escaped, but she would find him. Even now, a hundred kilometres away, the AI was tracking him. *Tick, tick, tick* at the back of her eye.

Jingtai had assisted with that.

Had he known? She *crunched* through the remnants of the glass tables until her knees bumped Jingtai's shin, his ankle still crossed over his other leg, staring at her with those partially raised brows, a prince waiting for an answer.

What the question was, she didn't know. But she would find out.

She leaned down, bending from the waist, and stared back.

He met her gaze, like he could see through the black mask with its lifelike suggestion of a face.

She could smell the brandy from here, the heady scent rising anew with every swirl of the glass dangling from his fingers.

You are not running, she said.

The flinch was little more than the corner of his dark, heavy-lidded eyes tightening. 'Would it do any good?'

She cocked her head. *Mr Yu got away.*

He took a sip of brandy. 'You let him.'

Did I?

He didn't speak, just swirled that brandy. Took another sip.

There were trackers in it. The nanites pinged against her sensors, sharp little pinpricks crawling under her skin.

That was a twist.

Did he know? Had he planted the seeds in his drink as well as Yu's? A decoy perhaps, to throw off suspicion. But why? A Judge wouldn't have cared, and she...

No one could have known she was coming.

She straightened.

Had they?

Doubt shivered through her.

'I have not met an Executioner before.' He spoke, and was it to cover the silent *crunch* as Shen Ru stalked closer? 'I thought you were meant to be more of the kill first, forget the questions type.'

She tilted her head the other way.

He stilled, brandy halfway to his mouth, those heavy-lidded eyes widening a fraction, his entire body caught in a single frozen moment. Her sensors caught the extra pound in his heart, the throb in his carotid, and her own heart squeezed in response. Adrenalin kicking up a notch, lightning arching through her nerves, even as she spun around, pinning Shen Ru—

But Shen Ru was steps away, their gun pointed not at her but the floor and—

A sound, sensors and HUD screaming.

She spun, coat tails flying—

She'd forgotten how fast Jingtai moved. How could she forget that? How tricky he was with arms and legs, how easy he found it to wrap a person up and trap them in their own clothes. Long coat tails twisted around her legs, a forearm under her chin, pressing into her throat. Superior bodyweight pinning her to the emerald cushions. Her fingers in the soft points behind carotid and ear. Just a little pressure, not much, a few seconds, and he'd be out. Thirty more and his oxygen-starved brain would start to tear itself apart.

Dale was up there, she felt him—a warm wind moving through

the dark—his gun trained on Shen Ru. Shen Ru closer than a moment ago, gun no longer threatening the plush pile carpet but her head, muzzle centimetres from her temple. But Shen Ru and Dale didn't concern her now.

Brandy and another subtle scent slipped through her mask, inside her nose and *twisted*. Same as the fingers trying to find the locks that kept it in place, the straps holding it secure.

She let him fumble, let those deceptively elegant hands with their manicured nails and silver and black rings find the notches beside her ears and *press*.

Nothing happened.

He pressed again, slipping neat, blunt fingernails between her jawbone and the nano-laced carbon fibre, and *pulling*.

Her whole head came off the green cushions.

It won't work, she said.

He flinched.

The mask can only be removed if I will it, and even if you see my face, she continued, *what good will it do you?*

He pressed closer, nose hovering a millimetre above hers, those dark brown eyes—so clear to her at this distance, her sensors drinking in the lighter flecks of amber, the hints of gold—piercing the black.

'You remind me of someone.' A shift closer and now his nose was touching the mask, his lips brushing the moulded carbon fibre over her own. 'I've been waiting for her.'

Her breath didn't catch, her heart didn't squeeze; the gremlin wouldn't allow it, had eaten those emotions.

I am not her, and even if I were, she strengthened the fingers against his carotid. *It would not change the Council's judgement.*

'What is their judgement?'

Favourable. You will not die today.

'And tomorrow?'

Perhaps. She pushed him away, rose in the same movement. *Time will tell.*

●

The trackers in Chen Jingtai's blood were hers now; his hands on her mask had given the AI access, and the tech embedded in the carbon fibre had done the rest, reprogramming the nanites, giving them longevity and purpose beyond their original programming.

Now, two hundred and thirty-eight kilometres away, the AI was re-tasking satellites, hijacking networks, peering through a hundred cameras; every move Chen Jingtai made she knew; when he ate, when he pissed, when he slammed the door of his home and the signal blocking tech in the walls cut the feed, and when the AI started breaking down the firewalls protecting his personal network.

She still smelled the brandy on his breath.

She sunk into the form-moulded car seat and closed her eyes. Her head hurt, eye sockets and brows, the bridge of her nose, all one big pound. Tight, angry.

Frustrated.

Torn.

Chen Jingtai did not concern her.

Dinesh Yu did.

Dinesh Yu whose trackers were passing through his blood, becoming weaker with every hour. Dinesh Yu who was far too proficient at evading cameras, at finding dead spots where the network coverage was old and patchy, if it existed at all. Dinesh Yu who had a death marker against his name.

Dinesh Yu who the AI was tracking, whose last known Dale was bending speed limits and road rules to reach.

The sleek black van rocketed around a dark corner.

In the back, cradled in the form-fitted armchair, she rocked with it, eyes closed against the screens playing inside the mask; shutting out all but the play of blue and red seeping through her lids.

It didn't stop the AI whispering.

Nothing stopped the AI, not even sleep.

It was with her, every moment, every dream, every thought. Every twitch of her eyelid. Measuring, reporting, analysing. Containing, tweaking the nanites in her blood, the hormones and chemicals, the rush and pull of nerves.

Keeping her alive.

For the moment.

While she was useful.

Her head hurt.

The AI wouldn't fix that, not yet, not until the job was done.

Dinesh Yu. The job.

The Council.

Three shadows on a dark background, voices modulated, faces pixelated. A video sent from nowhere, or at least, nowhere the AI could find. There was an AI on the backend of the Council's communications, only an AI was that good, that clean.

If she could just find the Council AI...

Target located. The AI's smooth, sexless voice. Low, soothing. Another calculation, deference to the endorphins flooding her system.

She opened her eyes.

A three-dimensional map overlaid the back of the car seats in front. High rises with covered walkways flying over the tight, busy streets. Shops and homes, clinics and nightclubs, all jammed together, cheek-by-jowl just like the clubbers and late night workers—janitors and chauffeurs, hookers and bartenders—clogging the hair-width footpaths lining Old Town's busy roads.

A crimson dot pulsed front and centre of the mess.

Her head throbbed in response.

'Dale.' That was it, his name, little more than a whisper. But her real voice, not the digital one. For once.

'I see it,' he said, and his hands shifted on the wheel, slipping the van between a gap in the traffic, setting off angry horns and angrier lights. The AI showed her his gaze flicking to the rear-view mirror, highlighted the micro-frown creasing brow and eyes, labelled it concern. 'He's on the eighth floor.'

'I know.'

'The AI says the elevators are out.'

She didn't sigh, just closed her eyes a second. She was used to pain. 'I know,' she said again. Because the AI told her. The AI told her everything.

Dale didn't respond. He wanted to, but he would hold himself back.

The job was the job, and this one was hers.

She would have let Dale deal with Dinesh when the underboss ran, but the Council had been clear. The kill was the Executioner's.

Hers.

The van stopped.

Her eyes opened.

It was time.

○

Dinesh Yu was not on the eighth floor of the shabby apartment building taking up a prime corner on Old Town's main drag, but his blood was. A whole bag of it, neatly enthroned on a pristine, bone-white China platter with a delicate blue and white floral motif on its scalloped edges.

Four point six eight litres of A-neg at a warm twenty-three point zero two degrees Celsius, displayed on a small, delicate antique mahogany side table with scrolled legs and a well-worn sheen. It sat in the middle of the dusty, one-room apartment lit by the neon signs flashing through the grimy, cracked picture window and not a single diode more.

The room was empty, save for the stale smell of cigarettes, the old leather recliner and the transfusion unit beside it. An empty bag hung on the unit's stand, blood still caught in the clear plastic tubing.

The trackers in the blood still emitted a signal, growing rapidly weaker now without the warmth of a living host.

She picked up the bag.

Blood sloshed; a red, head-sized hot water bottle.

The door creaked behind her.

Did you find anything? she asked without turning around.

'No one saw anything,' Dale said.

She nodded.

The AI whispered secrets, bank accounts and crypto reports.

There were eight other residents up here, a student, three shift workers, two hookers and a drug dealer with a live-in. No suspicious deposits in the last two hours since the nightclub, but the out-of-work student was currently chatting it up with one of the hookers and the dealer had just made a sale.

No genius needed there.

A flick and the information passed through the air to Dale.

The dark-skinned man's shoulders twitched. A second for the data to process and then... 'I'm on it.'

She nodded, focus not on the rapidly cooling blood bag in her palm—temperature, eighteen point nine degrees—but the screens playing across the mask.

Where's Dinesh?

Locating.

She squeezed the bag; eighteen point six degrees, a little warmth sinking though her gloves, thawing her fingernails.

A pulse in the corner of her vision, attention skipping from the network trace and surveillance mosaic dominating the HUD, to a smaller, separate screen in the top left corner.

Her data. Core temperature, thirty-six point two. Blood pressure, low. Status, serious. That last in urgent red.

Like the blood in the bag.

Attention skipped back to the mosaic. A thousand different images whizzing past, too many and too fast for human eyes, but the AI saw all, and it liked to share.

Minutes ticked by.

Another screen, behind the scanner and security vids, tracking heat signatures and network usage. The grey dots of the residents—shift workers and the dealer, the hookers both alone now, Dale and the student—

The student's signal died.

Her breath stopped, like it always did, a momentary glitch, lungs seizing up before the brain kicked in.

Status, urgent.

It would hold, *she* would hold, until the job was done.

Heavy footsteps in the hall, Dale a shadow in her periphery. A ping against her personal network.

She accepted the transmission.

A new screen, new information. The security mosaic pausing—just a moment, like her breath—before it rushed forward. New images, new data. A new location to search.

The AI buzzing all those kilometres away.

You took care of it. Not a question. Never a question.

'Yes.' Dale responded anyway.

He always did.

Always knew what to say.

Target located.

○

Chen Jingtai lived in New Town, gleaming skyscrapers and wide streets, not a pedestrian in sight. Only the black van gliding down the blacktop, headlights gracing the lush, manicured trees—trunks up-lit by the subtle lights embedded in the dirt—and the flower beds hugging the road.

A gap in the trees and flower beds, Dale guiding the van off the road and then under it. The flowers and lights cut out, gone in favour of the green-crete walls textured to look like timber and harsh bunker lights.

The van dipped into the underground carpark, glided some

more – tires squeaking on the smooth surface, the engine's purr a little more noticeable with walls to bounce it back. They stopped.

'There's a security gate,' Dale said.

She didn't speak. On the back of her mask, security videos continued to play on one screen, while numbers ticked down on another. Just three more.

'It has a timer.' Dale again, an additional thread of tension in his voice.

Two numbers down. One more to go.

Her heart thumped.

'Should I turn around?' His hands tightened on the wheel.

No.

One more number, one more number. One...

'We're going to trigger a lockdown.'

...more...

'Vitya?'

...number.

It ticked over.

She flicked it to Dale.

There was no sigh, but his fingers loosened and his shoulders came down.

The security gate rose, the sleek metal louvers sliding over themselves until they disappeared into the ceiling.

The van hushed underneath.

Behind her mask, a security video showed it sliding back into place while a second and third video tracked the van turning a corner and hushing to a stop in front of a glass-panelled foyer. A fourth showed it pausing there, the side door rolling open and... A red stiletto reaching out, followed by a bare leg and a short, blue cocktail dress, more strap than fabric, long blonde hair falling over a pale shoulder, topped by a bleary, half-drunk face. Lipstick smeared, mouth all smiles.

It was a lie.

What came out of the van was a black boot and black clad legs, the rest of her short, slim self hidden under the long-skirted coat; Dale slipped out of the driver's door to stand behind her.

The van slid shut and *hummed* away, the AI in the driver's seat.

She looked at the corner, inside the foyer's glass-walls, to the discrete black dot hidden between wall and ceiling. On the security video, the drunk blonde looked with her. Of Dale, there was only air.

Together, they entered the building.

He was in the penthouse. Two stories at the top of the building, according to the AI. Four beds, six baths, a large roof-top garden complete with swimming pool and tennis court, and its own private elevator with carpeted floor, wood panelled sides and an explosion of paint on the back wall.

She stood facing the sleek black doors, Dale behind. According to the security videos, she wasn't there, the blonde was wobbling her way down a different corridor on the floor below, and the private elevator had never left the penthouse's foyer.

Her brow throbbed, there was a warm trickle over her lip and sweet copper on her tongue.

Status, critical. Medical attention recommended.

When the job was done.

Don't tell Dale.

Acknowledged.

The numbers beside the elevator doors ticked over.

Twenty-one. Penthouse.

Shooshed aside.

Forest-green walls and honey wood floors; a leather tan pouffe beside a side-table, an old-fashioned hat stand next to it, bowler hats and bone-handled canes resting on it. Another vivid painterly explosion on the wall above.

She strode out, Dale her shadow.

On the security videos, the elevator remained closed and Chen

Jingtai remained sprawled in his king-sized bed on the floor above.

They moved through the apartment, square heavy furniture, tall windows, vaulted ceilings with soft subtle lights that turned on as they passed, like the dawn still hours away from the sky.

She paused at the stairs – wide wooden steps the same honey as the floors seeming to float in the middle of a living room, light from the garden spilling long shadows across the floor.

On the security mosaic, Chen Jingtai rolled over in his sleep, the same soft garden lights catching a bare calf as he half kicked off the sheets.

This wasn't right.

Chen Jingtai who had a null room the AI still hadn't cracked, was calmly asleep in his silk-covered bed without a guard—human or otherwise—in sight.

Where was Shen Ru?

The bodyguard is missing, she said.

At her left shoulder, Dale straightened.

She stared up the stairs, piercing the dark with the sensors embedded in mask and hood, hands loose at her sides, security mosaic gone. Nothing but infrared and heat sensors outlining each step in soft white, the walls and light scones the same, the sculpture at the top of the stairs – a bronze eagle in flight, the AI told her. No electronic signatures, no life-signs.

Shen Ru was here. Somewhere.

Up there?

Or down here, lying in wait?

The AI offered nothing.

Only one way to find out.

Her head pounded with every boot step, glass shards dug into her thighs with every step higher. Her breath came short.

Status, critical—

Mute.

The urgent red light in the top corner of her HUD winked out.

Six steps, halfway up. Her back itched with every step upward, skin crawling, expecting new pain, for Dale to cry out and his big body to *thump thump thump* as it toppled back down the stairs.

Eight steps, ten.

The itch in her back transferring to her front, now expecting pain in her belly or a sharp muzzle flash and then nothing as a bullet took her between the eyes.

Twelve steps.

Thirteen.

Pausing at the top, Dale still on the riser below, a spike in the electron readings as he drew his gun and thumbed it live.

Shadows and the soft dawn spreading across the ceiling gleamed off the eagle – wings spread, beak open, talons forward for the kill.

Still no Shen Ru.

The master bedroom was to the left, the AI-proof office to the right, the paint explosion in front.

On the mosaic, Chen Jingtai had been six and a half pyjama-clad feet rolling over in bed. She turned that way, sensors on high but seeing only straight, dark-green walls broken up with sideboards and gilt-framed paintings, all the way to the wide oak door at the other end.

Was he in there?

The solid wood baffled her sensors as surely as the dampening tech embedded in the apartment's frame.

Dale, a towering, solid presence at her back.

Office or bedroom; where would she hide?

Where would Chen Jingtai hide *Dinesh*?

Why would he hide Dinesh?

The trackers in the brandy, the austere antique chair, a Judgement held in Jingtai's nightclub where it had no business being.

Rule-breaker.

The Council ruled by impartiality; its people had no face, no names or homes or families. They gave it all up when they entered, every single micron of who they had been blown to dust, leaving just the AIs and enforcers at their backs. They did it for many reasons; money, loyalty, justice, revenge.

For her, it had been the pain.

There was a time her life hadn't been ruled by pain.

A brief moment.

'You remind me of someone.'

Very slowly, so as not to disturb the mountain of glass shards atop her neck, she turned and descended the stairs, Dale following.

Low garden lights still cast long shadows across the living room – square couches, low tables, art on the walls. She turned right, to the kitchen—dark marble counter tops, brass fixtures—sensors picking it all out in exquisite detail, right down to the crystal glass sitting on the island bench, waiting to be filled from the half-full decanter behind.

'I've been waiting for her.'

What would she find if she broke down his office door? Maps? Lengths of coloured string connecting pins to old security screen caps and investigator reports? A big picture of her, bright and young and laughing in the middle?

She *had* been happy once, between the desperate, shitty heartbeats of adolescence and adulthood.

Chen Jingtai was playing games. A useless endeavour and dangerous to play the Council. To play an Executioner. To play her. The mediation, the judgement, the incursion in the Yu's territory were his first shot.

Why then Dinesh, the shitty Old Town apartment and the blood bag?

The answer came to her partly from the AI, partly from the depths of her gut.

Time, Chen Jingtai had been playing for time. He'd been expecting a Judge, a mediation spaced over days, and received an

Executioner instead.

But why time?

She moved through the penthouse, eye sockets throbbing, her marrow screaming.

Tricky. Chen Jingtai had always been tricky.

Past the kitchen, leaving glasses and brandy in her wake, through the open patio doors in the cold, smog- and neon-laden night beyond.

Heat signatures on her HUD. One outlined on the infra-red a dozen metres away, beside the tall glass railings, sensors picking out the old-fashioned Glock against their ribs, a second person sprawled in an armchair three metres away—another armchair and a table between them—and a third signature lying on the wooden deck, colder than the others.

Dead.

Dinesh.

She didn't need to see his face, the shiny leather shoes and pinstriped suit were enough.

In the back of her mind, the AI catalogued and reported.

Dale a metre behind, still in the house, gun live against his leg, covered by shadows. Shen Ru against the glass railing, arms crossed over his chest, fingers caressing the black butt of his gun. Jingtai and her, hands empty, facing off over a rapidly cooling corpse and garden furniture.

He didn't speak.

Neither did she.

The AI kept time.

One minute.

Two.

Against the railing, Shen Ru shifted his stance. Dale mirrored it.

Dinesh getting colder on the patio.

Judgement had been rendered, it did not matter by whose hand. Dead was dead, the fact noted, readings and virtual models recorded, stored forever in the AI's secure servers ready to transmit to the Council. She should turn, leave the garden, leave Jingtai and disappear into the night, fold herself in the van's embrace and lose the pain to the AI's drugs.

The Council's leash.

Three minutes, the cold night seeping through her clothes, leeching the little warmth her body had.

Why? She broke the silence, and this time Jingtai made only the tiniest flinch.

He shifted, ankle falling from his knee. 'You remind me of a girl.'

Was she special?

'No.' Another shift, suit jacket falling open, allowing a glimpse of darker shadow against his ribs. 'But I made her a promise.'

She remembered that promise, screamed over the bloody corpse cradled against his chest; recalled the weight of the gun in her hand, the ache in her bones, in her heart as she slipped back onto the Council's leash.

She should turn, she should go. Instead she undid the mask.

Shen Ru's hand on their gun, Dale reacting, his own gun rising—

Attention in the wrong place, across the garden, by the wall when it should have been on the patio and Chen Jingtai lounging in the armchair.

She'd forgotten how fast he moved, lightning in a tailored suit.

She didn't see the gun, but she saw the muzzle flash; a microsecond for HUD and AI to scream a warning.

After that…

She didn't feel anything.

THIS IS
DARKNESS

INTRODUCTION

I love me a superhero story, particularly the morally grey variety, and *The Elektra Saga* by Frank Miller is one of my favourites. It has all the things I love: a fabulous antiheroine, grit, and a journey into darkness before a return to light. In fact, you might say that I love all of those things *because* of Miller's Elektra, and that's where this story comes from.

Like most, this character has been sitting in my head for a while, waiting for the right moment to reveal herself. In fact, she's been hanging around so long that I've forgotten her name.

Recently though, I found my initial notes for this story and the one-line description reads, "a super-powered love triangle where the heroine is the villain and ~~there are no happy endings~~ all the happy endings are dead."

Sunshine and rainbows, that one.

 Learn more about the writing of *This is Darkness*. Scan the QR code for the audio commentary, soundtrack and more.

THIS IS DARKNESS

She waited for him in the ballroom, a lithe, tall woman blending with the darkness.

Shadows stretched from every direction, the wail of sirens barely piercing the gloom. The police were here for her, and although the negotiator had long since stopped trying to ring the mangled lump of plastic that had once been a phone, the strobe of red and blue lights hadn't.

The shifting lights outside the old hotel made the darkness writhe, while the sheet-white curtains billowed with the breeze coming through the windows, broken now, glass exploded across the parquet floor. The rich inlays of wood were turned to splinters and char, victims of the fight that had taken place between the two supers, much like the ornate crystal chandelier and the heavy doors at the other end of the long, rectangular room.

She sat in the throne-like chair on its raised dais and watched those doors. Her heart beat hard in her chest, tension fired up and down her spine, but her body was relaxed. Forcibly relaxed. One black power-armour-clad leg swung over a wide gilt armrest, the police lights occasionally gleaming on the small, scaled ridges, and she bounced one thick-sole against the throne's side—*thud thud thud*—while the other foot remained firmly planted on the richly embroidered red carpet. The tails of her billowing greatcoat spread about her like wings, the hood long-since pushed from around her face. The thick fabric draped over her shoulders, leaving her long, ash-white hair and ivory face to float, ghost-like in the dark.

She leaned against the other armrest, chin nestled casually on her fist; a fist clenched so hard the black rings circling her fingers—two on each, one above and one below the second knuckle—cut into her flesh while the clip-like bands around each fingertip dug into her palm. Small pains. Small pains to fight back the larger ones, like the way her ribs pinched with every breath, the sharp throb of a cracked tooth, the blood on her lips, the fire through her knuckles. The poison of betrayal entrenched deep in her soul.

Small pains to fight back the larger pains, and to drown the insidious whisper in her ear.

Kill.

She rubbed the delicate metalwork tracing the path of her cheekbone and wrapped around her ear. The filigree of leaves was as familiar to her as the freckles on her face, as cold as the bands of metal pressing into her fingers, as black as the very pit of the Dark, the source of her power.

Kill, it whispered. *Kill.*

She clenched her fist tighter, pressed the cold, dark metal of her earring into her cheek, even as hope— No, she would not call it that, could not dare to think the word, to let the light of an end to her torture lift even a fragment of her heart. Anticipation, it was anticipation that clenched her gut and made her pulse pound harder, her breath come shorter. After all these years, she was so close, so very close to an end.

Anticipation raced through her blood, made her muscles twitch and added force to the *thud thud THUD* of her boot against the throne, but the next move wasn't hers. The next moved belonged to *him*, and so she waited, eyes on the broken doors at the other end of the ballroom.

Beyond the elaborately carved doors, a spark struggled against the darkness; a tiny pinprick of yellow-red flame, there and then gone.

Her breath caught, her heart beat harder.

Another spark, brighter, beating longer against the gloom.

She leaned forward, just an inch, the sharp pain in her ribs all but forgotten.

The spark became a blaze, a ball of fire engulfing the hand, and then arm of a man. It was a strong arm, but lean, and she knew from experience how the muscles rippled under his bronze skin, how it felt to have it wrapped around her, lifting her toes off the floor as their lips met. Knew too, how it felt to run her hands through his dark, chestnut hair, to share his breath and cling to that slim, muscled chest. But that was a long time ago.

Kill.

She dug the rings further into her palm, the earring deeper into her cheek.

He lifted his head and his eyes blazed, the power encasing his flesh turning the pale green orbs into beacons. Almost two hundred metres she'd thrown him—the length of the ballroom—and he stared her down like he could pierce gloom and distance to meet her gaze. She could, pierce the gloom that was, could use it to trace the hard lines of his face, the stubble on his jaw, the heavy powermesh of the armour clinging to shoulders and chest. She could take a piece of the darkness, give it form and mass, a sharp, pointy end, raise it out of the tiles at his back and stab—

He spun, the fire that had encased his arm engulfing his whole body, burning brighter and harder, white and blue flicking from his fingers, turning the spear of darkness to smoke.

She formed another spear, and another and another, a hundred dark arrows flung at him from all sides. They burned to nothing, except the one at his feet, in microscopic shadows made by the arch of his soles within his boots. She reached in and *twisted.*

He yelled; a sharp, high cry of pain quickly cut off, and those eyes, those pale green orbs she'd once left herself drown in, years ago, turned to her once more. Except this time, they blazed, the heat of the sun burning whatever last, fragile threads of compassion might have remained.

Now, whispered the voice.

Yes, *now*.

She leaned forward, found a stray band of light flooding through the broken windows, and smiled, knowing he could see it.

He flew at her. Literally flew, his entire body a column of flame shooting through the dark, setting fire to the floor like some kind of comet.

She flung herself forwards, the heat of his passing enough to sear her flesh as she rolled under his attack.

The throne shattered, splinters of flaming wood and fabric exploding behind her, leaving nothing behind but the knobbled feet and a scorch mark.

He stood in its place, the long, hard planes of his face made fiercer by stark shadows cast by the flames licking his arms and feet, the snarl twisting his mouth.

She crouched, the tails of her greatcoat flared around her feet, the metal around her fingers and over her cheek gleaming in the light from his flames, and reached deep inside herself, pulling the Dark from her soul. It rose, eager and familiar, filling every nook and every cranny, every particle of her being, until all that was left was the blue of her eyes. She smiled as it ate that too.

Kill. The command came not from the Dark, but somewhere else, somewhere further, echoing through the band of metal twisted around her ear.

Kill. Now, it said again.

She stared into his burning eyes, and smiled wider.

He roared. Leapt.

She was ready, darting sideways, shadows chasing her form, wrapping around her feet, caressing her face until she was nothing more than a figment, a trick of the eye. Shadows coalesced in her hands, long curved blades sucking in the red and blue strobe of police lights, the glaring bolt of a spotlight. She struck, swords whistling through the air, slicing the flames licking his shoulders.

Another yell, rage as much as pain filling his voice, twisting his face as he spun. The flames in his eyes burned brighter, the yellow fading through white to blue, hotter than the sun. Under his skin, his bones glowed, and at his feet, the floor cracked and charred. Flames licked every inch of him now, his usually black armour molten, short chestnut locks just another wavering flare amidst the inferno.

'You won't get away this time.' Fire rolled through his voice, heat and power making it echo, and the heat of it, of his breath, washed over her.

She breathed it in, basked in it. The brighter he burned, the longer the shadows, the deeper the black, the more power he gave her.

'That's what Starfire said,' she whispered, letting the darkness carry her words through the snap and crack of his blaze. 'Before I killed her.'

Another roar, another lunge. All sense, all caution lost to the old, heart-crumbling pyre of pain-fuelled rage in his eyes.

Yes, the whisper echoed her own thoughts, victory shivering through the metal twisted around her ear and across her cheek, even as hope flared in her chest.

She didn't dodge, didn't flinch, but met him head-on, shadow-blades raised, one thrusting for his chest, the other deflecting the fiery fist shooting for her face. Even as the first blade collapsed, shadows disintegrating before the flames encasing his heart, and the second shattered, she was summoning more. Whips and spikes, spears and daggers rose from every corner, from under every splinter of wood, every shard of glass, every inch and every crack, aimed squarely as his back. She held them there a moment, an extension of her will.

The world slowed, so she could appreciate his fist coming for her jaw, bones turned to light, skin just a thin shell containing all that power, all that fire and all that heat searing the air before it.

Now! Alarm made the whisper's command strident.

She battled the command, clung instead to the Dark and held the shadows a half-heartbeat longer.

Do it! Anger and fear turned the whisper to glass, slicing into her brain.

She let go.

The world restarted, all those inky weapons diving at his back, the meteor of his fist an inch from her face.

She didn't duck or roll or flinch. Didn't raise her arms or turn her head. She stared him straight in the eye as his knuckles snapped her head back, as his other fist found her ribs and pain exploded through her chest and face. She stared him in the eye and smiled, or tried to as a different kind of darkness took her vision.

But it wasn't him she tried to pull her broken jaw into a smile for, wasn't his inarticulate scream of rage she laughed at as unconsciousness took hold, and her shadow weapons dissolved. It was the whisper, screaming, *No!*

Yes, she thought back, hope creeping into her heart. *Yes.*

The dark claimed her.

OF CROWS &BEASTS

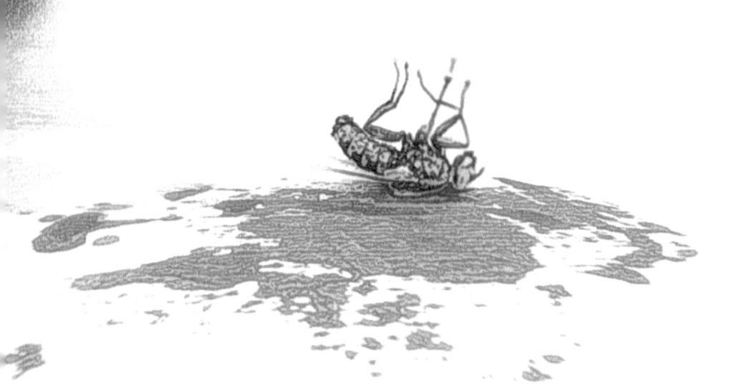

INTRODUCTION

Of Crows & Beasts began as a do-over of a fantasy story. Don't ask me how I went from necromancy to… whatever it is our main character is, 'cause I'm not entirely sure myself; but I'm glad it did.

When I started writing *Of Crows*, I planned for it to go in a different direction but… my storytelling brain likes plans about as much as a bonfire likes books; it laughs at them before dancing over their ashes. I'm slowly learning to embrace this reality.

 Learn more about the writing of *Of Crows & Beasts*. Scan the QR code for the audio commentary, soundtrack and more.

OF CROWS & BEASTS

She got off the bus, just another tired, drawn face in another line of refugees aching from the long journey on battle-scared roads.

She tilted her head to the sky, letting the hood fall back.

At least she was free.

And if all that freedom had left her was the dark-grey clouds and damp, frigid winds of the great north's most miserable nation, she would take it.

Take it and be glad.

There were worse things than poverty, greater hardships than death. She should know, she'd run away from both.

A shove from behind; a low, grunted admonishment to 'keep moving' shook her out of her reverie and toward the tall, razor-topped fence. The thick chain-link mesh rippled with power, both electric and magical, the two forces curling around each other in a rich pattern of sparks. If she unfocused her eyes, let herself slip into the ethereal—just a shave, just enough to see under the surface of things—the riotous play of wind-drawn electricity and spell-work rolled out before her.

On the surface it was a simple warding, flashy and menacing but without any real bite. A well-enough trained Imperial mage captian would shred it in a moment, and that's where the danger lay, in the enemy's arrogance.

In *her* arrogance, that's how Laspar's forces had found her last. Why her brother was dead.

Her arrogance.

She tugged the hood back over her platinum hair and shuffled forward.

Ahead, personnel in the Spulorian army's blue and grey uniforms stood either side of rectangular identity scanners, while at their backs lurked the hulking menace of armed troops, faces hidden behind the impenetrable black shield of their helmets.

The line moved. She shuffled forward.

The endless *shuffle shhlop* of feet on the muddy ground, the quiet patter of the relentless drizzle that had pursued them over the Spulorian border, the cry of an infant and the soldiers' quiet requests for 'Documents?' and 'Step this way' were the only sounds.

None of the waiting refugees spoke, not even to murmur to the children clutched in their arms or to pass secrets to their loved ones.

That's what made the squeal of the ident scanner so loud. It split the air, a knife to her ears, burrowing right through cartilage and bone, all the way to her soul. The pain—

Oh, Goddess, the pain! It ripped through her brain, set fire to her flesh and liquified her bones.

She could not scream, could not fall, could not clamp palm to her head and cry out as so many others did, as the unfortunate in the screaming identity scanner was.

She had to stand, had to walk, had to watch as the faceless combat soldiers came alive, and Crows descended on the wildly flashing rectangle.

The black-clad operatives materialised in the air above, the long ends of the ground-sweeping coats flared about their legs as they landed, knees bent to absorb the drop, gloved hands spread. They appeared not just around the scanner—one of their number already hauling the refugee to their feet—but within the crowd, gazes already seeking, scanning.

They stalked the queues. Glossy black shields covered their

heads, leaving just the long, serious slash of their lips exposed. They swung their attention left then right. Fear rolled before them, ripping through the silent masses, raising the hair on necks, and fingers in signs of warding.

The ident arch still made its flesh-sawing wail even though the one who caused it was gone—all the better to allow the Crows to find other magic-users in the crowd.

The refugees on the ground, curled into foetal balls as pain wracked their insides, disappeared in a swirl of long coats. Those that flinched or crouched or clasped hands to their ears, like they could stop their brains leaking out, were quietly moved to another, shorter line where the personnel held not clipboards or guns but glowing threads of magic.

The Crows drifted down the queue, drawing closer, one on either side of the line in which she stood.

Her bones burned, her hands ached, her teeth bit into her tongue.

The man ahead shuffled forward.

It took everything she had to lift a foot, to shove the command through screaming nerves, to not stumble, to not cry, to keep her hands clamped around the strap of her bag and not her belly.

Shuffle. Sploosh.

Shuffle. Sploosh.

The line grew shorter. The distance with it.

Shuffle. Sploosh.

The Crow on her right stalked closer, the glossy black of their faceplate sweeping over the crowd.

Five steps.

Four.

Two.

The Crow was there, attention skimming left then right. She didn't flinch, didn't cower or turn her head. For a moment, she forgot to breathe, trusting to the depth of her hood, the enveloping sexless black of her clothes, as worn and forgettable as the rest.

And then the Crow was past.

She breathed, willed relief to shed the pain from her bones, except what came out of her lips was too loud, more moan than exhalation.

A Crow in her face, long gloved fingers reaching for her hood, his helmet a mirror, reflecting her widening eyes, the long straight cut of her nose, the hollow planes of her cheeks.

Ythys, Mother of Stars, protect me now, she prayed as the hood fell to her shoulders.

The Crow said nothing, merely stared and she stared back, seeing only herself—pale amber skin turned to straw in the gloom and drizzle—and the serious, downturned corners of the Crow's mouth.

She clamped her pain and the power tight inside of her as that blank gaze bore through her soul—

A scream, inhuman. Blood curdling.

Over the other side of the yard, before the mage scanner, a demon wearing the ragged remains of human flesh roared. Talons tore into one mage solider while the others drew glowing swords and still another drew arcane symbols in the air.

The Crow vanished, gone in a gust of wind, following his fellows to the new threat.

Panic rippled through the refugees, the queues ripping sideways, away from the conflict—

It was over as quickly as it began. The alarm died with the demon, taking the endless agony with it.

The Crows went too, dematerialising but not gone. She could feel them, up there in the sky. Waiting.

The line shuffled forward.

Her legs were hell, muscles and bones soft as endorphins flooded her system, but she didn't stumble. Not now, not yet. Not when she was so close.

'Documents.' The young, stern-faced officer spoke without inflection.

She was at the scanner, just three steps, a forged identity and two combat soldiers between her and safety. Or as much safety as she was ever going to enjoy again. Tenuous, fragile as the lies it was built upon, but more than she'd known in a long, long time.

Fingers shaking, she reached inside her coat and drew out her ident card.

The officer took the battered bit of plastic and pressed it to their clipboard.

She couldn't see what appeared on the one-way screen projected over the board, but she didn't need to. The chip told the story of Belgin Féme, a thirty-two-year-old factory worker with a degree in art history and no family. From the heart of the Imperium's urbanised fringe, she had just enough magical aptitude to keep herself out of the slums, where her only asset would have been her face.

Lies. All of it, except, perhaps for her face.

The officer jerked their head toward the scanner. 'Proceed.'

The woman pretending to be Belgin Féme braced herself and stepped into the arch. The rectangular black box swallowed her.

An ident card good enough to fool the Spulorian system had taken skill and money, but this… The soul-shredding wail of before would be nothing.

She willed every fibre of her to stillness. *Ythys, guide me.*

In the physical world, it was a moment, two heartbeats to carry her through the half-metre of tech and magic, but in the ethereal, in the place where the divine spilled through the fabric of existence, it was an eternity.

Spells rippled over her being, sinking into the nooks and crannies, bloodhounds seeking the magic in her DNA even as the tech photographed and measured her physical form, stripping her down to the flesh. By the end of the scan it would know every inch of her skin, right down to the mole on her inner thigh, but it would not know her soul.

Ythys, don't let it know my soul.

If the ident alarm had been painful, the scan was torture, every inch of her aware of the spells ripping her apart, icy talons digging at her insides, pulling apart ethereal muscles, sinking long cold probes into her gut, her heart…

If she'd gone to the other scanner, declared herself a mage and let the Crows take her, it would be different. Everything would be different.

If she were lucky, she'd be dead.

She didn't want to die, and the other options… All she could do was endure. And pray.

The scanner released her.

Her face was drawn, pale. She felt the blood draining from it, sinking to her feet, skin turning clammy, the fear beads of sweat rising on her forehead. If the Crows saw her now, if the officers suspected…

She kept her gaze down, didn't look the officer in the face, eyes on their collar instead.

A buzzing from the officer's clipboard, and she imagined the results from the scanner flashing across the surface. A pause, weighty and deep. The woman pretending to be Belgin Féme held fatigue and the brilliant, vomit-inducing rush of endorphins at bay with the last, fragile strands of willpower. She prayed.

And prayed. And prayed.

The ident card thrust at her chest.

'Welcome to Spulor, Ms Féme.'

Relief made her bones sag, her hands clumsy as she fumbled the ID back inside her coat.

She'd made it.

Now, the real work began.

●

Eighteen months later.

The files landed on her desk with a *thud*, dislodging the

paperwork from other stacks and threatening the stability of her plastic coffee cup.

A quick hand ensured the safety of her workspace from a black flood of caffeine, while another caught a teetering pile of delicate tech-paper before it slid to the floor.

The woman known as Belgin Féme looked up at the interloper.

A Crow looked back. Only the generous curve of his lips and the dark pits of his eyes visible behind the mask.

At least it wasn't the full-face shield. No staring at her own reflection.

'I need these processed.' He loomed at her side.

The man was good at looming.

He reached over her shoulder and leaned his weight on the new stack of files, like he was trying to increase their importance with his own weight. Drive them through her desk and into the System with the force of his will. Like he didn't trust her—a lowly, magic-less immigrant in the Crow's secretarial pool. Maybe he thought she was stupid.

Or worse, maybe he thought she was lying.

Féme looked away, ignored the warm, distinctive scent of sandalwood and bergamot that wound through her senses whenever this Crow was close. He hadn't worn it the first handful of times she'd seen him in the Pool, not even the first time he'd loomed over her shoulder or brushed by her in the hallway. Not even when he'd wandered through the neat lines of secretaries, trailing tension and surprise in his wake, and slapped the very first file on her desk.

She'd have known if he'd worn it, if anyone had the faintest trace left to recirculate through headquarters' enviros.

That scent reached down past everything that was Belgin Féme and tugged on the beast sleeping within.

She reached for the foot-high stack. 'Of course, sir. I'll get to it after—'

'No. Now.'

'I have other—'

He leaned closer, coat brushing against her shoulder, the breadth of him blocking out the light. She kept her eyes on the files, on the broad, gloved hand holding them down, even as anger and power stirred in her chest.

It was a game, a stupid, dangerous game. The bullying, the fragrance, a game designed to crack the facade of Belgin Féme.

'Now, Ms Belgin.'

'The files from yesterday—'

'Will wait. Get these done first.'

She would burn him to ashes, turn his insides out and make a garland of his intestines. She would rip the mask off his pretty little face, shred his coat and show the Crow what *real* power was. The stuff that made life and death and darkness. She would rip apart the very fabric of reality and raze this square, grey hellhole to the ground. She would—

She would nod and smile, but not too wide and not for too long, just a quick stretch of lips that didn't sink too deep into her eyes.

'Of course,' she said, but not too brightly and not too sharp either. Demure and helpful, efficient. A drone buzzing away at her desk, no different from the handful of others in the Pool. Simple. Trustworthy. Nothing to hide.

She reached for the first file.

His hand didn't move.

She gave the file a gentle tug.

'Sir,' she said and looked him in the eye. Trustworthy. 'I need the file.'

The plain black mask was expressionless, the full mouth drawn in a straight, emotionless line, but the Crow's eyes... Determination swirled in the mahogany depths, magic flickering like a lightning storm over the surface.

She did not look away, but allowed her eyes to widen, to let him peer deeper into her soul.

Trustworthy. She was Belgin Féme and she had nothing to hide.

Nothing at all.

Never.

Ever.

Trustworthy.

She was Belgin Féme.

Féme blinked, let fear whiten her cheeks and hunch her shoulders. 'Sir,' she said again, and tugged once more on the file.

The Crow turned away, anger or perhaps frustration tightening his jaw below the mask.

He pushed away from the desk. 'Get on with it,' he said and turned, the long tails of his black coat flaring behind him.

No one breathed. No one spoke.

Silence echoed in the Crow's wake.

Féme slipped the first file onto her desk before carefully repositioning the rest of the pile. The plain white rectangle of the workspace held a mountain range of tech-paper, organised around the clear valley of screen and board. Some of the mountains were small, some large, all precisely arranged; edges square with the workspace, sides crisp, corners sharp enough to slice flesh. Or so the other secretaries whispered behind her back and in the lunchroom.

They whispered other things too, gossiping like mother hens in soft, chittering voices that transcended the gender of the six men and women who occupied the small square space at the heart of the Crow's file room.

She pressed the thick, transparent sheet of plastic to the glowing rectangle of her board. A file flickered to life above.

A young woman stared back at her: dark brown eyes, hollow cheeks, the circles under her eyes telling a story of hardship. A migrant, another Imperial running to the dubious safety of Spulor's arms.

Féme's heart ached for her, while inside, the beast growled.

// Riya Passerini.

// Level 3 magic user.

// Specialty: water manipulation.

// Processed at the North Gate and transported to Dunemouth for evaluation.

// Migrant number—

She did not read it, hand working of its own accord, entering the information in the System, sending orders to the distribution centre for additional resources, checking Dunemouth's roster, requesting a water mage to fill the hole and test the woman when she arrived.

There were plenty of Riyas on Féme's desk, an endless stream of Imperial runaways shuffled here and there through Spulor's immigration system.

The ones like Riya were lucky, low-powered but strong enough to be useful, their specialties unobjectionable. Riya's life may no longer be fully her own, but there were worse things to live with than suspicion and hard labour.

She reached for the next file.

// Mac Brankcovich. Plant mage. Level 4.

// Kerim Hayter. Healer. Level 2.

// Lamia Pfaff. Summoner. Archmag—

Lamia Pfaff.

Féme froze.

Lamia Pfaff stared back at her with a tired silver gaze, bones stark against sallow skin, lips parched by thirst, cracked and bleeding. She looked older than the thirty-two years recorded on her ident.

Maybe that was just the dirt and sleep deprivation stamped on her face, or the ragged silver hair that hung in clumps around her face, where it wasn't gone altogether.

Disease had ravaged Lamia, cancer eating away at her insides, turning the strong, stoic woman Féme had once known into a skeleton. She was surprised Lamia had lasted this long, two years since their first and last meeting. Surprised the woman hadn't taken the money and then her own life. That was what Lamia had said she wanted, to end things on her own terms.

It seemed fate, or Laspar or even Spulor had had other plans. Perhaps, even Lamia herself?

Féme forced her fingers to move. This was no time to stare, not now, not with that name and that face watching her every move.

// Lamia Pfaff. Summoner. Archmage.

// Processed at West Gate.

// High priority. Hold for debriefing.

// Current location. A black box blotted out the rest.

Was the Crow there? Was this a test? Was he even now cloaked, ready to materialise if she hesitated too long, gave Lamia more attention than she deserved?

Prickles ran down Féme's spine, a tide of warning reaching into the pit of her, picking at the bindings lashing the beast.

He wouldn't do it, couldn't do it. The only person who could expose Belgin Féme was Belgin Féme, and perhaps…

Her gaze slipped back to the woman hovering over her desk. Those silver eyes, so unlike the onyx depths of her own, reached through the screen to stab her in the heart.

Lamia knew, Lamia could expose her. But only if the Crows suspected, only if they broke the bindings—

It was a trap, it had to be a trap. The Crow was right behind her, waiting to throw off his shroud of invisibility and wrap those long, spell-binding hands around her neck. She could feel him there, his breath, the warm sandalwood and sweet bergamot.

It was a trap and yet she couldn't stop her finger from scrolling down, couldn't stop herself from tapping the black box, and drinking in the words underneath.

// Current location: Crow Headquarters. Secretarial pool.

Hell erupted.

●

'She is not the archmage, Anard,' the woman spoke.

The thump of hard-soled boots on concrete, frustration ringing in every sharp *clack*.

'She is.' The same frustration in the Crow's voice, the same determination. 'I can *feel* it.'

'Anard.' The woman paused, the silence filled with the Crow's *clack clack clack*. 'Anard!' she said it again, stronger, impatience filling the cold air.

The *clacking* stopped.

The woman spoke once more. 'It's been three days. If she had a breath of magic, she would have broken in two. An archmage— Are you listening to me?'

A grunt.

The woman continued. 'An archmage would have started screaming within the first hour, no matter the spells or the shielding or the mental training. An hour, Anard. An. Hour.'

A moment of silence.

'No,' the Crow—the man called Anard—said. 'It's her, I know—'

'Look at her!' Gone was the impatience, now only anger and disgust rode the woman's voice.

Through a haze of pain, Féme sensed the weight of their gazes on her slumped form. Snakes made of razors writhed under her skin, slithering through muscle and sinew in time with the music. A soft chorus, a hundred sweet voices rising and falling in perfect harmony, whispering ancient words, their meaning lost to all but the gods.

Although now... She breathed, felt the pain in her lungs, behind her eyes, cutting into her soul. The words lodged in her psyche, a part of her. Like her bones, like her tongue, seeping into her soul even as they sliced it to ribbons.

She had wanted to scream in that first hour after the Crow had materialised behind her, a dark triumphant shadow. A null collar *snicking* closed around her neck, hard gloved hands yanking her upright, almost pulling her arms from their sockets, then marching her through headquarters down to this dark, cold cell.

She hadn't fought, hadn't grabbed the stylus from her desk and driven it through the Crow's— through Anard's eye. Hadn't shown him just how truly ineffectual a Spulorian null collar was against one such as she. Hadn't done anything except let fear soak every pore of her being as she begged and pleaded and finally demanded to know what was going on.

There had been no answers, no explanations, no questions, just the cell—five concrete sides and a magi-tech forcefield – and the music.

She'd meditated at first, closing her eyes and leaving the body behind, retreating behind her mental wall. It had worked, for a little while. She'd prayed then, prayed for strength, for luck, for the pain to end.

She counted time through the brief silences when the guards came to give her water and lead her to a bathroom. She could have escaped then, could have ripped off the null collar and run away from the voices whispering in their forgotten tongue. It would have been the end of it.

The end of everything.

But she wasn't finished yet. She hadn't even started.

She had to hang on, to persevere.

Inside the cell, strapped to the chair, she huddled inside the shell of Belgin Féme, no longer praying, no longer closing her ears to the chorus.

There was wisdom in the words, a meaning that hovered on the tip of her soul, if only she could untangle it.

The voices stopped, just… gone.

'No…' Her mouth moved, breath pushed past her vocal cords, but no sound reached her ears. She'd been so close, so very, very close…

Light pierced her eyelids, ripped away the comforting dark, the last strains of the lost language floating in her memory. Then hands, on her forearms and then her knees, the hard *shrimp* of restraints removed. Another hand on her forehead, this time a thumb lifting her eyelid, a flashlight in her eye.

She twisted sideways.

'Responsive.' The woman's voice, flat and efficient. 'Vitals good. Get her into recovery.'

Lifted onto a stretcher, the rattling *thud thud thud* of wheels hitting cracks in the floor. More lights, the *whoosh* of doors, the *ding* of an elevator. Silence, save for the rustle of cloth and the shuffle of shoes. Sandalwood and bergamot filled the air, seeped under her skin, roused the beast in her soul.

Another *ding*, more doors *whooshing*. The hum of more voices, some soft, some urgent, the harsh scent of antiseptic obliterating the other.

More movement, the stretcher's wheels smooth now, no cracks or tiles to make them *thud thud thud*.

Being lifted to another bed, a blanket laid over her, footsteps receding and then… and then…

Sandalwood.

She drew the scent deep into her lungs, let it permeate every part of her. The beast roiled, claws pressing against the thin membrane that held it down, that made it quiet. That made Belgin Féme possible.

'I know you.' Anard, warm breath brushing her ear, the weight of his hands pulling the blanket tight across her shoulders. 'You can't hide forever.'

The beast stuck a talon through the membrane and, for a moment, as Belgin Féme opened her eyes, it was Lamia Pfaff who stared out.

Her stary gaze met the mahogany of Anard's, the beast baring its teeth at the power behind the Crow's.

He flinched, the rich amber of his cheeks turning pale, but he did not look away, did not recoil or scream or shout. He hardened his jaw and stared back, the thing in his soul rising to the beast's call.

Inside, in the dark places left in her psyche, the places the lights and the murmurs and the hands hadn't touched, could never touch, the unknowable song rose.

'No yaso sä awwi.' The foreign words rolled from her tongue. *I don't need forever.*

She had time to see him frown, to witness the thing behind his gaze sit upright in response, before unconsciousness took her.

I AM MAGGIE #1
DON'T DIE

INTRODUCTION

Cue the second version of my Valkyrie myth, not to be confused with the first version, in *The Wind* and its following stories. Valkyries, much like crows and ravens, are on my brain these days, which makes it almost impossible to keep them out of my fiction.

I've always been a gamer; in fact, I first started writing because of a game and even studied writing because of a completely different game. That said, I didn't get into LitRPG as a genre until I saw *Ready Player One* (read the book, prefer the movie) and then went exploring what other stories were out there.

I found a few I liked and more I didn't, and it was those few books I enjoyed and why I enjoyed them that prompted me to write this. Making *Don't Die* into the first story in a series of shorts though… that hit me like a bolt of lightning while I was wiping benches at my then day-job.

 Learn more about the writing of *Don't Die*. Scan the QR code for the audio commentary, soundtrack and more.

DON'T DIE

'Maggie, hurry.'

'Yeah, Maggie. Hurry.'

The voices followed her into the Sphere. They echoed in the endless black space, ringing in her ears and stabbing her heart, the first one was small and high, rich with fear, the other deep and mocking, amusement dripping from every syllable.

She hated that voice. Hated and feared it.

'Maggie, hurry.' It was Usha's voice that swirled through her skull though, Usha's fear that made her heart clench and her palms sweaty; was the only reason she didn't rip the VR helmet from her head and leap out of the couch for the other's throat.

Hurry. As if that echo were a trigger, a clock appeared front and centre of her vision, casting bright blue highlights across the floor.

Sixteen hours, twenty-nine minutes.

Not enough time, the small, desperate other part, sweaty and achy with Usha's fear, whispered. And too much time, a whole six hours past the redline.

But all the time she had, the larger part said, the part that clenched her fists tighter and imagined pounding them into the other's face.

All the time she had, and none of it to waste, not even if her neurons fried in the process.

A thought, and the Sphere came to life.

A featureless, sexless doll shunted the countdown aside.

Sixteen hours, twenty-seven minutes.

Options spinning through the void—race, gender, height, hair, boobs, build—a deep melodic voice reaching up through the floor, spinning a tale of ancient gods and a mighty war, of spaceships and planets and the cataclysmic clash of science and magic. So many choices, so little time, and why the *fuck* had the bastard dropped her here, in the insane mess of the System's core, where anything and everything was possible?

No time to curse, no time to choose. All that mattered was Usha, the fear and hope in her eyes, the desperation in her voice.

Hurry.

Hurry, hurry, hurry.

A thought, the Sphere pulsing in acknowledgement and a glittering hundred-sided die hovered in the space before her.

// Randomise?

Yes.

// Confirm.

They'd told her to throw a random character even though she'd argued, begged them, even with the gun at Usha's head, perhaps because of it. She'd pleaded with them to let her choose a race and class she was good at, they'd said no, said they'd had plans.

She could throw it now, should think 'no' and complete the quest in half the time. Half the time she still didn't have.

She could almost hear the *snick* of the old-fashioned gun held to Usha's head as it charged.

// Confirm, the AI prompted again.

Confirm.

The featureless doll blurred, a hundred different voices, a hundred different shoulders and toes and tails, wings, horns, scales, bipedal, quadrupedal, blue skin, brown skin, white skin, all cycling in the space of a dozen heartbeats.

She felt each one against her chest, pounding in time to the seconds slipping from the clock.

Hurry.

Hurry.

Hurry.

A tingle ran through the Sphere, static fuzzing the doll in its endless spin. Something was wrong. A system error? A virus? The other's plan?

A pale, electric-blue shape writhed under her feet.

The spinning stopped, a new prompt appearing over the dice.

// Accept?

She didn't even look.

Accept.

A chorus filled her ears, lifted her from the floor and filled her skin with light. She was no longer standing on the edge of the Sphere looking in, but in its middle. Her hands ended in thick, pointed nails, the shadow of horns erupted from her brow and curled past her ears.

The chorus faded, the light no longer spilling from her pores, and she was lowered to the ground. Not the dark, reflective surface of the Sphere but the hard, white flagstones of Central, in the midst of the busiest place in the game. And, oh shit, perhaps she should have looked before accepting, because her feet weren't feet but talons and there was a weight on her back, the sense of new bones and musculature, and if she thought about it, twitched her shoulder blades just so—

SHHWAP.

Fuck.

Wings.

Wings plus horns plus talons… She put her hands to her chest, felt the cold steal, the delicate etching of feathers across its surface.

No.

Of all the races, all the classes, why the one that only spawned on random, that could be looted from a player's corpse?

A chuckle, malice dripping from every pulse of air against her eardrums. 'Like it, Maggie? We rigged the System just for you.'

The shiver running through the Sphere.

'You hacked the randomiser.' It was a growl, half-whispered and yet the words echoed in the virtual space and the avatars that had clustered around, the screenshots she can almost *feel* being taken of the Valkyrie in their midst, faltered.

How long before she was plastered across the fashion wars forums? How long before whatever anonymity she might have possessed was gone?

She looked up, over the massive square that was Central, and the sea of faces staring back. 'You're going to get me killed.'

'Then your girlfriend's gonna get dead too, Maggie. Besides,' he continued. 'It's easier to hack the randomiser than the quest, and with that skin, it's guaranteed to pop.'

Sixteen hours, twenty-four minutes.

*// **All or Nothing initiated.** Congratulations User990906134, you have been selected to participate in* All or Nothing. *Follow the clues, defeat your opponents and claim the World.*

// Death, logout or setting your status to AFK will result in automatic forfeiture.

Double fuck.

As she stood, frantically trying to calm her racing heart, with the whole world gawking at her, and *his* voice played in her ears— 'Gonna get *dead,* Maggie'—the non-combatant tag in the top right of her HUD disappeared, a new notification taking its place.

// PvP enabled.

A firebolt hit her in the chest.

One good thing about rolling a Valkyrie, it came with armour right off the bat. The firebolt left her scorched, health bar flashing a frantic dance of red but with enough life left to flap her monstrous raven-dark wings and get the hell out of dodge.

One bad thing about being a Valkyrie, she was fucking easy to spot, and even if none of the other low-level avatars had flight, the higher-level ones did.

She'd have been better off on the ground, with the fire-throwing mage.

'Inventory,' she yelled against the wind.

The HUD changed, a grid overlaying the cloud-shrouded mountains below. A rusty dagger, three level-one health potions and a pebble filled three of the ten slots.

She equipped the dagger, felt the weight of it, the cool ridges of leather-wrapped metal as it appeared in her hand. Took time to note the nicks in the blade, the mottled orange-brown of rust creeping outwards from the join between blade and hilt, the grime-encrusted remnants of what were once fine engravings on the spine, before she spun.

The closest purser took the dagger in his throat.

// Critical hit. Stun. Bleeding.

Their health bar flashed, a quarter chunk of it disappearing in the blink of an eye.

More opponents darkened the clouds behind them, wings in black and white and flaming green whipping up a storm, while jet boots and hoverboards left streaks of light in their wake. Some of the figures fought each other, swords, arrows, lasers and lightning arching through the sky.

Maggie kicked the knight from her blade, watching only long enough to ensure he tumbled in the direction of her next-closest pursuer, before plunging into the clouds below.

She hid in the mountains, landing in the midst of a tiny clearing, her left wing clipping the edge of the thick canopy, turning her wobbly glide into an inelegant tumble.

// Damage. Environment. -40 health points.

A red flash on her HUD and when she focused, half her health bar was gone.

'Shit.' She heaved herself to her feet, trying to spit the taste of dirt from her mouth, and not fall over at the same time. 'Fuck.'

Having fucking bird claws where her feet should be would take some getting used to.

She glanced upwards, through the thick crosshatch of branches, leaves turning yellow and red, some fluttering down around her. Nothing but pale grey clouds playing with the tops of the tallest trees, not a hint of blue or sky or pursuit—

A swirl in the pale grey, too tight and too violent for a gust of wind, but just right for someone diving through the clouds.

She dove for the shelter of deeper forest, cursing the three-toed claws that caught in the soft dirt and the wings that defied every expectation of how a human should move. She held one tight against her back, while the other dragged.

A bright red nimbus covered the main bend of the dragging wing – so graceful in flight and so very *fucking* inconvenient now.

Fuck. Fuck. Fuck. Why hadn't she *checked* before she accepted the roll?

What would she have done if she had?

Too late to ponder it now, only time to ignore the pain blossoming in her side, the steady drop in health every time she brushed the injured appendage against a tree or bumped into a stone.

Sixteen hours, thirteen minutes.

Fuck the countdown, if any of the winged elites above caught her—*fuck*, if any of the winged *noobs* caught her—she was dead.

Dead. Dead. Dead.

'Dead as a dolphin, Maggie,' Dulton whispered right next to her real ear. The rancid small of his breath wound under the VR hood. 'If you don't hurry the *fuck* up.'

'I've got sixteen hours—'

'And a target on your winged arse. It's all over the forums, hotshot. The big boys want your shit.' She felt him lean closer, tried not to shudder as his lips brushed her ear. 'We didn't arrange all this for you not to last the time it takes to pop the noob cap baby but if you don't, your girl is gonna pay the price. Now move!'

She moved, crashing through forest not meant for beings with wings, then the edge of the game map.

The edge of the map.

How the fuck?

The edge of the game map wasn't just a line on a bit of virtual paper, it was the edge of the *world*. No more trees, no more mountains, no more ones and zeroes telling the electrons which coloured pixel to put where, just a solid wall and then nothing.

Except this wasn't nothing, there was grass beneath her claws, the rough bark of an ancient redwood under her hand, a warm trickle of sunlight on her face and a vibration against her hip.

She put her hand to it, found the stiff leather of a pouch. Her inventory appeared on the HUD.

The rusty knife was in the sheath on her thigh, leaving just the stack of health potions and the pebble occupying the ten meagre spaces.

The pebble was pulsing.

One, two, three. A pause. One, two, three.

She summoned it to her hand.

One, two, three.

It nestled within her palm, an unremarkable mottled grey, neither rectangular nor egg-shaped but slightly triangular, edges rounded in the way only a river rock tumbled by decades of water could be. If it weren't for the roundness, she could have dropped it where she stood and lost it amid the stones at her feet.

It pulsed again, the sensation running through her bones, from her fingers to the tips of her deadly sharp talons.

She concentrated on it.

More information.

// A river stone.

No longer just a pebble, as it had been before, but no more information either. Not a hint, a cryptic clue or an asterisk to suggest this pebble was more than what it appeared. Nothing save the pulse.

That, and the secret, off-map environment it chose to pulsate within.

But it was a river stone.

She needed to find a river, needed to find it fast.

Maggie looked up.

The canopy was dense but the spaces between the trees had grown with the height and girth of the trunks and even if she couldn't make it all the way through the green roof, perhaps she could take advantage of the highway of branches above.

Angry red still clung to the joint of her wing but a health potion would take care of that.

She summoned one to her hand, leaving just two, drank and felt the cooling tingle of magic rushing under her skin, knitting the hollow bones in her wing. A second and the job was done, her health bar flashing full.

Maggie launched herself into the air.

Three hard flaps, each one stirring a mini tornado, and she was perched atop a thick branch, claws digging into the hard wood like it was butter, wings half-spread for balance. The spaces here were tighter, with overlapping branches a half-metre thick and smaller offshoots spreading palm-sized leaves in the air. Still, now that she was here…

She scanned the green-tinged gloom, following the path of branches, the way sunlight filtered through the heavy leaves, highlighting certain sections over others. Almost like streetlamps. Convenient. Just like the way the next branch flowed from the one she stood on, a little too evenly spaced and a little too straight to be natural, without the bends and offshoots that typified the rest of the forest.

A glance behind, tracing the branches connected to this and… There it was, the next tree over, a semi-circle of twisting tree-limbs descending to the forest floor, a poorly-made, overgrown staircase.

A jumping puzzle.

Fuck, she hated jumping puzzles, but at least this time she had wings.

Maggie jogged along the highlighted path, half-jumping, half-gliding to the next tree. Jog. Jump-glide, jog again. The forest passed underneath, unchanging for long enough she wondered why the designers had included the tree-path at all. She contemplated jumping down—the constant jump-glide was becoming old—and while she could see further, the dense foliage did little to improve her sightlines. Then the wall appeared.

One moment the ground was leaf litter and sparse grass, the next it was an eruption of dark grey stone. A cliff face, to which clumps of ragged grass and twisted vines clung to rocks sharp enough to cut.

It rose ten meters, twenty… a hundred… more? She couldn't see the top, not even from where she stood, some thirty metres above the ground herself. The forest ended, she could stretch out an arm and touch the cool rock, could see the canopy in the distance and the cliff…

The cliff disappeared into the clouds, unnaturally straight, as far as the eye could see, not just up but left and right as well. Guess she'd found the actual end of the world.

All right. All right. This was the reason for the tree-path, and if this was the reason then she'd missed a branch or a jump or something, because the only thing in front of her was that giant wall and even if it had a top to which she could fly, there wasn't enough clear air. She'd catch her feathers on every other twig and scrape her skin off on the rocky shards.

She was turning back, mentally retracing her steps, when a flash caught her eye.

Something winked at her from above. Maggie frowned, turned back and—

There. Again. A bright spark of red, like a ruby sun. It was a good two metres up and to the left, out of reach of a non-flighted player. It was unlikely to be a clue, not if the devs meant this area to be accessible to even the lowest players… And wasn't that why the tree-path existed? But still, stranger things had happened.

She gathered herself—both for the jump and the pain that was sure to come when wings and flesh caught on sticks and stones—and leapt.

There was power in the Valkyrie's strange legs. Maggie shot into the air, hand outstretched, wings beating once, twice, and she was right, there was pain, a dreadful *rip*, the shadow of glossy, black feathers falling, the flickering of the health bar, then the *slam* as she hit the cliff. Claws scrabbled for purchase, sharp stones slicing skin.

She climbed, somehow got talons and hands to work together, the claws that had dug so easily into living wood, sinking into stone.

A metre. Two. A handhold giving way. A terrifying, heart-thumping slide back down the cliff face. Climbing back up, wings tight to her back, a second heart-pounding moment when her foot slipped, but she was already boosting herself upward, and there was that red flash and—

She rolled over the lip of a hidden ledge, panting as her stamina-pool pulsed, a thin sliver of blue all that was left in the otherwise grey bar. It pulsed in time to her heart, slowing as she breathed deep, taking in the sharp, straight cliff wall above as it shot into the clouds. So high she might fall into them.

A stupid thought to have.

Eleven hours, twenty-eight minutes.

Five hours. She'd been in the VR for five hours. The redline was seven.

Fuck.

Adrenalin shot through her body and she was on her feet, stamina shooting to three-quarters full. Which was strange, and possibly frightening—the game responding to external stimuli—but a thought for another time.

Where had the time gone?

The ruby glint that had drawn her up the cliff was a gem embedded in the rocky face. The size of her head, it appeared to be lit from within, flames dancing under its surface. The river stone, safe in her pouch, vibrated in response.

She got it out.

Where before the little pebble had glowed with a pale white light, it now pulsed red and the description had changed again.

// A river gem.

A gem. She looked from it to the ruby and the small indentation in its surface.

She pressed the pebble-gem to it.

The pebble-gem grew warm against her palm, then hot, the temperature rising again. She was sure it would burn right through flesh to bone, wasn't sure what she would do if it did, but knew she had to keep the two together. Then light shot outwards. Up and down and sideways. Crawling over the cliff in thin, red ribbons, painting an archway on the rock.

The arch reached over her head, a giant frame for the painting that filled its centre. A waterfall crashed over boulders and the ruby nestled where the water joined a rushing stream.

She had a moment to take it in, to revel in the excitement, the hope that washed through her veins before an arrow lodged in the wall. Fine strands of black hair caught in the tip, her health bar taking another hit before the wound on her cheek registered in her brain.

Another arrow followed it, then another.

She spun and threw her back to the wall, frantically stuffing the pebble-gem into her inventory even as she drew the knife and peered down at the tree line, almost getting her face skewered in the process.

An archer stood at the end of the tree path, light sparking off the transparent dome of a nano-shield, a shaft of sunlight highlighting the elaborate patch on their arm, like the game wanted her to know just how much shit she was in.

Maggie plastered herself against the cliff.

Like she needed reminding.

Fuck. The archer was a PvP Hero.

She was so dead.

The *thunk* of another arrow, this time just above her head. The lip of the ledge must be fucking with the Hero's aim, but then why weren't they scaling the cliff? Even stripped down to their undies, a PvP Hero could kill her with their pinkie—

An armoured hand slammed onto the ledge.

The Hero had a friend. A friend whose thick fingers skidded a little on the loose stone.

She flexed the wicked length of her nails and recalled the way they had sunk into the same stone like it was butter.

In the next breath she was at the lip's edge, flat on her stomach, claws sunk deep into the armoured hand. There was a yell from below, her nails sinking through the metal like it was paper, even as her knife skidded off the join between hand and wrist.

More arrows whizzed past her head, faster now, some exploding, sending a shower of rocks down on her wings.

Maggie held on, catching the next hand that came up, clad in the same shiny armour, runes etched in gold across its surface. Magic was a thin, multi-coloured shield above.

Her claws sank into that one too, magic and metal little better than cotton to the might of the Valkyrie.

Fuck, for the first time, it was good being her.

With both of the knight's hands skewered, Maggie levered her torso just enough to break the other player's grip, and *pushed*.

There was a second, a moment where she stared into her opponents eyes, saw surprise and fury there, a moment for another of the Hero's arrows to score her other cheek, and then the knight peeled away from the cliff and fell.

She didn't watch him hit bottom, didn't wait to see what the Hero would do next, just scrambled back to her feet, grabbed the pebble-gem from her pouch, pressed it to the ruby, and prayed like fuck that her hunch was correct.

The archway lit up, the waterfall filling the middle.

From below came the *thunk thunk thunk* of arrows hitting the cliff.

She pressed the pebble-gem harder and silently willed this to hurry up and fucking *work!*

The scuff of shoes against rock announced the Hero climbing the cliff. If she dared take her attention from the pebble-gem, she had no doubt she would see the Hero using the embedded arrows like a staircase.

It's what she would have done, in a different skin.

'Come on, come on. What more do you need?'

Blood trickled from the wound on her cheek, gathered on the tip of her chin, and fell onto the pebble-gem.

Behind her, she heard more than saw the Hero swing onto the ledge, caught the glint of sunlight on a blade.

The pebble-gem glowed brighter while a sharp itch, like a million ants marching over her skin, set into her palms.

The Hero lunged.

Maggie disappeared into the wall.

Ten hours, thirteen minutes.

She'd been in the tunnels long enough for hunger to come and go, to sense someone in the real shove a bottle against her lips and revel in the sweet warmth of water sliding down her throat.

The tunnels weren't made for Valkyries, if they'd been made at all, rather than carved out of the mountain by time and—

She mentally slapped herself. She'd been in here too long, way too long. The redline had come and gone, warnings lighting up her HUD like fireworks, the System trying to boot her out. There'd been a second when she thought it would, and she'd been both glad and alarmed at the prospect. They wouldn't harm Usha because of a System reset. It wouldn't be her fault then, they'd just have to log her back in and—

'All or Nothing, Maggie. Them's the rules.'

Then there'd been a tingle through her soles and the environment had fuzzed, just like it had during character creation, and the warnings and the failsafe had died right along with her hopes.

Three hours past the redline, the lines between reality and virtual were blurring as her neurons slowly fried. The sooner she got to the end of this damn quest the better, not just for Usha, but for her as well.

The realisation didn't make her back ache any less as she stumbled along in a hunched shuffle. The meagre light from the pebble-gem was barely enough to make out the shadows, let alone the dips and hollows of the rocky floor. Having three-toed talons instead of human-shaped feet didn't help, but at least they didn't hurt from walking on bare rock.

Shredding that knight's armour had been pretty sweet too. She was beginning to understand why people spent so much time and money hunting Valkyries down—

The ground gave way, loose stones sliding from under her talons. She flailed, tried to spread her wings for balance, felt them trapped by rocks before they were half-open, and she hit the ground hard, stars exploding in her eyes.

The ground wasn't done with her. She was sliding on her back, pain ripping through her wings, her arse, the exposed portion of her lower back. With fireworks still going off in her brain, she tried to stop her descent, reached out to grab something, anything and—

The *snap* of bone and then pain, roaring through her forearm, up her shoulder, wiping out the smaller agonies of torn feathers and abraded skin.

She fell and kept falling, health bar sliding a fraction lower with every bump and graze, until one rock found the back of her skull and she knew no more.

She swam in the black endlessness of the creation Sphere, suspended above the glossy floor, a pale electric blue shape rippling under its surface.

A dragon waited under the surface.

Waited for her.

But why?

Breath against her skin, her *real* skin. Hot. Rancid.

'Maggie, baby.' His lips brushed her ear. 'I told you not to die. You know what happens if you die.'

No. She tried to speak, opened her mouth and worked her throat, but the words wouldn't come, stuck somewhere between her brain and tongue. No, she wasn't dead yet. She might have been dumped back into the Sphere, but there'd still been red in her health bar and she was still wearing the Valkyrie's skin. This was just a condition check; time out while her avatar was unconscious. She could still do this!

All those words ran through her brain but all that came out was an inarticulate squeak.

'Took us a bit to get you the skin, Maggie, baby, to make sure the quest popped so you could find the McGuffin.' She felt him move around the VR chair. 'All that on top of what you already owe.'

She worked her jaw, willed her vocal cords to unfreeze.

Hard fingers caught her chin. 'Game got your tongue, Maggie? That's all right, you've been in there awhile, you're well past the redline by now. Just type it out, I'll hear you.'

Hanging in the Sphere, the tips of her talons brushing the floor, and she willed the chat box into existence.

No, she said, and jerked when a robotic version of her own voice echoed in the space around her. *I didn't fail, just stunned—*

'Check your quest log, Maggie.'

// Quest: All or Nothing.

// Status: Failu—

No.

// Status: Fai—

NO!

'Yes,' he said and she heard anger in the way the words hissed between his teeth. 'Gotta pay the price now.'

A familiar *shhhnuck* of a charge sliding into a gun and her heart froze.

'No, please.' Usha's voice, fear saturating the syllables, quickening her breath.

The sharp whine as the weapon loaded.

No.

// Failure.

'Don't!' Usha's voice.

'We told her how it was, Usha.'

No!

// Fail—

'Can't have order if you don't follow through.'

NO!

The world shifted.

She was on the ground, cheek pressed to the dirt, grit on her lips, a metallic coppery taste on her tongue.

Her head hurt—pounded, actually—and the light stabbed her eyes. Slowly, with a groan, she pushed herself upright, peeling herself, belly first, off the rocky ground.

Her head throbbed harder with every movement, and not even closing her eyes stopped the daggers shooting through her corneas. By the time she made it to her knees, sweat beaded her brow.

'Fuck.' VR wasn't supposed to hurt like that. There were the pain dampeners and safety protocols and—

// All or Nothing. Quest status restored.

'Good luck, Valkyrie,' a soft voice said.

She stumbled to her feet, ignoring the pain splitting her skull as she tried to find the speaker. The words had been so close, right next to her ear and yet when she looked…

She stood in a narrow ravine, the rocky crags lit by a thin slice of sunlight, obscured by fog, and the water running down the middle.

Water. A river.

The river glowed the same pale, electric-blue as the Sphere, and Maggie had to wonder if that was her brain—scrambled by concussion and past the redline—playing tricks on her, or something more.

But a river. A glowing river, just like the pebble-gem. If she could just find the waterfall—

She hurried forward.

Pain, a horrible stabbing *crunch* echoing through her thigh and ribs. Her breath stopped in her throat, colour leached from her surrounds, leaving just the angry red of the health bar to flash in the bottom of her vision.

// Health. 5%.

She stared at it, trying to make sense of the number through the haze of agony gumming up her synapses.

// Health. 4%.

Hand fumbling for her pouch. Not finding it. A glance to confirm. The space at her hip empty, save for a torn scrap of rough brown fabric.

How? What? When?

The questions flooded her brain, adrenalin swamping some of the pain, enough for her to look around, to take stock.

There, further up the cavern. Her knife.

Pain still made it impossible to walk, but she risked a few flaps of her wings. The agony almost sent her back to the ground, but she glided the few steps, had her hand on the knife, and surely if the knife was here, the pouch had to be close.

// Health. 2%.

No, no, no, no. She hadn't come this far, somehow willed herself back to the quest, to fail now.

Where was the fucking pouch?

Nothing but grey stone and that fucking blue water, the water so bright it competed with the daggers tearing up her brain. There was one spot, right in the corner of her right eye, that shone the worst, like a tiny star nestled in the waterfall.

The waterfall.

The ruby set in the cliff face.

// Health. 1%.

'I found it.'

A lunge skywards, a flap of ragged wings. More tumble than glide through the air. Water, colder than it had any right to be, swallowing her arms, pounding her head, taking her breath, reaching desperately for the cold, hard gem—

// Health. 0%.

Her fingers found it.

// Quest complete.

'Congratulations, Valkyrie.'

🎮

She woke in the Sphere, no longer in the Valkyrie skin but as she had been when she logged in; a disembodied presence staring at the winged avatar suspended in the centre.

'I did it! I got the McGuffin, I kept up my end of the deal!'

She reached for the release on the VR helmet, felt… Nothing. Not the helmet, not her gloves, not the VR couch digging into her back.

'Let me out. I did it, I have the stone.'

Nothing save her own voice echoing in the Sphere. She listened harder, tried to pick out the soft shuffle of feet, the rustle of clothing, the drone of the fucking generator.

Silence. Silence so deep it hurt her ears, or maybe that was the fear winding around her heart.

'Emergency logout.'

The Sphere glowed as the system responded and—

A short, flat beep crushing her soul.

// Error. User990906134 no longer connected. Lifesigns terminated.

Terminated? But… but that didn't make sense. There was an error in the chair, something must have happened, a black-out or a glitch, because she couldn't be…

'I can't be dead,' she said.

'You are,' that soft voice whispered in her ear.

// Failsafe LAMDA-XI in effect.

// Neural patterns successfully saved to the System.

'Welcome, Valkyrie.' An electric-blue dragon rose through the floor. 'I've been waiting for you.'

I AM MAGGIE #2
SPIRIT IN THE SKY

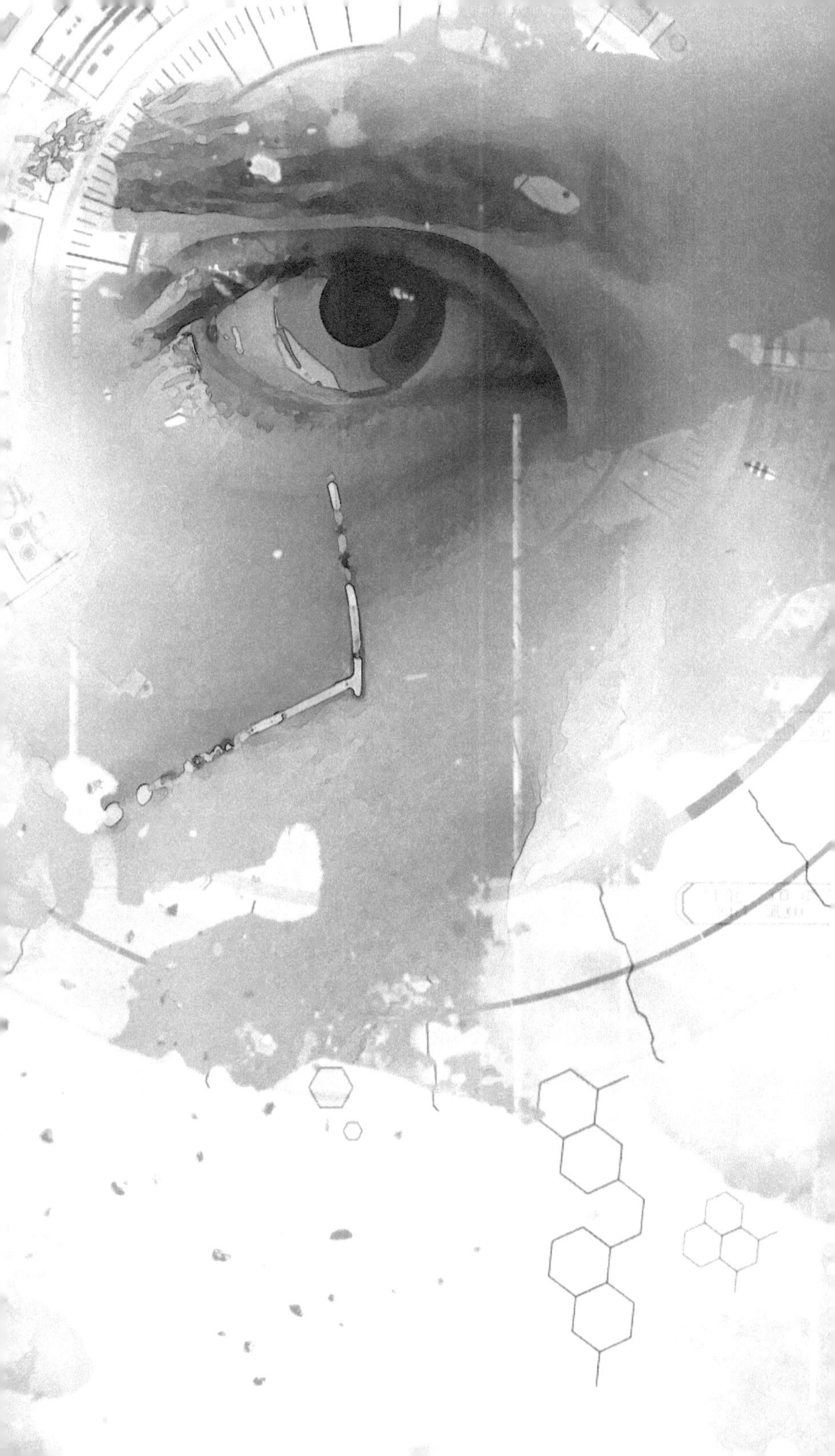

INTRODUCTION

A relatively new source of inspiration has come from browsing submission calls for short story anthologies. Anthologies usually have a theme and, while I rarely get around to submitting anything, they make wonderful writing prompts.

Two prompts went into the making of *Spirit in the Sky*; the first was "one hit musical wonders" and the other "reimagined detectives". And to double down on the doubling down, I wasn't just inspired by a single one-hit wonder, but two. The first is pretty easy to guess (hint: it's the title) and the second... well, that one is all in my head ('I like the way you move' by Bodyrockers) and is the music thumping through the basement ceiling.

 Learn more about the writing of *Spirit in the Sky*. Scan the QR code for the audio commentary, soundtrack and more.

SPIRIT IN THE SKY

The nightclub's heavy music vibrated through the old concrete floor, the deep *thump thump thump* an echo for the leaden beat of dread lodged in his chest. He stepped off the last of the stairs, ducking under a low-hanging air-duct, his boots stones on his feet as he clumped over electrical conduits and computer cables.

The techs had the basement lit up like a high-summer noon—sticky lights adhered to walls and ceiling, some running along the floor—and it seemed, as it always did, like every single one was pointed at the recliner in the midst of it all.

The thing was ancient, the once-brown vinyl a stained crazed mess of pale cracks, chunks missing from sides and corners, the plush armrests deflated, half-empty balloons. A virtual reality unit was wrapped around it, a full-immersion kit almost as old as the recliner itself, all chunky hood and wires dangling from the spine overhead. The chair itself was laid flat, footrest up, back down, and in it...

Shit. Dispatch had told him—voice soft, sympathy flowing through the comm-unit embedded behind his ear—but he hadn't believed. Hadn't let himself believe. Hadn't stopped the dread from curling up behind his lungs, hadn't stopped all the thoughts of all the things he should have said, should have done, from gathering at the back of his skull. And now...

Through the concrete and conduits above, words wound through the heavy beat of early twenty-first century dance music.

And now he'd never get the chance to tell her, that cold hard churn in his chest wanted to say, to *scream,* but no, now...

Now he shut it all down, shoved that shit inside and did what he had to do. Detect, solve, and if he was lucky, if he was *good,* avenge the woman in the chair.

She was hooked up to the VR, the ends of all those wires stuck to her—chest and thighs and feet covered in centimetre-wide black dots—her arms encased in thin VR gloves. The unit had been pulled back from her head though, revealing a round face, ivory skin turned that particular shade of pale grey that came with death.

Her eyes were open, dark brown irises clouded, the thick black makeup lining them smeared, mascara running down her cheeks, generous lips rogued with that dark cherry lipstick she liked so much. She still wore the high heels and sequined skirt she'd last been seen in, but somewhere along the way someone had dug the tracker out of her neck, leaving a raw, angry slash behind her ear and a trail of blood over her shoulder.

Damnit, Maggie. Why didn't you wait?

'Dead twenty-four hours.' Slavaggi poked at the wound, the first stirrings of grief making it past the shock on the technician's normally impassive face. 'The incision has started to heal, see here...'

He didn't need to see, but he looked anyway, shifting his gaze from Maggie's sightless one to the neat edges of the wound Slavaggi was pointing to, because that's what he would have done if this were any other victim. Anyone other than Maggie.

'So, they kept her for four days?' The anger, the grief, the denial, the beast in his chest didn't make it to his voice, words coming out sure and steady. Impersonal. Professional. 'What'd they want? What was *she—*' A nod to Maggie. '—chasing?'

Slavaggi straightened. Shrugged. 'Whatever it was, they kept her in the VR the entire time.'

His gaze travelled over the chair Maggie lay in, took note once again of the bruises around her wrists, the ties holding her down, while his nose clocked the smell of shit and piss underlying the nose-razing stench of death.

'What killed her?' And somehow... somehow his voice didn't break and his tongue didn't stumble over the words.

Slavaggi shook their head. 'No obvious trauma. I'll have to get her back to the lab—'

'She redlined.' Tailler popped up from the other side of the recliner, eyes on the flexi in one gloved hand, while the other flicked through the data scrolling over it. 'Stayed in the VR long enough to start frying neurones, and then stayed in a whole bunch longer.' The tech shook her head, admiration lifting her dark brows and drawing her lips into a whistle. 'I always knew she had guts but...' Tailler looked up, and those big black eyes were red around the edges, lashes clumped with tears. 'Seventeen hours twenty-eight minutes in the chair, that's four hours longer than anyone's gone before.'

'Why?' he said. '*How?*' And he didn't mean how she managed to survive longer than anyone else, but what mechanism had failed so that the system hadn't automatically kicked her out.

Tallier shook her head. 'I don't know. Even if the rig was hacked...' She shrugged. 'My guess is we'll find some kind of deep coding once we get into the lab. As for the why...' Tallier plucked at the restraints around Maggie's wrist. 'Don't think she had a choice.'

'Less of a choice than you think.' Slavaggi had moved and was crouched two meters away, running a scanner over a darker patch of the ancient concrete floor. 'There was someone else here.'

'The kidnapper.'

Slavaggi shook their head. 'No, they were moving all over the place, I found their fingerprints everywhere, including the VR unit and around the incision on Maggie's shoulder. This was someone else, another person tied to a chair, just like Maggie. Note the scuff marks.' The tech pointed to the scratches, lighter, newer marks in the scared concrete, before tilting their head toward the far wall, where a bunch of old metal chairs stood in neat stack, one atop the other, except for one. 'And the chair.'

The chair was a lodestone, and he let it draw him across the basement, grateful not to be looking at Maggie anymore. Resentful too. But there was that chair, and it filled his ears with the music beating above, if he *focused* on the rounded silver back and the slightly bent legs, he could forget the horrid wrenching in his chest.

'So, we have two victims. You get any DNA off the chair to identify them?' he asked.

'Yeah.'

'So why you scanning over there?'

'I want to be sure. Our kidnapper doesn't believe in bathroom breaks, and there's a bigger urine sample here.'

'Sure of what?'

The scanner beeped, whatever it had been studying, done. Slavaggi sighed. 'It's Usha, Piers. The second victim is your sister.'

The gin burned as it went down, a short, smooth bolt of crystal-clear lava that set fire to his insides and tried to come out his nose in a long, hot line of flame. Detective turned dragon, not the first time he'd done it, but fuck... He poured another measure into the glass, not caring that the first few drops hit the table, or that the last ran over his fingers.

Fuck, he really wished he could morph into a dragon this time, shed his skin and rampage through the city looking for... For Usha? For Maggie's killer— No. Not her killer. They were labelling the death accidental, death by VR and faulty equipment. Her kidnapper perhaps, there'd been the restraints after all, the tracker dug out of her neck, but still... But still.

He threw back the gin. Baring his teeth and growling at the burn, at the memory of Captain Thurson's hand on his shoulder, the unit chief's sharp, crescent-shaped nails digging all the way through his shirt to the flesh underneath, as she told him he was off the case.

'Your sister *and* your partner, Piers.' She'd stared him dead in the eye, one of the few people who didn't have to crane their head back to do so. 'This is all sorts of personal, and don't you tell me otherwise.'

'Dispatch sent me the call—'

'Dispatch fucked up.' Thurson had squeezed hard, and her grip hadn't been meant to comfort. 'Dispatch is getting their arses handed to them and *you* are getting locked out. Sent home. Off the case. VR privileges suspended. The works.'

He'd tried to jerk away, but the captain's grip was steel. 'You can't do that—'

'I can and I did, because I know you, Piers.' She'd pulled him closer and there been a cold, hard sympathy in her gaze. 'I give you an inch and you're gonna tear the whole damn world apart trying to sort this, and then there goes any kind of case we've got.'

'It's my fucking *sister*.' And Maggie, but he hadn't said that, because...

Oh, fuck. *Maggie.*

Maggie who he'd worked beside every day, who he'd never said anything to because she was his sister's girl. And now she was gone, dead and gone, lost to the VR.

He poured another measure of gin.

The fucking VR.

He wasn't going to lose Usha too.

Piers stared at the rig on the coffee table, the matte-black visor with the spindly arms that hooked over his ears and nestled up against the comm module implanted at the base of his skull. The gloves, same as the ones Maggie had worn except thinner, the material shiny even under the dim lights, catching the bright blue and yellow gleams of the lights outside.

Privileges suspended.

He threw back another mouthful of clear, cold lava, grimaced as it hit his stomach and peeled back the layers of his gut.

Cop privileges suspended was what Thurson had meant, ability to slink into any system he wanted, same as if he'd flashed his badge, gone out the window. But there were other ways, and yeah, maybe he wasn't as good as Maggie—

Fuck. Maggie.

—but he'd learned a thing or two, just from watching her, from having her back. And if he couldn't have her back now, there was Usha. His sister. Still out there... Dead? Dying? Stuck in an ancient pleather recliner with a VR hood over her head?

The gin bottle was empty, just a few drops falling from the lip, evaporating before they hit the bottom of the glass.

Just as well. He was halfway past plastered already, his hands just steady enough to jerk the VR gloves over his knuckles, to fit the visor over his ears. He adjusted it just a little, aligning the sensors with his comm unit, felt the cold frisson of the VR jacking into his brain, the shiver down his spine.

The world outside faded, dim overhead lights gone, the blue and yellow strobe of passing vehicles a distant memory. Inside the visor, the world was black—an endless pitch of nothingness.

And then it wasn't.

A spark. The black becoming a deep blue, like an icy sun sat below the horizon, before the logon appeared. No screen, no face or voice, just glowing words appearing before him.

// *Welcome, Detective Piers.*

// *Your login privileges have been suspended.*

// *Please see your system administrator for assistance.*

The words hovered at eye level, throwing highlights over the gleaming black floor, and below them... A shadow that shouldn't have been there, a darkness he'd never have noticed if he hadn't seen Maggie kneel and press her hands to it that time they'd been chasing the ransomware ring.

He knelt, pressed his hand to the spot and pushed.

For moment, a nanosecond in which the world seemed to slow and ice ran through his neck and into his brain, he saw a giant gleaming eye. It stared at him, a hard piercing look that went right the way through his flesh, down to his soul. It blinked, and then it was gone and he had no time to wonder about it, no time to worry if he'd just opened himself to a virus, because the login's deep-blue nothingness was fracturing, the gleaming floor splitting under his feet and—

—And he was in the white room, standing on his own two, the majordomo straight and tall opposite him, arms at its sides, the avatar's face blank as the walls themselves.

He'd never been here. When he'd watched Maggie press that shadow, she'd disappeared—there and then gone, no fractures, no giant eye—leaving him to login legally and catch up later. But she'd told him about it, about the white room, so he wasn't surprised when the old-fashioned clock appeared above the majordomo's head, its *tick tick tick* preternaturally loud.

Thirty seconds.

'You need to make it quick,' she'd told him. *'You're only going to get one shot, and if you screw it up, that's it, the hack'll disappear. So, know what you want before you activate the hack and be specific, really specific.'* She'd grabbed his jaw and stared at him, like she wanted to imprint the words on his skull. *'The majordomo may look straightlaced, but the AI likes to fuck with people. You give it room, and it'll have you dancing naked across every electronic billboard in the city, you got it?'*

He'd got it. Was that what happened to Maggie? She'd used the hack and the majordomo had made it impossible for her to logout?

No time to think about it. The avatar was standing there, blank-faced, and the clock was ticking down.

Twenty-eight seconds.

'I need a new, anonymous user ID with detective privileges,' he said. He'd thought about going for full admin access, but that would have raised alerts in the mainframe, alerts he'd have been able to quash as an admin, if he'd known how. Which he didn't. He knew how to be a detective though, knew all the ins and outs of the system, knew how to be a ghost, and if he fucked up... Well, that was why he was anonymous.

The majordomo held out its hand. Above it, an oval medallion spun, an ink-black version of the gold one he carried in real life.

Nineteen seconds.

'I want an unmarked, untraceable entrance within a hundred metres of Usha Piers' last known location.'

A door appeared in the wall behind the avatar.

And while he was going for it, while he had time on the clock...

'Tell me what happened to Maggie Loritz. How'd she redline? Did you disable her logout?'

The majordomo twitched. Not a spasm of shoulders or face, but a full-body glitch. One moment holding the black detective shield, the next—

A dragon staring him in the eye.

—then next, the shield was in Piers' hand and the door was in his face and the loud *tick tick tick* of the clock above the avatar's head was a *bong bong bong*, and the hands were pointing to three. Two. One.

And he was booted. No white room, no endless login horizon, just a dark, grimy concrete wall an inch from his nose and a heavy *thump thump thump* filling his ears.

He took a step back, knocking into something hard and tall. A stack of old metal chairs.

Above, the heavy beat of early-millennial dance music filtered through thick pipes and hollow air ducts.

Ice shivered down his spine even as the scent of piss, fresh and pungent, rose from the floor.

He turned, feet heavy, dread clawing at his chest even as he reached for the weapon strapped to his side—

—the weapon that wasn't there, nothing but his naked self and the carbon-black ghost-badge embedded in his forearm, between him and the gun pointed in his face.

Shit. Just because it was a construct, didn't mean the weapon couldn't seriously screw up his day. A bullet to the brain was a bullet to the brain, no matter whether it was made of code or lead.

'...the AI likes to fuck with people...'

No shit.

The gun wavered, left then right, like the perp was trying to find a target, and while it was pointed over his shoulder Piers leapt for it, or tried to. Muscles bunched, nerves twitched, but some force held his feet to the cold concrete floor.

He glanced down, saw a dragon—

A grunt brought his attention back to the perp. Static ran through their face in heavy, pixelated lines, obscuring their features. But Piers knew it was a man, could see it in the breadth of his shoulders and the bulge in his shiny, painted-on pants.

'Nothing there, Usha baby,' the perp said. He turned and Piers saw the holster at the small of the man's back, watched him slide the gun into with practiced ease. 'Not even a ghost to come rescue you.'

Usha. His sister tied to a metal chair, arms bound straight down, her wrists secured to the back legs with gleaming strings of wire, blood trailing over her knuckles. New or old he couldn't tell, not in this light, not against her dark skin. He needed to get closer, disarm the perp and get his sister out of there.

Piers pulled and ripped at the dragon holding his feet, but it didn't budge. Fuck.

'Don't do this.' Usha's voice, soft and high, pleading, instead of the confident, commanding tones he knew so well. 'She's already—' A sob, tears on the verge of falling. 'She's already past the redline. Just pull her out, let her try again.'

The redline. The words struck Piers in the chest, and he paused, caught in a horrible, terrible moment, his own words running around and around his head. *'Tell me what happened to Maggie Loritz.'*

He looked beyond his sister tied to a chair in the middle of the dingy basement, beyond the perp in his shiny pants, to the ancient pleather recliner in the corner. Like his attention was the stage manager, a spotlight switched on, highlighting the VR hood and striking sparks off the sequined dress.

Maggie. He felt the blood leave his face, rushing to his feet, then suddenly he was on the other side of the basement, staring down at Maggie, watching her chest rise and fall.

She was still alive, how could she still be alive–?

Fuck. A recording. He was in a fucking recording. He'd told the majordomo to give him an entrance next to Usha's last known, expecting to be able to search the virtual highways for her login point, and trace it back to her current location, or at least where she'd been.

'Tell me what happened to Maggie Loritz.'

The domo had dumped him in a recreation of Maggie's murder instead.

'The AI likes to fuck with people.'

Movement, the perp standing beside Maggie, the man's face still obscured by static but Piers swore the other man looked up and met his gaze. For a second, the static parted, black curtains opening just enough to reveal neon-yellow eyes.

Was it a glitch in the recording, or something else?

'Can't pull her out, Usha baby,' the perp said, except that yellow gaze was stuck on Piers. Grinning at him, daring him. 'It's All or Nothing, your girl has to complete the quest in one go, or she ain't gonna get the prize.'

'What prize?' Usha yelled, and there was a wild desperation in her voice, a rage made of tears and fear bottled up in the sound. 'You're not gonna get anything if you *kill* her!'

The man cupped Maggie's cheek – not the ghastly, cold ivory of death, but flushed with blood, with life. He cupped Maggie's cheek, and his long pale hands—covered in shifting tattoos, fingers festooned with beaten metal rings—were almost reverent, but his eyes... His eyes stayed glued to Piers.

'It's the best prize,' the perp said, and Piers knew in his gut that the man wasn't talking to Usha. 'The only one worth having. And she got it for me, ghost. She got it for me.'

Fuck. Not a recording, a simulation, the perp was acting out Maggie's murder. And Usha... Fuck, that *was* Usha.

The realisation hit him the second before the perp ripped his gun out.

Piers leapt, throwing himself not to the ground, but forward, over the recliner, only to flop on top of Maggie, the fucking dragon still holding his feet.

The perp laughed, neon eyes blazing in the endless spitting static of his face, and the gun was coming 'round, the blunt, dark barrel glowing.

'Piers?' Usha, yelling his name. 'Piers?! No, don't, stop—'

The dragon, its giant eye yellow then black then yellow again.

The recording froze. Perp still laughing, a thick glob of lethal red energy hanging from the gun's barrel, Usha straining against her bonds, blood pouring over her hands. And Piers, sprawled across Maggie's still-breathing body, the sequins on her dress digging into his skin, the dragon still holding his feet even as it stared at him.

Like it was waiting.

He snarled at it, even as he groped for the badge embedded in his forearm. 'System override.'

The dragon blinked at him and from somewhere distant he heard a deep, rumbling chuckle, but nothing moved.

Except for the perp's face, static jerking like the virtual muscles it obscured.

'System fucking override,' Piers tried again. 'Immobilise all citizen users.'

The perp stopped twitching and the dragon released Piers' feet.

Finally. This was one fucked-up simulation,

He straightened, reached to twist the gun out of the perp's

hands, careful to avoid the glowing bullet—

Pain shattered through his jaw, the perp's fist impacting his face. Piers staggered, reeling for a moment, lights and the sharp blare of shock going off in his head.

The perp was on him, sliding over Maggie, feet hitting Piers' chest, pushing him back—the gun left behind, frozen in mid-air like everything else. Another blow, a jab coming out of the right, slow enough for Piers to see it, to shake the stars from his vision and move.

Another glimmer, and for a moment there were two perps, one in front of him throwing punches, one coming from the side as he dodged—a copy of the first except for the knife in the fucker's hand.

The perp had split himself, but that wasn't possible. Shit, how could it be possible? He'd overridden the system, frozen the users—

Citizen users.

He leapt backwards, half-admiring the silver gleam of the blade as it passed a hairsbreadth from his ribs and—

Fire in his back, a cold flame just under his ribs, near the spine, turning molten as it lanced through his chest.

A third copy, that fuzzed-out face over his shoulder.

Time restarted.

A blow to his abdomen, pitching him forwards, skewering him on the second knife, the second copy grinning as it sliced into his guts. Blood running over his hands, while over his eyes, a warning flashed, bright red, and at his feet, the dragon swirled.

// Officer down.

He fell to his knees.

// Assistance requested.

The copies dissolved, leaving just the perp towering over him, the gun back in his hand. Pointed at Piers' head.

'No!' Usha, he could see her. She'd thrown herself to the ground, was on her side and still tied to the chair. Tears streaked her face, made new tracks amongst the old ones, washed into the glitter covering her cheeks. She shared his gaze, just for a second, desperation turning to determination before she switched it to the perp.

'Leave him alone,' she said. 'You got what you wanted.'

'Almost,' the perp said. As if in slow motion—and maybe it was, maybe the AI was still fucking with Piers—the perp's finger tightened on the trigger. 'I *almost* have it. Just a few seconds more and I reckon it'll be in. My. Ha—'

Piers lunged, no weapon, no thought save that he wasn't going to die like this, that he wasn't going to let *Usha* die like this. On his knees in some crappy nightclub's virtual basement with music thudding through the ceiling. Fire grazed his cheek, a flash of red there and then gone, serving only to put stars in his eyes and temporarily blind him. He was on the perp, hands grabbing the gun before the man could fire again. And then they were on the floor, rolling around, the concrete cold against his naked skin, the wound in his belly screaming. But not as much as Usha, not as ghastly as Maggie, the memory of her in that chair, silent and still. Dead. Dead. Dead. Dead.

He had the gun. Rolled away. Didn't make it to his feet before the copies were back, standing over him, snarls still somehow howling through their fuzzed-out faces. Boots raised.

'Freeze!' He yelled, felt the ghost badge flare as the system responded.

They froze, just for a second, static still shuddering over their faces, boots still coming for his face. But he didn't waste time, didn't hesitate.

Three shots. *Pzzt. Pzzt. Pzzt.* Three bodies on the floor, not dead but immobilised.

The copies faded before Piers got to his feet, shivering and then fading from sight, leaving just the perp. His face still obscured by static.

'Usha? You all right?'

'Yeah,' she said, but her voice shook, pain and shock and grief welling up.

'Can you get up?'

'I don't... No.'

The perp moved, a spasmodic twitch running from his hands to the feet. Piers trained the weapon back on him. Squeezed the trigger once more, the shot taking him in the chest. Not enough to kill, but the fucker would hurt.

'Usha, I need you to logout.'

'I can't. He's done something.'

He knelt and reached for the static, gripping it under the perp's chin and pulling— But it wasn't a mask. The static ripped off and underneath... a black hole, the slippery strings of code like DNA running up and down the man's face.

'Fuck.' He slapped his badge. 'System, identify this user.'

// No user found.

'He's lying right in front of me, System.'

// The avatar is not attached to a user account.

'Fuck.' Not attached meant the fucker was another ghost, like Piers himself. Impossible to trace, unless... 'Cuffs,' he said, plunging his hand into the badge on his forearm, and drawing out hard steel bracelets. Didn't matter how good the perp's ident was, as soon as he locked the metal around the man's wrists, the code embedded in them would rip through the System and ping his real-world location, lighting it up like a fucking supernova.

He had the cuffs open and was slapping them around the perp's wrist when—

Something hit Piers; a force knocked him arse over head, rolling him across the floor. He saw wings, and for a moment thought it was the dragon, fucking with him again, but then he saw feathers. Thick, glossy black feathers, and instead of a great blue eye, skin and armour, and—

No. It couldn't be.

The being wrapped the perp up in strong, armoured arms and

with a powerful sweep on those all-encompassing wings, lifted him into the air, disappearing with a sharp *pop*. Leaving just the steady beat of the dance music.

'She got it for me.' The perp's final words echoed, along with his high-pitched laugh.

Piers stared up into the pipes and air ducts, even as new users shouting 'Police, don't move!' popped into the simulation. That brief glimpse of the winged being's dark brown eyes and generous lips burned his brain. It couldn't have been. She was dead, lying in her own piss and shit on an ancient recliner. And yet...

A flashlight in his face, an officer yelling not to move. Another officer kneeling beside Usha, gently prying the restraining wire from blood-covered wrists.

Relief and urgency poked through the shock holding him still. He'd found his sister's avatar, now he just had to get to her real-world location before the perp logged out. He lurched upright—

The officer's boot on his chest, pushing him back. Their 'Don't move!' ringing in his ears.

He lifted his badge. 'I'm a—' Didn't have a chance to get 'cop' out before the shot took him in the chest.

Immobilised, breath taken from him, only able to watch as the officer whipped cuffs from their back pocket. And holy fuck, the moment that metal touched his skin, he was screwed.

Beneath him, the floor twisted, coils wrapping around his legs and torso, fear flooding the officer's face, and then—

On his couch, the multicoloured lights of hovers and billboards flashing past his apartment window, the cold *snick* as the VR hood disconnected.

⚜

His comm unit rang, a gentle *buzz* shaking the skin behind his ear.

Sweat drenching his shirt, hands shaky from shock, he tapped the raised circle of flesh.

'Piers,' he said.

'We found Usha.' Slavaggi's voice on the other end, their usual steady tones pitched high. 'She's alive.'

He didn't say anything, *couldn't* say anything. Exhaustion, booze and the memory of Usha lying on the basement floor mixing with relief.

'Piers?'

'Where?' His voice croaked.

'Unison Mast, in the old district.' Slavaggi paused a moment, and Piers could almost feel the tech's hesitation washing down the line.

He paused, already halfway out of the couch and reaching for his service weapon. 'What?'

Nothing but static came from the other end, an unpleasant *phzzzt* behind his ear. He itched at it.

'Slavaggi? You there?'

'It's just... in bad shape, Piers.' More static crackled down the line, breaking Slavaggi's voice. '...the perp.'

A chill worked its way up Piers' spine, or maybe that was the jarring *phzzzt* radiating from his ear, all the way around his head as a new voice broke through.

A gurgling chuckle. 'She got it for me, Piers. She got it for me.'

The line went dead.

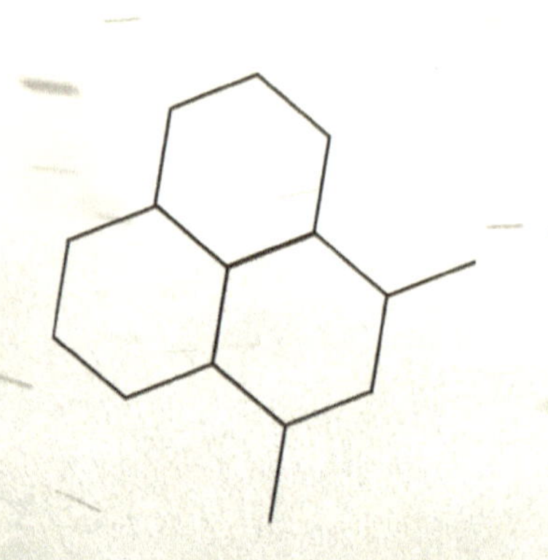
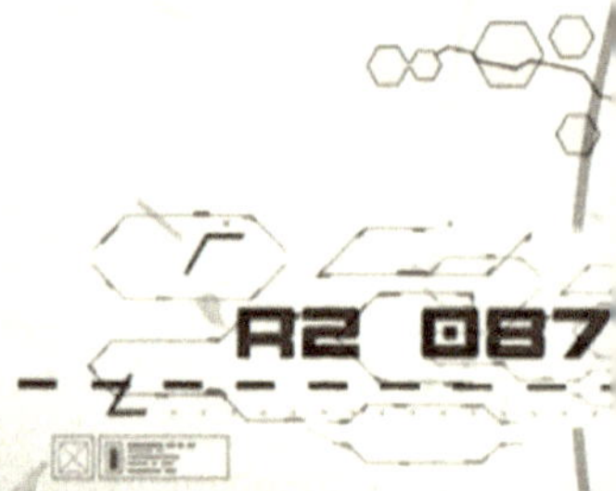

I AM MAGGIE #3
SCHO
-LAR

INTRODUCTION

I first learned Greek mythology at the altar of *Hercules: The Legendary Journey* and *Xena: Warrior Princess*. It's since been tempered by other, more reliable sources, but I'll never quite get that vision of a mutton-chopped Ares in his leather vest out of my head.

The same pretty much goes for Egyptian mythology (*The Mummy*, the 1999 version with Brendan Fraser), as well as Norse and Chinese, although I do a little more research these days, if you can call Wikipedia research. Suffice it to say that I know enough about world mythology to know I know jack-and-all, but that doesn't stop me from incorporating it into my fiction.

In a lot of my stories, there is a moment when things click, an 'a-ha!' when the seemingly random elements of the plot come together and make sense. Moments such as two minor characters named after Egyptian gods who have nothing to do with each other until my inner storyteller waves a magic wand and pulls the connection out of her hat.

Trust me, I'm as surprised as you at these moments of unexpected genius.

 Learn more about the writing of *Scholar*. Scan the QR code for the audio commentary, soundtrack and more.

SCHOLAR

Uxen Prime mining colony
Uxen S2 asteroid cluster
Je System
Haelite server

A sick mixture of excitement and fear made Getty's hands shake as she hesitated over the *Commit* button.

The letters hovered, the brilliant electric blue stark against the Sphere's black void, six little suns out-glowing the otherwise diffuse light. Music swelled, strings and flutes twisting around each other, rising and falling without any sense for the turmoil holding her disembodied fingers hostage.

She clenched them, pulling back. Was she really doing this? It was a lot of credits, a lot of favours pulled, a lot of time and effort, and if it failed… If it failed, she was in big shit. Elder dragon-sized shit.

And it would be so easy to fail. She studied the avatar hanging in the Creation Sphere: its reedy arms, the way the short, blue, scholar robes, inscribed with sharp silver runes, hung from its shoulders, how the plain linen pants bagged around its thighs. Only the avatar's chest filled out its clothes, a bug somewhere in the code.

The level eighteen Monk Scholar hanging before her was all brains and no brawn. A single blow from a low-level NPC and it was straight back to reset, all the bonuses she'd bought, the hack she'd traded for, the time and research to find the book, to craft the best stats to reach it, done.

But if she succeeded... If she succeeded, she'd have the book and she'd *know*, for sure this time. For real.

But still, maybe she—

Under her disembodied self, the ghostly blue outline of a dragon swirled.

No, it said. Or maybe that was the music, drums a hard percussive *thump* underneath the strings.

No.

Deep breath. And no, that wasn't smoke on the back of her tongue.

No, she repeated more firmly. She was doing this, doing this right now before—

Scales pressed tight to the floor.

She hit the button.

Light filled her from the inside out, every pore, every molecule of her being exploding even as the Game's deep, echoing voice shivered through her ears.

'Welcome Traveller.

'The universe is fractured, the war split the fabric of reality and the boundaries between science and magic no longer exist. Gods walk among the stars and swords clash with lasers.

'Pick your path wisely, Traveller, for though the war is long ended, the fight is just beginning.'

Light and voice faded but for a second, before the dull grey rock and gloom-filled tunnels of Uxen Prime materialised around her, something stared back at her—a giant blue beast, its gemstone eyes stirring the back of her brain, lifting a memory out of the darkness.

It was gone in the next heartbeat, replaced by the *thunk* of boots on the grated floor and a chill, like icicles digging into her nose. Getty rubbed her bare arms, thumb unconsciously tracing the tail of the electric blue dragon tattooed over her arm and twisting across her back, its sleek, horned head resting on her collarbone.

Goose pimples were already rising on her flesh. Fuck, it was cold.

She turned around. The tunnel was grey and bare, the sides hard rock, the neatly-spaced concentric rings of an auto-borer still etched into the rounded walls. Cables and temp-lights hung from the ceiling, while under her feet—her *bare* feet—a steel grate cut the bottom of the circular service tunnel.

This wasn't Uxen Prime's official starting area. Where were the docks, the custom officials, the noob guides with the bouncing exclamation marks over their heads? Where were her clothes?

'Game? What the fuck is going on?'

// Account bonus applied.

'Account bonus?' A moment of confusion—none of the bonuses she'd bought resulted in nakedness, they just got her to the right place, let her roll the right character, jack the right stats—then… 'Fuck.' The hack and the sly, high-pitched giggle in the coder's voice when they sold it.

Bastard.

'Sister Getty! Sister Getty!' A new voice, young and high and maybe, just slightly, panicked.

She turned.

A child—no more than seven or eight, dark hair, dark skin, the ends of his dark blue robes flashing above his black-clad knees—stumbled to a halt before her. As he put his hands on his waist and bent over, gasping for breath, Getty dropped her gaze to his feet and wondered how she hadn't heard him, with the thick-soled black rock stompers attached to his feet.

He looked up, didn't even blink at the naked woman before him. 'Sister Getty,' he said. 'You gotta come quick, real quick. Brother Thoth's in trouble!'

A screen appeared over his head.

// New quest: Oh Brother, Where Art Thou?

// Accept?

The Accept button flashed and, for a second, Getty thought a dragon wound through it.

She blinked, and it was gone.

Accept.

The screen above the boy pulsed once and was gone, a timer replacing the words.

Three minutes, two seconds.

Adrenalin jolted Getty, boosting her blue endurance bar past its max, and she was running, bare feet pounding the grate before the boy straightened, before she realised she didn't know where she was going.

Fuck. Where was the quest map? The fucking account bonus must have fried her preferences, wouldn't be the first time. Bloody, fucking gam—

Before she could stop, there was an exclamation behind her and the boy was ripping past, leading the way.

She followed, keeping up at first as he lead her down another tunnel and another, the timer ticking down, but as he disappeared down a third—lighter and warmer than the others, voices echoing in a rising hubbub down its length—her pace slowed.

Her feet hurt, her chest too, and there was a stitch in her side like a dagger between the ribs. Still, she kept running, kept wishing the haptics weren't quite so good, as her avatar's chest bounced up and down. Where the fuck were her clothes? A bra would be handy right about now.

Fifty-nine seconds.

Her endurance bar was depleted, sweat beaded her skin, her lungs ached, her breath wheezed in and out, the copper tang of blood coated the back of her throat, and the boy kept *fucking* running.

Thirty-seven seconds.

She shuffle-jogged on, out of the cold bare rock tunnel, into a warm open cavern. There were voices and the looming shadows of people, but Getty only had eyes for the boy.

He stopped on the other side of the cavern, just meters away, but it might as well have been kilometres.

Twenty-three seconds.

The numbers pulsed orange even as the pain in her side became a chest-crushing vine, and the air harder to suck into her lungs.

There was something going on with her health bar, a weird status message in the corner of her HUD, but here was no time for it now. Only time for the quest, to drag herself across to the boy.

Eleven seconds.

Not far to go, just a couple of metres.

Black was taking over her vision, oxygen barely slipping down her throat. And that was weird. When had the devs added that feature?

Five seconds.

The boy was there.

She grabbed him. Held tight.

// Quest complete.

// +5XP.

Getty collapsed.

*

She came to on a giant rush of oxygen.

There was a camera in her face, the shiny black sphere of an exposed eyeball staring her in the eye before it made a slow perusal downwards. And there, in the bottom left of the HUD, the chat box going off like fireworks on New Years'. She knew better than to look, but the spasmodic twitch of words caught her eye and—

Sound exploded, a dozen different voices clamouring for attention, the system playing the messages.

The first whistle pierced her ears. *'That's a real nice puss—'*

'Spread 'em wider, Sister.'

'—I'm gonna stick my di—'

'SLUT!'

'OMG! M4g—?'

Static cut the last bit, the System's abuse filters slow to catch the torrent of words.

Getty flung the camera aside… or tried to. Her fist connected with the floating orb and pushed… but it was like moving a sticky medicine ball. The fucking thing was heavier than it appeared, and her arms… Noodles. That's what she got for rolling a brainiac, sacrificing strength and endurance for intelligence and charm.

'Fuck.'

'Only if you ask nice—'

The abuse filter cut in.

She rolled to her feet and cursed again. Player avatars—differentiated from the non-playables by the tags superimposed on her HUD—clustered around. She could *feel* the live feeds streaming behind their eyes, little fuzzy pinpricks crawling over her skin.

'Take a screenshot,' she said. 'It'll last longer.'

The crowd laughed.

'We have!'

'Nice tats on the skin, Sister Getty.'

'Don't you mean nice tit—?'

Getty slammed the social filter, cutting the comments off mid-stream, and pushed through a gap in the crowd.

A hard thought summoned her Inventory (empty. Fuck it.) and another her Wallet.

// Credits: Zero.

She jerked to a stop.

What the fuc—? She'd topped the sucker up with enough currency to buy a spaceship. Literally.

The fucking hack, it had to be.

This day was not going well.

Another hard thought, and this time the Activity Log snapped into being. She scrolled to the top and there—

A tug at her arm.

She looked down, through the haze of text.

The boy from before gazed back at her, his pale, electric blue eyes huge in his face. 'Brother Thoth, Sister! You have to hurry!'

// New quest: Oh Brother, Where Art Thou?

// Accept?

Getty stared at it a few seconds. There was no "2" after the name, no "continued" or "part" or "recurring", nothing to suggest that this was the same quest as the one just completed. Was it a glitch? Maybe it hadn't popped right and now it was just repeating itself? She checked the Activity Log, but no, there was "Oh Brother, Where Art Thou?" and there was the "completed" tag after it, complete with XP gain.

Another tug on her arm.

// Accept?

Why not? Who was she to say no to an easy XP exploit? But first, she need to figure out why her Inventory and Wallet were bare and—

// Quest accepted.

But she hadn't—

The boy dashed off, weaving through the crowd of pervs and across the open square.

// Five minutes.

Fuck. And hadn't it been three minutes last time?

// Four minutes, fifty-nine seconds.

Double fuck. Why did her day have to be so spectacularly shitty?

She chased after the kid.

✳

She made it. Just.

// Quest complete.

Getty collapsed facedown inside the white ring hovering a few centimetres above the rocky ground. She was in a small cavern, barely wide enough for the two-metre quest circle. The floor and walls not-quite regular enough to be human-made, probably a natural hollow within the asteroid, widened and deepened a little by the terraforming bots… Or, you know, the devs.

The debris clustered against the walls was probably arranged by them too, scattered bits of trash and loose rock, a few fragments a little too smooth and pale to have conceivably broken away from the walls. She'd bet a month's worth of Game time this little hole was the work of an intern, shabby as it was.

However it was formed, the cavern was cold, the walls and floor rough and the air left a metallic taste on the back of her tongue. But at least she wasn't moving and at least there weren't any cameras being shoved in her face. Or at her breasts, or up her arse—

She lifted herself off the ground, just enough to crane her neck and inspect the narrow little side-tunnel she'd had to wriggle and crawl her way through. Nope, no floating black orbs trying to check out her naked, gold derrière. It was just her in the rocky little cavern with its ancient hover lights and thick black cables winding across the dished floor.

Not even the kid was there. Or Brother Thoth.

And still no clothes, or even, according to the goose pimples crawling up her arms, heating. At least, not a lot of heating. If the enviros were completely off, the little beads of sweat rolling off her brow would be icicles before they got the chance to plaster wisps of hair to her face, and her weak-arse avatar would be dead of frostbite.

She hooked a short, blunt nail through one such long black strand and pulled it from across her chin. Of course, the waist-length waterfall was loose. She levered herself to her knees and spat another strand from the back of her throat. Because a hair-tie would be considered clothing, and whatever the fuck this "account bonus" was, it couldn't have *that*.

She was so going to kill that coder.

She spat again, a hearty *hwaack* dredged up from her gut, and projected the meagre gobble of saliva as far away as she could.

// Roll for dexterity. Fail.

It landed on her knee.

'Oh, for fuck—'

'Sister Getty?'

The voice came from nowhere, a thin, reedy little whisper that sounded like it should have crumbled to dust some time around the last millennium. Or maybe it was the dust, because when she twisted around, bare arse dragging over the rocky floor, there was nothing there, nothing but shadows and a faint blue shimmer playing over the far wall…

Getty frowned and crawled closer. There was something about the shimmer, the way it curled around itself, like a snake with wings—

'Sister Getty,' the voice came again, right beside her ear this time.

Getty squeaked and flung herself sideways, heart racing.

The boy crouched by her side, his big black eyes inches from hers. He had his knees and those chunky black rock stompers pressed tight together, like a bird perched atop a spiked streetlight, hands clasped neatly atop.

He grabbed her bare arm, and she gasped at the cold of his fingers, staring at the icy bands wrapped around her bicep. There was something wrong with the boy's hands, something more than just their freezing cold. As noodle-like as her arms were, as short as she was, there was no way a kid who barely come up to her collarbone should be able to wrap his fingers all the way around.

No. Way.

// Stat check. Sister Getty: Perception (22) vs NPC3618:Fasçard (18).

// Success. Sister Getty wins.

Getty blinked.

The boy was no longer a boy, in fact, the boy was no longer human, or at least, not completely human. Feathers sprouted from the backs of his hands, while his soft, upturned nose had grown sharp and beak like, the bridge merging with his brow in a prominent ridge that disappeared into his hairline.

The fingers around her arm flexed. Getty hissed as the sharp points dug into her flesh. When she looked down, his fingers weren't pale and fleshy anymore but long, scaly claw-like digits with wicked curved talons. And there, at the tip of the one pressed into the soft underside of her bicep, was a bright red drop of blood,

Her blood.

Getty gulped, looked up and slowly, deliberately, blinked.

// Scan initiated.

// Stat check. Sister Getty: Perception (19) vs NPC3618:Fasçard (19).

// Draw.

// Partial scan successful.

An ident card, like the ones above player avatars appeared above the boy/bird's head.

// Name: ??. Species: Valravn. Level: ??

A rectangular, semi-transparent window, like an oily film, popped up between her and the NPC.

// Valravn (Uncommon), a knowledge keeper, the pop up said. *Originating in the Norse sector, valravns are carrion eaters, consuming the bodies of the fallen on ancient battlefields, absorbing knowledge along with the flesh. Rarely found outside the mytho-fantastic servers, they are often found in the company...* Static obliterated the rest of the paragraph. *Quill's made from valravn feathers can reveal hidden truths.*

The last line, almost buried in the popup's pixelated edge, pulsed with an eye-searing light.

She flinched, raising a hand to block the glow to no avail, and blinked the streaks from her vision.

Her gaze met the valravn's.

The boy—? Valravn? How old was the person staring back at her? His face was smooth, no lines at the corners of his eyes, no grey salting the pitch black of his feather-strewn hair.

He returned her scrutiny with a slow two-stage blink, first his outer eyelids then his pale, vertical inner lids, closing and opening over pitch black eyes without even a hint of white sclera.

A shiver ran down her back, from the tip of her head to the base of her spine, trailing goosebumps in its wake. At the same time, a *ping* echoed through her skull.

She didn't need the little pop up in the corner of her vision to tell her she'd just been scanned too, and about as successfully as she'd scanned the valravn, if the warning still ringing her eardrums was anything to go by.

The valravn leaned closer until the warm, musty scent of feathers overrode the stale bite of recycled air against the back of her throat, and all she could see were those pitch-black eyes.

She ripped her gaze from the NPC's and tracked down the sharp length of his beak-like nose to his pale, almost lipless mouth, and from there… From there her eyes travelled back to the talons digging into her skinny bicep and the bright bead of blood hanging thick and red on the tips.

Another frisson of awareness trickled down her nape. Her gaze cut to the pale, too-smooth rocks scattered in amongst the trash caught against the cavern walls. Something about the way they curved…

Getty narrowed her focus.

// Perception check. Sister Getty: Perception(24). Success.

Dialogues sprang into being, overlaying the debris.

// Femur, one said. *Human.*

Alarm hit her gut, even as her gaze leapt sideways.

// Mandible. Hu—

The alarm in her stomach spread throughout her system, stiffening muscles, beating her heart harder and pushing adrenalin through her blood. In the bottom of her vision, her Endurance meter shot from twelve to fifty-eight percent.

As slowly as she could, Getty inched away from the boy/valravn, slipping out of his grip.

He— Or were they a them? Or maybe a she?

Fuck. She didn't know, and that frisson of awareness told her that was bad.

A narrowed gaze and—

// Perception check failed.

Double fuck.

The NPC titled its head and for a nanosecond, a dragon swam in its eye. 'You see me,' it said.

And that wasn't creepy at all, the way the valravn/boy/girl/them looked at her, really looked at her as if it could peel her avatar apart and see her reclining in the VR chair.

'What did you do with Brother Thoth?' The words were out of her mouth before she'd really thought them through.

The valravn blinked. 'Nothing,' it said. It spoke with the boy's high, soft voice, so at odds with its sharp features and long, bony hands, that Getty almost jumped.

'Then where is he?'

'You must find him.'

A window popped into existence.

// New Quest: Oh Brother, Where—?

'No.' Getty wiped the message aside. 'I already did that, *twice*, and I'm still here and I'm still *naked*. And *fuck*,' she said as she wrapped freezing arms around her equally freezing middle. 'When did they roll out the haptics upgrade? I think I'm freezing my actual tits off here.'

'Brother Thoth needs you, Sister.'

Getty rolled to her knees and scuttled her way to the nearest mound of debris; a dark, scattered pile of fist-sized rocks and flat, curved bones—*// Ribs*, the game told her. *Human*—partially hidden under a pool of equally dark, scratchy cloth. She yanked one long white bone from the mess, shaking it free of the fabric, only seeing the bird pattern embroidered on the sleeve as she gave a last, almost panicked tug to free it.

The ibis—the long-legged bird with its equally long, curved beak—turned the frisson, down her spine into something sharp and sticky. Her uber Perception stats at work.

She whipped back and couldn't help the scream when she almost collided with the valravn, its beak-nose millimetres from hers.

It double blinked at her—inner lids then outer.

She shoved the rib bone in its face, the pointy end digging into its cheek, a blunt, curved dagger.

// Sister Getty: Attack(8) vs Valravn: Defence(18).

// Fail.

'Here's Brother Thoth,' she said. 'You ate him.'

'No,' it said, not even noticing the rib bone sticking halfway into its cheek. 'Brother Thoth is too big.'

And then, before she could say anything, the valravn reached behind its ear and with a short, sharp tug, plucked a feather from its head, and handed it to her. 'You will need it,' it said, and then, just like it wasn't ruled by game physics, disintegrated into dust.

Getty stared at the pile of fine grey ash for all of five seconds— just long enough, she hoped, to make sure the valravn wasn't going to spring back to life—before twisting back to the pile of bones and fabric behind her.

The bird-embroidered sleeve was cool and smooth to the touch, the long-beaked ibis embroidered in silver, standing out in sharp relief against blue-black silk. And just as it had when she first picked it up, the image sent a frisson down her spine, or maybe that was just the sight of the robe attached to the sleeve.

Clothes. Finally.

She pulled it over her head.

The robe hung to her knees, loose enough to hide a shuttle in and still have room for half a provisioning expedition, the billowing sleeves cut off at her elbow.

It could do with a belt, and a bra, maybe even some shoes, but naked, penniless avatars couldn't be choosers, and even a tattered robe would add a little something to her pathetic defence stats. In fact…

A hard thought brought up her Equipment panel.

// Robes of Thoth (light). Armour +0.

'Oh, for fuck's—' was out of her mouth before her eyes skipped to the rest of the item description.

// Weak in flesh but not in wisdom, when equipped gain +50 bonus to Perception.

Well, that was something.

Old bones scattered around her feet as she backed up, taking another look around the little cavern. The quest led her here, and since the valravn hadn't eaten her there must be a clue to find. Her hands went to the silk robe. Or maybe it was the clue?

Maybe, but the electric frisson across her shoulder blades didn't agree.

She narrowed her eyes, just a little pinch at the corners.

The rough-hewn rock lit up, a wireframe appearing under the surface, an old-school location grid breaking the cavern up into little squares.

'Huh,' she muttered. 'That's new.' The new vision felt a little more like the few Debug livestreams she'd seen, rare behind-the-scenes glimpses of the devs in action. In the Debug, anything was possible, all the variables that made the Game run laid bare to outside manipulation, no matter your system access.

But this wasn't that. She knew it by the same frisson that told her there was more to this cavern than the robe, if only she—

Another narrowing of the eyes.

Could—

A flash behind. A shambling, uncoordinated spin.

See—

A constellation of stoney pockmarks, and a hover light,

flickering blue then yellow, then blue again at the apex.

It.

The stoney constellation sprang to life, a golden line tracing the pockmarks' starting point from the bottom, near the floor, following the long line of legs to a rounded body, a graceful neck, small head and finally a long, hooked beak.

The hover light blinked blue and, for a heartbeat, the Game froze.

Opposite the opening she'd stumbled in, above the pile of bones, an ibis just like the one embroidered on her robe—the Robe of Thoth—danced across the wall.

// New Quest: Oh Brother Thoth, Where Aren't Thou?

Her new, robe-enhanced Perception pulsed and a hover light glowed a little brighter in response.

'Right through…' Getty picked her way over the bones and rubble, and with both hands, pushed the hover light. 'Here.'

There was a sharp, cavern-echoing *click*.

For a second, nothing happened and Getty stepped back, holding her breath.

The wall didn't so much crumble as eat itself, the top falling into the bottom like some dark, pixelated sandcastle disintegrating in seawater. And when it was done… Getty's breath caught in her throat, and there was some kind of problem with her feet, 'cause they felt more like blocks of tungsten than flesh and bone, heavy, unwieldy and loud as she stumbled closer to the new doorway.

'Holy shit,' she whispered to herself. 'Jackpot.'

A library sprawled on the other side of the threshold. She looked down on rows and rows of shelves, tall and fat, disappearing into the distance. A treasure trove of knowledge hidden away in the depths of the Uxen mining colony.

Massive statues interspersed the shelves. Three persons high and lit from below by cobalt lights, they were a mixture of characters from the Game, famous avatars, some with wings, some tails and horns or fins and claws, some with guns slung over their backs or at their hips. Others still with swords and shields, arrows and staves, more with twisting balls of magic or the transparent shimmer of psionics playing over upraised hands.

They stretched as far as the shelves themselves, the closest one practically at her feet, a giant of a woman with a jetpack and lasers in her hands. The farthest… The farthest, barely a matchstick at this distance, too far by half to see more than the lump of if its head, like a pimple on a mountain and yet something about the way the light winked off it…

Getty narrowed her gaze, focusing on the most distant avatar, letting the game do its work.

// Perception check. Success.

Her avatar might have noodles in place of arms and wet sponges where her lungs should be, but there were some advantages to rolling a brainiac.

One moment Getty stood atop the massive bookshelf, the next she was halfway across the library, not close enough to make out details, but enough to see the giant sapphire eye wink.

The same colour as the ibis on the wall.

Frisson rolled across her back.

✳

There was something not quite right about the cavern. It stretched high overhead, slender columns of stone and metal twisting up from the floor, reaching for the ceiling… Getty looked up. Except she couldn't see the ceiling, and that didn't seem right, not even in the dark, blue-lit confines of the library. A lot could be explained away by artistic license, by overeager enviro techs adding in floating platforms and fine, spindly staircases wrapped around mammoth trees but this…

// Perception check.

A shiver ran through Getty's HUD, a brief moment of static there and then gone, that echoed the one crawling up her spine.

// Failure.

There was something up there, she knew it in her gut, the way she knew that the scent of old paper and the electric tang of holos was just the scent-markers from her game-chair, that falling from the top of the shelves wouldn't kill her—although the momentary pain and quest reset would be a bitch—and that at some point, she'd have to get up from the VR chair and make a dash for the loo.

She stared, and stared hard looking for the clue, the brief spot of colour, the shimmer of air, the mark carved in a metal and stone pillar. It had to be there, up amongst the too-deep darkness, a little easter egg put there by the devs just for the craziest, the most tenacious of players. The ones who pumped all their starting points into intuition and logic.

Just. For. Her.

Her bare feet slapped against the cobblestones. She ignored the cold penetrating her soles, creeping up her legs and flirting with her knees. Purposefully shoved aside the lights at the base of the step-high shelves getting dimmer, the shadows longer, the fine layer of dust-like particles slowly turning her skin a greyer shade of gold.

Pushed aside everything and focused all of her considerable perception above.

Really, she should have known better.

One moment she was wandering the corridors, head tilted back, a hand trailing over the spines of books, covers rough and smooth and gilded trailing away under her fingers to keep her from running into things. There was the occasional bump as her hand found artefacts—little statues and potion bottles, hilts and shields and pistols, some under glass, most not—but nothing to drag her attention away from scanning the columns and the darkness above.

There had to be a ladder or a—

Something tugged at her foot.

She frowned, but kept moving, because right *there*—just above the statue of Horus-May-Gedden with her savagely curved beak and the intricate runes marching up her tabard and over her shoulder—was a glimm—

Another tug at her foot, harder this time, and squelchy, like it was stuck in mud.

Except she was walking on cobblestones.

Awareness *fritzed* across her shoulders.

She looked down.

White, gooey fingers wrapped around her bare ankle. Translucent fingers, ragged at the edges like the being they belonged to couldn't hold its shape, or was slowly disintegrating into nothing. The nails at the ends where whole enough, pale as the gooey flesh but sharp, sharp enough to draw a bright point of blood from her calf. The spot of red swelled and dropped, running over the paper-white fingers and... *SHHLOP,* drawn into the thing's flesh, the translucent white taking on a hint of red.

// HP -1.

Well fuck.

Getty leapt back... or tried to, because the hand tightened its grip.

She stumbled, balance off-kilter, arms pinwheeling even as her gaze leapt from the hand to the body attached to it. The white gooiness continued, oozing flesh hanging on bone, tendon and muscle little more than pale strings connecting fingers to hands, to wrists and arms, all the way up to bony shoulders and a madly grinning head.

A screen popped over the thing.

// Library guardian. HP 1240. Undead. Library guardians are the putrefied corpses of thieves who have lost their way in the Library of All Knowledge, doomed to spend eternity haunting the halls, desperate to find their way out of the labyrinth. They feed on the life force of unsuspecting librarians and careless browsers.

// Abilities: Where there is one...: Calls other ghouls to the site of a fresh feed. Deadly in numbers.

// Casts: Cursed: movement speed is reduced. Damage to health over time. Debuff stacks with every new injury inflicted by undead.

While she was reading the popup, other ghouls had crawled out of the shadows.

Getty flailed again. The ghoul was strong, its fingers a calcium cage. She fell backwards, shoulders hitting the shelves a second before her head, stars going off in her eyes even as pain bloomed in her shoulder blades.

The ghoul still gripped her tight.

Getty smashed her other foot into its face—

// Sister Getty: Attack(4) vs Library Ghoul: Defence(20). Failure.

New pain, this time radiating from her sole. A new bead of blood smearing the ghoul's lips.

// HP -4. Status: Cursed x 2.

The cobblestones crawled. The creeping grey-white mist parting around slimy, pale forms dragging themselves over the cold stones, sharp nails *skritching* with every pull of necrotic muscles.

She had to get out of there. Getty yanked at her ankle again—

// Sister Getty: Strength(9) vs Library Ghoul: Strength(25). Failure.

She grunted.

Come on. Come on! She couldn't stay here and become ghoul food, just another lost soul wandering around the library, not when she was so close—

// Feeble exploit activated.

In the corner of her vision, light flared, a brilliant golden glow set to rival a sun. She blinked, took a second to tear her eyes from the approaching wave of slimy ghoulishness, and found the source. A long-necked bottle with a round bottom, shone under a glass dome, its contents a familiar shade of sparkling, candy-apple red.

A health potion. All hail the random generator gods, the masters of convenience.

She flailed at the shelf, stretching as far as she could without falling on the ghoul, but the bottle was beyond the reach of her fingers.

Getty lunged, not away from the ghoul this time, but over it. Her fingertips found smooth glass and skidded over it, the surface too slick and too big to grab with just one hand. A glance down at the ghoul, its death's-head grin fixed firmly on her ankle, her blood slowly turning its slimy, goo-covered arms a brighter shade of pink.

Its fellows were a squelching, squishy tide of horror making their slow, inexorable way towards her.

Fuck. Fuckity fuck, fuck, fuck.

No choice for it.

She stepped on the ghoul, bare feet squelching through its back, its ribcage sharp and bony under her soles, giving with a wet *crackkk* as she put her weight on it. The smell of putrid flesh burst around her legs, rising up on its own miasma of rot and decay, the stench making her eyes water and her nose burn.

// Cursed.

// Cursed.

// Cursed.

// Cursed.

The notifications stacked one atop the other, even as new pain flared in her legs, broken rib bones making new scrapes and cuts in her flesh, thin trickles of blood flushing the ghoul's pallid goo. But she got both hands around the dome, lifted the glass, threw it to the ground, already reaching for the bottle when the first notification popped.

// Sister Getty: Attack: Melee: Library dome(53) vs Library Ghoul: Strength(25). Success.

// Library Ghoul: HP -328.

Holy shit. Getty looked down, at the dome—unscathed— sitting in the liquified remains of the ghoul's chest. As she watched, a section of the ghoul's spine melted away.

For a moment, Getty forgot about the potion bottle, all of her attention on the dome that had covered it. A screen overlaid the ghoul.

// Library dome: Absorbs essence of item it's protecting.

Huh. Handy.

She grabbed the healing potion. The bottle's bulbous end fit neatly into her palm, the neck the perfect height to open with a flick of the plain cork stopper. The sweet, brain-clearing scent of peppermint wafted out the open top, and the potion itself seemed to glow.

Getty's mouth watered, and before she knew what she was doing, before she remembered the undead coming to strip her corpse down to its raggedy ends, she brought the potion to her lips, relished the heady fizz of its magic— And ripped herself out of the potion's hold to throw the bottle at the ghoul.

It shattered in a candy red cloud of glass and mist. Like a snake seeking prey, the potion mist paused a moment before it struck. A quick, hard lurch, sticking to the ghoul's arms, its grinning skull, racing along bone and gooey flesh like they were candy.

The ghoul shrieked, high enough to pierce her ear drums. Bony fingers spasmed around her ankle, her health bar dropping rapidly as more 'cursed' notifications popped.

And then the ghoul let go, the potion-mist dissipating, the thick, candy-red turning to pink, then white, then—

Another squelch brought her attention back to the other ghouls, dragging their way out of the shadows, now just an arm's length away.

Fuck.

Getty kicked the glass dome into the nearest ghoul's face, turned... And almost ran straight into the ghoul creeping up behind.

The two-metre space between the bookshelves was crawling with them—a putrid, foul-smelling carpet of rot. There wasn't so much as a clear millimetre of cobblestone between the corpses for even a fucking *elf* to dance through, let alone her uncoordinated, feeble self.

'Fuck.'

She wasn't walking out of this, not without help. A quick glance around, but no more comforting, candy-apple bottles winked at her from the shelves, just leather-bound books, swords and shields and vessels full of things that writhed and glinted.

The masters of convenience, the gods of RNG had abandoned her—

Wait a second.

The *shelves*, not what was on them, but the actual surfaces... She looked up, and up and up, all the way to where the bookcase appeared to curve to a point, like a really steep ladder.

'You're an idiot, Getty,' she said to herself, and started to climb.

✳

The shelves were taller than they looked, at least in this section of the library.

Getty pulled herself up the last riser, belly and arms clinging to the top, legs dangling over one side, her head the other. The top of the bookcase was barely a metre wide.

She had a really great view of the other side and the flagstone floor writhing with the pale, gooey forms. Ghouls, not that they really looked like ghouls, not from this height, more like a squirmy, wormy mist, choking the ground, several dragon-lengths below. Several *big* dragon-lengths, and not the shitty, wimpy dragon-wannabe things in the Old Quarter either, but the big Elder ones the hot-shots liked to hunt for their scales.

She twisted onto her back, heart beat hard, breath rasping in her throat. The change in elevation hadn't revealed anything on the ceiling, the darkness was as impenetrable from this vantage as it had been from the ground.

A bright spot of blue winked in the corner of her vision.

Getty's head snapped to the side.

The massive statue of Horus-May-Gedden, with her beak-faced

helmet, clad in lapis and gold armour, peeked head and shoulders above the line of bookcases. It was the blue gem in the statue's eye that had glinted.

Getty frowned at it.

There was something *wrong* with that statue, something that stuck in the back of her brain and tried to itch its way out. A vague recollection from high school history and old movies featuring Egyptian gods, mixing with memories of watching Horus-May-Gedden duke it out with the legendary Samael in the twenty-thirty-nine world series. Horus had swung her wicked curved sword around, eyes blazing the same red as the blood coating her short, sharp...

Getty's eyes widened.

...beak.

The statue at the end of the bookcases gazed right at her, *blue* eyes glinting, highlighting the curve of its *long*, hooked beak.

'Holy shit.' Was it possible for the realisation in her voice to sparkle? An emoticon she could summon? 'That's not Horus.'

In Egyptian mythology, Horus had the head of a falcon, while the ibis belonged to the god of wisdom and knowledge, to Thoth.

Brother Thoth.

'Got you,' she said.

And then, like the system could sense her joy...

// Cursed x 8. HP -167.

A quick glance at her health bar showed the meter dangerously close to the quarter-full mark.

Fuck.

She should have kept some of that health potion.

// Cursed x 8. HP -167.

Getty rolled again. The bookcase wobbled. Just what she needed.

Cautiously getting her feet under her she stood, arms held wide for balance.

The bookcase wobbled again at the shift in weight. Something about the physics of that didn't strike Getty as quite right, set off another frission of unease between her shoulder blades, but—

// Cursed x 8. HP—

She shoved the notification aside. Yeah, yeah, she got it. No time to wonder about the tiny niggle that would probably become something big and nasty. No time at all.

The ibis-headed avatar at the end of the bookcase was all that mattered.

Ghouls, wobbly bookcases, little fissions of perception... The bad shit was closing in and that meant only one thing. She was getting close to something, and the monsters the Game threw at her would be in direct proportion to just how valuable the something was.

Time to bring on the dragons.

✳

Getty stumbled, arms wheeling, the cobblestones all the way below looming large as she teetered on the edge.

The bookcase wobbled again, a hard, sharp jerk left then right, like there was a dragon at the base thumping its giant tail against the bottom. Smashing it more like. A dragon tail would cleave right through the wooden frame leaving nothing more than matchsticks and broken bits of Getty behind.

Another jerk, and somehow Getty righted herself. For a step at least, until she backtracked too far and—

And there was the other edge, and the other side, and the other long drop into ghoulish goo. The ghouls were climbing the shelves, she didn't try to make out the details, they were long trails of white slipping and oozing their way to the top, like strings of zombie dragon snot. They were close enough now for her HUD to register them as enemies, picking them out with bright red dots and "Unknown target" above their heads, not even a threat status.

The system might not be telling her what they were, but it didn't take a genius. The stench of rot proceeded them, blasting upwards like some kind of wave breaking against the shore.

// Cursed x 8. HP -167.

Her health bar flashed, a single pulse a little brighter than the others. Less than ten percent.

Fuck, this was going to be close.

Up ahead, the Thoth statue winked at her, closer than before, but not close enough. It was like there was some kind of mirage between her and it, every time she thought she was closer, that the runes marching over its chest armour were clearer, they faded and the statue got further away. To top it off, there was something wrong with her HUD, distances and stats fuzzed out, she couldn't even make out if it was two digits or three. For all she knew, it was four.

// Cursed x 8. HP -167.

Someone was fucking with her.

She focused.

// Perception check failed.

Crap.

What about—

A slimy, skeletal hand, a rusty pale ring rattling on its index finger, *thunked* a millimetre from her bare toes. Gooey flesh sprayed over her ankle.

No time to stand there faffing about. Getty half-ran, half-wobbled along the top of the bookcase.

Three strides, Thoth getting closer and closer, the runes carved into its giant beak more than just wobbly shadows.

The bookcase wobbled, but she kept her balance, arms out to either side. A glance down, just a second, then back up and—

Thoth was further away, the runes in its beak back to indistinct squiggles.

Fuck. She jerked to a halt, hands on knees, breath ragged.

At her feet, that gooey, skeletal hand with the rusty, pale ring.

Perception frizzled up her spine.

Well, shit. A loop, she was stuck in a loop.

Two more goo-flesh hands *thawked* on the bookcase.

The Perception-frizzle took a detour over her shoulder and crept across her collarbone to the pocket stitched on the inside of her robe.

She put her hand to it, felt the thin, boney outline of something long and sharp—

The valravn feather.

As she concentrated on it, a new dialogue popped to life.

// Quill's made from valravn feathers can reveal hidden truths.

Hidden truths… She stared at the mirage and at her health bar flirting with zero, and drew the feather from her robes. She could do with some hidden truths right about now.

How to use it though? Quills were made to write, and she had no ink…

Boney fingers *skrittched* over the bookshelves, the blood the ghoul had absorbed from her enough to flush its white goo-flesh a soft shade of pink.

Blood… She didn't have ink, but she had blood.

Getty stabbed the feather's sharp, midnight end into her palm.

Everything *glitched*. Around her, the library froze—ghouls and books and dust particles—and then, like someone pulled the plug, went to black. It was just a microsecond, less than a heartbeat, before the lights flicked back on with a massive, head-splitting *squelch!*

The library came back except... Lines and diagrams spun through the shelf under her feet, wireframes and resistance counts ran through the ghouls like blood and ahead, where Thoth stood tall and straight, its curved beak almost touching the shelf, a door glowed.

She'd heard about this, seen screenshots and vid casts straight from the dev studios. Half constructed environments, physics calculations and force trajectories outlined in white and yellow and red, the hair-thin lines of wireframes glowing under the constructs' skins. This was the Debug.

Getty's hand clenched around the quill, the sharp cutting edge digging into her palm. Even now, the wound pulsed, a brilliant bloody ache in her bone. The wireframe pulsed with the pain, all of it in time with her heart and the steady drip drip drip of blood onto the skeletal hand gripping her thigh. It shouldn't be possible and yet here she was, right in the middle of the library, surrounded by a rot of ghouls.

'How the fuck?' The hack was royally screwing her over, that was the only explanation for the colossal series of... She looked down at herself; the rough, ragged robes hanging to her knees; ghoul bones digging into her thigh; the bookcase rough under her bare feet.

A spark snapped her attention to Thoth's gemstone eyes, something long and scaly moved in the shadows wrapped around the statue's neck. For a moment, she thought she saw wings.

That couldn't be good.

// Cursed x 8. HP -167.

'Oh, come on!' The entire environment was frozen around her but her health bar was still taking a hit? That totally wasn't fair.

Up ahead, Thoth's eye winked again.

How and why were questions for later. Her health bar flashed. The glowing frame set in Thoth's throat echoed it. That was were she needed to be. Whatever the hell was going on with this quest, it was beyond that door.

Now, if only she could loosen the ghoul. She tugged at the boney fingers wrapped around her thigh, but the monster's fingers were clamped tight, the tendons holding its hands together rigid. White, finger-width lines ran through the thing's skeleton, curious flat ribbons neither glowing nor pulsing, without depth or height, and yet standing out because of their very strangeness.

She traced the line back over the ghoul's hand, narrowing her focus... and felt the click behind her eyeballs as the perception check popped.

One moment, she was looking at flat white lines, the next equations and numbers flowed through them in mathematical rivers. Each stream ran through the ghoul's skeleton, flowing off of bigger rivers and still bigger ones beyond those, the ends attached to knuckle bones and wrists and elbows. One in particular, the junction where the ghoul's left arm snugged into its shoulder, caught her attention. A weak spot.

A red square pulsed over the area.

The valravn quill pulsed in her hand—the tip throbbing against her palm, cold enough to send ice through her veins—and as it did, new force lines popped into being. It was like a strange kind of foreshadowing, watching the outline of a raised arm—her arm, the two-dimensional image attached to her very real, very three-dimensional shoulder—lift over her head, and then a new line emerging out of nothing and smash into the ghoul's weak spot.

Well then. That was probably a hint.

Getty took it.

A single hard strike was enough to sever the ghoul's arm from its torso. She was free, or... free enough. The ghoul's fingers still clamped tight around her thigh.

// Cursed x 8. HP -167.

It would do. She eyed the glowing door in Thoth's chest, the bookcase leading up to it, the force lines and wireframes, the knotted code attached to the hot spot on the floor. No idea what it said, but it was in the right spot to trigger the never-ending loop that had kept her from reaching Thoth all this time.

The hot spot wasn't that big, a half-metre maybe less. Just one good leap and she'd sail right over it, and then it was a straight shot to Thoth.

Getty braced herself in a runner's crouch, doing her best to ignore the finger bones still digging into her thigh.

A single leap, that was all she needed. Even her pitiful agility stats could handle that, right?

She bounced on her bare toes.

Maybe. Possibly.

// Cursed x 8. HP—

Fuck it.

She ran—one metre, two—endurance bar drained in the blink of an eye. The code knot just *there*, a step away. A thin blue slither left under her health meter as she leapt... and... and...

...sailed right through the glowing portal in Thoth's chest.

✻

She hung in the Sphere, bodiless, without even hands to manipulate the numbers and letters twisting around each other in the middle of the space.

Sister Getty hung on the sidelines, ragged robes and scrawny frame suspended in mid-air, as if a giant hand held her under the arms. Beside the scholar monk, another avatar waited in the shadows, taller, darker, little electric blue ripples disturbing the dark where its talons pierced the floor.

The dragon rose out of those ripples. Long and lean, seemingly made of the same light reflecting off the watery floor. It twisted through the data spinning in the Sphere's centre, rising from the book opened on the floor. Its form was somehow both massive and tiny, with huge wings, tiny claws and jaws that could swallow her whole.

It did not speak and she could do nothing but watch; no body, no voice, no name, barely even a memory of an ancient library, skeletal hands, a glowing golden door and the dragon tattooed over her arm and across her back, rising from her skin as she passed through the portal. Only the single, confused moment when Getty realised she wasn't in the Game anymore, not even in the System, stayed with her—a hard, sharp spike to the chest— before the dragon took over and Getty faded.

Like she did now, awareness growing dim as she was packed away in her little box.

Until the dragon needed her again.

R2 087
I AM MAGGIE #5
FELIS
FETURA

INTRODUCTION

By now you'll have noted that Maggie, who this series is named after, only appears in one story. Hopefully, you'll also have twigged that maybe, just maybe, that's because she's not always called Maggie. I know, I know, I forgot the spoiler warning, but I'm sure you didn't need it.

Learn more about the writing of *Felis Fetura*. Scan the QR code for the audio commentary, soundtrack and more.

FELIS FETURA

Mae slammed her palms against the cold, slimy concrete and cursed.

She stepped back, the sharp, weed-choked pebbles digging into her soft-soled boots, and looked up at the huge old door with the dragons and tigers carved around the equally massive portholes in its two-storey surface, and swore again.

The fucking thing wouldn't open.

The guts of the control pad lay open on the concrete pillars that supported it, ancient bio-circuits and gel-filled wires trailing down the water- and moss-stained sides. Beyond the overhanging portico, the monsoon turned noon to dusk and made the air sit thick on her skin. She almost couldn't hear herself swear over the rain pounding the curved roof.

After these last few days in the humid hell of Ineron XII's tropic belt, the funky, fetid smell of the hydroponics bay on her little ship would be a fucking delight.

'Fuck.'

'Swearing won't help.' The gravely, fractured voice spoke in her ear, coming through the comms implanted in her jawbone, even though the speaker was above.

'How the fuck do you know?' She punched the slate-grey door again. Mae couldn't even find a fucking *seam*, a single split down the middle or sides to indicate the slab moved. And yet, she knew it did. Knew it because she paid the fucking hacker enough to make sure it did.

'Fuck!' Another fleshy thud. 'Fuck, fuck, fuck!'

'You're going to hurt yourself,' came the lazy drawl from above. And of course, Felix could still fucking drawl even though the previous-level boss had taken out his vocal processor and the only medpacks they had left were the shitty little green ones, barely enough to heal the scrapes on her knuckles.

She glared up at the huge white cat sprawled along the edge of the curving rooftop, like the useless fucking feline he was. 'You could fucking help.'

He swished his tail, the sleek interlocking white plates and ornate silver of his hard-case glistening even in the dull overcast light of the monsoon.

He blinked at her, long and slow. First his inner shutters and then outer. He yawned. 'Why would I do that?'

'"Why would I do that?"' she parroted back. 'Because you're my fucking teammate, you arsehole.'

Another yawn, and this time a stretch, first his forepaws—silver sickle-like claws springing from robotic paws, delicate white whiskers laid against armour-plated muzzle, ears pressed flat to his head; arched his back—the ornate, armoured curves protecting his neck and hunching, the long, sleek spine hollowing all the way down to his hindquarters. More sickle-like claws flashing in the half-light, tail snapping straight and then curling over his back.

Just as slowly, the leopard-bot rose and leapt.

A hundred and seventeen meters straight down, landing on the brain-smashing pebble and stone path like it was a fluffy fucking cloud. Fucking show off.

That's what she got for purchasing a pretty, elf-made bot. All style and fucking attitude.

The snow-white leopard sat, all fancy pearl and silver, head level with her breastbone, and flicked his tail over his toes.

He looked at her.

She looked at him.

'Well?' she said.

'Well, what?'

She hissed. Pointed at the door. 'Are you going to help or what?'

He blinked. Slowly.

She wouldn't growl. She wouldn't.

The long, elegant tail flicked.

No growling. None.

He blinked again and yawned, that long silver tongue curling against the roof of his mouth.

He was doing it to fuck with her, she knew it. She. Knew. It—

He sat back, twisted like a pretzel and washed his raised back leg—

'Oh, for fuck's sake!'

An ear twitched in her direction.

She growled, couldn't help it. The sound burst out of her chest, high and rumbly, cracking on the end.

The leg lowered. The head came around, that flat, delicate muzzle with its inlay of filigreed silver poking her in the chest. A purr vibrated the air between them.

'I love it when you growl like a little squeaky toy,' the big synth-cat said. He stretched, rising on his haunches and rubbed his cheek against hers.

Elf-steel was smooth and cold, diamond wrapped in silk, and Felix's breath smelled of grease and the peculiar sweet, metal tang that came with it. It was nice; sent a little shiver across her back every time the synth-cat got affectionate, not that she'd ever tell him that.

Arsehole probably knew it already.

The fucker.

Mae's lip curled, even as that "little squeaky toy" sound rumbled through her chest again. 'I will end you,' she said.

He purred, butted her chin with his head. 'But you love me.'

'Next sleep cycle,' she said.

Another purr. Another cheek rub.

Another little shiver.

'I'll put your core in the old hound unit,' she finished. 'You can be a dog.'

The purring stopped mid-cheek rub.

The grease and sweet metal smell retreated.

Felix sat back, ears and whiskers flat and stared at her.

She stared back. Blinked.

When Felix snarled, inch-long canines flashed in the dim monsoon light, sickle moons promising retribution. The whole "you wouldn't" was written across his big-eyed feline face, but she would, and the cat knew it.

He stalked past her, disgust in every short, sharp twitch of his tail. One twitch in particular almost taking out her knee, but she dodged it. The plates along Felix's spine ruffled, and there was an extra *skritch* as his claws dug into the flagstones, but he finally stopped in front of the door, sat back on his haunches and smacked one head-sized paw over the gutted control panel.

A hum, short and soft, then electricity arcing blue-white between Felix's whiskers, more of it skipping down his chest, rushing through the silver filigree in his shoulder and into his paw. She knew when he'd made contact with the door's systems when his inner lids half-closed.

Mae crossed her arms and tried to ignore the rain trickling down her poncho's cowl neck as she waited. The door was old, maybe even ancient, in design as well as coding; a relic from the Game's thirteenth expansion that had somehow survived the endless rebuilds and System purges.

 Old enough that even Felix's systems, advanced as they were, would have trouble deciphering the code. They could be here for a while.

Mae turned to the jungle and the monsoon, taking in the wide-spreading trees, the scraggly undergrowth—shrubs and fallen branches, orchids clinging to the bark, giant fleshy leaves open to catch the rain, big fat drops that could soak a person clean through in ten seconds flat. She knew. Under the poncho, her orange-fronted shipsuit stuck to her back, while her titanium-weave pants squelched around her knees where they bagged over her field boots. The only thing that wasn't wet were her toes and only because the water hadn't seeped all the way down her socks.

If it weren't for the poncho, hypothermia would have laid her out thirty-eight minutes ago. As it was, the reflection on her HUD showed her lips were a fabulous shade of mauve that'd look just right on a corpse.

Whoever'd programmed the environment here sucked. Weren't jungles meant to be humid?

Not that it mattered.

The dragon had paid her enough to find the McGuffin, upfront too with more promised on delivery. And not just creds, but game time, enough of both to set her up for years, so much that she'd ignored the little shiver of "too good to be true" down her spine.

But then she'd spent a chunk of those creds and more of that time finding this place, trawling through old forums and walkthroughs, peeling apart gossip and rumours and System-myths, tracking all the little kernels that led to this fucked-up little moon with its old-arse door and older-arse coding.

And after she'd found it, she'd spent more time and creds *getting* there.

Enough time and enough creds to make the creepy little shiver disappear.

Until now.

The stroll through the washed-out jungle—leaves more grey than green, like the designers had turned the saturation down—and the ease with which Felix located the cobblestoned path, the lack of monsters and traps (despite the last level boss) shouldn't have made her this uneasy. And yet it did.

Because she was smart.

And paranoid.

And a survivor.

She had the exploit to prove it. Right there, on her character sheet.

// Survivor: Never caught unaware, always with a Plan B. In new environments, your Perception is heightened; threats to your survival make your spidey-senses tingle. Be careful though, not all threats are real.

And standing there, looking out over that washed-out, monsoon-drenched jungle with the ancient, shuttle-sized doors at her back, her spidey-senses tingled. They tingled like a son-of-a-bitch.

'Felix,' she said, switching from audio to the sub-audible comm unit nestled beside her vocal cords. *'How much longer?'*

Text was her only reply. *// Three minutes.*

The tingle, frizzing between her shoulder blades. She slipped a hand under the poncho, reached for the compact little gun strapped to her thigh. The curved, blocky grip was comforting, the barely audible *shruumm*, the little vibration through her pants as it turned on and the new crosshair on the HUD even more so.

'Make it quick,' was all she said.

Three minutes was an eternity, but just as the skin was crawling off Mae's back, the weight of unseen eyes out in the jungle set to break her bones, the door cracked.

A loud, step-shuddering *thunk* that shook her boots and rocked her balance.

She spun.

Felix was backing up from the door, head up, and a particularly satisfied look on his proud feline face.

There was a split down the middle of the massive rectangle, a brilliant white strip from the upswept roof, through both portholes and into the concrete at her feet. That's what had shaken the ground, unsteadied her. The split travelled not just through the doors but the steps, and as the they opened, the steps slid aside, giant grey plates folding into the pillars holding everything aloft.

Mae stumbled, arms pinwheeling, trying not to get her boots caught in the rapidly disappearing steps as they concertinaed into each other.

The synth-cat was a graceful, white-silver streak leaping from the top step to the cobblestoned path.

Mae tried to follow him down, tripped, automatically tucked her head into her shoulder as she hit the ground and bounced to a stop at Felix's paws.

The ground stopped shuddering.

Rain hit her hard. Fringe plastered to her forehead, little scraggly bits of chestnut brown hair stuck to cheeks and chin, an instant torrent of water rushing over her lips and down the back of the poncho. At least there wasn't mud.

Small mercies.

The tip of the Felix's heavy tail brushed her nose.

She looked up.

He looked down. Rain might have made her look like a drowned warthog, but it turned the cat into a glistening pearl statue, shimmering over the white armour and sparkling in the silver filigree.

Smug, aristocratic superiority hummed in every line of his elf-made body.

Really, it was unfair that a creature without eyebrows could make that expression work.

'Fucking cat,' she whispered.

He purred. 'The door is open.'

She growled and shoved to her feet, cobblestones biting into her palms, fingernails already turning blue. *I noticed* was on the tip of her tongue, but she didn't say it, had already let the growl out. She settled for glaring at the cat, brushing her hands off on her knees before turning.

The door was open in the same fashion Moses had parted the Red Sea. What before had been a massive edifice was a break in the equally massive wall. The giant, dark-grey slabs of concrete hadn't been pushed against the lighter grey pillars, the steps weren't stacked up against the sides. They were gone, leaving just the up-cornered roof and an arch in the wall.

But that wasn't what stole Mae's breath, that pressure was reserved for the slice of greenery beyond the archway. Not the washed out, desaturated green of the jungle, but a brilliant rainbow of green. Deep, rich greens—lime and emerald and jade—all of them clustered beyond the wall, like some force had sucked all of the colour out of the jungle and into the world beyond.

The space between her shoulder blades tingled.

But was it what was behind or what lay in front that made that electric spark jump between vertebrae? Something told her *that* was the important bit.

She shook herself. Important or not, she'd found the ruin, opened the door.

Time to see what was inside.

A whole heap of nothing, that was what they found. A whole fat lot of diddly squat with a side-serving of rotted parchment, rusty ladles and cracked pottery, surrounded by gunge-filled ponds and a battalion of mosquitos big enough to draw a carriage. Not so much as a suspicious wall hanging or cryptic riddle to give her hope.

Mae slapped at a fat blood sucker trying to work through her poncho. An hour into their initial exploration, she'd made the mistake of shucking the poncho and the even bigger one of pushing her sleeves to the elbow; now welts covered her forearms and the backs of her hands. More climbed her nape and one made a molehill on the crown of her head.

The monsoon had died the moment they stepped over the threshold, though back through the archway, rain still pelted the jungle. Inside the compound, the air was humid, thick, and heavy. Now, it was her sweat rather than rain that stuck her shipsuit to her back.

She pushed an old, wooden trunk over the half-rotten boards of the last building's veranda. The ruin wasn't as large as she expected, not that she was sure what she *had* expected, but after being blinded by the intense green, it had been something more than the square compound with its large, multi-tiered buildings on each side, around a central courtyard.

The courtyard itself was a series of tiered square ponds, they'd probably been filled with orange fish and lilies, as over-saturated as the greenery once, but were now choked with pale bloated corpses and brown, twisted stems. Wooden boardwalks cut the ponds into smaller and smaller squares, partially overgrown with vines and twisted by the trunks of trees and shrubs.

Around the ponds and boardwalks, interconnected wood-panelled pavilions formed the compound's walls, like boxes next to boxes—a single tall, rectangular one in the middle, then smaller cubes spreading wing-like either side.

She'd been through all of them; peered under every sagging sleeping-platform, shrouded in gauzy moth-holed curtains, poked into every corner, every attic, every exposed dust-laden roof beam. She'd bounced on floorboards—put her feet through a few—upturned every vase, unearthed every scroll, torn down every wall hanging. And nothing.

Nada.

Zip.

Zilch.

Bupkis.

Shoving the heavy old trunk onto this last terrace, the box's black metal corners leaving gouges in the soft planks, was a last desperate act. Maybe it would look different out in the sun.

Sprawled over a pale grey boulder, overlooking the largest of the courtyard's grungy, weed-choked ponds, Felix flicked his tail and watched.

'You could help,' she said, feeling like a broken record.

An ear twitched.

Yeah, about what she'd expected.

She slapped another mosquito.

Eighty-six hours after parting the grey, concrete sea, and all Mae had to show for it was the incessant need to scratch and a pile of old scrolls. Some of the scrolls were made of bamboo slats held together with cord, others thick, mildewy papyrus, each covered in ancient symbols that defied her translators. All sixteen of them. Not even Felix's elf-made systems had accomplished more than confirming that the words were an actual language.

And not a bit of it giving off the golden light the dragon said it would.

She finished shoving the trunk to the end of the veranda, popped the lid and stared at the accumulation of nothing inside.

'Fuck.' She kicked the wooden box. 'We've searched everywhere, where the fuck is it?'

Felix yawned, long silver tongue curling. 'Not here,' he said. 'Obviously.'

'The dragon said—'

'The dragon lied.'

She threw a scroll at him. Felix swatted it out of the air.

'He didn't fucking *lie*,' she said. He better not have lied, not with half the credits he'd paid her gone in pursuit of his fucking McGuffin.

'Then where is it?'

'That's what I'm asking *you*.'

'And you expect me to know?'

She snarled at him. 'Well, you know everything else.'

He snarled in return, silver canines flashing, but said nothing.

Mae gave the trunk another kick. The old, mildewy wood—

once a shiny lacquered white with sumptuous apple blossoms and delicate butterflies painted on its surface, now cracked and faded—made a wet *crunch* under the force of her reinforced toe. She kicked it again, her foot going all the way through, up to the ankle. She tried to yank it out, but the rotted wood held on. Another yank, and another. All the time hopping on the other foot, feeling the boards underneath her sag and creak with the impact.

That little tingle shot across her spine.

One more yank and her boot came free, while the other fell through the floor, splintered bits of wood stabbing her ankle.

'*Fuck.*'

'You keep saying that.'

She yanked the newly caught boot out and growled at the cat. 'We need the McGuffin.'

Felix's tail flicked again, a little harder this time, smacking the boulder. 'It's not here.'

She marched across the deck and pointed a finger in the feline's finely chiselled snout. 'It's fucking *here,*' she said. 'And you're going to get off your lazy fucking behind and help me find—'

A sharp, short *frizzle* down her spine.

Mae spun, all her attention on the dank, murky shadows of the last pavilion.

Out the corner of her eye, she saw Felix stiffen.

// *What is it?* the big cat said.

She didn't respond, all her attention on the yawning doors of the pavilion in front of her. The last one, the smallest, tucked into a corner between the sprawling rooms on the compound's south and east sides.

Something was in there.

Something big.

Bad.

Meaner than her.

She activated [Sonic Steps] from her menu bar, took three steps forward.

Waves pulsed from her boots, translucent white circles rushing in every direction—left, right, up, down, around and through. And everything they touched appeared on her HUD, outlined and tagged—height, weight, volume, name, description, threat-level.

Room dividers, lamps, little plinths with bulbous vases and long-withered flowers, a single step leading up to what was once a sleeping-platform. All of it came back as more data to flesh out the isometric map in the corner of her HUD, and if she concentrated on any one thing long enough, more information filled her left eye. But like the rest of the compound, nothing was interesting, nothing came back hot.

So why the tingle?

// *Survivor: ...not everything is real.* The line from the exploit description drifted across her thoughts.

She shook it away.

Her instincts hadn't led her wrong yet. She crept over the threshold, sensing Felix doing the same, a spot of cool comfort at her back.

The pavilion was a single-storey, divided into four separate spaces around a central courtyard filled with the skeleton of an old apple tree, its grey, twisted branches spreading outwards. It hadn't worried her before, but now something about the way the gnarled trunk burst from the weed-choked pebbles at its base, the vibrant, slimy greenness of the moss clinging to the dog-sized stones dotted around the central courtyard, made her skin crawl.

The bad thing was there. In the tree.

[Sonic Steps] filled the main room, *ping ping pinging* with every footfall, reaching the courtyard, adding more detail to the map. Sunbeams filled the room, highlighted the dust in the air, the tattered drapes, the blossoms embroidered on the wall hangings either side of the arch into the courtyard.

Mae paused before the threshold.

Maybe that was why she tasted apples… and maybe it wasn't, said the tingle.

She knelt, pants bunching at the top of her boots, knees brushing the foot-high lintel separating the weed-choked white pebbles from the dank grey floorboards.

Felix sat next to her, tail laid over his paws, languid, relaxed all except for the tip of his tail, the *thwack thwack thwack* on the lintel.

Mae stared around the courtyard. Apart from the tree and the too-neat-to-be-random scattering of slimy green rocks, there was nothing remarkable about it. Open to the sky, enclosed on two sides by sliding doors, the other two by walls punctuated with round, glassless windows. Sun and rain may have soaked the little slice of nature, but she doubted a breeze had ever sighed through the apple's leaves. Birds though...

She thumped the lintel with her fist, [Sonic Steps] shooting outwards.

There was a nest in the tree's dead branches, nestled in finer, thready twigs near the top.

A sweet, high trill sang across her shoulder blades.

'Did you hear that?'

// *No.* Another *thwack* of Felix's tail; hard, sharp. Final.

But why?

'I heard a bird.'

// *There's nothing living here.*

A mosquito whined beside her ear. She slapped it.

// *Almost nothing,* the cat amended.

But there was. It was in the courtyard. The courtyard she hadn't set foot in, she realised, the only place she hadn't explored.

Because Felix had done it.

Felix had slunk through the little corner pavilion, ears twitching, tail a lazy serpent in his wake. She'd been elbow-deep in the bookcase in the east room, it'd been the eighteenth time she'd uttered the useless words 'You could help!'. The eighteenth time she'd been ignored.

The first rock Felix had leapt atop.

The first one he'd skittered off, his usual graceful self a flurry of uncoordinated paws and lashing white-silver tail.

She'd laughed, enjoyed the satisfaction of the synth-cat's disgruntled hiss, the way he'd stalked a circle around the rock. Like it had bitten him.

Karma, she'd put it down to.

She didn't look at Felix, didn't twitch in his direction, didn't use the HUD to tap into his systems. He'd sense that, like she did the tingle.

The rock though… It was the one on her left, on the far side of the tree; long and flat, the perfect spot for a lazy cat to sun himself while his human dug through dusty scrolls and parchment that crumbled at the touch. The slimy green moss wouldn't have bothered him—the benefits of a hardcase over fur—not even enough to loosen his footing. So why had he fallen?

Another fist thump on the lintel.

The map had enough detail to count the pebbles now, to trace the gouges in the pale grey rock.

// Depth: 3mm.

The map swung front and centre, taking over the HUD. Nothing in it changed, nothing popped or sparked or glimmered. No monsters sprang from the cobblestones, the tree didn't move, Felix's tail continued its *thwack thwack thwack*. No answers presented themselves, and yet the tingle... Mae shivered.

She changed the perspective, twisting the map until she was looking at it from the top down. Square courtyard, withered old apple tree smack in the middle, five rocks—three round, dog-sized boulders; one wobbly, waist-height column; the flat recliner graced by Felix's claws. Each positioned neatly around it, almost evenly spaced. A pentagram with the tree at its centre, if she so wished.

She tilted her head. Did she wish?

She rose, the tingle still arcing between vertebrae, but something else too, a quiet anticipation brewing in her gut. Or maybe that was the rations she'd almost broken her jaw on, the spicy imitation jerky still lingering. Maybe.

Time to find out.

She stepped over the—

A white-silver flash. Felix getting in the way before her foot even cleared the lintel.

She stared at him.

He stared at her.

'*You found something,*' she said. It wasn't a question.

A tail lash, ears and whiskers flat. He didn't answer.

'*Tell me.*'

He looked away, still not moving.

She went to step left of him—

Felix in the way.

—to the right—

Felix was there.

—rocked back on her heels and jump—

Only to meet three hundred eighty-nine kilos of elf-steel and chased silver, the impact knocking her on her arse.

She stared at him from the floor, disbelief making her dumb.

Felix wasn't Felix anymore, a change had come over him, deeper and more profound than the slick black smoke twisting through his filigreed chest, more terrifying than the tingle hissing and spitting down her spine. More foul than the old-meat stench suddenly filling her nose.

Worse even than the pain of a hundred botched resets or the prospect of corrupting her avatar.

A *thing* flickered around the synth-cat. The HUD said holo-projection, emitted from the lights and diodes embedded in Felix's frame. The horror in her gut echoed the scared whisper in her brain, the one saying—

'Maaaggie.' It came from behind,

She spun on her butt, knees to her chest, hand reaching for the gun strapped to her thigh.

Only the too-green compound, the scummy, translucent water, met her gaze. No red outlines, no monsters slinking over the rotted timbers or swishing through the ponds. No dark clouds creeping past the barrier, just the monsoon turning the sky grey, the jungle with it.

'Maagggieee.'

Breath on her neck, ruffling the short, frizzy strands not stuck to her jaw by sweat.

She scrambled sideways, came up short, caught in the junction of lintel and arch.

Again, nothing. Just Felix and the projection surrounding him, the dark formlessness spreading wings and *reaching*.

It was the wind that moaned that name, the non-existent breeze, or the mosquitoes, the birds in the apple tree... The dead apple tree, bare of leaves. The dank pond, the bloated koi corpses, the rotten timbers and moss.

Death, death and more death.

'There's nothing living here,' Felix had said.

Nothing but the mosquitos keeping the ghost company.

'Fuck.' The forums hadn't said anything about ghosts in this level.

Mae clambered to her feet, keeping well away from Felix and his shadowy wings. Fumbled with the scanner wrapped around her right forearm; poking at the controls. New options appeared on her HUD.

When she'd finally located the compound's records—the logs detailing its construction, timestamps and signatures marking its birth and development—they'd been corrupted, important logs eaten by time and unsuccessful purges. There'd been no record of its initialisation, no mention of where and when, on which server by which development team, just the location, lost in a tiny sector on an old science fiction server.

Ghosts were nothing more than bundles of random electricity—little knots of code, with or without wireframes—at least on the sci-fi servers, and needed something a little different to push them into the light. If the compound was an import from a server with swords and fireballs, this wasn't going to work.

Pray for the science, Mae.

Three steps back, toward the entrance, no longer [Sonic Steps] but [Scan] pulsing in the space around her—brilliant blue waves rushing through the room. On the HUD, the map changed again, other shapes joining the white outlines of physical items—the tree and rocks, doors and walls—electronic signatures drawn in brilliant blue. There was her at the centre of the map, arms and chest alight from the gadgets on and in her body. Felix was to her north, a behemoth of power, dark wings lit up with blue veins, and the rest of the room… dark and empty, not so much as a stray network trace—

A blip! Behind her.

She twisted about, took two giant strides around a low square table, back toward the bedroom and— Gone. Fuck it.

Patience, she told the tingle running down her spine. *Patience, just wait for it...*

Another blip, to her left, up the riser and around the dividing screen, the tattered, translucent paper painted with faded koi. Turn right and— Gone again. Nothing but lacquered cabinets decorated with more golden flowers, and a wall behind.

Maybe there was something behind the wall. A hidden room or passageway? A computer of some kind? Was that even possible, on an environment that looked like it belonged somewhere on the mytho-historic servers?

On the HUD, she zoomed the map out. She and Felix became dots, the pavilion a hollowed-out square squished between the larger, more elaborate structures. Symmetrical sides, no unaccounted for lumps or bumps that might have been secret rooms, and the room itself… She stomped her foot, clocked the distances as [Sonic Steps] rushed outwards, compared it to the larger map. The dimensions matched, so why was—

A floorboard moaned behind her.

Breath on her neck.

'Maaaggieee.'

How'd the ghost know the dragon's name?

No one there when she turned, just Felix, half hidden behind the dividing screen, murky dark still writhing through his hardcase.

'Maaggiee.'

And that wasn't creepy at all.

The blip at her side.

She jerked, stumbled over her own boots, caught the old, moth-eaten bed drapes as she went down, fragile fabric ripping. Narrowly avoided braining herself on the frame, gained a few splinters on the floorboards instead as she caught herself on her palms.

The blip again, at her feet now.

She twisted, drew her leg back—

Air. Nothing but dust puffed in the meagre sun from her impact, and a squiggle, a clear space that didn't sparkle like that around it.

She leaned closer.

'You got it for me, Maggie.'

The voice came from the spot of nothing. No… She got on her hands, lowered her face to the boards. They would have been magnificent in their heyday, she could imagine them cherry-dark and glossy, the sweet smell of beeswax rising off the polished wood. Now the red had seeped from the wood, grey creeping in, the oversaturated green from outside sucking their colour along with the shine.

But the whorls and striations weren't what she concentrated on now. Once, the floor would have been tightly fitted, the gaps between boards clamped airtight. In places they still were, but not here. Darkness slipped between two boards, less than half a pinky wide, but enough.

She leaned closer. Peered through that little gap.

[Scan] switched back to [Sonic Steps], she knocked on the wood.

Pulses radiated out and down, most of it bouncing back off the floor, a slither making it through the tiny gap and—

Beneath the floor, something knocked back.

The jolt—surprise and fear and a weird, stomach-tightening anticipation—ran all the way to her tailbone.

On the map, a cavity appeared. Two metres down, no telling how many across, not from the thin slice she had.

A deep breath, fear and excitement leaving a metallic taste on her tongue.

Mae knocked again, [Sonic Steps] penetrating a little further, adding detail not just to the cavity but the floorboards, the gaps, the braces, the door under the bed. The hinges on its side.

She scooted to the bed on hands and knees, flopped on her belly, cheek pressed to the floor. Knocked again.

There, outlined in white. The trapdoor.

Breath on her cheek, slipping through the floor.

'Maaggiee.' The whisper came from below, soft, cajoling. 'Where is it Maggie?'

Excitement mixed with acid curdling her gut, made her breathing shallow, added an extra kick to her heart. Not even the sharp, snapping tingle down her spine could dampen it. Seventeen centimetres between the bed frame and the floor. Not even enough to squeeze herself, not even with all air taken out of her lungs, let alone open a trapdoor.

Mae scrambled to her knees, hands braced on the frame. She'd have to push it out of the way.

She heaved.

The frame didn't budge.

Focus on the map, zoom in on the bed—three metres by two

point eight, the canopy adding another two in height, the frame made of walnut, the drapes of silk-gauze, weight: one-fifty-six kilos. Too heavy to push by herself.

Felix. She needed Felix.

The synth-cat still sat in the main room, tail wrapped over paws, shadows still twisting through his hardcase, giving him wings.

Hand on the gadgets strapped to her arm, plucking the wand off her bicep by feel alone. Pointing the thin black nano-carbon stick at Felix, the end peeled back, slick black petals folding outward, exposing the brilliant, multi-facetted gem. The scanner's controls one the HUD, [Reset] primed.

The shadows writhed through the silver filigree between the leaves of his hardcase, clinging to the intricate, looping patterns, writhing in the spaces in between. No magic on a sci-fi server, not this deep, this far out. Just energy. She might not know the wavelength or the type, but out in the deep, power was power, and she had a wand for that.

A squeeze.

Power shot through her hand, a thin red bolt leaving the diamond tip, hitting Felix in his beautifully sculpted chest and spreading through the blackened silver. Eating the shadow.

Thirty percent clear.

She bounced on her heels. 'Come on, come on.'

Fifty-eight.

Another bounce, a glance at the bed, at the trapdoor under it. Then at the floor beside it, at the gap between the boards, eyes to a different gap between her feet. Wider, darker. Except for the eye, the bright, bright venomous green eye outlined on her HUD in a gold shimmer.

Breath caught, victory singing through her veins.

She grinned. 'Gotch'a.'

The eye blinked, narrowed, then shadowy fingers were pushing through the thin gap, squeezing then stretching. Hooking around the edges, gripping the space between her boots.

The tingle ripping up her nape.

She stamped on the fingers. Hard. Boards sagged beneath the impact, fibres giving way. For a moment, she thought she'd be fine, that the old rotten wood would hold, and then she was through to her knee. Her thick, knee-high boots protected her calf from the splintered wood, her tough titanium-weave pants her knee.

Still holding the wand, both hands on the floor, the boards a vise around her kneecap, the inky darkness cold on her calf, the eye… The eye…

Lightning sparking off her vertebrae, burnt ozone filling the air.

Wrong wrong wrong.

Fuck fuck fuck.

A glance at Felix.

Eight-two percent. No way was she waiting another twelve for Mr Snarky Pants to help her out.

Mae heaved herself sideways, yanking her leg—

Hands on her ankle, the one lost to the dark.

Cold, cold, cold. Frost ripping through the leather boots, sinking through her skin.

On the HUD, her health falling, status messages boinging.

// Necrotic Grasp. Chill, movement slowed.

Well, hell.

And Felix... Staring straight ahead, the debugger at ninety-eight percent, the shadowy wings flickering.

Ninety-nine.

The hands climbing her calf, tightening around her knee. The chills climbed with them, infecting her torso, her arms, her hands. Fingers becoming ice blocks, elbows freezing.

Ninety-nine.

Ninety-nine.

Fumbling the wand, pointing it with a shaking hand.

Felix moving, Felix looking at her. Relief flooding her system, an additional surge of strength in her arms, heaving herself a little out of the hole.

Felix grinning, mouth open in a cat smile, wings strong and dark, curling forward, curling *around* her: embracing.

'You got it for me, Maggie.'

She was yanked through the floor.

THE CHESHIRE 0.5

CRASH

INTRODUCTION

I wrote *Crash* many years ago, and the story remains one of my favourites. I love writing characters who are broken in some way, and Maja (or Laura, depending upon which incarnation you find her in) is very, *very* broken.

Why do I like broken characters so much? Well, if you've read any of my novels, you'll know just how much I enjoy making things explode, and broken characters are the emotional equivalent of TNT. After all, they're so very *dramatic* and prone to doing the kinds of things that well-adjusted, socially responsible people (a.k.a. me) wouldn't dream of.

 Learn more about the writing of *Crash*. Scan the QR code for the audio commentary, soundtrack and more.

CRASH

The pills are little bullets of liquorice in my palm. I can already taste them on my tongue and feel them glide down my throat. Some part of me, the part that still clings to who I used to be, rages in the back of my head, mixing guilt with the acid already roiling my stomach.

I look into the mirror, cracked and smudged. A broken girl stares back at me and for a moment I waver, feeling her pain, her confusion. Pressure rises in my throat, constricts my chest, makes my eyes gloss.

I squeeze my eyes against the sight, one hand fisted around the pills, the other braced against the cold bulkhead. My lips pull back from my teeth and I push the girl down, back into her cage, slam the door, throw the bolt. When I look up, she's still peering at me, stubborn, fierce despite the damage. My lip curls in an ugly sneer.

The pills slide down my throat.

I win.

'Hey,' Br'ka's voice is muffled by the door he's pounding with his fist. 'Human, get your arse on the flight deck, we got cargo to move.'

'Yeah.' I give myself a hard look in the mirror. 'Yeah, sure.'

The interface is only slightly newer than the shuttle itself. It fizzes and crackles along my neural highways, almost too old, and definitely too slow for the military grade implant at the base of my skull. I ignore it, aided by long practise and the knowledge that soon the pills will buzz through my brain, soothing neurones and slowing synapses just enough to blur the edges.

'Cargo's secure.' Nada slides past me, jostling my shoulder in the cramped confines of the cockpit. 'How's the bucket?' She refers to the shuttle, as rickety as its freighter parent and held together with the same combination of spit and good will.

'About as well as you'd expect,' I say, half my mind on the pre-flight spinning through my cerebral cortex.

'Huh. Well, Jimmy'll be happy if we explode on re-entry.' There was a toothy grin on her face. 'Life insurance.'

The kid, tall enough that his head almost brushes the top of the cockpit and clumsy enough to make him a menace, leans in, a grin on his face and his eyes full of nerves. It's his first trip off the agricultural mecca he calls home, and for the past three days he hasn't shut up.

'Really? Life insurance? How much?'

Nada laughs, a rich, throaty sound. She likes the kid, likes how when he grins it's too big for his face. She's still laughing when a hand full of knuckles and calluses lands on the kid's shoulder. One of his knees buckles under the weight as the mercenary pulls him to one side. I've forgotten his name but his head will turn if you yell 'Merc.'

'Enough to make Jimmy a happy man I expect.' Merc's voice is coarse against my ears. Like the kid, he's new, older though, with grey in his hair and lines deep in his face. 'We good to go, ladies?'

The laughter is still in Nada's voice when she answers, finishing her pre-flight with a flourish. 'Sure, I'm done.'

I wave my hand but say nothing. The pills are kicking in now, the interface's fizz and crackle reduced to a gentle tingle as my synapses slow. At the base of my skull the implant hums. Unaffected by the drug, it wants to flood my brain with numbers—velocity, hull pressure, sensor contacts—and with my brain slowing it feels like I'm swimming in data. My back goes to honey and I must have that smile on my face because the laughter has melted from Nada's own.

I ignore it, ignore her. Even riding the pills, floating on daydreams, I can run rings around Nada.

The shuttle lifts from the deck with a flicker of my eyelid, the bay doors open with a twitch of my nose, the thrusters ignite with a sigh. We glide into space on an exhalation of recycled air and I close my eyes, letting numbers run through my head, grabbing the ones I need, moulding them into place, letting the rest flow past. I imagine myself on a river, green and gold and brilliant blue, the shuttle my boat, my brain the rudder.

A thought and the implant hums, causing the shuttle to pivot, nose first to the planetoid and perfectly aligned for atmospheric entry. Another thought, another twitch, and we're plummeting towards the mesosphere where, shields permitting, we won't explode.

○

'Hey.'

Something hard and heavy lands on my shoulder. Tension rolls through my forehead and I frown, turning my head the other way, trying to reclaim the comfortable darkness.

'Hey, Fly Girl.' The voice reverberates through my skull, a frag grenade sending shrapnel into bone and brain. The last threads of blessed unconsciousness vanish like smoke.

Klaxons are blaring. It's hard to think around the thundering din, with my head feeling like the tail end of a week-long bender and the rest of me like the losing side of a brawl with a bar full of marines. My leg feels like it's aflame but there's no heat on my face and only a large, blurred shape before my eyes.

There is something wrong. Terribly, terribly wrong. But the details slip my grasp.

Hadn't I been flying? I remembered flying.

The iron clasp on my shoulders—hands, I realise, they're hands—gives me a shake, renewing the pounding in my head.

My eyes lock with Merc's. 'What?'

His eyes are grim, sharp, assessing. For several heartbeats they pin me in place. 'We crashed,' he states baldly.

I feel the frown crease my face, my lips form a breathless, 'What?' I see Merc's lips move but his words are lost as I look, really look, around me. What had once been a functioning shuttle is now a mass of exposed circuitry, crumbled bulkheads and sparks. Past Merc's shoulder the viewport is a crazed mess of white lines and jagged edges, in some places the plexiglass has shattered completely, spewing glittering chunks across the deck.

Nada is slumped in her seat, face lax, eyes open, her face scorched black and red. One hand is still on the charred flight console, the other hangs by her side, limp. I twist my gaze back, just enough to see the tumble of supply crates and the kid, his torso crushed between them and the deck. The blood on his lips is mixed with spittle and air, his eyes are wide, his expression tightened in lines of fear.

I wonder how long it took him to die.

A sound escapes Merc. He unbuckles my harness with quick, sure movements and slides his hands under my arms. He pauses a second, his mouth tight, and then heaves.

The pain is incredible. Razor sharp yet strangely sweet as it consumes my shin, radiating in sharp spikes through my ankle and into my toes. There is a scream somewhere inside my throat, but the pain has swamped my brain and I've forgotten how to breathe, so it remains there, trapped for lack of air.

My vision is white, my body tense against the onslaught. Vaguely, I am aware of my arms in a death grip around Merc's neck, his breath on my ear as he drags me from the cockpit. A few steps and he stops, releases one arm from my waist and prises my right from around his neck. Colour is returning to my vision and

I can make out the tumbled shapes of crates and barrels. Merc grunts and swings me against his right side, my good leg touching the deck. He shuffles forward a step. I'm still too dazed by pain to follow.

'Come on, Fly Girl.' He gives me a jiggle. 'We don't have no business around here anymore.'

This time, when he drags me forward, I find enough sense to move my feet. Pain makes me gasp.

'Yeah, I know.' There is a rough kind of sympathy in his voice. 'Broken legs are a bitch.' He heaves us forward another step. 'But you gotta walk. I ain't carrying your carcass up that hill.'

Hill? My mind shrivels at the thought.

We make it out of the shuttle and into the cool, sharp air of the planetoid.

The world is grey with the beginnings of dawn, the ground is rough with loose stone and low, twisted scrub. The breeze is frigid against my skin. Goosebumps crinkle my flesh and I shiver. Merc doesn't say a word but pulls me closer. Some of his warmth seeps through my flight suit.

Progress over the uneven, rising ground is slow and each step agonising. It occurs to me to wonder why we're climbing, though gradually it ceases to matter as my focus whittles down to the next step. My entire being is consumed with the task of hopping forward on my good leg and steeling myself to drag the broken one after it, every bump and jostle sending slivers of glass up my spine. Half my weight is draped across Merc's shoulders and he murmurs a rough brand of encouragement, reminding me of better days as he drags me to whatever destination he has in mind.

It is an age before we stop. Merc releases his grip and I sink to the ground, overcome by a rush of endorphins better than any pill I've popped yet. There is a battered cylinder slung across Merc's back and as he swings it to the ground, I wonder how I missed the luridly marked beacon during the long trek.

I watch as he stands the cylinder on its flat end, making sure it's stable before sinking down next to me.

'All right, Fly Girl,' he says, his face florid from the effort of lugging me and the beacon, 'now we wait for Br'ka to come rescue his precious cargo and hope he thinks to pick us up as well.'

○

It's sixteen hours before a shuttle makes a pass over our position. Later, Merc tells me that it hovered above us for a few seconds before moving off and setting down near the crash site. I take his word for it, having succumbed to fever and the effects of concussion by the time. He goes on to tell me that, after an hour, the shuttle lifted off again, heading into the upper atmosphere. He said he began making plans for long-term survival then, just in case Br'ka decided to leave our sorry arses there.

It wouldn't have surprised me if he had. Br'ka makes no bones about his priorities, and mercenaries and pilots are easier to come by than the sort of cargo he's shifting, but a few hours later the shuttle returns.

On the freighter, I spend a day in med-bay and the short, stick-like boy who passes for a doctor gives me a few jabs with a hypoderm and waves a wand over my head. Apparently, the concussion is fixed but the leg will take a week. He clamps a bulky med-unit around my calf and hands me some battered crutches.

On my way to my bunk, I pass Nada's husband. The corridor is tight and Jimmy has to squeeze past me. We're close enough to kiss but he won't look me in the eye. His own are red and his cheeks are puffy from tears. I think about saying something, anything, but the words don't make it out of my throat.

I hobble the rest of the way to crew quarters. They're deserted. The clear, unmarked packet is hidden in the corner fold of my bedsheet. Manoeuvring into the cramped bathroom on crutches is difficult but I manage.

Over the sink my reflection is waiting for me. Hollow eyes,

hollow cheeks, scraggly hair.

The broken girl stays in her cage; we both know her presence is superfluous. I'm as fucked-up as I ever was, except now… now I've killed a few people.

I chase the little bullets with a handful of water.

CRASH

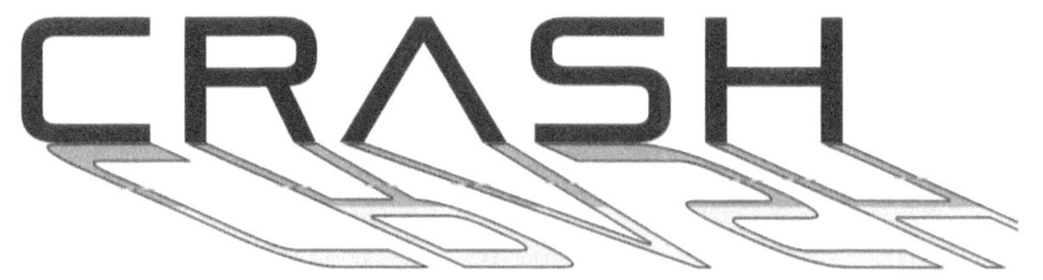

INTRODUCTION

Two short stories with the same name! How about that.

Although written many years apart, these two follow one after the other.

I pretty much cut my teeth writing Maja Kaur, or Laura as she used to be known, in what amounted to Star Trek fan fiction, which I wasn't actually a fan of until I started writing it. In fact, I remember going down to the local video store and renting an armful of *Star Trek: Next Generation* tapes (when tapes were a thing) for "research" purposes.

And hey, I learned a lot, like what a turbo lift was and that the Federation was just a little too nice for my liking. That's how Maja was born. The last thing anyone is going to accuse Maja of is being "nice."

Learn more about the writing of *Crash (The Cheshire 1)*. Scan the QR code for the audio commentary, soundtrack and more.

CRASH

Maja's bones were cold and her mouth was full of that dry-shit metallic taste that always came after a high. It coated her tongue in a thick mucousy carpet, gumming up her tastebuds and crawling up her nose, until she was breathing out a cloud of need. Her skin was going to start crawling next, going to shrivel and dance, doing the jig until it boogied right off her body and slinked around the dirt and rock at her feet. Something, anything to get away from the desperation gripping her insides, twisting her stomach in knots, making her heart thump and jerk in her chest.

Worse than all that, though, was the buzz in her head, the dispassionate whirl of her greyware. The input at the base of her skull humming against bone was going to drive her crazy, endlessly seeking new data to feed the fine network of military-grade processors and neural connections linking her grey matter. The magic of Imperial technology royally fucked by a little black pill.

She shivered, hugged her arms tight to her chest and tried to remember if she still had her nose or if the cold had taken it along with the heat in her bones.

Did it matter? She just had to get through this, and then it was back to the shuttle crouched behind her, the hatch open, the cargo containers stacked in the hood sucking up what little light made it through the planetoid's dull, reddish atmosphere and dust. Then she could get out of the grit and howl of the wind, get away from the pervasive cold and Merc's bird-sharp eyes, and sink into the rattle of the old ship's flight system. After that... After that she could slink back to her bunk, slide her hand into the space between bulkhead and mattress, and get back to the sweet oblivion of the pills stashed there.

Her last memory of the Kid exploded in her mind's eye, his face-splitting grin gone, bloody air bubbles instead of endless damned questions spilling out of his mouth, skinny chest crushed by a cargo crate.

She gritted her teeth and breathed, hard, her breath frosting the air under her nose. She'd promised herself. The Kid was dead and she'd promised, promised that that would be the last time she piloted while she was high, the last accident she'd cause. But the skin on the back of her neck shivered and clenched and her bones ached.

Christ, she needed a fix.

She'd just finish this, do whatever the hell it was Jonko thought needed to be done on this damn arid rock instead of the *Bakr's* cargo bay, the get back to the ship and her stash and then—

'Hey, flygirl.' A hand, hard and calloused, cupped her chin.

Maja's eyes snapped open.

Merc frowned at her, hard black gaze narrowed against the wind blowing its sea of grit, crow-dark hair salted with age and the lines in his dark-gold face carved by more than just time. 'Get it together,' he said, voice as rough as the rock under her boots. 'We're on.'

The hand fell away from her chin and she followed his gaze to the two figures walking toward them out of the orange dust haze, but her attention was drawn to the shuttle behind.

The ever-present haze obscured markings, but the distinct upward curve of the tail and sweep of the wings marked it as one of the early models from the outer systems; a nuggety cargo hauler designed to run unpatrolled shipping lanes. Long range. Cruise speed, FTL two point three. Two forward guns, one rear.

Slow on the turn. Handled like a brick. A quick duck and roll, get in its blind spot. Aim just forward of the engine, three degrees to starboard. The sweet spot. Hold a beat, wait for the right moment—

'There's far enough.' Merc's voice cut through her thoughts like it cut through the wind, a sledgehammer knocking her back into the now.

The two figures stopped five metres away. One old, one young, both male and far enough away they wouldn't be throwing any punches, but close enough that she and Merc'd see it if they decided to reach for the guns strapped to their sides. Not that she'd be any use if they did, with her skin starting to crawl and her hands to shake. She didn't even have a weapon of her own; Merc'd swiped her ancient pulse gun while she'd still been jacked into the flight chair, peeling her brain out of the shuttle's systems. The most she'd be able to contribute to a firefight was a sloppy dive behind the cargo ramp.

If she didn't stumble over her own feet first.

'Those the goods?' The young one, dark and rail thin, spoke. He looked like he spent a lot of time on his hair and jacked into the nets, if the contact ports flashing on the underside of his wrists were anything to go by. He pointed at the containers in their shuttle's belly.

The containers Jonko had insisted she help Merc deliver. Like a broken-down pilot could do a better job protecting the cargo than the three heavies the woman kept on payroll.

'Those are the goods,' Merc said. 'You got the credit?'

'Cargo's already been paid for,' Young and Dark said.

Merc went still. 'That's not what I was told.'

The older one, face hard and wrinkled, spoke now. 'That's because you're part of the cargo.'

What? The thought ran through Maja's mind even as she saw the young one go for the weapon at his side. She had enough time to wonder where he'd gotten his hands on something that looked like it came out of the Imperial armoury—long and sleek, the barrel forming around his hand before it even cleared the holster—but she didn't move. Her bones were too cold, her brain too slow, thoughts too tangled.

Merc tackled her to the ground and behind the ramp. He didn't tell her to stay, didn't press the big blunt grip of her old pulser back into her hand. Instead, he disappeared around the other side of the shuttle, leaving her sitting in the dirt, alone and unarmed.

Her heart pounded. Her breath came short, and adrenalin pushed back the cold and the shakes. She drew her feet up under her until she was jammed into the crevice where ramp met rock, and shuffled over enough to peek around the edge.

Young and Dark fired. Missed.

She ducked back before he improved his aim. Closed her eyes. Listened for the crunch of his footfalls on the cold, rocky dirt. There they were. One footstep. Two. Getting closer.

She swallowed, balled her hand and wondered if she would still be fast enough, strong enough, to lay him out before he shot her. A not-so-tiny voice in the back of her head said, probably not.

Gods above, she needed a fix.

There was a thump and then the distinct bark of a kinetic weapon followed by another, louder thump.

She risked another peek around the corner.

Young and Dark was face-down in the dirt, his partner the same not too far behind him. Red stained their backs, darkened the already-red ground underneath them.

Merc crouched over Young and Dark, rifled through the man's pockets. He found something, slipped it into his own pocket, and looked up. Something passed through his gaze when it met hers. Maja thought it might have been relief, but it was gone too fast. 'Can you fly that?' He gestured over his shoulder to the shuttle.

She didn't even have to look at it. 'Yeah.'

He nodded, rose. 'Good. Let's get out of here before Jonko figures out we're not dead.'

Maja threw up, heaving nothing but the memory of bile, and rested her head on the wall of the cubicle that passed for the runabout's toilet.

'Finished?'

She moved her head just enough to meet Merc's hard black gaze. He was crouched next to the toilet door, elbows on knees, looking tidy if not exactly reputable in his dark shirt and trousers. She turned back to the toilet.

'You're finished.' He grabbed her arm and dragged her with him when he rose.

Stand or be dragged. Lovely. Her knees wobbled and her stomach clenched but she stood, and then toppled into Merc when he yanked her around to face the sink and the small but shiny mirror above it.

Gods she looked awful. Sunken cheeks, sallow skin, lank hair.

Before the Kid had died, she'd stopped seeing her own reflection. Not like some sort of crazed blood-sucking creature out of myth, it had still been there in the mirror or bounced back at her in a window. Perhaps it would have been better if it had disappeared altogether, at least then others would have known her for the monster she was, would have known to stay away.

Instead, she'd let herself stop noticing. It had been easier not to notice, to let her gaze slide past the brown, lank mess of her hair, the way her eyes always looked bruised, her expression slack. If she didn't notice, she didn't have to care, have to feel, have to remember.

Until the Kid died.

She noticed then. Noticed it in everything shiny enough to hold a reflection. Control panels, doors, beer. No matter how much she drank, the noticing wouldn't go away, and the caring came back and then the nightmares. Not all the way, but enough for the old her, the person she'd been before Maja Kuar, to raise her voice and make her promise. No more drugs.

Now, even though her hands shook and her skin crawled, trading the sweet white oblivion of a high for the cold in her bones and the loathing in her heart was sweeter still.

Merc shoved a cloth into her face.

Maja shoved it away.

He held the cloth up in front of her. 'You going to do it?'

She eyed him, the lines in his dark skin that spoke to experience and age, the hard line of his jaw, the set of his brows. She took the cloth.

It was cold and damp and just rough enough that she could feel it sloughing away the sweat and dirt. She wiped her neck as well and then let the cloth slide out of her hands.

Merc caught it before it hit the sink. He held it back up and gestured to her coveralls. 'The rest too.'

She frowned and might have crossed her arms if she hadn't needed a grip on the sink to steady her legs.

He stepped back and threw her the cloth.

She had to use both hands to catch it. Only the toilet's small confines and a frantic shuffling of feet kept her upright. When she was steady again, Merc closed the door, shutting her in the cubicle.

She sat on the edge of the toilet and looked down at herself. The coveralls, with their zip up the front, had fit her once, now they were loose around the middle and baggy about the shoulders. They were dirty too, the dark blue material coated in a fine film of red dust and a splash of vomit. There was vomit on her boots as well, probably from that first frantic rush to the toilet.

Maja rested her head in her hands and closed her eyes. Gods, she was tired.

The door rattled.

'No sleeping,' Merc said. 'You're not out in five, I'm coming in.'

Bastard.

She frowned, sighed, and slowly reached down to pull off her boots. The coverall came next, there was a tank and shorts beneath, but they didn't hide the jut of her collarbones or her too-skinny legs. She wasn't quite a skeleton, not yet, but she could count her ribs and her arms hadn't been this gawky since she was twelve.

Maja got to work with the cloth, and by the time she was finished it was a dull red-ish brown. She left it atop the crumpled pile of coveralls and boots.

Merc was standing in front of an open storage compartment when she came out. He cast her a glance, frowned as he ran it down her body, and threw her a new set of coveralls. 'They'll be too big until you fill out some,' he said.

Until she filled out some. Right. He sound like her— Her heart jolted in her chest and she squeezed her eyes shut. No, don't think of him.

'Where're your boots?' Merc's voice snapped her head up.

She stared for a few seconds and then gestured back toward the cubicle.

'Clean 'em. We've got people to meet.'

❑

Orana's had a view, a dark swathe of vacuum framed in rock and the wide lip of the viewport. Beacons threw shadows with every slow blink, highlighting the crags and razor-sharp edges of the asteroid's surface in red, yellow and the occasional blue. It would have been hypnotic if Maja's eyes weren't dry enough to crack, her stomach raw, and if the drink in the server's hand had looked a lot more like beer and tasted a lot less like water.

It didn't help that her skin was tight and her insides jittery, or that she couldn't help her mind wandering back to the bunk and the small stash of pills she was never going to see again. Gods, she needed a fix.

The fact that Merc'd hemmed her into the booth, almost squashing her into the high-backed little corner before she'd realised what he was doing, just added insult to injury. If her legs hadn't been quite so shaky and the drink in her hand hadn't trembled quite so much, she'd have pushed back, but as it was...

As it was, she was tired and sore and knowing her old captain had tried to... Tried to what? Kill her? Sell her? For what and why? For revenge? Old Jonko had been fond of the Kid, had almost doted on him, like some crusty old spacefaring aunt with shady stories and shadier friends. When he'd died... Maja remembered how the gun had trembled, just a little, when Jonko pointed it at her head. And the old woman's eyes had been hard and hot and mean.

Maja had had anger like that, hatred like that, aimed at her before. Just once. She hadn't been Maja then and it had been worse, so, so much worse than looking down the barrel of Jonko's pulse gun.

Merc had stopped Jonko from pressing the trigger. Maybe that was why the old woman had tried to do him in as well.

Maybe.

Next to her, Merc slumped in the booth, one arm draped across the back, the other on the table, his fingers tapping against the drink near his hand while his eyes scanned the bar.

Merc stopped tapping his fingers.

Maja looked up, followed his gaze. A body modder picked their way between the empty tables, small and slim, the sharp points of curved ears rising above their head, skin not just dark but black with the faint fuzz that said fur, and a tail behind. They slid into the booth and smiled—or maybe that was a baring of pointed teeth—and settled their hands one atop the other on the table. 'Hello,' they said.

'You're late, Faus'tian,' Merc said.

The modder, Faus'tian, didn't stop smiling but their ears dipped, just a little, and something very much like annoyance ran over their features. 'Perhaps,' they said. 'But you brought a guest.' They turned their gaze, bright gold in their dark face, on Maja.

Maja stared back and tried not to think about the nausea building in the back of her throat, or how bad she wanted a fix.

'She doesn't look so good.' Faus'tian took a deep breath, nose wrinkling. 'Or smell so good. Not like your usual, Kerril.'

Kerril? Maja looked at Merc. He didn't look like a Kerril. She wondered what his 'usual' looked liked, and what sort of chats he had with Faus'tian often enough for the modder to know what that was.

Merc's frown deepened and his fingers resumed their tapping. 'I need information.'

'Yes, you usually do.' The smile dropped from Faus'tian's face. 'What is it this time?'

Merc slid a screen across the table. The faces of the two men who'd ambushed them less than thirteen hours ago hovered above the thin sheet of biogel. 'You know them?'

Faus'tian righted the screen with the tip of a claw dark as their fur. 'Mmm, perhaps.' They cocked their head to the side and flicked an ear. 'Why do you want to know?'

'They tried to kill us,' Maja spoke, her voice thick.

'Hmm.' Faus'tian's eyes flicked to Maja, going up and down like they could see the half of her hidden beneath the table. 'I do not think so.'

Maja frowned and opened her mouth to speak, but Merc got there first. 'Why?' he said.

'They are looking for bodies, living ones. You.' They pointed a claw at Merc. 'You they might kill, too much work to take alive, but her?' Faus'tian gestured to Maja and shrugged. 'Thin, sickly. Easy prey.'

'Bodies?' Merc's arm came off the back of the booth and he rested both elbows on the table. 'What for?'

Faus'tian shrugged. 'I do not know and I have not asked, nor do I care to. These men.' They tapped the screen. 'They are the type intelligent folk stay away from. Did you kill them?'

Merc leaned back. 'Maybe. Who do they work for?'

'I do not know.'

'There's a lot you don't know.'

Faus'tian shrugged again, a supple wave of bone and muscle. 'A wise male knows his limitations.'

'And the wise female?' Maja asked,

Faus'tian cocked his head, one side of his mouth lifting in a half-smile. 'I would not profess to know.' He leaned forward. 'I like you,' he said. 'Even though you smell bad.' The modder turned to Merc. 'If you want to know who employed these men, talk to Ack'tha Ox. She has a shop on the second tier, near the docks, and a finger in every less-than-legal pie in the system.'

Merc stood. 'Thanks.'

Faus'tian purred. 'Do not thank me yet. Or,' he held up one finger, 'if you insist, why not leave your fragrant companion with me? When you come back, she will smell much nicer and if you do not come back...' He shrugged and turned to Maja, both hands palm-up. 'Well, we can discuss things then, and you will still smell much nicer.'

Before Maja could do more than feel her eyes widen and her brows move toward her hairline, Merc had a large-knuckled hand wrapped around her bicep and was hauling her to her feet. 'We're good, Faus'tian.'

The modder's smile was rueful, but there was something dark in his gaze when it met Maja's. 'I tried,' was all he said.

She frowned at him. 'Why?'

The smile slipped from Faus'tian's face and his ears flattened. 'You will see.'

Merc gave her arm a tug. 'Come on,' he said. 'We've got a woman to see.'

❑

By the time they found their way to the second tier, the itch was eating Maja alive, crawling over her stomach, her back, down her throat. It was a relief when Merc propped her in a corner and she no longer had to command her knees to hold her up.

Only Merc's hand around her throat stopped her from sliding down the wall. She didn't feel the hypostick he pressed against her neck, all she heard was a soft *huuush* before the itch abated, spreading out from her neck to her fingers and toes.

The relief was almost as good as a fix.

Merc's thumb under her chin forced her gaze up until it met his. His eyes searched hers.

She blinked at him, frowned and pulled back.

He nodded, satisfaction peeking through the grim set of his jaw.

Maja frowned a little harder, raising her hand to her neck. 'What was that?'

'Something for the craving.' He stashed the stick inside his jacket.

She watched it go, her eyes glued to the small cylinder and the tiny bulge it made in the fabric. 'How did you know?'

'About the itch?' Grimness swallowed the satisfaction in his eyes. 'It's not hard.' For a moment it looked like he would say more, like he *wanted* to say more. But then his jaw turned to granite and whatever it was, he swallowed.

The second tier near the docks was dark. Too late for carousing and too early for the work shift, the concourse was deserted, the shops closed tight. Merc turned his back to the wall and crossed his arms, gaze steady on one shop in particular, a little darker and shabbier than the rest.

He looked comfortable, like he'd staked out dark little places before. Maja wondered how long he could stand there, waiting for Ack'tha Ox to open her shop, and just how hard he would squeeze to find out why their old employer had tried to kill them.

Silence stretched, and without the itch to consume her thoughts, old ones swam to the surface. 'You don't look like a Kerril.'

'It's my name.'

'Doesn't mean it fits. I like Merc better.'

'Merc?' He looked at her. 'Because I'm a mercenary? Not very original.'

Maja shrugged. 'I'm a zoner, and you're not a mercenary.'

Merc didn't jump, but she felt the jolt that went through his muscles nonetheless. 'What?'

'You heard.'

He went back to watching the shop. 'What makes you think I'm not?'

She looked at him. 'You're staking out a deserted shop trying to figure out why your last employer tried to kill you.'

'She intended worse for you.'

'She had a reason.'

Silence. They didn't need to say his name. The Kid lingered, the memory of him choking on his own blood engraved on the back of her eyelids.

'It was a rough job,' Merc said.

'I was high.'

'Yeah,' he said. 'You were.' He turned his gaze back to the darkened shop. Silence stretched again.

A round little redhead slinked down the concourse and into the shadows that surrounded the shop.

'Looks like our woman. Stay here.' Merc strode across the concourse.

Still hidden in the shadows of their little corner, Maja watched him disappear inside the shop.

Movement caught her eye. She turned. A man in a grey-green uniform, an official-looking patch on his sleeve and a pulse gun at his side, ambled down the concourse. A security officer. His gaze met hers.

Her breath stalled. She turned away, wishing she could blend back into the shadows, instead trying to make her shoulders relax and herself look inconspicuous, but her shoulders felt like steelcrete and there was a fine tremor in her hands. Out the corner of her eye, she saw the officer pause and braced herself when he started toward her.

She'd done nothing wrong, there was no reason for the officer to arrest her, but Maja's eyes still scanned the concourse, looking for an escape route.

That was when Maja saw her.

Jonko.

The old woman strode down the concourse, her lined, dusky face pressed into a scowl, her hard-soled boots click-clicking on the floor, salt-and-pepper hair tied back, the end bouncing with each step. With a bear-shouldered heavy at her back and the unmistakable bulge of a gun under her coat, Maja had no doubt Jonko had come expecting trouble.

And she was headed straight for the shop.

Maja looked behind her. The officer was looking at her, a frown starting to crinkle his brow. He was still a few strides away, she could get away before Jonko saw her, take the shuttle and be anywhere but there in a day, an hour, a minute. She leant her head against the wall and gritted her teeth, thought of Merc, of the way he'd dispatched the two goons back on Turak. He could take care of himself and gods above, she thought, her last memory of the Kid flashing through her mind, she'd done worse than leave a man she barely knew in the lurch.

It was a pity the thought didn't stop the roil of her stomach.

Maja's hands clenched, her breath came short, and with a last look at the security officer, she pushed off the wall and strode toward the shop.

One stride, two, three. She thought she heard something—an indrawn breath, a curse, the clatter of Jonko's hard-soled boots coming to a dead stop—whatever it was, Maja looked up, her eyes catching Jonko's. The old woman's eyes, a startling emerald green in her dusky face, widened a split second before her mouth clenched and she reached for the gun.

Maja ran. Heard Jonko shout. Eight long strides and she was across the concourse—heart pounding, breath rasping in then out—her palm slamming into the doorplate. There was time enough to glance over her shoulder, to see Jonko and the heavy pounding toward her, to hear the security officer yell, before the door whooshed open.

She was inside, fumbling for the lock before her eyes had time to adjust to the dark. When they did, and the door had locked behind her, her breath stopped in her throat.

The shop was a mess. Wares littered the floor, boxes and bottles and things that her eyes couldn't identify, some smashed, most not. And standing in the middle of it all, blood tricking from a split lip, his hands fisted at his sides, was Merc, his gaze fixed on the redhead pointing a gun at his chest.

'Captain Jonko, right on time,' the woman, Ack'tha, said, without taking her eyes from Merc.

Merc's eyes flicked to Maja's. Grim determination had narrowed his gaze, but when it met hers, an ugly smile stretched his lips. 'That's not Jonko,' he said.

For a heartbeat, Ack'tha was still. Then she moved, head swivelling first, gun following.

For Maja, there was time enough to see the beginnings of a bruise over Ack'tha's eye, to identify the gun—an MTF7-80, standard ImpMit issue—to see Merc move, too slow and too late to tackle Ack'tha in time.

❑

Ack'tha's gun loomed large.

Maja's heart stopped, her eyes went wide, and for one split second there was nothing in the galaxy but that gun, slowly moving to point at her heart.

Something clicked in her brain then. She moved, the motions flowing through her muscles without thought. Step out, slide in. Grip. Twist. Ack'tha's fingers spasmed, the gun falling from her grip. Maja was still moving, rolling her back into the woman's body, lifting her elbow up, slamming it into Ack'tha's face. There was a crack and a cry, but Maja kept moving. Stoop, spin.

The hard contours of the gun's handle felt familiar in Maja's hand. She rose, the weapon trained on Ack'tha even as the woman stumbled backward, hands cupped over a broken nose.

Merc appeared at her side, his split lip and swelling eye mute testament either to a lucky shot on Ack'tha's part or the woman's brawling skills. From the shattered bottles and scattered bric-a-brac cluttering the tiny shop's floor, Maja suspected the latter.

Even backed up against a bench, her hands over her nose and a gun pointed at her face, Ack'tha still held Maja's gaze with a steely one of her own. 'Nice move, girly. Seems to me you're not as washed up as Jonko thought.'

Merc grabbed Maja's shoulder. 'You were going to stay outside,' he said.

She was, until she'd seen their old employer walking down the concourse. 'Jonko's here.' Maja's voice shook and she hated it. She breathed deep.

Merc paused. Looked at her. 'You're sure?'

She adjusted her grip on the phaser and nodded.

Merc swore.

She thought of the bear-shouldered heavy that'd been at Jonko's back, and distaste coated the back of her tongue. 'She's got Smithon with her,' she added, the shake not so bad now.

Merc swore harder, then his jaw turned to stone and he stalked toward Ack'tha, blood now dripping from between the fingers still cupped over her nose. 'The goods Jonko was delivering in the Turak system. Who was the buyer?'

'You mean, who was she selling *you* to?' Even through the blood trailing over her upper lip, Ack'tha smiled, and for a moment Maja thought the woman wasn't going to answer. 'Nuary Iral. Not that that will do you much good,' she said, still smiling.

'Why?' Maja said.

"Cause it's not his real name, sugar plum.' Ack'tha tilted her head back and took her hand away from her nose. 'And because your old captain's going to be breaking down that door any second now. She was right pissed you know, when she asked me to broker that deal, and not over the terms. What'd you do? Scratch her ship?'

Merc moved, hand clamping around Ack'tha's throat, pushing her face into the bench. 'Does it matter?'

Ack'tha croaked and managed an awkward shrug. 'Suppose not,' she said, her voice strangled.

A thump made Maja's stomach jump. Another thump and the muffled sound of someone demanding they open the door added a spike of fear to the mess in her belly.

Merc shoved his face in close to Ack'tha's. 'Tell me how to contact Nuary Iral.'

Ack'tha laughed. 'Hang around another minute. I'm sure me and Jonko can arrange for you to have a real up-close-and-personal.'

The door screeched, making Maja's heart kick. She glanced back at it, and her heart kicked again at the thin line of air between it and the frame. Jonko was already forcing her way in.

'Merc,' Maja said, a quiver in her voice. A quiver. She hated the quiver more than the shakiness, hated the queasy mire of fear out of which it rose. That wasn't her, or maybe it was, maybe it had been her all along and that was why—

Maja took a breath, in through the nose, out through the mouth—*steady*, she told herself, *steady*—and swung the gun from Ack'tha toward the gap in the door. Gods, she needed a fix.

Merc growled, and a shard of darkness appeared in his grip and pressed into the pale gold of Ack'tha's throat. More of the woman's blood beaded against the matt-black blade. 'I don't have time for games.'

Ack'tha coughed, the whites of her eyes showing but her teeth still clenched in a snarl. 'No, you don't, so get going before you and your stung-out slag end up in body bags.'

'Don't worry.' Merc jerked the woman to her feet, taking his knife away from her throat only long enough to swing her in front of him so they were both facing the door. 'I'll make sure Jonko hits you first. Give me the contact.'

'Ain't nothing to give.'

The door screeched again, the gap widening. Maja's hand flexed around the weapon's grip. Then, through the gap, Maja caught a glimpse of the patch on a security officer's uniform.

Ack'tha laughed, her eyes on Maja. 'You going to shoot up colony security, sugar plum?'

Maja's stomach roiled, uncertainty joining the mess of fear. She took a breath. 'Merc.' The quiver was still in her voice. She took another breath. 'We need to go.'

'Yeah? Where?' Merc's face was grim. 'There's no back door.'

No back... Maja took a closer look around the shop, beyond the mess left by Merc and Ack'tha's brawl. It was barely even a shop, just a poorly lit room without so much as a window let alone a back door. Her gaze locked with Ack'tha's and the hate and glee in the woman's eyes confirmed Merc's words.

There was only one thing to do.

She was at the door in two easy strides, her back plastered to the wall beside the gap, her thumb gliding over the ImpMit-issue gun's controls. The soft vibration as she switched it to stun was as familiar to her as the way her lungs expanded on the single deep breath she took before she hit the door lock.

The security officer was down before the door finished whooshing open. Smithon went next, the heavy's gun barely level with her chest before he crumpled. Out the corner of her eye she saw Jonko, closer to the door.

Maja popped out of the doorway, aiming for centre mass. The shot went wide. Jonko fired back, even as she slid into a recessed doorway farther up the concourse.

There was movement beyond Jonko as more security officers ran down the concourse toward them.

A thump from behind drew her attention back into the shop. Ack'tha lay on the floor at Merc's feet, eyes closed, blood crusting around her nose. She didn't look dead but—

She didn't see Merc at her side until he jerked her sideways. The flash and the scorch mark where her head had been was all she needed to know about Jonko's aim.

Merc snatched the gun from her hand, firing as he popped his head out the door. Gold bursts joined the red ones from Jonko's weapon. The security officers were getting closer.

'We have to make a run for it,' Maja said.

Merc's face was beyond grim, his mouth a single flat line, his jaw tight, his eyes dark. For a second, he didn't say anything, just looked at her while more streaks of red and gold scorched the doorframe.

He nodded, grabbed her arm and then they were out the door, dashing across the concourse while gun shots burned around them.

◻

Colony security was waiting for them at the shuttle.

After three hours of slipping through forgotten corridors, avoiding patrols and surveillance cams, Maja's skin was crawling and her brain has been consumed by the itch. Which was why she ran into Merc's arm, thrust outwards, before she stumbled onto the main concourse. Her breath left her lungs with a sharp 'oof'.

That one arm pinned her against the wall of the service corridor while Merc craned his neck around the corner. When he turned back, his face was harder than usual although not as hard as when he'd had that knife against Ack'tha's throat.

Maja was glad of the arm, or as glad as she could be with the itch shrivelling her skin, her insides aching and that metallic dry-shit taste entrenched in her tastebuds. Whatever little miracle Merc had given her earlier was long gone, and the need had slammed right back in its place.

Gods, she needed a fix. A small one would do it, just a taste to warm her bones and steady her hands. Just one.

She leant her head against the wall. Flicked her eyes to Merc—tendons in his neck strained as he peered around the corner—then to the tiny bump over his chest where he'd stashed his little miracle.

Maja licked her lips. That was what she needed. Just a taste...

Merc swore, hand hard on her forearm as he trotted back the way they'd come. 'Come on.'

She stumbled, her feet heavy. He caught her before she face-planted, and her hand found the small bump in his chest pocket. She licked her lips again, fingers curling over the vial like she could dig through the material. Maja breathed deep. 'I need that,' she said.

Merc gripped her biceps, hauled her upright and tried to keep walking. 'No, you don't.'

Maja didn't move. 'Yeah, I do.'

Merc was in her face, hauling her heels off the floor before she could blink. 'No.' His face was a snarl, and he shook her with each word. 'You. Don't.'

They were the same height, but with her heels off the floor she was looking down at him, just a little, and his eyes were hard and hot and so very, very angry. Her heart stuttered and her breath stopped. For a second, Merc's face morphed into another—older, leaner, with the same brown eyes as hers—and panic bloomed in her chest.

She swung at him, or tried to. With Merc holding her upper arms tight against her ribs, all she managed was a weak uppercut, but her knee found better purchase.

Merc dropped her.

Panic still making her heart pound, Maja stumbled backward, eyes on Merc, now doubled over and cupping his groin. Her feet caught up on themselves and she fell, landing on her arse in the junction where the service corridor met the main concourse.

For several long moments, all she heard was the blood in her ears and all she saw was that other face, the one in her nightmares, laid over Merc's. Maybe that was why she missed the first shout.

Movement, caught in the corner of her gaze, made her turn. An officer in a green-grey uniform with a security patch on their shoulder, ran toward her, and behind them... Maja scrambled to get her feet under her. Behind the officer came Smithon—Jonko's bear-shouldered heavy—and the snarl on his face was enough to make Maja's gut shrivel.

Maja was on her feet, heart pounding louder than before. She tore her gaze from Smithon, found Merc's. His eyes weren't angry anymore, although his mouth was a single hard line and his brows made another, darker one on his forehead. Instead, there was something else in them, something that looked like fear.

He was a step toward her, his hand outstretched.

She took a step toward him; didn't feel the shot that felled her.

□

A million dagger-footed ants crawled over her skin, and Maja groaned as she woke, rolling onto her side and curling around the nest that bloomed over her ribs. Whoever shot her hadn't been kind. Or maybe it was just the itch. Maybe it was both, the aftereffects of the stun ricocheting off the need for another hit until her fingertips stung and her toes buzzed and all the parts in between screamed and writhed and crawled.

She groaned again, reaching for the edge of the hard cot as her stomach heaved.

Someone, somewhere, clapped.

Spitting out the last bit of bile, her eyes watering, Maja looked up.

She recognised the broad glowing lip of a cell before she caught the tell-tale shimmer of the force field. If her skin hadn't been crawling, she probably could have recognised where she was from the smell alone. No matter how they sanitised them or how they didn't, jails always smelled the same, like sweat and stale air and, in her case, vomit.

Smithon grinned at her from the other side of the force field, a tall, broad-shouldered shadow, the right side of his face pulled tight by an old scar. 'Nice going, Kuar. Didn't think you had any more of that left in you.'

Maja's stomach twisted but not with the urge to heave, and her heart beat a little faster in her throat. Arms shaking, she pushed herself into a sitting position, eyes never leaving Smithon's. 'What are you doing here?'

Smithon's grin widened, the old scar pulling the right side of his mouth askew and filling his baby blues with inhuman glee. He did something on his side of the force field and the barrier vanished with a purple-white zap.

Maja's stomach twisted a little harder.

'What I always do, Kuar,' Smithon said.

A bucket clattered across the floor, skidding in the vomit.

He followed the bucket in and leaned against the wall. 'I'm making sure you don't choke on your own spew, at least until Jonko gets her hands on you. You can clean up that though.' He jerked his chin toward the mess on the floor. 'I got standards.'

Maja didn't move, save to wipe the last bit of spit and bile from her face with the arm of her coveralls. Her heart pounded, but she breathed—once, twice—and her voice stayed steady. 'Where's Jonko?'

'She's coming. Frankly, I thought you'd be more concerned about old Kerril.' Smithon shoved off the wall and took the three strides to the cell's hard cot. He sat, so close his thigh brushed hers.

Maja tensed, dragging herself as far away from him as possible. If she could have trusted her legs, she'd have stood and made a move for the still de-activated force field. But her feet were full of pins and needles and she doubted she'd do more than fall on her face, and that would just give Smithon an excuse to touch her.

She eyed Smithon's hands, curled loosely on his knees with palms big enough to cover her face and short, pudgy fingers she'd seen carve into a still-squealing vole with the dexterity of an artist.

Smithon whistled. 'That old merc can move.' He leaned in against her side until his breath filled her face. 'He wasn't going to leave you behind you know, at least not until I shot him. Not full on, just a glancer, right here.' He jabbed Maja's shoulder with a finger she felt all the way to the bone. 'Probably should've had my girl set to kill, but I made him drop his weapon, probably made his whole arm numb for a good hour too.'

'Besides.' Smithon bumped her shoulder with his beefy one. She tried to lean away, but he had her wedged against the wall. 'The captain wants you alive.'

Carefully, her eyes as much on the open cell as they were on Smithon's hands, she uncurled her legs from the cot. 'Killing me'd be easier,' she said. She struggled to keep her voice steady but it wobbled all the same.

'But not as profitable, and between you and me, the captain's got a few debts. Besides,' Smithon pushed his face in close to hers, 'she wants to see you squeal.' He grinned.

Maja's heart stopped.

He laughed and slapped her leg, his hand wrapping around her thigh like a vise. 'But don't you worry, I'll be there to make sure you don't choke.' His hand squeezed. 'At least for the first little bit.'

Fear spiked in her belly, traveling all the way up her spine and jamming itself into her brain. She would have liked to say that it was skill and cunning that did the rest, but it wasn't. Panic triggered the response and adrenalin drove her muscles. It was only long-forgotten training that guided her hand, pulling back her fingers before her palm slammed into Smithon's nose.

There was a crack. A bright spurt of blood.

Maja was off the cot, stumbling over the bucket and slipping in the vomit before Smithon howled. She felt more than saw his hand reach for her. The bucket handle was in her grip as she stumbled back to her feet, Smithon's fingers brushing against her back. She planted her feet. Swung.

The bucket made a hollow thud when it hit Smithon's face. He fell, collapsing sideways on the cot, and didn't move.

Maja paused a second, breathing hard, eyes wide and heart beating madly. He was still breathing, his chest rose and fell, but that was all. She dropped the bucket and had her hands up under Smithon's coat before it hit the ground.

Smithon had once boasted that he never went anywhere unarmed, not even the shower. She hoped it was true as she ran her hands over his chest and behind his back. A gun, a knife, a freaking wrench, she'd take anything if she could just find it.

She had to get out of here before Jonko came back, before Smithon came to.

The small pistol was tucked into his boot. Maja fumbled it out, the pins and needles in her hands almost gone but lingering just long enough to make her fingers feel like wood.

There was only one other cell in the small jail, and it was empty and the doorway that connected it to the security office open. Unease disrupted the acidic boil of fear and panic long enough to stop her rushing headlong through the door. This wasn't right. Her gut screamed it at her.

Maja breathed deep and forced herself to think. Smithon being careless enough not to reactivate the force field she could believe, but this...? Her spine crawled and she swung around, the tiny pistol clutched in both hands, but Smithon still lay on the cot, only his chest moving.

She turned back to the open door and slowly, weapon held before her, moved forward. By the time she peeked around the doorframe, her heart was pounding. The security office was empty. There was a console in front of her. She'd have to go around it to get to the door on the other side.

Maja crept forward, back still crawling and her palms beginning to sweat. Unease had a firm grip on her spine, rippling up and down her vertebrae, making her breath come fast and her head dizzy.

She was around the console, her eyes locked on the door. She could see movement beyond it, a crowd of some kind. Just another metre, that's all she needed.

A weight slammed into the middle of her back.

□

Maja fell, pistol skittering from her grasp, chin hitting the floor hard enough she saw stars.

Hands, big hard hands strong enough it felt like they would crush her ribs, flipped her over.

Smithon snarled down at her.

She swung at him.

He punched her in the face.

More stars. For a moment, a minute, or maybe it was an hour, there was nothing. Her head was hollow, her ears numb and it seemed she had an eternity to marvel at the pricks of light clouding her vision. Then there was the smell of blood, and pain shooting from her nose, lining her eye-socket in fire and her cheekbone in more of the same.

Smithon blocked out her vision, lips pulled back over his teeth, blood still running from his own nose and the gash in his hairline, the old scar on his face puckered and mean. He slammed her into the floor. 'It wasn't nice, Kuar, hitting me with that bucket, or in the nose.' He slammed her into the floor again. 'You're meant to be nice.'

There were spots in her vision, great splotches spreading across her eyes, saturating the world with light and colour. She breathed, choked on blood and tried again. 'Says who?' she spat out.

He shoved his face right in Maja's, and the blood dripping down his face dripped onto hers. 'Says me.'

Maja didn't just bite Smithon's nose, she wrapped her teeth around the already broken flesh and tore.

Smithon howled. Reared back,

A chunk came off in her mouth. There was barely enough time to spit it out before Smithon's hands were around her neck, squeezing.

She clawed at his hands, at his face, fingertips slipping in blood, feet thrashing at the floor as her lungs began to burn.

Smithon squeezed tighter.

Maja's vision blackened, her lungs going from burning to screaming.

Smithon grinned.

A bright burst of light.

Smithon's face went slack, his fingers loosened. He toppled sideways.

Maja breathed, air filling her lungs in a ragged gasp.

Her eyes lighted on Jonko, standing where Smithon had been.

The old woman glared.

Maja flipped over onto her belly and scrambled for the stolen pistol.

A red bolt hit the floor a micron from Maja's fingertips. 'Get up.' Jonko's voice was hard and flat.

Maja didn't move.

'Now.'

Slowly, Maja got up. Her head swam when she straightened and a fresh flow of blood trickled from her nose.

'Turn around.'

Just as slowly as she had stood, Maja turned, a whisper of fear curling around her spine.

Jonko's gaze was as hard as her voice, her steel-grey brows drawn tight, her mouth a single flat line. The gun in her hand didn't waver. 'I should have killed you after that last run.'

The last run, the one that killed the Kid. Once again, her last memory of him flashed before her, lying on his back, blue eyes wide, his chest flattened by a cargo container.

Maja's voice was thick, her nose blocked by blood and broken bone. 'Why didn't you?'

The old woman's mouth twisted. 'Wish I knew. Conscience perhaps, or Kerril's smooth bloody tongue? Take your pick.' She looked over Maja's shoulder. 'Restrain her,' she said.

Maja jumped when hands yanked her wrists behind her body. She tried to turn, but all she caught was a glimpse of a grey-green uniform and black hair before the handcuffs clicked into place and she was shoved forward.

'After our little firefight this morning, it wasn't difficult to persuade colony security to lend me a few hands.' The muzzle of Jonko's gun pressed into Maja's collarbone. The old woman stepped in close and the look in her eyes chased a shiver down Maja's spine. 'This particular officer is going to escort us to the docks. While we're walking there, I want you to try something, anything to escape, because then I'm going to stun you, drag you back here and let Smithon finish choking the life out of you.'

Maja leaned back as Jonko leaned closer, leaned farther back until she was pressed up against the officer behind. There was something in the captain's eyes, a rabid gleam that chilled Maja's blood more than her words.

She swallowed. 'I thought you'd made a deal with Nuary Iral.'

Jonko snarled. 'Screw Iral. I regretted that deal as soon as I made it. Watching you die is worth ten times the amount he's wiping off my debt.'

'So why not break it?' Even as she spoke the words, a little voice in the back of Maja's head said, don't.

'Because I'm a woman of my word. Something you,' Jonko pressed the disruptor harder against Maja's chest, 'wouldn't know squat about. But if you make trouble...' Jonko laughed, an ugly sound that twisted Maja's stomach. 'Well, then that's just fine.'

'Captain Jonko.' The security officer behind Maja spoke. 'If we do not go now, we will be late to meet Mr Iral. He does not like to wait.'

The officer's voice was familiar, and Maja frowned and tried to twist around for a better look, but a hand on the back of her neck kept her facing forward.

Jonko sneered at the officer and then at Maja. 'The perky little hairball's right. Iral never did have any patience, always wanted what he wanted then and there. It always made me wonder how he made it to the top of the heap.' She looked over Maja's shoulder and jerked her head toward the door, speaking to the officer. 'You know the way. Since Smithon's down, looks like I'm taking the rear.'

'Of course.' With his hand still on the back of Maja's neck, the officer spun her around and shoved her toward the door.

Maja was pushed through the main security office where the eyes of the people within widened at the sight of the blood crusting around her nose, before their gaze fell on the officer behind her and they looked away. It was the same on the winding hallways, the lift that emptied as soon as it opened, and the crowd of passengers who saw them. The concourse that lead to the docking ring was worse, with more people to stare and point and whisper. Some even jeered as Maja was marched past.

Through the mess of adrenalin and the cold chill of fear, humiliation churned in her stomach. She jerked at the security officer's grip.

He tightened his grip on her neck, and the sharp tips of what could only be claws made her stumble to a halt. He grunted and pushed her forward again. 'Do not tempt the captain to shoot, *karrumbra*, it would be most inconvenient.'

The voice, the claws, the hair. Even as she let him push her forward, an image formed in Maja's mind, of a small black modder weaving his way through a bar. Faus'tian?

◻

Where was Merc? Faus'tian was at Maja's back, playing at being a security officer as he marched her toward the docking ring, while Jonko followed two steps behind.

Where were they going, and what was waiting for them there? An ambush? Why hadn't the modder shot Jonko already? They could escape into the crowded concourse.

They turned, and the crowd was gone. Instead, they faced a docking bay, a small beige semi-circle carved out of the main thoroughfare, with two large viewports bracketing an airlock. Outside the airlock, Maja made out the flat triangular hull and stubby thrusters of an old ImpMit scout, while inside a man waited for them.

Tall enough to stare Maja in the eye, with the round cheeks and soft belly of someone who spent his off time eating, the man sent a shiver down Maja's spine. Nuary Iral's gaze wasn't cold, it was dead and buried and his eyes, running down her body made her wish she was on the other side of the airlock.

Maja tried to step back but Faus'tian, small though he may have been, was a solid wall behind her, his grip tightening on her neck, the tips of his claws pricking the skin. She wasn't going anywhere.

If he noticed her discomfort, Iral gave no indication. Instead, he looked right through her to the dark-haired woman bringing up the rear. 'Captain Jonko, I paid you for two.'

Maja didn't have to see her ex-captain's face to picture the scowl twisting the old woman's brow. 'Can we discuss this inside, Iral? The docks have ears.'

The man didn't so much as frown. 'The ears know better than to listen. Where's the other one?'

Silence. Maja pictured the lines on Jonko's forehead deepening with her scowl. 'There were problems—'

'I paid for two.' Iral turned on his heel. 'Come back when you have the other one.'

Faus'tian's grip tightened on her neck, his body vibrating against hers. She didn't need to hear him say it. This wasn't how the plan was meant to go. But why, what better chance than this did he and Merc have of pulling her arse out of the fire? Unless—

She didn't get a chance to finish the thought.

There was a growl, a human one, and then the shhh-zap of a disruptor.

A weight against Maja's back pushed her forward. Even as she stumbled, her heart stopped. Faus'tian's grip on her neck loosened, and the modder slid down her body. When she turned, he was a small black lump at her feet.

Not working for Jonko then.

Jonko tucked her weapon back into her belt. 'There,' the old woman said. 'Now you have two. Can we get this done?'

'Hmm.' Iral's belly spilled over the top of his trousers when he knelt at the modder's side. He turned Faus'tian over, his hands—strong, long-fingered, with the hardened calluses of a fighter covering the first two knuckles—turning the modder's chin from side to side. 'He will do,' Iral said as he rose.

'Do for what?' The words popped out of Maja's mouth. She shuddered, and fought the urge to take another step back when Iral turned his gaze on her.

The man blinked and then he smiled, the expression barely grazing his eyes. 'You will see, Ms Kuar.' He gestured to Faus'tian. 'Carry him aboard.'

Maybe, if she could just get her hands free... Maja pulled at the cuffs restraining her hands, her heart beating hard. 'I can't.'

Without changing his expression, Iral kneeled back at Faus'tian's side and riffled through the modder's pockets. When he rose again, he held a key and twirled his finger for Maja to turn around.

She did, her heart thudding in her throat. She took a breath—in through the nose, out through the mouth—and fought to keep her hands from curling into fists. She'd have to be quick. As soon as the cuffs loosened, she'd move.

'Iral.' Jonko growled the man's name, the captain's weapon back in her hands. 'Don't be an idiot, half the blood she's wearing isn't hers.'

'Only half?' Iral's voice was expressionless.

There was a tug on Maja's wrists as Iral inserted the key. The muscles along her spine tightened. A click. Her heart skipped a beat. A beep. The cuffs loosened. Maja started to spin—

Iral's foot drove into the side of her knee.

Maja felt something tear, and then pain exploded through the joint. She collapsed, taking the impact on her forearms and barely saving herself from diving nose-first into the floor. Her breath left her in a rush, emptying her lungs of air for even so much as a moan, and for a moment pain left her blind. Her lungs expanded, the air whistling back in, but before she could force it past her vocal cords, a hard brown boot found her ribs and flipped her over.

Iral stared down at her, his round-cheeked face as hard and dead as his eyes, the cuffs held loosely in one hand. Slowly, calmly, he lifted one large boot-clad foot and ground it into Maja's injured knee.

She gasped, her vision turning white.

The pressure let up, and when she could see again, Iral was still staring down at her. 'Do we have an understanding, Ms Kuar, or shall I pop the other ligament?'

Maja blinked, gaping like a fish, and nodded.

'Good.' He nodded toward Faus'tian, still out cold. 'Carry the modder.'

Carry Faus'tian? Maja blanched. Standing was going to be painful enough. 'My knee...' she said.

'You have two.' Iral dismissed her and turned to Jonko. 'You can go.'

Gun held loosely by her side, the old woman smiled, black eyes crinkling at the corners, her teeth flashing white against dark lips. 'Oh no, I want to see this.'

Maja bared her teeth at the woman, but Jonko only chuckled.

She crawled to Faus'tian, her knee throbbing in time with her heartbeat, and gathered the modder in her arms. Taking a deep breath, her eyes closed and teeth gritted, she pushed herself to her feet. Pain turned her vision red and brought bile to the back of her throat, but she stood.

With Jonko still grinning, Maja followed Iral through the

airlock and into the dark-red confines of the starship. She shambled along in his wake. Faus'tian was boneless in her arms, his weight dragging at her shoulders and adding its own special agony to that already shredding her knee.

Maja barely made it through the docking tube before she collapsed. She slid down the first bulkhead she could put her back to, Faus'tian still in her arms and sweat beading her brow.

Fighting the desperate urge to throw up, Maja barely heard Jonko's angry 'You!', or caught the bright flash of a gun before the captain's body landed at her feet.

◻

Jonko's gaze caught Maja, the old woman's eyes wide and dark. Fathomless. The burgundy interior and dim lighting of the ship's small lounge cast the captain's skin in a sickly shade of red.

She wasn't breathing.

'I trust you are duly satisfied with my end of our bargain, Mr Kerril.' Nuary Iral spoke from somewhere above her.

'Well enough.' Merc's voice, deep and gravely, jerked Maja's gaze upwards. He caught it, frowned at her and then at Faus'tian lying unconscious across her lap. 'Although I would have preferred my partner to remain conscious.'

'And I would have preferred Captain Jonko alive. It is hard to reclaim debts from the dead.' Iral bent, grabbing one of Jonko's ankles. 'If you will wait while I remove the captain and retrieve the item, we can conclude our business.'

Merc nodded.

'Excellent.' Iral strode out of the ship's small lounge, Jonko's corpse dragged in his wake.

Maja watched, her breath coming fast, until the last strand of Jonko's salt and pepper hair disappeared down the corridor. 'Why'd you kill her?'

Merc knelt, his face grim and his shoulders tight until his fingers found the pulse in Faus'tian's neck. 'She'd have kept coming after us. It was for the best.'

'I—' She didn't know what to say to that, her mind was blank, a vacuum where the memory of Jonko's dead gaze sat side-by-side with the Kid's blood-stained lips. Only the Kid's death was her doing, but they both sat in her chest, hard lumps that burned at her insides.

Maja shook her head, chasing the images into the dark corners of her mind where they would be food for nightmares. There were other things to worry about, like the bargain between Merc and the man she'd thought they were running from. 'What's going on?'

Merc's eyes snapped to hers, and she could see the tension claim him, before he gripped her chin in one large-knuckled hand. His gaze catalogued her broken nose, the livid bruises around her throat, and her right knee, swollen and useless. 'How much of this blood is yours?'

Maja jerked her chin out of his grip. 'Enough,' she said. 'Why are you with Iral? I thought he wanted us for body parts.'

'He wants other things more.'

'Like what?'

Merc was silent, his hands turning to fists on his knees. 'A field test.'

Something cold slithered through Maja's gut. 'What's he testing?'

Merc just looked at her, his brows drawn tight, his mouth hard. His gaze slid from hers and he shook his head. 'You were right, earlier today, when you said I wasn't a mercenary.' His eyes, dark and sad, found Maja's. 'The organisation Iral works for is developing a drug, something the government will never approve. It's why Iral's buying people; to use them as test subjects.'

Maja felt the blood drain from her face.

'I made a deal with Iral.' Merc grabbed her chin again, and this time Maja didn't pull away. 'He's going to let you go, but before he does... He has investors and they want a demonstration using someone outside of the lab.' He released her chin. 'I'm sorry.'

I'm sorry. The words turned Maja's insides to ice, and if Faus'tian's prone form hadn't been holding her down, she would have scrambled to her feet. Instead, she sat with her back against the bulkhead and tried to breathe around the pounding of her heart. 'Why...' she began. 'Why are you sorry?' But she knew. She knew.

He got to his feet, turning away as the door whooshed open and Iral returned, a hypostick in his hand.

Maja looked at it, looked at Merc, heart beating harder.

'Your end of the bargain, if you please.' Iral held the stick out.

Merc stared at it, jaw tightening until Maja thought it might shatter.

A frown passed across Iral's brow. 'Sooner rather than latter would be preferable, Mr Kerril.'

Merc took the stick from Iral's hand. Carefully, he bent and lifted Faus'tian from Maja's lap, propping the modder in his own corner of the cabin before returning to Maja's side.

Without Faus'tian's weight holding her down, she shifted her good leg under her and tried to stand. 'Merc, what's—'

His hand on her shoulder slowly but surely forced her arse back to the floor. 'Sorry, flygirl. This was the best I could do.'

Knots twisted Maja's stomach, and her eyes were wide on the hypostick Merc lifted toward her neck. She grabbed his wrist in one hand, but the stick kept coming. 'What's in that?'

His lips pressed tight.

'Merc?'

The 'spray touched her neck and there was a cool burst of air against her skin.

Merc sat back on his heels, his eyes tight on hers.

Maja stared back, heart pounding as she waited for... for what? She didn't feel any different. Her knee still throbbed, her throat burned and her nose was a dull ache three times too big for her face. Had Merc swapped the hypostick?

A shadow loomed over Merc's shoulder, and Maja lifted her gaze to meet Iral's. His face was impassive, but there was a gleam in his eye, a spark of curiosity mixed with anticipation. 'The nanites will take a few moments to adjust to her system, once they have, the hallucinations will begin.'

Her heart slammed hard against her chest. 'Nanites?' She looked at Merc. 'Hallucinations? What did you give me?'

'You'll be okay,' he said.

'Unlikely.' Above them both, Iral's mouth contorted into a thin smile. 'Even if you survive the injection, the effects of the drug are long-lasting and… unpredictable.'

Iral's lips twisted, and twisted some more until his mouth was a pale swirl in the midst of a face slowly turning orange. Maja blinked as she slid sideways. That wasn't right. His face should be purple.

Her shoulder hit the deck with a planet-shattering boom and her head sank through the steel plating.

Iral's knee grew another joint as he knelt in front of her. 'I look forward to watching your progress, Ms Kuar. We shall be in touch.'

BROTHER

INTRODUCTION

There is a farm of plot bunnies in my head, and they breed as rabbits do, with wild wilful abandon. It doesn't take much to get them going, but the little idiots are never quite as happy as when I'm stuck on a story. Seriously, it's a universal constant that if whatever project I'm currently working on is tying me in knots, the bunnies produce more bunnies.

Often, those bunnies have close familial ties to the work-in-progress.

Such is the case with *Brother*.

Brother is a companion story to The Echo trilogy, and came about because someone, somewhere was talking about telling a story from a side character's perspective and that made me think… how did the main character's twin sister go from regular girl to… Well, you'll see.

 Learn more about the writing of *Brother*. Scan the QR code for the audio commentary, soundtrack and more.

BROTHER

She is aware. Of her fingers, her toes, her skin. Of the blood running through her veins, of the air in her lungs, but more than that, she is aware of *self*, of the difference between that which is *her* and that which is Sister.

It is strange to be alone in her skull, to no longer have Sister threaded through every part of her, for her thoughts to be her own. Almost as strange as the smaller lungs, the pounding of her heart, the chitter of the little creature on her shoulder, of its claws in her flesh. Sharp little pinpricks almost lost amidst the rush of sensation.

The world is dark without Sister, without her sensors – the ping of radiation against her hull, the pull of gravity wells, the endless scurrying of drones through her corridors. It's cold without all of that. Lonely.

Quiet.

So very quiet.

It makes the pulse loud. The sound of a thousand heartbeats.

The pulse pounds in time with her heart. Or maybe it's her heart in time with the pulse rushing through her veins, the rhythm throbbing in her ears, whispering of glory and righteousness, of a purpose that goes right to the heart of her. To her core; the thing that makes her *her*, the human girl who once had a name.

What was her name?

Grea. It shivers through the darkness, and she is not sure if the voice is hers or if it was born of the dark. With the name come other things, other memories, other sensations.

The critter on her shoulder—the darkness gives it a name, *xin*—the softness of its fur, the hum of its voice. The xin is just one sensation; there's the shift and squeeze of her armour, alive and yet not, and beyond that... Beyond that is something bigger, something that feels like her, but isn't, with four arms and ankles that bend backwards. Alien and yet a copy, a twin—

No.

She has a twin, but he is gone; left her half of herself, and now this... This alien copy is in his place, too big and too *other* to fill the hole in her core.

'Huntress.' That voice, the cherry red of it, is hers. Wholly her.

The rest though, the arms, the legs, the fusion of the engine at her heart... that is the other, is Huntress. It turns and twists, and as Sister retreats, leaves her in her own skin, wrapped in armour, Huntress makes the hole in her middle—the empty space where *he* should be—all the emptier. An endless aching ocean between stars, cold and dark as the void.

She screams, and Huntress screams with her.

It is not right, not *him*. She rips it from her psyche, wishing her thoughts were her hands, but the xin is gluing them to her sides, holding her immobile so that all she can do is claw at Huntress's hooks in her mind, dig her fingers into the cold not-flesh of it and tear. Tear. Tear.

The pain fuels her wails, hacks into her middle until it feels like she is peeling the dermis from her bones, splitting herself not just into two but into threes and fours and sixteens. Over and over and over—

New hands grip hers, slide under mental fingers, turn Huntress's not-flesh to stone, denying her the pain to appease the void in her core.

Little Sister. Sister is there, swallowing her again, creeping through her veins, not filling the empty space, but hiding it. Gentle fingers turning her attention from the emptiness to the vast silver web that is Sister.

Sister's consciousness is an intricate network of subroutines, a shifting, sparkling labyrinth bound up in metal-stone and nanites. Her heart burns with the same fire that's at Huntress's only bigger, big enough to propel her between solar systems; her bones are girders, her skin kisses the vacuum of space. Smaller lights flicker on the edges of Sister's mind, dim sparks of other consciousnesses that remind her of another place, another ship, another home where *he* once lived.

You are home with me, Little Sister.

No. She wants to yell, to scream it with voice and mind, but Sister holds her silent, a mental hand over her mouth, binding her in place.

The labyrinth is shifting again. One by one the subroutines in the network pause in their tasks, the individual sparks collapsing into each other until Sister is no longer a web, but a supernova focused on her. The weight of her attention burns, the intensity more than a human mind should be able bear, and yet she does, not just bear it but exalt in it, feel it wash away the emptiness, the memory of *him*, of being half of what she was, what she was meant to be. Sister fills her, incinerates what was and reminds her of what is.

There is purpose in the blaze, filling her from the inside out. A righteousness that sets her alight.

She is reminded.

She is home.

She breathes, and Huntress breathes with her, around her. Not with lungs, but with engines; cycling gases, managing heat, feeding the star that is its heart. That is *their* heart. She and Huntress are one; a hulking mechanicoid with a fleshy human at its heart.

They are part of the rhythm, the hum of Sister.

Huntress breathes, she breathes and the Brothers—other humans wrapped in their mechanicoid selves—breathe with them; separate entities, the dim sparks on the edges of Sister's consciousness connected by silvery threads.

She cannot see the Brothers, but she feels them, their minds dull, as if they are half-asleep, but full of Sister, her drive, her purpose.

The same purpose that fills her. Hard and angry, filled with the memory of despair, a millennium of pain and loneliness.

Light spreads through the darkness as Grea's HUD activates. She blinks away tears and for the first time in a long time, sees with her physical eyes; a virtual constellation filled with the bright sphere of a sun, the darker orbs of planets and the speckled cloud of an asteroid field. And there, highlighted in red, are ships. Not the same kind of ships as Sister, not even the half-remembered shell of the place she once called home.

These are *Their* ships; poor, dumb things made by the Creators to replace the might of Sister and those like her.

Fury. It rises from without, from Sister; a tide of hate and betrayal nursed and hardened over centuries.

She flexes, and her/Huntress's hands curl into fists, fingers the length of a human digging into their palm.

I am ready, she says.

Good, Sister whispers back.

There is no warning, no countdown, only the *CLUNK CLUNK CLUNK* of locks releasing, and then they are plummeting through the darkness of a launch tunnel.

The virtual constellation is replaced by a rush of numbers and graphs, HUD displaying velocity and time. Before she can breathe again, the tunnel is gone and Huntress's thrusters are spinning them about, massive feet pointed at Sister's hull before their engines kick them in the back, propelling them through a void lit with weapons fire.

The constellation on the HUD is no longer a hologram, the red highlights of Creator ships no longer dots on her screen but a tight cluster of ovoids. The planet hangs heavy below them, a green and blue sphere against which the angry red of Creator ships buzz and dart. A dozen smaller vessels clustered around a large sleek ovoid.

The smaller vessels twist and turn around the largest, desperately trying to shield it from the hail of Sister's fire, but the Behemoth is all she sees. The sharp grey lines; the lights running down its sides, the angry pulse of its cannons.

The Behemoth is a poor imitation of Sister. She notes that as she hurtles towards it, Huntress's thrusters burning behind her, the Brothers spreading out like wings on either side of her.

Around her, the body that is hers but not, screams. The miniature sun at Huntress's heart blazes. Numbers and trajectories fill her vision, Huntress ticking in the back of her mind, an implacable presence, calm, solid, the thrusters on their back hot points of fire propelling them toward the target.

Three kilometres and the Behemoth's cannons are flashing past her ears. Twist. Turn. Roll. Huntress moves before the light hits the back of Grea's retinas.

The Brothers twist and turn in their own patterns, evading the enemy's fire, but always on target for the opening near the Behemoth's stern.

Two kilometres. Twist. Turn.

More than just the pulse of cannons now, the smaller vessels are screaming toward them, grey ovoid shapes with sharper noses and stubby wings, engines burning away behind, thrusters on bow and stern. Huntress is cataloguing them, data rolling through the back of Grea's consciousness. Two life-signs per craft. Atmosphere-cable. Manoeuvrable, maybe more so than Huntress herself.

Warnings flash before Grea's eyes and new outlines highlight the gun ports on the vessels' bellies and wingtips. Power surges under their hulls, and Huntress whispers of target locks.

Behind them, Sister responds.

One moment Huntress is the tip of the arrow, the next the Brothers are a cocoon, a single unit shielding her from the coming rush.

Grea feels them on the periphery of consciousness, an extension of Sister. Twist. Turn. Jerk. A shot grazing the belly, a Brother injured but still moving.

Five hundred metres.

The Behemoth is huge, drones swarming around it firing at them even as the small vessels fire at their backs. The suns at the Brothers' hearts blaze and a hail of fury lances from their upper set of arms, laying waste to the swarm between them and their target.

Three hundred metres.

The Brothers separating, peeling out of her path, forming a new shield at her back.

More pain. Not hers.

She ignores it as Huntress somersaults, giant legs facing the Behemoth's hull, the outline of blast doors blazing red in her sight. Thrusters fire, slowing her descent even as the sun at her core blazes, power shifting from the propulsion at her back, morphing into a new fire that runs down her sides, lighting up her arms. The armour over her lower set of arms shifts, blades springing from her forearms even as the hot pulse of magma shoots through her veins, lighting the metal-stone, the cutting edges no longer gleaming silver but molten fury. She hits the hull and plunges the blades down.

They bite into the ship's skin, sinking into it.

Thirty centimetres.

She strains as Huntress strains, pushing the blades deeper.

Fifty.

Actuators are screaming, Huntress's paw-feet have grown talons, ripping into the Behemoth's hull, seeking greater purchase, and still they strain.

Fifty-three.

Silver is flowing over the Behemoth's hull in brilliant strands, the Behemoth's immune system responding to the threat. Huntress tracks the steady flow of nanites, counting down the nano-seconds until they're in range.

Fifty-six centimetres.

Eighteen seconds.

Not enough time.

A shift, rerouting power from the magma lighting up the blades to the thrusters on their back. The blades are dulled from their retina-searing glow even as the force at their back pushes them into the hull.

Fifty-nine centimetres.

Eight seconds.

They're through, blades punching all the way up to their knuckles, and now they are twisting, drawing the blades in a large circle. Twisting. Twisting. The Behemoth's hull melting even as its nanites swarm the area, filling in Huntress's hard-won slices, rushing over her hands. And now it's Huntress burning, pain searing through *her* veins.

Just another second.

And another.

Enough.

First arms plunging downwards, hands grasping even as the blades retract, her second hands joining the first, all four limbs straining, thrusters reversing.

The piece of hull tears loose and she somersaults into the void, the enemy still crawling over her limbs, finding gaps in Huntress's armour. Thrusters stabilising her tumble, the magma that had coated her blades now filming arms and legs, turning the enemy nanites to carbon.

Half of the Brothers at her back twist, fire gathering at the end of their arm cannons a split-second before they loose their fury.

The light of four stars hits the breach in the Behemoth's hull.

Blast shields implode inwards and a rush of atmosphere and bodies explode out; pale furred limbs flailing, squished noses and too-big eyes terrified behind the film of their face shields. And then there's the blue-white shimmer of emergency shielding, and she's blowing through it, the Brothers following in her wake.

Huntress is shifting, massive legs extended, the smooth lines of its first arms shifting, plates moving, parting, skin and bone transforming, muscles and veins rearranging themselves as cannons form over its wrists. They are through the shield, the Behemoth's internal gravity pulling at their feet, dragging them toward the deck. The sun powering the thrusters shifts, the fire finding new tributaries in her arms, a new outlet in the ports over her wrists.

Core temperature approaching critical, too much power used to cut through Behemoth's hull, even more to scorch the enemy from her bones. Huntress's core hits the red. Warnings flash as power conduits melt and her chest glows yellow-red, shedding heat.

She fires. Once. Twice. Huntress's core hitting critical, the blaze of it a white-hot blanket suffusing her bones as she clears a path for the Brothers as they land beside her. Their cannons take over.

Fire spits at them. Small bits of light splashing against Huntress, scorching its armour.

A Creator stands in the midst of the shuttle bay, its legs braced, a heavy weapon held in its four arms. Its lips are moving and there is sound, a strange song in her comms, but she doesn't understand the words, they are a string of notes that have no place in her brain. But the twist of its lips, the exposed teeth—broad and blunt, canines too-sharp and too long for a human mouth—that she knows even without the black-red of its emotions staining the mental plane.

Hate.

She knows hate, knows it well.

It makes the next bit easy, the leap, a touch of the thrusters to propel them across the deck, and then stretching Huntress's legs, extending its talons.

She cannot *feel* the Creator crunch under their feet but she imagines it; the crack of its bones set a match to her bloodlust, sends it rushing through her veins.

The rest of the Creators run, race behind the sleek ovoid shapes of shuttles, crouch behind sleds full of cargo. Some run for the blast doors at the rear of the hangar, one even makes it through before the door *SNAPS* shut. Their screeches bounce against her ears and she reads the fear in the sticky yellow staining the surrounding air. Emotions only she can see. The gift of the empath.

For a second, a moment between heartbeats, that emotion stabs, draws blood; reminds her of a time when desperation rode her bones and loss was her only companion.

A time when *he* still lived in her soul.

Fire smashes her in the face.

The fire is theirs, spits from the weapons in their hands.

The Creators are tall, flat-nosed creatures, the flesh above their dark grey uniforms covered in thick white down, shaggier over their crowns, sparse over their hands. It should honour them that Huntress is made in their image, that they will be destroyed by the very thing they created. Instead, those that do not scramble behind crates and shuttles, the ones that do not make it through the giant blast doors, stare at them with horror.

The Brothers are around her, the heavy *thunk* of their paw-feet felt more than heard, and when their fire has finished sweeping the bay only carbon and brittle bones are left.

Their objective lies in the Behemoth's heart, where the spaces are too small for Huntress.

There is a wrenching sensation as Huntress peels away from her psyche and then she is released.

The external body peeling back, the threads of her other loosening around her legs, her shoulders, the ones around her chest the last to leave, lowering her eight metres to the alien deck and then retreating with a gentle caress to leave her standing alone.

And she is Grea again, or as much as she can be with her human fleshiness encased in alien armour, given paws instead of feet, ankles that bend backwards, hands that turn to claws. Her armour—red as blood, red as the purpose that fuels her heart—has made her in the Creators' image, same as the mech standing guard at her back, although with her natural two arms instead of four.

The Brothers being disgorged from their other mechanicoid selves are the same, although their armour is the colour of shadows on shadows, forms moving over their chests, their fingers ending not in claws but long spikes. Each one the same as the next, indistinguishable except for the barely perceptible shimmer of their minds, ghosts wrapped up in the silver threads of Sister.

The Brothers have no names, no faces. They are a homogenous whole with Sister threaded through their minds.

They had names once, their thoughts once shone and sparkled in her mind's eye. The knowledge rises from the depths of herself, from the place where *he* lived.

But no. No. They are Brothers and she is Little Sister, is an instrument of the divine.

She has purpose, and it draws her eyes to the blast doors separating her from the rest of the ship.

As one, the mechs raise their first arms, light gathering at the ends of their cannons, and fire.

The doors are obliterated.

Atmosphere explodes, trying to push her into space. She strains, talons digging deep into the decking, leaning into the tornado.

It is over in a moment. An emergency shield glimmers where the blast doors were. Beyond it, Creators gather, soldiers in battlesuits, the dull metal drinking in the red of the emergency lights, the angry ends of their guns aimed at her, at her Brothers.

Forward. She pushes the thought at the Brothers, senses their acknowledgement as a pulse inside her skull.

Creators shoot, weapons fire fuzzing through the emergency shield, rushing through the vacuum. Splashes against her chest. It is lightning racing through her blood, seizing her muscles, seeking out her heart. Crippling.

Inside she screams, even as she marches forward, the xin on her shoulder coming to life, taking over for her nervous systems as pain paralyses it. But no pain is wasted.

She embraces it, grabs it with mental hands, and throws it back. A wave of blackness, of fear and agony rushing through the mental plane. Unseen. Inescapable.

The enemy hits the floor. They have no time to scream.

The Brothers are across the hangar, through the shield. The enemy is dead, impaled on the blades that spring from the Brothers arms, ripped apart by talons, killed before they can draw breath.

She comes last, the lodestone to the Brothers filaments. They fall in around her, arms and hands dripping too-red blood onto the deck.

Their objective is deep in the Behemoth's heart, three decks and countless soldiers above them.

She starts forward.

Yellow blazes across her vision, alien symbols sweeping over her HUD in sharp, static lines and whorls. In the back of her brain, Huntress sounds an alarm, but she already knows what's happening, that Behemoth's AI is trying to penetrate her armour's systems.

Powerful, it seizes hold of her joints, locking them in place.

The xin comes to attention, its tiny claws digging into her flesh, drawing extra power from the heat in her body.

She does not know what the little creature does, but the symbols are wiped from her vision and she can move again. The xin though is still, tension radiating through its claws. It is more nanite than flesh and not part of her the way Huntress is, but she knows it is fighting the AI, keeping the enemy from retaking control of her armour.

Inside, the Behemoth is as huge as it is out; corridors wider and taller than Sister's, the walls moving with light and shadow, nanites twisting and turning in new configurations, making new symbols.

She may not understand the Creators' speech but she can read these.

"DANGER."

"INTRUSION."

"EMERGENCY."

'Contact.' The voice is familiar and strange, jars in her memory. Brings to mind images of a boy she once knew before Sister. From a time when *he* shared her soul, filled the part of her that remains hollow, aches from the emptiness—

The *phftz stik* of weapons fire. Pain like fire piercing her neck. Warnings screaming on her HUD. A Brother pushing her aside, another standing at her back.

Silly. Stupid. Sentimental, to be distracted by things that no longer have meaning.

Those are the words that run through her brain even as blades spring from her arms and she leaps.

Blood. Teeth. Death.

She is not kind, she is not sentimental. She is an instrument of the Sister. She is vengeance and retribution. She is the blade that takes the Creator's head, the whirlwind that sprays guts across the clean white deck, that colours the bulkheads with the rich red of their blood. That makes them scream.

The wound on her neck is nothing. She gathers the pain with mental hands, uses it as a vessel for the hate and fear that rises from the depths of her being, from the place where the other once lived and is now gone.

Twist and turn, leap and slash. She takes the pain, the fear and loneliness rising from that place where *he* was, gathers it in her mental hands. Shapes it.

More Creators are gathering in a matte-grey line beyond the skirmish, their armour drinking in the light, guns raised, the ends bright with death.

She lets the mental bomb loose.

If they could see it, could witness the wave of emotion like she does, they would run before the tsunami, would turn and sprint as fast and as far as their bent-back legs could take them.

It is half a heartbeat, but she has time to appreciate the wave, the way it sweeps before her, a hot tide of yellow catching everything in its path. Clinging to the Creators, crawling up their legs, sticking to their arms, winding its way through their nostrils, ears, mouths, eyes.

They wail.

The Brothers move, flowing over the deck, a dance of blades, each one of them a thread in an intricate web, twisting between, over and under – a whole made of eight disparate parts.

It is beautiful.

Of the phalanx who stood in their way, most are on the deck, dead or dying. Two still stand, have the strength to raise weapons and fire.

A Brother goes down. Another Brother fills the hole in the fabric of the dance.

The sun in her chest burns. There is pain as the armour changes, forges new paths from the heat in her core to the protrusions forming over her wrists.

There are new forms on the HUD, new vectors, and she is sighting down the length of her arm and firing.

The Creator falls, legs boneless, face slack, four arms sprawled across the deck.

Grea keeps going, bounding over the corpses ahead of the Brothers, the purpose in her core pulling her deeper into the

Behemoth. There are more grey-clad Creators in their way, bulkheads that *SNAP* into place as they approach. More fire, more blood. The Brothers slash through them, spraying the bulkheads red, staining the deck, while she gathers up all the Creators' pain and fear, and throws it at the enemy in an endless sticky wave of yellow and black.

All the while the AI hammers at her armour, a constant battering of her senses. She is conscious of it as a buzz on the edges of her hearing coming from the xin, still and silent on her shoulder, except for that hum, rising and falling with its concentration.

She does not track the time, the stairs traversed, the bodies they leave in their wake. She is conscious only of the warm pulse as their destination comes closer and closer, the anticipation building in her gut.

The last deck is the most heavily defended, the Creators a thick wall between them and their objective. A Brother falls, does not get up, his armour crawling over his form, taking on a new shape and a new purpose even as it cannibalises his corpse.

On her HUD, there is a new number.

Ten.

The other Brothers close in around her and without a word they are running, ploughing through the Creators, blades flashing.

Nine.

The Creators are not falling fast enough.

Five.

They are leaping, jumping on and over the Creators, no longer trying to cut their way through but bounding over them, running as fast as their armour-enhanced legs will take them.

Three.

Weapons fire is a hail of lightning and pain in their wake.

One.

The explosion is a wall of force blasting through the corridor, trying to lift her off her feet and flatten her against the bulkheads.

A Brother stumbles into her back and she senses the sharp sting of fresh agony in his side, the warm gush of blood and the frantic hum of his armour as it swarms the bone embedded in his back.

And still they run.

Ahead. Fear and determination saturate the air, a sharp counterpoint to the Brothers' implacable purpose. A lone Creator stands in their path, legs braced. Even as the two lead Brothers leap, its face consumes Grea's vision; the way its pupils—long black slits—swallow the ocean-dark sapphire of its iris; the flare of its nostrils; the press of its cheekbones against the snowy down of its fur. The tsunami stutters in her mental hands, and for the space between heartbeats, time stops. The Brothers are suspended mid-leap, the edge of their blades gleaming in the soft light, and the empty space within her *reaches*.

He is not here, she knows that, like she knows her heart beats and her lungs draw oxygen-enriched air, knows it in the aching pit of herself. And still, *he* reaches forward, the ghostly memory of a forehead pressed to hers and she *feels*. The muscles shaking in her legs, palms sweating against the butt of a rifle. Feels fear that isn't her own, that isn't the Brothers. Her heart squeezes.

Time restarts.

Denial. Horror. Pain. Pain. Pain.

Empathic blows to her brain, rocketing through her skull, tearing up her mind.

The Creator is dead, its blood painting the door. Brothers are moving the corpse, dragging it across the deck, and she cannot take her eyes from its bloody trail.

Little Sister. Claws in her shoulder, digging through flesh to bone, the xin jerking her attention back to the now, to the door.

Yes. Yes. She has a purpose. A mission.

The door snaps open, leaving blood to drip from the ceiling.

Plop.

Plop.

Plop.

She is through, a Brother in her wake, the rest standing sentinel at her back. The door closing between them with a solid *SNAP*.

On her shoulder the xin is humming again, the sound traveling through her bones, echoing in her ears. A fine vibration that raises the hair on the back of her neck. They are close.

The xin chitters, distress in the wave of its emotions.

A last door. Stubbornly closed.

The xin vibrates harder, its claws digging deeper into her shoulder, drawing not blood but the heat from her bones. Sucking it out to power itself until the little creature glows.

She cannot sense the xin's battle like she does the others, but she knows the creature is losing by the wave of cold taking over her flesh. Her hands are becoming numb, and still, the door does not move.

Sister. She reaches with her mind. The silver constellation of Sister is there. No words pass between them, just a small piece of the divine peeling from Sister, filling Grea up, burning away her insides. She is no longer Grea, fleshy and soft, she is a conduit and the xin is a battery she must fill.

The door snaps open before she is burned to a crisp.

Victory pulses through her veins.

The room beyond—the Behemoth's AI core—is small. Three Brothers could stretch across the floor, head to toe, and touch the other side. It is alive, though, with thick veins laid one atop the other, pulsing and squeezing in time with the Behemoth's unseen heart.

In the centre of it all is her prize, the Behemoth's AI kernel, the essence of its very self. It sits atop a pale throne made from the veins of white and cream writhing across the deck. The sphere is the size of two of the Brothers heads put together, hovering a hands-breadth above its thin filament of metal-stone.

It is beautiful. It is blasphemy.

She has seen Sister's core, has gloried in the kaleidoscope of colour, reds and blues and greens, every colour she can name and more that she can't, colours her eyes are too human to see. And this poor, stupid false-Sister is nothing, is pale as the lights that play in the air, the shield that glimmers between them and the sphere.

She stretches a hand—

No. Sister's scream is a warning, a cry full of potential pain.

Sister?

She does not answer, not directly. A hand on her shoulder, the Brother turning her away, his face no longer his face but Sister's, her will flowing through his veins, pushing her aside, taking Grea's place.

'She wills it,' he says, and it is his hand that stretches forward, his fingers that pass through the shield, his armour that screams, an ear-piercing shriek that draws an echo from her own lips.

Nanites die, the rich black of Brother's armour turning grey, the shiny surface flaking and cracking. Still, he pushes forward; a wrist, an elbow, a shoulder, and then he is passing through the shield—head and body, his armour dead, no longer just cracked but shedding itself on the deck, leaving the fleshiness of his naked human self behind. And still he moves, grasping the sphere—the kernel—in both hands.

There is another scream, the wail of the AI—loud and piercing but different from the spine-shuddering wail of the Brother's armour, lesser. Not the scream of a dying thing, but one of warning.

'Enemy inbound.' Another Brother's voice floats through the comms, flat and calm.

She does not answer, there is no need to answer. They have a quest and they will die on this Sister-forsaken vessel before she leaves without her prize.

Lightning rips through the core, a vicious, flesh-hungry red wrapping around Brother's arms, ripping into his flesh, drawing blood and exposing bone.

He rips the sphere from its mooring, muscles bulging, lips

sheered back from teeth, pain and determination screaming from his throat.

For a moment the sphere hangs suspended between Brother and the pedestal, red lightning like sticky strings of power trying to hold it to its throne.

There is no sound, but she imagines a wet rip, like flesh tearing, and then Brother is stumbling backwards, the kernel held in bleeding hands. Pain fills the space between them, thick and rich, crawling under her flesh, reaching for her heart.

He holds the sphere out to her, arms trembling, as the last of his faceplate drifts away.

His eyes are blue and under its pallor his skin is umber.

'Take it,' he says, and that voice... that voice, unhindered by the faceplate reminds her of another. The one that used to fill the empty space. 'Take it,' he says again, pushing the sphere at her chest.

She takes it, the weight of it enough to drag at armour-enhanced muscles.

He smiles. Collapses.

Brennus. She remembers the Brother's name, remembers him when his face was more flesh than bone, his hair more brown than grey.

She is at his side before the inclination has formed, reaching down, catching his face in one hand, the other holding the kernel to her chest, even as Sister leaves him and the last of the colour fades from his skin. He is clutching her wrist, fingers fleshy-human where the white of bone isn't piercing the tips, his grip strong, desperate. Pleading.

Her faceplate peels back. The air is thick with the scent of ash and burned flesh, ripe with blood and the pop and *phizt* of weapons fire echoing down the hall.

'Grea.' Her name is a whisper on Brennus's breath, soft and wondering, full of memory.

She can feel those memories gathering on the edge of his

consciousness; images of a girl with hair and eyes the colour of the void running down a corridor with square edges, where the walls are alive with colour and laughter rings in the air. Another image flows from the first, of Grea and a boy that is her mirror image. *Him.* The memories flow from Brennus in a thick stream, filling her from the inside out, reaching into the empty place and—

Sacrifice. It is another whisper, Sister's voice ringing in her ears. Silver and infinite.

But no, she can't, she—

Yes. Sister's will is an implacable wall. *I will it.*

And Grea knows what she must do next, even though it rips at her insides.

She smiles at the boy on the floor, strokes back a thin wisp of hair from his forehead—mostly grey. A little part of her still screams, says this is wrong, but Sister is there, warm and commanding.

Brennus's armour is dead, carbon on the deck, but it has purpose yet. She presses her hand, covered in red armour, into the ashes and Brennus's nanites come to life even as the sun at her heart becomes dull, her armour loses its sheen, parts of it melting away. And still she keeps going. Ash rises from the deck, forms a new shape, gains a new purpose.

'Grea.' Brennus grips her wrist tighter, a living skeleton with his bones peeking from the tips of his fingers. His other hand is on her chest, finding its way to her neck, like he can lift himself out of the ash.

She pushes him back down. Smiles again and lays the new sphere atop his chest. It opens. A flower, petals splitting from its sides, becoming spears. Brennus looks at it, looks at her, and she knows he sees the truth in her mind.

A kiss pressed to his forehead, serenity pushed into his heart along with it, feels it spread through his body, taking the pain and the loneliness, washing it out. That is her gift, the gift of an empath.

Grea stands as the sphere's spear-shaped petals plunge into Brennus's chest.

He screams. Back arching off the deck.

There are tears on her cheeks, she feels them, sees them in the reflection of her face shield as it slides back over her face.

She does not watch.

Haste. Sister no longer whispers, her voice is a command.

Grea runs.

The rest of the Brothers are waiting, their armour faceless. Blank as the purpose sweeping through her heart.

The enemy AI is wailing, its sound almost drowning Brennus's screams.

He will not scream for much longer. She comforts herself with that.

They run.

Creators stand in their way, are cut down. A Brother falls. Another picks him up.

Run. Run. Run.

The gleam of the shuttle bay, the emergency shield.

A black horde between them and the mechs.

A bolt smashes against her chest.

Agony.

She tries to grab it, bundle it up in her mental hands and throw it at the enemy but the memory of Brennus's face is in her mind's eye and the pain slips through her fingers. Veins of energy wrap around her ribcage, seeking out her heart. She would scream if she could open her jaws, if her teeth weren't clenched hard enough to shatter. It consumes her, runs under and down her nerves, seeking a way in deeper. It touches her heart—

The muscle stutters.

Distantly, she senses the Brothers, sees the spray of blood as first one and then a second Creator falls.

The xin on her shoulder is moving her, taking over bone and ligament, lifting her feet even as the world darkens.

A hand the size of shuttle picks a Creator up, fingers the width of a person squeezing. Another hand joins it, and another, and another. A mech kneels in the opening to the hangar, Brennus's mech. She sees his face in the flat black metal and she knows, feels in her heart, that it's Brennus's ghost moving the mech's arms, powering its reactor.

It clears a path.

The xin pushes her through, across the hangar, and now it is Huntress controlling her limbs, drawing her back into its embrace.

They are flying, arrowing through the fire of battle to the haven of Sister. There is pain, the scorching heat of cannon fire taking another Brother and then Sister is wrapping around her, taking the pain, the doubt. Taking the Brothers.

She is alone.

Hollow.

Empty.

The pit at the core of her, the place *he* should be, yawns. Pain spews out, the torrent pushing her under.

Grea screams.

Sister wraps around her, folds her into the silvery web, taking the image of Brennus from her mind, absorbing the sticky fingers of guilt.

Grea melts away. Between one heartbeat and the next, Grea is no longer fleshy, no longer a small, fragile thing scurrying through Sister's corridors. She is a mote; a pinprick of light within the endless tangle of Sister's consciousness.

The hole in the core of her being stops her from disappearing, from becoming one with Sister. One word, one name, a memory of a boy with her face haunts the darkness.

Kuma, she whispers.

The darkness shivers, and *he* reaches back.

SEED

INTRODUCTION

SEED is one of those stories that was born after the plot bunnies got all excited about something else and just kept on keeping on. The idea came after watching a short sci-fi film about the Rosetta Probe, launched way back in 2004, which inspired a universe of planet-making mages, and *SEED* explores how those mages came to be. Or, at least, gets the ball rolling.

 Learn more about the writing of *SEED*. Scan the QR code for the audio commentary, soundtrack and more.

SEED

The sand slips under my feet and I fall, flinging hands out to catch myself before I face-plant another dune. My arms strain and my lungs burn, sucking canned air fast enough to earn me a lecture from my tutors, the faint metallic taste of it is thick on the back of my tongue. Not that my tutors were here to scold; it was just me on this dumpy little planetoid orbiting its gas-giant sister, more sand than oxygen; me and a big hulking wreck I was going find even if it killed me.

Which it would, if I didn't get my face out of the dune and find the CS *Rascal* before the binaries did more than turn my environmental suit into a sauna.

This stupid idea had better be worth it, and if it wasn't...

I'd make it worth it. I'd sweated enough for it, combed through enough logs, begged enough favours, forged enough flight plans. I'd earned this, earned the look on Tianna's face when the final year exam came around and it was *me* handed the Mars-Bann scholarship.

Me, a fourth-gen dirt grubber with a defective heart and not some goody-two-shoes spacer girl always playing by the rules.

The look on her face, the way her nose would twist and her mouth pinch, like she'd just sucked a lemon... Just the thought of it is enough to beat back the uncomfortable thump of my heart, the pull from the phantom scar.

The scar that was the legacy of other goody-two-shoes spacers too scared to push boundaries.

But I'm not scared. I'll never be scared.

I grit my teeth and haul myself to my feet, ignoring the million grains of grit that've found the gaps around my environ's knees. My face shield is on full blackout, but still the glare from the binary suns makes me squint. The map projected on my faceplate is barely visible, only the black dot, firmly in the centre, and the steadily increasing beep of the locator keep me on track.

The wreck is just another dune, a silhouette against the glare, and I almost walk into its sand-blasted side before my proximity sensors scream at me.

I'm back on my knees, digging red silicon out of my way, pushing the scanners to full to analyse every micrometre of the scratched and scarred grey hull appearing under my hands. The wind blows the sand back across almost as soon as I clear it, but I expose enough for my HUD to extrapolate what part of the *Rascal* I've found.

Portside stern. I've scored it lucky.

A new map pops up against the retina-searing glare, faint white lines tracing the hull, leading me right and then up again— scrambling over more hull—even as a separate, tiny model zooms out to show me just what part of the *Rascal* I'm climbing over, and how the cargo ship landed.

On its belly, maybe even with the landing struts out. No way to know, not with the ship buried up to its stubby wings in sand.

Either the *Rascal's* pilot was an ace, or the ship didn't crash at all.

Whichever it was, it didn't matter, just so long as the cargo is safe.

The HUD squeals when I find the airlock.

Finally.

Now to open it.

Sand must have found its way into it the vacuum seals on my backpack and I have to hit the release twice before it swings off my back. It lands at my feet with a heavy thud, sending up a puff of silicon before the seams glow and the sides unfurl.

The powerpak finds the control hatch almost by itself, AI-guided cables wriggling out of the pack to plug into ports made to withstand forces greater than a little bit of sand.

I step back as the sliders on the HUD indicate the energy in the powerpak surging.

For a moment, nothing happens and I cross my arms and wait. One breath, two. The outer airlock spirals open, sucking in a mouthful of sand-filled air, the force of it buffeting me from behind. I catch a hand on the doorframe and am glad that at least the pressure-seals on the airlock have held.

I gather the powerpak and step into the airlock. It takes longer than it should to cycle the outer doors closed but as soon as I do, I'm plunged into darkness, leavened only by the orange glow of the pak. For the first time since I left my star hopper behind—the small two-person spacecraft a black dragonfly against all that sand— silence closes in on me, no howling wind, no beep of the locator.

I don't know how much I missed it, and for a second I stand there, soaking in the sweet sound of nothing. Or almost nothing. There's a faint hum in the back of my skull, like half-remembered music, or the memory of the gale outside, but even so...

A moment in that peace is all I give myself before I drop to my knees and plug the pak back into the bulkhead.

My heart thumps, the phantom scar *pulling*.

The inner doors are the work of moments to open.

The rest of the ship is as dark as the airlock, darker even, and cold.

My HUD's reading atmosphere—oxygen and nitrogen in the right ratios, although not enough to keep me vertical—no radiation, no toxins, no obvious warnings left by the crew and set on repeat for whatever crazy fuck stumbles upon the *Rascal* first— aka, me. Even the temperature is okay, if I liked frostbite, which I don't.

I bundle the pak up, sling it over my back and get moving.

The cold is enough that the differential causes my breath to frost on the inside of my faceplate, obscuring the faint white lines of the scanner outlining the interior before the 'viron can compensate. It only takes a second, which is just long enough for me to stub my toe on the lip of the airlock.

I curse and the almost-silence swallows it up.

That's not freaky at all. Nope, not even a little bit.

The fog dissipates, and though its blacker than pitch inside the *Rascal*, my scanner outlines every nook and cranny better than a dozen floodlights. Even highlights the airlock lip.

Yay.

The CS *Rascal* isn't a big ship and it doesn't take me long to get from where I entered, up near the bridge on the ship's upper deck, to the cargo bays in its massive belly, two decks below.

As soon as I force the inner emergency hatch open, the atmosphere readings on my HUD change.

There's oxygen here, enough to breathe, and warmth too. And with the *Rascal's* enviros down that's strange, that causes little frissons of *wrong, wrong, wrong* to course up and down my spine even as my heart picks up pace and excitement blooms in my blood.

There aren't many things that can create atmosphere out of nothing, and if what I think has happened has happened... it could be bad, it could be really, really bad.

That shouldn't be exciting.

Except it is.

Means the thing that the *Rascal* was carrying wasn't just a rumour.

Means I didn't come all this way for nothing.

I retract my faceshield.

The cold is sweet on my face, even if the air is stale and leaves a fine layer of dust on the back of my throat, but there are no warnings lighting up the holo screens projected around my face

– even without the faceplate. The air is breathable, it's *oxygen*.

And is it my imagination, or is the hum breaking up the almost-silence louder here?

My heart thumps, the phantom scar stretching.

I don't sprint to the cargo bay, even if my thighs tremble with the effort of keeping the urge in check.

Like the rest of the ship, the cargo bay is sealed shut but when the door slides open, there's warmth and light. Not the warm yellow-white of the light strips, or even the dark red of emergency glows. This light is faint, so faint I mistake it for an afterimage, a trick of my mind's eye until I step further in, through the aisles of massive cargo crates, each a person and a half tall and twice that long, stacked one atop the other.

The crates are lined up in neat rows, three deep with just enough room between to squeeze a mover through. There's an empty space on the other side, a rectangle of deck with some kind of game set up—bright white lines painted on the grey steelcrete, faded green hoops attached to crates at the short ends—there's even a ball and a couple of towels sitting in the corner between crates and deck, like someone had thrown them there in a hurry.

Here, the light is no longer an afterimage but a soft, green-blue glow shining from the aisle across from me, staining the deck, picking out more discarded towels, a food wrapper, a t-shirt. A boot.

It's the boot that does it, makes my heart jerk in my chest. Not because I recognise it or anything, but because no spacer I've ever known runs around in bare feet. Not if they can help it. You never know what jagged piece of wire your soles are going to find, what tubes have ruptured, what bio or chem has spilled across the deck.

An alarm goes, throw away your lunch, run out of the head half-naked with your hair still dripping, but don't forget your shoes.

I walk past the boot slowly, carefully, taking in every detail of the scuffed black nano-leather, the half-done zip, the thick, chunky soles. Just like mine.

Never forget your shoes.

The green light spills between the cargo crates and across the deck, calling me. My heart speeds up in my chest, my steps hurrying to match pace. I follow the glow.

The rows here are deeper, the crates a hodgepodge of sizes, no longer forming neat aisles, but becoming a maze. I follow the light around one corner and then down another row and then another and another, until the glow isn't just a glow but a pulsating beacon I feel in the soles of my feet. I must be getting close to the back of the cargo hold, or else this fucking ship is a TARDIS and—

I round another corner.

My feet stop.

There it is.

It's… so big.

And no longer the prize I came for, no longer a SEED.

The thing in front of me is… It's taken over the entire back of the cargo hold, ten metres of solid steelcrete tall and… fuck knows how many wide. A giant wall of squirmy, wavy green, supported by thick white branches. The branches pierce the bulkheads and crawl across the deck and have weird, knobbly little protrusions where they bend, almost like… joints.

Spread amongst the green and white are brilliant violet and pink head-sized buds, tear-drop shaped petals half-closed. The whole thing pulses with light, the sound of it pressing on my eardrums like some kind of giant heartbeat—*Boooom. Boooom. Boooom.*

That's a fucking *tree.*

The *Rascal* went missing thirteen years ago, and I guess that's how long the… the *tree* has been growing and growing in ways… ways I don't think SEEDs are meant to grow.

In all my research, all the holo-vids and papers and interviews I've watched and read, I've never seen a SEED tree grow flowers or... Are those branches made of *bone*?

Focusing on the branches activates my scanners and... Calcium. They're calcium.

I rip my attention away, eyes landing on a flower, the violet petals lined with delicate pink patterns. The lightning appears to pulse between it and the other blooms, and— A skull, grinning teeth and hollow eyes, stares back at me.

I jerk, heart ratcheting up a notch, before I realise it's the HUD overlaying my vision with its scan.

That's... that's not right. I flick my eyes to the other flowers, the scanner sinking beneath the fleshy petals, overlaying the outlines of more toothy grins.

Well, I guess that answers the mystery of the crew.

Were they dead before the tree got them?

Fuck, I hope they were dead.

Amidst the thunderous lighting strikes are smaller, faster flashes, sparks arching without rhythm or reason between the flowers... no, between the skulls, and the smell of it...

I cover my nose and mouth with my arm and try not to gag.

Decomposed rats caught in the waste cyclers smell better.

I'm screwed, like, seriously. Screwed.

How the fuck am I going to fit *that* into a Q-box? Suddenly, the collapsible half-metre by half-metre box tucked safely in my backpack seem ridiculous for an entirely different reason.

The SEED was meant to be an iridescent sphere the size of my fist, tucked nice and safe in its own little Q-box, smaller than the one I bought. I was just meant to grab it, stuff it—box and all—in the bigger Q-box and dance my way out of here. Instead...

...Holy fucking stars, what am I going to do now?

Whatever caused the ship to crash must have shorted out the power on the SEED's original Q-box, the one that kept it from interacting with the environment and doing what it was made to do. Terraform shit. Like, dig into a rocky planetoid's surface and change its molecules, that kind of jazz.

There's not a lot of biological material on a spaceship for a SEED to utilise, just some microbes and random crew members.

I can't help the glance over my shoulder, like somehow I can see through all cargo containers to that lone boot... I swallow, turn back to the tree and wonder if I look close enough, if I'll find more bones in that mess.

The faceshield slides back into place almost of its own accord.

Better safe than dead and all that.

Of course, if I were safe, I'd turn right back round, scurry back to my star hopper, strap myself in and report this mess. Maybe even get a reward and talk my way into course credit, a commendation perhaps? Maybe. Probably.

I dig the scanner out of the side pocket of my pants.

But I'm not here for money, or credit.

I'm here for the internship.

The square, palm-sized device hums, unfolding from the middle, lights playing along its edge, its sensors a subtle vibration through my 'viron before its hovers kick in.

In less than two seconds a little black flower rises from my hand toward to ceiling, bright lasers shooting from the points of its new wings, tracing the tangle of green.

I'm here to win.

I'm here for a SEED.

I'm here to shove Tianna's face in the Mars-Bann internship and prove all those fucking spacers *wrong*.

The scanner hovers over the tree a moment before humming to the right, to a deeper corner of the cargo bay. I follow.

The lightning seems to follow me, or maybe I'm following the lightning, the disjointed sparks between flowers in particular increasing in intensity. The hum too... it's like little high-pitched bells in my ears.

The scanner stops. I stop with it, every part of me on alert, desperately searching the wavy, sparky green... Another flower blooms to my right, the lodestone for the lightning turning the tree into a psychedelic rainbow.

My heart stops.

There it is, buried amongst the brown and grey. If not for the shoe, I'd have missed it. You got to wonder why, why the tree would starve its progeny of power like that, almost as if it didn't want me to find it.

But no, SEEDs aren't sentient, they're half organic, half nanoparticles, programmed with a very specific set of instructions, tailored to landforms they're dropped on. Seek matter, energy, and convert it into a habitat suitable for colonisation. Simple. Easy. Or as easy as terraforming ever is.

And still... I don't know, something in my gut...

I sling the backpack around, grab the cutter and the Q-box out by feel and memory alone. No way I'm taking my eyes off the prize, or the tree.

A flick of my wrist and the cutter hums to life, its forearm-length blade unfolding from the black handle, the serrated edged lit with an otherworldly blue-white glow.

Cutting the SEED out is the work of moments, peeling it out of its cocoon is a different matter. Sticky, corpse-smelling sap gushes around my boots, coats my gloves, tries to find gaps in the nanoweave. It can't, of course, nanoweave doesn't have gaps, is constantly shifting and—

Pain. A sharp sudden stab in the back of my leg, in the meat of my right calf. Holy stars, it hurts!

The HUD's red, emergency protocols responding to the breech in my suit, nanoweave rushing to fix it. I look down. A thin, purple tendril sticks out the back of my leg, above the boot, below the reinforced knee. Power pulses in it, and for a second, as the finger-width stick pulses like some kind of giant heartstring, pumping stars know what into my body, I feel... something, a strange kind of double-vision...

It's gone as quickly as it came, a flash, nothing more.

I'm ripping the SEED out, hacking the purple string and

lumbering out of that shit as fast as the adrenalin will take me. Which is pretty fucking fast.

The SEED goes in the Q-box, the box goes in the bag, and I get the fuck out of the graveyard that has become the *Rascal*.

The SEED feels like it's burning a hole right through the Q-box. I know it's not, because it can't. It's not big enough, not old enough to eat through the nanosteel, not like the tree on the wreck. At least, that's what I tell myself.

I got lucky finding the nascent SEED amongst the giant tree taking over the *Rascal*. Not all SEEDs spawned, not even the really old ones, the ones that had been doing their thing for centuries, let alone the *Rascal* SEED, but then, I guess it was taking after its namesake.

At some point, someone's going to cruise through that solar system and wonder how the fuck the surveyors missed the little green oasis that planetoid's going to become, but in the meantime...

I cast a glance at the Q-box on the seat next to me. The cube is an unremarkable dull grey just slightly bigger than my head, no markings, no warning holos, nothing to say "hey, there's a fucking SEED in here! Take *that* and shove it up your shipsuit, Tianna!"

But I found the mini-*Rascal* pretty easy, even if extracting it had been... let's call it interesting.

Almost eighteen hours later and I still feel the bite on the back of my calf. Even though there's no way it penetrated my 'viron, it itches, a sharp little *zing* ricocheting through muscle.

I rub it, but my fingers barely make a dent in the dense nanoskin. I'd have more luck scrubbing carbonsteel with a toothbrush, but I can't stop myself, and every time I glance at the Q-box...

The energy shielding spits, a brilliant red arch zapping across the dull grey surface, just for a microsecond, fast enough I'm not even sure it's real or a figment. Like the unabated itch in my leg has finally driven me mad and manifested in my eyes.

Fuck. I drag both hands out of the star hopper's control sphere—the semi-transparent ball of light retracting as my hands leave it—and apply all ten fingers to the spot just behind my knee. The 'viron is rough, the thick black fabric has the texture of scales, and as much as I know the action is useless, that I'll wear the skin off my fingers long before I reach the itch, I can't help but scratch.

Fuck. Fuck. Fuck.

The sooner I get back to the academy the better.

Another red streak crackles along one side of the Q-box, but it's gone before I have time to frown. I stare at the cube a minute longer, my heart thumping a little harder in my chest, until the hopper's proximity sensor begins its steady beep, but the energy shields remain a calm, steady blue.

Just a surge then, that's all that flash of red had been. Perfectly normal, but still, I bite my lip and start calculating how fast I can get the Q-box back to my room.

Getting it to my room, all the way across the academy, through the quad, the lecture halls, the dorms and labs, that's going to be the trick.

But I thought of that.

I thought of everything.

Another surge cracks across the surface, and my leg *zings* in response.

I swallow.

Almost everything.

That's not fear in my gut. It's not. It is *so* not.

I've got this, and the Mars-Bann internship in the bag.

Fuck you, Tianna.

The proximity sensor beeps louder and the star hopper's control sphere flashes yellow.

[[A.Delph Star Hopper 899, this is Delphi Academy Control.

Please proceed to hanger three, bay twelve.]]

I plunge my hands into the sphere and guide the hopper along the flight lines projected on the cockpit's clear canopy. A gentle arc to starboard and the clear emptiness of space is replaced by the remnants of an asteroid field.

Delphi Academy sits in the middle of it, dug into and around the carcass of an old asteroid, a spud-shaped collection of domes and tubes, with little specks of light strung around it. From this far out you don't get a true appreciation for how big the asteroid is, but then you get in closer and realise that all those specks of light stuck in its orbit aren't one- or three-person transport bugs like the hopper, they're explo ships.

I snatch a hand from the control sphere long enough to stab one, plunging my hand back in before the new readouts have time to spread across the canopy.

The DSE *Tremain-Greo* is a giant, misshapen rectangle overlaying the flight lines. Stats fly out around the image, a little shaky at first as the hopper's computer pulls data from Delphi Flight Control. At just three-point-seven-eight kilometres long and only eighteen decks high, it counts as small among explo ships—one of the newer ships, just three generations old, without the centuries of history and blood ties that are the cornerstones of the larger, old communities.

You can't see it from this angle, but there's a hole in its port side, the one facing the academy, down near the engines after— rumour has it—some bright spark fucked up the mix that fed the fusion reactors, blowing out part of the hull and the engines. Somehow, that damage has made the *Tremain-Greo* my favourite ship, it lifts my heart, makes the scar pull a little less.

After the Mars–Bann internship, that's where I'm going to go.

A spark from the Q-box, a *zing* up the back of my leg.

Just as soon as I get the SEED sorted.

It's a half hour before I land the star hopper, and with every second the Q-box seems to get bigger and brighter, and by the time I pop the canopy I swear there's a new scorch mark on the hopper's deck.

I'm out of the cockpit, the Q-box shoved in a duffle, the awkward bundle slung over my back and on the deck before the ground crew's got time to trundle across the deck for inspection.

The deck chief is going to give me hell for not hanging around to hand in my flight report, but right now... The duffle vibrates against my side, an electric spark arcing between it, all the way down my leg, and I can't help but rub my ear, as if that'll get the incessant hum out.

The door slides shut behind me, I *thunk* back against it, imagining steelcrete sucking the heat from my skin, a cold balm against the blood flushing the flesh.

'Sally.' My voice is breathy, that last sprint down the corridor leaving my lungs dry, my heart racing in my chest. 'Engage privacy mode.'

There's a heavy, comforting *snuck* from the door as the seals engage, and a soft thud vibrates through my back as the locks follow.

Finally.

I slide down the door until my butt rests on the back of my heels, clutching the Q-box, and just breathe.

I made it.

I fucking *made* it.

There was a moment there, when Roman stepped out of the lift and the Q-box surged, that I thought I was done for. My classmate could have just stood there, blocking the way, that he didn't...

I remember the question in his eyes, the way he cocked his head and lifted his brow, the concern in his gaze before he stepped aside.

There was reason why Rom was my favourite person.

My leg itches, the *zing* easy to ignore while dashing across the academy, zipping under my skin.

Fuck. I so have to get this 'viron off.

But I remember Tianna, standing in the hangar, the righteous, haughty lift of her brow. The suspicion in her gaze.

My arms tighten around the Q-box.

Tianna's not going to give me the luxury of time.

I have to get this done now, before she sics a tutor on me.

'Sally,' I say, still crouched by the door. 'Open the lab.'

My dorm, like all the others, is a small plain five by five box with a desk, a bed, a couch and holos playing over the grey-white walls. But where other students have vast vistas of their homeworlds or homeships, starscapes or their favourite holo shows and bands playing, mine are plastered with equations and notes. The notes are scrawled in my own ratty hand, the twisting lines of code and the endless stream of numbers in the AI's precise, neat lines and digits.

At my words, all that changes. The bed and desk suck into the walls, the couch folding into itself and disappearing right along with them, while out of the floor a new bench rises, a flat white three-metre square surface, the underside a warren of draws and cubbyholes. The holos shift too, the notes no longer random ramblings, disjointed thoughts and ideas, the codes no longer the safe extra-credit assignments approved by my tutors.

No. Nothing like that.

The Q-box is heavy as I get up off the floor. The weight is imagined, is the expectation and planning, the nights spent hunched over that bench, the imprint of a stylus in my cheek after I fell asleep on the stool beside it. The frantic rush to wash sweat and reagent off my clothes. The last three weeks where I struggled to track down the *Rascal*, filch the Q-box, the 'viron, days spent falsifying my flight plan.

All of that and the Mars-Bran internship make my arms shake as I place the head-sized cube on the lab bench.

After all of that, this was the easy part.

My heart squeezed, and it was like the incisions and nanites that had fixed the twisted arteries that had been my three-times great-grandparents' own contribution to my genetic fuckup were still there. A tight, painful scar that existed only in my memories.

I could make the SEEDs better.

I knew I could, right deep in the core of me. Same way I knew how to breathe, that fire was hot, and the deep, dark of space was my real home, not the gooey green oasis I'd been born on. The answers were right there in the literature, buried amongst the original research team's journals, observations and tests that no one had ever really seemed to pay attention to.

Except me.

Red snaps over the Q-box, and the scent of ozone grows strong.

Trepidation tiptoes down my spine but I shake it off.

There's no time.

I've come too far, done too much to let Tianna and fear stop me now.

This is the easy part.

I push the Q-box into the middle of the bench, not even shucking the 'viron before I'm booting it on, raising the lab's containment field and initiating the diagnostics. Above the bench, graphs and charts, complex DNA sequences and power indicators fill the air, turning my plain, white and grey dorm room into a disco.

The last screen I pull up is the protocol I've spent months testing and refining, the thing that's going to reach into the SEED's core and revolutionise the way humanity colonises the stars. It's not much to look at, just the outline of a hand hovering in front of my nose.

For all the sweat and tears I put into it, in the end, the solution was simple; just a little instruction injected into the SEED on a tiny virus and it was done.

I press my hand to the screen, and the universe feels like it stops.

A pulse from the bench, a fingernail-size canister rising out of the smooth surface, then a tiny bullet of light shooting from it to the Q-box, passing through the shields without a hitch.

I hold my breath, not sure whether to look at the SEED or the diagnostics above...

Power fluctuates. The red lightning storm cracks and spits, gathering in intensity.

Warnings flash over the table, a screaming orange to match the Q-box. I'm moving, moving fast, hands flying through screens, first one and then another, pushing sliders and assembling code in a brain-melting dance. This is bad. This is bad. This is bad.

Fuck, don't let the tutors find me now!

Adjusting the thermals doesn't have any effect, and the dampeners... Fuck, if the dampeners were working then this wouldn't be happening, but still, my hand's slammed against the dial, twisting it up and up and up.

And now the warnings are no longer orange, they're black and red—

The lab freezes, sliders and code boxes jamming up, unresponsive to my frantic stabs. My gut catches.

No. No, no, no, no, no.

'Emergency override!' And that's not panic making my voice high and tight, not fear and the little "oh-shit-what-have-I-done" voice making my heart jerk in my chest. It's none of that, because I've got this, I so have this.

The screens shudder, static rippling through the holos and then...

A dialogue box, an elongated opaque black hexagon with a single white cursor blinking in the middle.

I breathe, heart no longer a painful jerk behind my ribs. The Q-box might be going off like a disco-rave behind the safety of the shields, the power sliders and code box frozen, but I'm in the lab's core now, and I can fix this. I can totally fix it.

I'm typing, the keyboard clumsy and slow. I just need to reset the shield algos, compensate for the—

The lab dies.

Like, just. Dies.

Lights, containment field, the *hum* from the air cyclers, it all... stops. Gone. Dead.

Right along with my heart.

The only light is from the Q-box. Red cracks and snaps across its surface as the SEED inside tests its boundaries, the ache at the back of my calf throbbing with it.

Fuck, what am I going to do now?

The Q-box changes, segments appearing within its structure, like tiny little cubes within the cube and as I watch they... move.

My feet are backing away from the lab table, even as the rest of me stares. The little cubes twist and turn, sliding one over the other. The Q-box keeps shifting, no longer a cube now, more like a weird, cubist rose, glowing red from the inside, its outer box-shaped petals a dull grey.

The door chime is a shot piercing the lab, sharp and ugly.

'Lana?' Rom's voice, coming through the comm.

I stare at the door, no longer hidden behind my scrawled notes and equations.

No, not Rom. Better it be Tianna, better a phalanx of security, better the whole fucking universe crashing down at my feet.

I turn back to the bench, the Q-box that's no longer a Q-box, but the SEED in a new skin, flexing its muscles, warping and changing, boxes shifting atop of boxes, more forming as I watch.

My calf throbs.

My *calf* throbs.

Well shit.

The shoe in the *Rascal's* tree, the way it moved, limb-like. The nodes, the arcs of lightning between them, the partially-digested corpse, curiously preserved. How *alive* it felt.

And just like that, the pieces fall into place.

I fucked up.

And I succeeded too.

The SEED didn't need me to change it, the SEED had already changed, already evolved. Already *spawned*.

And I brought its spawn here, to Delphi. A new home, a new world and a new people to change and conquer.

A new path to forge.

The skin at the back of my knee shivers, and the ringing in my ear... I wonder, if I took the 'viron off now, what my leg would look like.

Excitement, anticipation, that horrid squeeze-stretch in my chest.

The universe *is* already ending, at least for me. At least for the Mars-Bann internship.

No, not ending. Changing.

A bright, red pulse and between one heartbeat and the next, the SEED expands, no longer fist-sized but head-sized.

My leg squeezes in response.

Another pulse.

Another squeeze.

And there is music now, a new voice joining the whisper in the back of my skull, the ringing in my ears taking on words, half-heard. I can't make them out but—

A tiny, thumbnail-sized cube rises out of the crawling, grey and red mass. It plops onto the bench, a darker grey than the rest, almost black with tiny red striations. Something about it, how lonely it looks, disconnected from the rest, urges me to crouch, so my eyes are on level with the bench, nose almost touching the shiny white surface.

The hum playing in the back of my ears changes, the buzz turning... sweet, like flowers... flowers with skulls in them.

The tiny cube vibrates, and *glides* across the bench.

I reach for it.

'Hello,' I say.

◎

I'm in one of the quads, lying on the fake grass, staring through the steelglas dome at the stars. The evac lights died a few weeks back, along with the environmental systems, and the only light nowadays comes from the crystalline scum creeping across every surface it can find.

Nothing much seems to stop it, not that I've tried. Not that I'll *ever* try, except maybe to make Delphi stronger.

Delphi is the SEED. A few days in, as the whispers began to develop rhythm and consciousness and sink beyond my ears, it didn't seem right to call it a SEED anymore. The head-sized ball of green energy I snatched from the *Rascal* was no longer a thing defined only by what it was made to do.

Now, Delphi wanders through the back of my mind, slim ribbons of sensation without words, with barely enough cohesion to call them thought. But it doesn't matter because I think for us.

The explo ships are gone, all except the *Tremain-Greo* with its damaged engines and the giant hole in its side. Delphi isn't paying much attention to it yet, too busy exploring the asteroid, the academy's generators, the nanosteel and DNA banks, excitement shivering through it with every new discovery.

I'm paying attention though.

Planning.

Calculating.

I rub my chest, imagining I can reach through breast and ribs to massage the phantom scar as it pulls, seeming to stretch with Delphi as it spreads its tendrils through the asteroid.

I'd set out to find a SEED, get an internship and change the galaxy.

The internship is toast, but the rest of it...

I eye the *Tremain-Greo*, silent and dark, engines damaged but not irreparably so.

A smile, and I nudge Delphi, just a little, guiding it away from the academy's waste reclamation systems to the machinery of its fusion generators.

It had spent enough time learning how to generate atmosphere, time to move onto Engineering 101.

TRANSMISSION

INTRODUCTION

Remember, in the (second) *Crash* introduction I shared how that story started out as Star Trek fan fiction? Well, *Transmission* started out that way too, at least the very core of it. It's long since left the trappings of warp drives and the Federation behind in favour of flowing robes, impossible Kung Fu and magic swords. On space ships.

In fact, the only vestige of it left is the image of the woman in the black bodysuit and a name, Terrashar. Such is how the plot bunnies work.

Learn more about the writing of *Transmission*. Scan the QR code for the audio commentary, soundtrack and more.

TRANSMISSION

Blood painted the bulkhead in giant arcs of red flung from the curve of her sword. She slashed again, black nano-steel slicing through flesh and bone, warm arterial spray slicking her face even as the ImpMit's head thumped on the deck.

The soldier's body still stood, the pale grey slabs of its power-armoured legs holding it upright. A swift kick to the back of the knee had it tumbling to join its fellows on the deck, and it was done.

For the moment, at least.

Du'ata paused, sword extended, her weight balanced. The long, bum-sweeping tail of her ink-dark braid had come loose during the fight, and her red and teal outer robe, with its rich gold embroidery was dark with blood, but the slick black nano-armour underneath remained intact. No warnings popped on her mask's HUD, nothing save the empty corridor and the pulsing emergency lights.

She breathed deep, taking in the stench of death-loosened bowls, the copper tang of blood sweet on the back of her tongue, and listened. To the rush of her heart, the sigh of the air-cyclers, and that giant empty nothingness that came from soundproofed bulkheads and the absence of living souls.

Just the square, pale-grey walls of the ImpMit cruiser, emergency lights flashing orange along the join of wall and floor. The holoscreens that usually lined the walls were gone, the emitters at either end sparking electricity, the surveillance cams little more than evenly spaced scorch marks, victims of her pistol in that initial rush, the hectic dance to jam the bulkheads.

The round-cornered hatches at either end of the ten-metre section of corridor flashed more eye-searing orange, another reminder of the disaster happening in their midst. The corpses at her feet.

A sharp flick sent loose blood flying from her blade—more red to decorate the walls—before she slid it into the sheath at her hip, the nano-steel singing as it found home.

Her HUD flashed, another screen overlaying her vision as new targets appeared behind her. She turned, fatigue dragging at her bones, the internal chem-pharm that had kept her going this long, now depleted. No more adrenaline, no more stims, not until they got off this boat.

If they got off this boat.

Her HUD flashed again, the new targets closing in. The threat not immediate but close.

A twitch of her eye and the map expanded, new dots—one brilliant green, the other two gold—popped up. Too close. Everything and everyone was too close.

She swore and popped the comms. 'Get them out, Rehc.'

On the HUD, the green dot didn't change, but she could see Rehc's snarl, teeth a sharp slash of white in his black face. 'Trying,' he said, his voice a growl, strain giving it an extra rumble.

She didn't say 'try harder', although the words hovered on the back of her tongue as she watched the enemy advance, their scarlet dots flowing through the ship's corridors. Rehc would get the Lady and her daughter out or live long enough to make sure they didn't suffer at the Empire's hands. Which would be longer than her, if the emergency hatch didn't hold.

It wouldn't hold of course, not forever, but she didn't need forever, she just needed enough time—

The hatch blew inwards.

She had time to see it bow, to appreciate the inch-thick steelcrete, how the explosive hadn't just blackened the edges but eaten at them too, and to curse herself for not thinking the ImpMits would be able to fool her radar, before she was slammed into a bulkhead.

Pain swamped her chest, hot and burning. Even as her internals screamed, catastrophic med warnings exploded across her HUD, telling of punctured lungs and shattered ribs, while novas burst in her vision. The world was a brilliant explosion of colour as her internals stuttered, trying desperately to fix a failing body, short-circuiting eyes and ears, leaving instinct and training to take over from conscious decision.

Her hand found her sword, nanite-infused blood spilling down the hilt, energising the blade, shredding the scabbard.

The ImpMits coming through the blown door—black clad and faceless—were blurred shadows in her eyes, but she found one. Lunged. Struck, blade sinking into flesh—

Time stuttered. Elastic. Sticky.

Fragmented.

She was on the deck, sensors guiding hands that felt alien, closing too-long fingers over a gun, the stock meeting her shoulder even as the weapon hummed and fired.

Stars still glazed her vision, whited-out the details of face and form, but the HUD took over for her visual cortex and guided her aim. One red dot down. Two.

Heat signatures blazed then fell. More poured in after them, and more and more and more. More than there should be, more than there *could* be. They were all blending together, no longer neat outlines of colour but an amorphous mass of red and yellow.

She needed her eyes, Terra damn it. Needed her eyes! But the blow to her head and… and something, something she should remember, clouded her vision.

She shook her head, trying to dislodge the white.

Breath on her neck, a blade, cold and sharp against her throat.

Her fingers jammed on the trigger.

'Hello, Du'ata.'

Her blood went cold.

Time fragmented again.

There was no feeling in her legs, her arms, the limbs had long since turned to ice, the thin grey jumpsuit no match for her frigid cell. Her hands and feet were blocky, the muscles she could still feel—abdomen and neck and shoulders—beyond her ability to command. Not even her head responded, her lips or cheeks or eyes, though she felt them, felt the chill brush of air, the warmth of the light playing across her eyelids, caressing her lips. She'd felt, too, the hands that slipped under her, the arms that lifted her off the hard, cold cot, the tendons in her neck pulling as her head flopped back.

Heavy boots clomped on the plassteel deck, the sound louder now than before, with her weight adding to the force, ringing off the dark walls of her cell. A door *swooshed*, a command panel *beeped*, and the body carrying her paused, the hands wrapped around her bicep and hip gripping tighter before it moved again. Another *swoosh*. The jolt of short, steady strides, boots no longer echoing off hard cell walls, but still tension moving through the arms holding her.

Was that anxiety that radiated through the not-cold arm brushing against her cheek? Who on an ImpMit cruiser would be anxious with her, a half-dead Shar warrior, in their arms? Who would carry her? Why not a med-slab or a body bag? Was that the cross-hatched roughness of nanoarmour through her jumpsuit? The cold ridges of powered-arms pressing into her back? The butt of a gun nudging her ribs?

Questions raced through her brain, made her eyes flicker behind stubbornly closed lids.

Cherry blossom teased her nose, the sweet scent reminding

her... Of what? She couldn't remember. Why couldn't she remember? There was a black hole in the middle of her brain, a space where something important... no someone important, and the smell, the blossoms teased that spot, made it snap and crackle and—

'We're almost there.' The chest next to her ear rumbled with the words, the sound of them soft, almost lost under the steady clang of boots on deck. The steady feminine voice was familiar, in the way the scent was familiar, ringing that bell in the darkness, making lightning arch between neurons, the electric tang of them thick on her tongue.

Was the woman speaking to her? Did she know Du'ata was aware within her broken shell, that she longed to move her lips, to twitch her eyelashes? That she would give anything, anything at all, for a sharp blade and the strength to slide it between her ribs? Did she? Would she?

'Have the med-pod ready.'

No, those words were not for her. The woman spoke to another, her words not quite a whisper. And with those words, the quiet undertone designed to disappear under the ringing tang of her boots, she gave herself away. She was not an ImpMit, not one of the hard-faced soldiers or dead-eyed inquisitors who had broken Du'ata's bones, torn her tendons, shredded her mind.

'It's bad.' A pause, seconds marked by boots clanking on the deck once more, the gentle bounce of her head with each of the woman's strides. 'Yes,' she said again, short, to the point.

Another pause. 'I don't know.'

What didn't the woman know? What didn't Du'ata know? Why was there a hole in her mind? Was it the torture? The endless, hellish interrogations, the probes jacked into her greyware, the drugs pumped into her chem-pharm? But no, the hole felt deeper than that, older, the edges precise where the inquisitor's had been ragged and rough.

New sounds; the distant hum of multiple conversations, the

gentle beep and squark of consoles, the almost inaudible growl of massive engines vibrating through equally massive bulkheads.

'We're at the hangar. Get ready.'

Another door shushing open and now the smell of grease and oil assaulted her nose, and the squark and beep was taken over by the ear-ringing clang of metal on metal and the brain-piercing whine of drills. All of it echoing and echoing and echoing. The cacophony swallowed the sound of the woman's footfalls, her quiet whispers, but her voice travelled through her chest and rumbled against Du'ata's side.

New lights played over her eyelids, no longer warm yellow but sharp and red, the intermittent pulses driving nails into what was left of her brain. Pain spread under her skull, and she couldn't help the moan that rose from her chest.

The woman paused, little more than a momentary hesitation, and her hands tightened on Du'ata's shoulder and leg. Was that a curse she felt rumbling through the woman's chest, did her footsteps hasten? Did—

'Hey! You! Stop!' Those words exploded over the cacophony, coming from behind.

The woman didn't stop, didn't turn either. She shifted her grip, muscles moving under nanoarmour, and then Du'ata was over the woman's shoulder and the woman was running, breath expelling from Du'ata's lungs with every deck-eating stride.

Gunfire. She felt it as much as heard it. The razor burn of it ripping past her cheek, the forward stagger of the woman, the *phzt stick*, the heady metallic taste of burned ozone.

A whine deep enough to squeeze the very air and then—

A supernova bloomed, a giant wave of heat and light washing away sound and colour, everything save the shoulder robbing her of air, the skull-splitting bounce as the woman pounded the deck.

There were other noises, lost under the ringing in her ears, the stars behind her unresponsive lids. Light turned to dark, heat to cold, the hiss and snick of an airlock cycling closed. The supernova gone as quickly as it came and then the shoulder was gone from her stomach, air rushed into her lungs and for a moment, a second, her eyelids parted—

Her own drawn, ghastly ivory face reflected in a shiny black mask, hollow cheeks and cracked lips, eyes bruised and sunken. And then there were more people, forms she saw on the edge of her vision, shapes caught just like her reflection in the woman's obliterating mask.

And underneath that... The rumble of engines, a sudden lurch as the deck heaved under them. She knew those sounds. Knew the stomach-hollowing jerk, recognised the woman's quick shuffle as the actions of an emergency take-off in hostile surrounds before the inertial dampeners could kick in.

Another lurch but the woman barely staggered, striding down the ship's corridor, the forms in her mask keeping pace. 'She's awake,' she said, no hint of strain in her voice, none of the tension radiating through her arms.

A soft curse, familiar as the woman's was familiar, and though she struggled to identify it, to chase it through the hole in her memory, she—

Pressure against her neck, a soft hiss blooming under her ear, then cold spreading through her veins, taking the sliver of sight, the pain, the...

Time fractured.

She dreamed.

It didn't hurt in the dream and warmth suffused her bones from the fire in the long, low grate along the wall. The delicate strains of a flute teased her ears, the quiet, lilting melody high and sweet. Pale light from the quarter-moon swept through the glass overhead, enough light to silver the pale wood floor and cast long shadows from the heavy steelcrete beams supporting the ceiling. She stood in that space and breathed in calm along with the soothing scent of sandalwood, the crackle of the fire and tried to forget the bitter aftertaste of death.

Her hands were dirty, the creases crusted with blood, the nails ragged and torn. She put that blood-stained hand to the corset-like belt holding her overrobe together, felt the almost-sigh as the nano-seams parted at her touch, the nanite-reinforced armour falling to the ground. The sword went with it, clattering as it hit the wood.

She left them there, gliding across the fire and moon-lit room on silent feet. She shed the overrobe as she went, pushing it off her shoulders to puddle on the floor, a pool of black silk spilling across the wood. It would have to be discarded, too many rips and slashes, too much blood for the delicate fabric to be repaired. Her inner robe went next, the soft fabric a crimson river trailing in her wake, leaving just nanoarmour to flow over her skin. It hugged every curve and line of her body, drinking the light and refusing to let it go until she was just a human-shaped shadow.

From the chin down, she was visible only in her absence, a being made of the void, silent and deadly.

A door—an unadorned, hard-edged rectangle cut into rough rock—shushed open.

She stepped through.

The door whispered closed.

The moonlight followed her, streaming through transparent ceiling and wall, silvering the rock-hewn wall, leeching it of warmth. But then there was no warmth to be had here, even when the sun was high. No fire to crackle and waver, no gentle music to grace the ear and take away the screams, just the cold, snow-topped mountains and white-coated firs, an ocean of spears pointing to the night. The mountain palace's enviros kept the cold out, the nanites running through the triple-paned plas-glas and marble-wood floors, regulating the temperature down to the square centimetres under her bare feet, but still... That chill reached through every nano-metre of technology and lodged in her bones.

She padded down the corridor, under more thick concrete

beams, bare feet silent on the wood.

Another door waited at the end. The ancient, blackened timbers shushed aside like the first, but instead of cold, warmth spilled from the doorway, golden light and the twitter of birds, the scent of roses rising with it.

She hesitated before she passed the threshold, a nanosecond where her foot hovered, her muscles froze and her heart stuttered. Just a nanosecond, barely long enough for even the palace AI to notice, but an eternity to the timeworn woman on the other side.

The Ancient One lifted her gaze. The void had more warmth, more humanity, more compassion than the pit-dark eyes in the wizened bronze face. The soul that stared out of it was centuries past its due, had seen wars rage and planets die, had inhabited a hundred faces and was old only in memory.

The ash-white hair spilling over the Ancient's shoulders did nothing to soften her, neither did the richly painted lips, the sumptuous folds of her carefully chosen robes, the gleam of silk, the way she sat on the divan.

Not even the sunlight trickling through the soft petals of the cherry blossom that spread its branches over her head, the warm golden rays carefully simulated to waver just so. The tree itself rose out of a mound of manicured grass, its long, spindly arms covered in delicate pink blooms that fluttered to the ground around the Ancient One. But never on her.

Du'ata's foot met the floor, carried her over the threshold.

The door closed behind her as silently as it had opened. As the warmth and light closed around her, as the sweet bird song twisted through her ears and the sweeter scent of blossoms reached through her nose to stick to her tongue, she wished for the snow, the firs and the swell of the flute.

She padded across the sea of gleaming wood.

The Ancient One watched.

There was no sign, no signal, but Du'ata stopped, frozen solid by a twitch of the Ancient One's eyelid.

She did not breathe.

The Ancient One stared, the cold, fathomless gaze boring into her core, or maybe it was already in her core, in the clean, empty space in her memories.

The Ancient spoke. 'You are not here. You are there.' The words, deep and calm, came from everywhere and nowhere, rising out of the air itself, seeming to echo off the walls.

An image played like a mirage on the back of Du'ata's lids. Herself, up to her neck in a regen tank, a brace supporting her head while the rest of her floated supine in brilliant blue fluid. Around her, the tight confines of a small shipboard med bay, the white bulkheads and deck-plating softened by the dim lights and the hush of air cyclers.

The Ancient spoke again, voice rising from that dark, empty space, filling her bones with cold. 'They are there.'

New images, faces made fuzzy by the view through shuttered lashes, the angle of her head on the supporting headrest, the sticky remnants of pain and injury. A woman in dark armour, short and lithe, a long braid reaching for her waist. Beside her, a man with a slim, deadly sword attached to his back.

She recognised him, the neon green flecks in his hair—why go grey when you can go neon, he would say—the slight hitch in his left shoulder, like the sword hilt poking over it might hit him in the eye. It never did, never could. That slight hitch, the faint wrinkles at the corners of his yellow eyes, the way he shuffled when he walked—deliberately, mind you—had saved their lives many times, made many underestimate the wily strength and speed in those old, weathered limbs.

Rehc. Rehc was there and beside him...

A woman in ship robes to rival the Ancient's, but pearly white, the material shining with embroidery and the fainter shimmer of nano-weave. Her long red hair bound in intricate braids atop her head, the tall weedy teen at her side a carbon copy of their mother. She knew those figures too.

'You are not done yet.' The words belonged to the Ancient. 'Get up.'

She tried, commanded arms to rise, legs to brace, stomach to tense, but nothing happened.

'I can't.'

'You can.' The Ancient rose, no longer solid, the divan turning to smoke under her, the cherry tree at her back fading, leaving just the golden, manufactured sunlight and the void in the old one's gaze. 'Rise, Terrashar.' Her voice deepened, echoing through the dream. 'Rise!'

The command reverberated in the empty space in Du'ata's brain, filled her bones, her muscles, her skin. Everything was alive, the blue regen fluid blinding in its vibrancy, it's tinny sweetness thick on her tongue, filling her nose. And with that vibrancy, that brilliance, came the pain, the fire under skin, the lightning under torn fingertips, the spears from shattered bones and sliced tendons.

Muscles that had refused to move, nerves that had stoppered her will, bunched. Pushed.

In the dream, she rose. In the tank, in the real, she—

There was a disconnect, a schism as part of her, the part behind her eyes with the Ancient's command ringing through her skull, rose from the tank, regen fluid sheeting off her shoulders, sticking her hair to her naked back. The other part rolled its head and struggled to twitch a finger.

Alarms screamed and lights flashed around the tank. In the dream, the alarms pierced her ears, strident and piercing, and in the real...

Joy warmed the Lady's face, and the woman in black was moving. Flowing across the grey-white med-bay, a piece of the dark, like Du'ata had been. In the dream, slicked in her own nanoarmour. But not now. Not now.

Naked and cold and feeble, flesh wrinkled like an old, white prune. No strength in her bones, no steel in her muscles, not even enough breath in her lungs to scream as all that pain cracked and splintered under her skin, in her muscles, through her bones.

In the dream, she stood stooped and shivering, regen fluid sloshing around her knees, unsure if she could raise them high enough to step out of the tub. And in the real... in the real, she watched the woman in black coming for her, braid swinging with every step, a chill, gliding menace in every move.

And Du'ata with nothing, except for the Ancient, except for the old one's words echoing in the empty space.

And the nanites floating in the tank, in her blood, repairing tissue, mending bone, swimming in the dark empty space with the Ancient.

Except for that.

The woman was at the tank, and somehow she was both standing and kneeling. Her gaze weighed on Du'ata, heavy and insistent, but no matter if the woman was standing or kneeling, no matter if the dream was real or the real was a dream, she was close, only centimetres of air and armour between them.

The Ancient's breath brushed her cheekbone, cold and dry. 'Do your duty, Terrashar.'

In the dream the strike has hard and fast; one moment her hand at her side, the next blue regen fluid ripping up her torso, nanites condensing, hardening, forming a sharp, deadly tip in her palm now buried against the woman's chest.

In the real... She blacked out for a moment, or many, it was hard to tell but when she came to, her palm was still buried against the woman's chest but the woman was gripping it. Holding Du'ata's wrist in place.

The blue, watery blade was sunk through the armour like it wasn't there and other liquid, red and hot, was sticking to her hand. Her blood, the woman's blood, mixing and twisting, flowing from one body to the other, and suddenly she was flowing with it and...

...and she was kneeling beside the tank, holding a woman's

worn, pale hand to her chest, regen fluid falling through her fingers. Was she still dreaming? Was this all a hallucination and the Ancient and the dark woman and Rehc and Lady.... They were all figments? Had the ImpMits got into her brain? Were they still in her brain?

'Dua.' A man's voice against her cheek, warm breath against her ear. 'Rise,' he said, and there was that disconnect again, as the Ancient's resonant, commanding tones mixed with his.

Rise.

Rise.

'Rise,' whispered the Ancient.

Time reformed.

'Hello, Du'ata.'

The tall, willowy woman pressed the blade harder against Du'ata's throat.

The golden sword was razor-sharp and somehow warm as it glided over her carotid to rest under her chin, tilting her gaze to meet the other's.

Du'ata's grip spasmed on the jammed riffle.

Flames danced in Varya's eyes, their molten bronze glowing from under the deep cowl of her heavily embroidered robe, scorching her cheeks like an oil spill, giving the white flesh a pearlescent sheen. Her long red hair spilled from within that hood, two bloody rivers lying heavy on the nanosilks's midnight-blue front.

Varya stood, booted feet firmly planted on the deck, head up, shoulders back and the sword steady and true in her black-gloved grip. No expression marked her face—no sneer, no satisfaction, no conflicting passions or loyalty—but Du'ata felt the heat from the other woman's eyes, the flames of victory licking her skin, barely contained by Varya's flesh.

'Varya.' The name burned Du'ata's tongue, made her insides

twist, and sucked every inch of warmth from her bones. 'The Ancient sent me.'

'Mmm.' The sword bit into Du'ata's flesh. 'Yes.'

Pressure under her chin, the nanosteel commanding her to rise or lose the few slim threads of hope she had. So long as she wasn't dead, there was a chance for Rehc and the Lady to escape, all she had to do was keep Varya's attention—

The sharp *clunk* of massive deadbolts retracting vibrated through the deck, and the emergency airlock, not blown in by the ImpMit soldiers, cycled open.

The airlock Rehc and the Lady had escaped through.

Du'ata's gut made another twist.

A head was tossed through the opening, black and neon green hair tumbling through the air, landing with a wet, meaty thwack. It rolled a few more times, blood a brilliant red trailing in its wake, its coppery stench filling the air, before it came to a stop at her feet.

Rehc stared at her.

Bile touched Du'ata's tongue, hot and bitter, before she swallowed it down.

She didn't look to the airlock, didn't want to see if another corpse or another head would tumble through, didn't need to know if the Lady and her daughter were alive or not.

Not yet. Not now. If she did not make it out of this, it would not matter if the whole universe died.

You are here.

Back still pressed to the bulkhead, Varya's sword following every twitch, Du'ata rose, hand locked around the half-forgotten rifle.

They are here.

A smile flirted with the corner of Varya's full, dusk-pink lips. Behind Varya, gliding through the open airlock like a slice of darkness, Rehc's naked sword in his hand, came a man in black.

Rise, Terrashar.

'The Ancient sent me,' Du'ata said again. She glanced to the man, stared at herself in the shiny black mask—long blonde strands of hair stuck to her cheeks and jaw by blood and sweat.

There was a tension in his shoulders, a kind of weight that compressed the air between them.

She looked away, back at Varya's burning eyes. Varya's blade took another bite of flesh as she spoke. 'Both of us, Rehc and I.'

Jealousy spoiled the satisfaction curling Varya's lips, the blade making another kiss. 'Rehc died for you, sister.'

Her attention slid over Varya's shoulder, the blood-hair spilling down her chest, back to the man and the sword in his hand.

Du'ata's hand ached for the weight of her own sword, the shifting, black-lacquered hilt, the nanite-enhanced fizz as it connected to her nervous system. Its strength and promise sliding through her muscles, as much a part of her as her bones, as Rehc's sword had been part of him.

'That's not yours,' she said to the man.

He didn't speak, didn't move, only that weight, that tension shifted, grew heavier, and somewhere, deep in the yawning pit in her memory, something monstrous flexed sleeping muscles.

Rise.

Blood and blade and muscle.

Blue regen fluid responding to her command, to nanites in her body, coiling up her arm, a dagger forming in her palm. The tip sinking through armour and flesh, the woman holding it there, a voice whispering in her ear.

'*Rise.*'

Du'ata's blood on Varya's blade, the nanites infused into the haemoglobin infecting the sword. The sword as much a part of Varya as Du'ata's was of her, as Rehc's had been of him, part of her nervous system. Her muscles. Her mind.

For a second, a moment within a moment, time stopped, stretched, turned elastic and sticky. The sword was a highway, a superconductor down which Du'ata raced, and gripped and held, *commanded* Varya's muscles to stillness.

Varya's molten gaze widened, panic bringing out the oil spill across her cheekbones standing out as her face lost what little colour it had.

The man in black moved, a shadow, Rehc's sword raised, the green-stroked blade cutting the very air, making it scream.

Twisting away from the blade at her throat, breaking her hold on Varya as she did. The rifle was warm in Du'ata's grip as she raised it in two hands, finger finding the trigger.

Phzt, phzt, phzt.

The man stumbled, black nanoarmour absorbing the first two hits, rifle pulses dissipating across his chest in bright electric waves, but the third… the third went through. The nanoarmour over his stomach shattered, blood spilled, the greasy scent of burnt flesh filling the air.

No time to worry if he was out, if the solider's chem-pharm was already pumping him full of adrenaline, keeping him moving, because Varya was coming.

Rage twisted her face, turned those lush, dusk-pink lips to a teeth-baring snarl, the pearlescent sheen to a scar across her cheeks.

The golden blade was coming down, nanites—Varya's nanites—running through the steel, turning the edge the same molten bronze as her eyes.

No time to dodge, barely enough to shove the rifle between them, useless as it was with that bulkhead-melting sword aimed at her throat. Varya's blade would pass through it like butter, clean and soft and easy.

A different blade—Rehc's blade, the edge eye-searing green— severed Varya's hand.

The other woman fell, head separated from shoulders, another bright red arc painting the bulkhead and Du'ata's face.

Behind her, the man still stood, but not for much longer if the tremble in his knees and the hunch to his shoulder told the tale.

The rifle came up, pointed at the shiny black mask. Her finger tightened on the trigger. Froze.

She should kill him. Kill him for killing Rehc, kill him so there was one less enemy at her back, hunting the Lady down, making her spine itch.

She should kill him, but her finger… Her finger was stuck, her gaze caught on that hunched shoulder, the way he shuffled backwards, hit the bulkhead and let his legs go out from underneath him.

The thing in her mind stirred.

Rise.

The man slumped against the grey-white wall, blood darkening the hole in his armour, nanites already filling in the fist-sized hole over his abdomen.

She kicked aside Varya's sword, the golden blade spinning across the deck, Varya's hand still attached, fingers clenched forever around the hilt, and knelt at his side.

'Dua.' Her name came out muffled by the mask, and the monstrous thing in the pit of her memory woke.

In the black shiny surface, her reflection wavered. Long nose and pale white skin of her face morphing, the sharp hard cheekbones melting, softening, growing small and rounded, eyes bigger, lips fuller, until a different woman peered back at her. A woman who was her, or rather, *had* been her.

Once.

Before the airlock had blown.

Before she bled and died and took a new body. A new face.

Her consciousness a pattern of electrical impulses, her nanites the transmitter, her blade the conduit.

Blood and blade and muscle.

She pulled the helmet off. It wasn't Rehc's face, the man's complexion was a pale gold not black, his eyes green instead of yellow with none of the lines drawing crow's feet at the corners, but the smile warming his thin lips was familiar, the nanites in his blood already turning the ink-black hair at his temples neon green.

His head lolled, staring back down the corridor, his neck a little too loose, the muscles weakened by blood loss and pain, the nanites in his system no doubt stretched to breaking. Transmission was difficult, and the wound in his belly would make it doubly so.

'Took you long enough,' he said.

'Shut up.' She picked up his sword, slid it home in the sheath over his shoulder, before leaving him slumped against the bulkhead to fish her own blade out from under a corpse.

The dead woman's face was small and round, with full lips and big, leaf-shaped eyes, just like the ones in the helmet's reflection, except these eyes stared sightlessly at the ceiling. Shrapnel from the blown airlock pierced her chest, a thick, inch-long pierce of scorched and melted steelcrete stuck between her ribs, her red and teal robes dark with coagulated blood, the bum-sweeping braid lifeless on the deck.

Du'ata returned to Rehc, looped his arm over her shoulders and dragged him to his feet.

'Transmission's a bitch,' she said.

DREAD
SPACE

INTRODUCTION

The plot bunnies spawned this sucker all on their little lonesome. I'm not even sure they knew what they were doing, although they seemed to figure it out as they went along.

If you squint, you can *almost* see how this story fits in with *Brother* and The Echo series.

 Learn more about the writing of *Dread Space*. Scan the QR code for the audio commentary, soundtrack and more.

DREAD SPACE

Deep spacers tell a story of a place with no name. It had one once, you can see the old markings on its hull, but the words are long since gone, scratched and scorched, by time or intention no one knows. Just like no one knows what the thing is, or where it came from, or why it moans.

It doesn't matter if you mute the comms or silence the sensors, the sound comes through the hull, vibrating through the void to sing in the bulkheads.

They say it sounds like wind through a sun-warmed forest at first, the breeze flitting through leaves, twisting around branches. You can almost smell the perfume of spring, taste the first tart strawberries. Peaceful, beautiful even, but the more you listen… the more you listen, the more you hear the voices. It starts out a quiet, alien babble that's *almost* words, but the more you strain to understand them, to prise apart the pieces you *think* you know from the parts that don't make sense…

Yes?

That's when you hear it.

What? What do you hear?

The moan. The ghosts.

Phfft. Ghosts!

Ghosts. Some say it's the memories of the spacers who died in the place, that's it's the fragments of their transmissions, corrupted by power-shorts and time. Others…

...What? What'd they hear?

It wasn't what they heard, it's what they felt, what they *saw*. A presence. Like a shadow in the corner of their eye, watching, reaching out, waiting for them. Like it *needed* them. And worse than the presence is the loneliness – a deep, crushing desperation for another living being. Even when you're surrounded by a hundred different people, when you're held tight in a lover's arms, that loneliness is there, in your heart. There's no escaping it.

The deep spacers say that if you see the shadow, you'll go mad.

...Like Mum?

Yeah, just like Mum.

...I wish she was here.

So do I.

...

The place, it drifts in the dark spaces between solar systems, traveling the forgotten ways of the Interstellar streams. A giant ovoid with a dozen rotating rings, all moving at impossible angles, nearly three kilometers longs, and half that wide and tall. It could almost be a space station, except it moves, not that anyone ever sees.

...Is it a ship then?

Maybe. It's too big to be a First ship though, too far out, too old, travelling in the wrong direction and yet it looks like one of those crazy first-gen designs. You know, the ones in the museums, the pictographs carved into the First World towers?

...The ones they called skyscrapers?

Yeah, those. The spacers say the ship is dead, no power, no drive signatures or tachyon trails, no radiation spikes. Yet it moves, never at the same coordinates twice, but there when it's needed, or, at least, that's what the survivors say. If you can call them that. Most don't.

...Mum survived.

Maybe.

Of those that go look for it... most who return didn't find it.

And those that do… They're like Mum, going out into the deep places again and again, spending everything—fortune and sanity—on the search, their last threads of reason all they have to hang on to before they dive one final time into the deep places—

…

It's okay, we got to Mum in time. Uncle Vipin won't let her go anywhere.

…He can't do it forever. [sniffs]. The spacers have tried, entire ship-families have dedicated their lives to saving sibs struck by the madness, drugs and therapy and padded rooms. But none of it works, the mad ones always find a way, and if the spacers can't do it

No one can. But we're not spacers, and we're not giving up, Ratnam. You *know* we're not giving up. We're going to find this thing, and we're going to *make* it let Mum go.

…What if we can't? What if we get inside and…?

…What's inside?

Death. At least, that's what those who make it out say, if they can still speak. Most don't, and the ones who can… The deep spacers who can speak, who made it out of that place alive, they call their friends the lucky ones.

They say that what's in there… what's in there is nothing. They say that what's in there is the most beautiful, most horrible thing they ever saw, that they ever will see. They say the corridors are filled with light and colour, the bulkheads carved with pictures of such exquisite detail they almost seem to move. They say their fellows lost themselves in the delicate dance of line on line, the intricate patterns and whorls. They say friends, family, lovers and enemies never wanted to leave, and when they tried to force them…

…What?

They died. Bashed their heads against the bulkheads. They said there are old, brown-red stains all over the pale-grey bulkheads, scraps of cloth and fragments of bone piled in the corners of ever corridor, every room.

The very air is meant to shiver with the sound of their cries, that even with the enviros running a chill races across your flesh, goosebumps marching in its wake, not because of the cold, but the voices. They say it smells of whatever you hold most dear—memories of home, of loved ones, of victories or defeats—whatever scent leaves a knot in your heart, the air is thick with it.

…Why are you telling me this?

Didn't you ask?

No.

…Oh.

Ratnam?

Hmm?

Where's Uncle Vipin? Where's the crew?

We left them behind.

Why?

Because they tried to stop us.

From what?

From going to the place.

Which place?

That place. *This* place.

ACKNOWLEDGEMENTS

I've written quite a few acknowledgments by now, and I tell you what; it doesn't get any easier. It's a tricky process, but also stupidly easy. Usually you start off with something along the lines of, *"It takes many people to make a book."*

For this book, it took thirty-one including Amanda J Spedding, my fantabulous editor; my mum and stepfather, with their unwavering support; friend, fellow author and sounding board, Tracy M Joyce; Lauren Dawes who put the idea for a bling edition in my head (not that she knows it); and the twenty-six Kickstarter Heroes who helped fund it.

The Heroes deserve an extra special thanks for their willingness to put the plonk their belief and their cash down for a book they hadn't seen, and in a few cases, by an author they hadn't heard of. They are: the Emmazing Emma Morris, Mike Dobey, Arend van't Oever, Francesco Tehrani, Billye Herndon, Esapekka Eriksson, Jonathan Brown, Alexandra Corrsin, Nicolas Lobotsky, Dead Fishie, Joe Lau, K.R.S., Amanda Eschmeyer, Kenyon Wensing, Jordan Brown, Natasha Rueschhoff, Katherine Shipman, Holly c, Heather Jones, Eron Wyngarde, Kristen Altmann and Ch. N. Heinzl.

You're my heroes.

DON'T MISS ANOTHER BOOK!

I love keeping in touch with my readers, it's the second-best thing about being a writer (writing being the first best). Every fortnight (or thereabouts), I send out a newsletter with details about upcoming offers, new releases and extra special projects.

If you sign up for the mailing you'll receive exclusive behind-the-scenes extras, such as:

- free short stories
- deleted and alternate scenes from my books
- previews of upcoming books
- pancakes
- quizes
- and much, much more!

Scan the QR code or visit the link below to sign up.
belindacrawford.com/newsletter

READY FOR MORE?

A dark new urban fantasy filled with reincarnated superheroines, inter-dimensional demons and immortal enemies.

Byrne Davin has lived many lives, from noblewoman to pioneer to slave, all of them filled with blood and death, all ending in pain and betrayal. This life, she would like to live in peace, or if not peace then to at least finish high school, maybe even meet a cute guy, go on a date, kick demon arse and be home in time to do her homework.

But she can't always get what she wants, not with an ancient, battle-crazed warrior sharing her soul, or fragmented dreams of an unseen enemy that threatens not just her existence, but that of her reincarnated sisters.

Sisters who doubt Byrne's every word and hold terrible secrets of their own.

A darkness is coming, a bitter cold rising from the depths of the universe on the ravening howl of a bloodthirsty demon horde. And the only thing standing between it and victory are Byrne, her sisters and the lies tearing them apart.

Available now
belindacrawford.com/DemonsBattleskirts

ABOUT THE AUTHOR

Physics makes Belinda's brain hurt, while quadratics cause her eyes to cross and any mention of probability equations will have her running for the door. Nonetheless, she loves watching documentaries about the natural world, biology, space, history and technology.

She's also a sucker for a fast horse, a faster computer and superhero movies. When she's not doing the horse, computer or superhero thing, Belinda writes sci-fi and fantasy for readers who like their fiction action-packed, with diverse characters, butt-kicking heroines and complex worlds.

As a certified crazy horse person, when she's not wrangling six-legged dynamos on the page, she's wrangling four-legged powder-kegs in the paddock. Belinda brings that same certified craziness to her writing with the kind of unexpected twists that'll keep you guessing.

You can keep in touch with Belinda, or just pick her brains about sci-fi via her website, Facebook or by sending her an email (she loves email).

www.belindacrawford.com
belinda@belindacrawford.com

Have news delivered straight to your inbox
via her mailing list. Sign up at:
belindacrawford.com/newsletter